E.G. FOLEY

THE GRYPHON CHRONICLES, BOOK TWO:

JAKE & THE GIANT

Books by E.G. Foley

The Complete Gryphon Chronicles Series:
The Lost Heir (The Gryphon Chronicles, Book One)
Jake & The Giant (The Gryphon Chronicles, Book Two)
The Dark Portal (The Gryphon Chronicles, Book Three)
Jake & The Gingerbread Wars (A Gryphon Chronicles Christmas)
Rise of Allies (The Gryphon Chronicles, Book Four)
Secrets of the Deep (The Gryphon Chronicles, Book Five)
The Black Fortress (The Gryphon Chronicles, Book Six)

50 States of Fear Series:
The Haunted Plantation (50 States of Fear: Alabama)
Bringing Home Bigfoot (50 States of Fear: Arkansas)
Leader of the Pack (50 States of Fear: Colorado)
The Dork and the Deathray (50 States of Fear: Alaska)

Credits & Copyright

The bigger they are, the harder they fall.

~Old Saying, 19th Century

TABLE OF CONTENTS

Next Up!
About the Authors

PART I

PROLOGUE
The Giant Who Fell From the Sky

Thunder rumbled over the fjords—or so the humans thought down in Midgarth. But up above the clouds, it was only Snorri taking out his frustration on the rocks that cluttered his sheep meadow.

He pried another boulder as big as a human's cottage out of the turf and hurled it onto the pile, clearing a nice, smooth field for his flock to graze.

The scowl on his low, sweaty brow had his woolly charges worried, however. Bleating anxiously, the sheep ran to and fro to escape the flying boulders.

The angry giant paid them no mind.

He was too busy fuming over how Prince Gorm had made a fool of him—again!—in front of the entire great hall. Even worse, in front of Princess Kaia-of-the-Yellow-Braids.

The truth was, giants never *were* the brightest folk in all the Nine Worlds. But Snorri the Shepherd was, sadly, dumber than most.

So he had been told.

So he had come to believe.

For sometimes, even a giant could be made to feel small.

Wham!

With a glower, he tossed another boulder onto the pile and shook the world of men below.

That's it, he decided. *I am never going back to the great hall.*

He was sick of being humiliated by Gorm and the other warriors. Nobody appreciated him around here.

If only there was somewhere else to go!

But Odin and Thor had sealed off Jugenheim from the world of men below. This, the boastful gods decreed, was to stop the giant folk from running amuck. Humans did enough of that sort of thing on their own, he'd heard.

Snorri had never actually seen a human, but he'd heard they were very tasty. Stuck here, of course, he'd probably never know.

He laid hold of a particularly stubborn boulder nearly as large as himself and fought against it, trying to wrestle it out of the dry dirt where it was lodged.

He struggled and pulled with all his might, sweating and grunting against its stubborn bulk, and getting angrier at himself by the minute for being the stupidest dolt in the village.

If he had to be stupid, at least he should be strong! he thought as his muscles strained. Gorm was always bragging about how strong he was, that vain know-it-all. Oh, how he'd like to show him!

Everyone said Prince Gorm was the smartest, bravest warrior who had ever come to serve King Olaf. Indignation bubbled like a great cauldron in Snorri at the thought of that wind-bag marrying the chieftain's lovely daughter and becoming the next king of their people. Gorm would be intolerable once he was in charge.

The thought filled Snorri with an extra, angry heave of strength, and all of a sudden, the boulder budged.

As it left the spot where it had wedged in the earth for a thousand years, there was a tremendous pop, like a cork being pulled from a bottle.

Snorri fell onto his giant backside as the boulder rolled free, a sudden updraft of wind gusting up from the hole where he'd removed the rock.

"Huh?" How could wind come out of a hole in the ground? That didn't make any sense.

Puzzled, Snorri crawled over on his hands and knees and gasped to see a HOLE in the earth! Not a simple crater in the dirt, but sheer air, like the middle of a donut—clean through.

Dread filled him.

"Oh no! What have I done?" he whispered under his breath. "Idiot! I've gone and broke the earth…"

He could already imagine Gorm howling with laughter at him over this blunder, but it was no laughing matter. No, indeed, this was serious. Snorri realized he had just ruptured Odin's seal between the worlds.

He blanched. What if Thor found out? That hammer of his could take a giant's head off. Aye, those wild Norse gods scared the daisies out of him.

They were so unpredictable, angry one minute, laughing over their drinking horns up in Valhalla the next, and always threatening to turn you into something horrid, especially that bewildering trickster, Loki—the bad one of the gods' royal family.

Oh, Loki was a slyboots...

Nevertheless, curiosity got the best of Snorri the Shepherd; he peered over the edge of the hole into empty space below.

He drew in his breath in reverent wonder as he found himself staring at the mighty Tree of the Universe, Yggdrasil, that held all the Nine Worlds of gods and men in its vast branches.

He stared at its endless trunk, whose length stretched down into the mists, and whose width was so enormous that to encircle it would have taken a string of olifants joined trunk-to-tail.

Fascinated, Snorri leaned out farther over the hole, peering at the particular branches that held up the only world he had ever known.

A world he really would've liked to leave, since everyone was mean to him around here except Princess Kaia.

Even Gorm spoke of leaving Jugenheim, even though it was not possible. It went against their adventuring Norse nature to stay always in the same place.

I wonder what's down there...

Snorri lay down on his fat belly at the edge of the hole, trying to see as much of the other worlds as he dared. Reaching ever so carefully to pluck a leaf of Yggdrasil as a gift for Kaia; he focused all his attention on his task.

He leaned a little farther—and suddenly heard a dire crack.

"Uh-oh," he mumbled as the dirt gave way beneath his tremendous weight.

The next thing he knew he was falling...

Falling, falling...

Down, down...

Down...

CHAPTER ONE

Airborne, or, The Mighty Pigeon

"Up, Jake! Into the sky! Give me a push now, and make it a good one! The more speed, the more lift!"

"You're insane," Jake replied.

The two boys stood on a windy cliff overlooking the waves far below. Incredible vistas encircled them: Green drop-away mountains ringed the glassy fjord.

As Jake peered doubtfully over the edge of the sheer rock face, an upward gust of wind blew through his blond forelock. He tossed his hair out of his shrewd blue eyes and sent his cousin, Archie, a skeptical glance. "You're sure about this?"

"Absolutely!" the boy genius said with his usual dauntless cheer. His crazy dark hair was sticking out in all directions, thanks to the goggles on his head. He pulled them down, adjusting them over his eyes, then strode toward his wondrous flying machine. "Now's the perfect time! Henry's distracted, taking a walk with his lady friend. Miss Helena's busy helping the girls unpack before the Welcome Dinner. When else will I get the chance?"

Jake's stomach grumbled at the reminder of the Welcome Dinner. At age twelve, it was safe to say he was always hungry.

Though he had never tried Norwegian food before, it had to be better than watching his slightly younger cousin risk his neck off the side of a cliff.

"Besides," Archie continued, "that thunder we heard earlier seems to have stopped, so I shouldn't get struck by lightning—"

"Shouldn't?" Jake exclaimed.

"Well, I've got to take the old girl out on a test run before I unveil her to the scientific world, don't I?" Archie countered. "Make sure she wasn't damaged on the voyage over from England, what?"

"I'm sure she was safe down in the cargo hold with Red."

"Jake, I'm not about to make a fool of myself in front of Mr. Edison and Alexander Graham Bell, to say nothing of Nik Tesla."

"I suppose," Jake said with a frown. But considering he had only just been reunited with his peculiar relatives about a month ago, after spending most of his life as a penniless orphan scrapping to survive on the streets of London, he could not bear to think of anything happening to Archie.

Risking his own safety was one thing, but the boy genius, for all his eccentricities, was the closest thing to a brother that Jake had ever had.

His final checks of wheels and tail and wings completed, Archie vaulted into the cockpit and hunkered down in the seat of his marvelous contraption.

Jake watched uncertainly while his cousin fooled with the various knobs and switches on the little dashboard he had built. The propellers tucked under the back end started turning—slowly at first, gathering speed, noisy as they whirled. Mysterious pipes puffed steam and exhaust.

Archie moved levers to adjust the canvas sails, and the Pigeon's light metal wings began to flap, like a giant pair of bat-winged kites. "Ha! There she is! Good girl!" He gave the wooden side of the Pigeon a proud slap. "Ready?"

Jake sighed. "Very well. But if you plunge to your death out there, don't come haunting me. I'll only say I told you so."

"Nonsense. If I start to crash, just use your *Fernwirkung* to catch me." His cousin waggled his fingers at him in a teasing imitation.

"That's not how I do it," Jake answered flatly. "Anyway, I don't know if it even works from that far away."

"Don't worry. Parachute's packed if anything goes awry. But it won't. I've tested this model a hundred times. Besides, I'm a genius, remember? That's why we're here."

Jake snorted. "Don't let it go to your head."

Archie laughed and pulled on his driving gloves, then buckled the safety strap across his waist. He made a few final adjustments, then gripped the steering bar. "Righty-ho! Now give me a push, coz, and I'm off into the history books!"

"Lunatic," Jake mumbled. Nevertheless, he braced his hands on the stern end of the flying machine and took a deep breath. "Here we go." He pushed with all his might, and the Pigeon began to roll.

It picked up speed, faster and faster, heading down the little path, barreling toward the cliff's edge and the smooth boulder Archie had chosen for his launch point.

Still pushing, Jake ran alongside the contraption. "Good luck!" he yelled. Nearing the cliff's edge, he gave a final shove, then stumbled to a halt.

"Woo hooooo!" Archie whooped as the Pigeon leaped away from the rock and sailed out over the water.

Panting from his sprint, Jake visored his eyes with his hand; his cousin floated on the breeze hundreds of yards above the waves. He shook his head, amazed.

It worked!

Well, of course it worked, he thought. Archie knew what he was doing. Jake shook his head, smiling ruefully. "You're still a lunatic," he whispered, pride in his brilliant cousin filling him as he watched the Pigeon climb on the currents of air, its odd wings flapping rhythmically. Blimey, what would that freckled madman think of next?

For a moment longer, he watched Archie's invention soaring like an awkward white-winged bird on the clear Nordic air.

The fjord below was a brilliant shade of peacock blue, a finger of ocean crooking into the rugged Norwegian mainland.

While the University of Oslo and its quaint little capital city nestled on the valley shores below, the mountains were wrapped in a green shawl of dense forests, crisscrossed with plunging streams that offered some of the finest salmon fishing in the world, Jake had heard.

It was a wild and beautiful place, this homeland of the Vikings. Of course, Jake was still a city dweller at heart, and being left alone in the woods a fair distance from civilization suddenly started making him uneasy.

The silence was profound, any noises muffled by the thick blanket of pine needles underfoot. *Too quiet.* No rumbling carriages, no clip-clopping hoof beats. No fishwives screaming down the street, no newsboys hawking papers on the corner.

Even the birds seemed to have stopped tweeting, and then, all of a sudden—*BANG!*

A giant boom like a mighty clap of thunder nearly knocked him off his feet.

Jake steadied himself with a gasp, instantly thinking Archie had crashed or the Pigeon had exploded in midair.

But, no, thank goodness.

When he whirled around, heart pounding, there was his cousin in the distance, gliding smoothly through the sky.

Whew. He clutched his chest in relief. Then, furrowing his brow, he wondered if one of the other scientists down at the University had exploded something. They were testing all sorts of weird things down there, showing off their latest discoveries to their colleagues.

Inventors had brought their oddball experiments from all around the world for the Invention Convention.

Whatever had caused that mighty boom, its deep reverberations were still rumbling, the very ground vibrating a little beneath his feet, though it was beginning to fade.

All of a sudden it dawned on him. *Earthquake!*

Of course! On the boat ride over from England, Henry DuVal, the boys' tutor, had taught them that all of Scandinavia was dotted with ancient volcanoes, and these, in turn, could cause occasional earthquakes.

They had neither of those things in England, so Jake could not be sure. The boy genius would have known, but up in the sky, Archie wouldn't have felt the boom nor the shaking of the ground that followed.

But if it was just a passing earthquake, then why did he have this sudden, peculiar sensation of danger lurking somewhere close?

Jake stared into the woods, but saw nothing out of the ordinary and could only conclude that it was just his imagination. He shook off the strange, uneasy feeling with a scowl, ordering himself to stick to the business at hand. The Pigeon would be landing in the fjord soon, switching into boat-mode.

Archie would need his help pulling it out of the water. With a last, uneasy glance over the cliff to make sure his cousin was still in one piece, Jake set off jogging down the mountain path.

He'd had quite enough of all this Nature for the moment. He could hardly wait to get back to civilization.

* * *

"Ugh," Snorri rumbled after a long moment.

He had finally finished falling, and the great *BANG* that had echoed across the forest had been him, of course, hitting the ground at last in a giant belly-flop.

The fall had knocked the wind out of him as he finally landed facedown in a high mountain meadow.

He rolled onto his back, stunned and blinking.

Fortunately, giants have very strong bones. He was bruised and a bit dazed from his long plunge out of Jugenheim, but as he lay on his back staring at the blue sky, he gingerly wiggled his toes, then moved his arms around and was relieved to find he had nothing broken.

At last, he sat up and shook his head to clear it. *Where am I?*

Glancing around, he saw Yggdrasil in the misty distance of another mountaintop. He memorized where it was just before the magical mists closed and hid the vast, legendary Tree from view again.

He did not know if he would ever be able to get back up to Giant Land—or if he'd even want to. Maybe he could make a new life for himself here, wherever here was.

Good question. Lumbering to his feet, Snorri noticed that the treetops were only as tall as he was. *That's odd,* he thought with a frown. Then he saw some sheep grazing in one corner of the meadow.

They had stopped chewing to stare at him, but as he stared back, Snorri was even more amazed than they were.

Why, they looked just like his dear little sheepies back home, only they were miniscule—as small as kittens.

I'm in Tinyville! he thought. But then it dawned on him he must have landed in Midgarth, the world of men. *Well! This isn't so bad, then.* He'd miss Princess Kaia terribly, but at least he wouldn't have to listen to Gorm mocking him anymore. He was free!

He decided to have a look around and try to get his bearings. Who could say? Maybe he could start a new life for himself in this quaint little place. But when his stomach rumbled, loud and long, he clapped his hands to his round belly.

First things first. A hungry giant had to eat.

He'd have to catch something for dinner—or a lot of little somethings—and build a cooking fire. "Hmmm," he rumbled, musing to himself.

Glancing around at the woods, he saw all he'd need for building traps. He snapped a few branches off some spruce trees and got to work building cages in which to catch his supper.

With any luck, he might soon get the chance to find out if humans were as tasty as he'd heard.

CHAPTER TWO
A Gathering of Geniuses

Twenty minutes later, Jake burst out of the woods at the bottom of the trail, sweaty and breathing hard after his vertical sprint down the mountain. He felt a bit silly for letting himself get rattled over nothing—nevertheless, it was good to be back in civilization again.

People were in sight, thankfully, strolling along the waterside Promenade. Nearby was the University of Oslo, which was hosting the Invention Convention. Beyond the campus lay the quaint Norwegian capital city—which wasn't a city at all, by London's sprawling standards, but a nice large town, tidy and green.

He propped his hands on his waist, pulling for air as he walked on legs that still felt rubbery toward the genteel graveled path that edged the fjord. From there, he saw that Archie had landed the Pigeon safely in the water.

The young aviator's feat had attracted the attention of an audience. The people strolling along the Promenade were staring toward the waves; ladies with parasols and gentlemen in bowler hats were pointing at Archie's strange invention with their walking sticks.

Some of the other scientists who had come from all around the world for the conference had also gathered at the water's edge to cheer for Archie's successful demonstration.

"Bravo, Archimedes!"

"Good show, lad!" they cried.

But not everyone was impressed. Henry must have glimpsed the Pigeon in the sky while taking a stroll across the campus with his lady-archeologist friend. He came running, but stopped at the shore and cupped his hands around his mouth. "Archimedes James Bradford!" he bellowed across the water. "Bring that thing to land at once! I did not give you permission to take it out!"

Uh-oh.

Ninety-nine percent of the time, Mr. Henry DuVal, the boys' tutor, was an easygoing scholar in a bowtie with a book tucked under his arm. It was the *other* one percent of the time that made Jake think twice about angering this particular teacher.

Henry and his twin sister, Miss Helena, the girls' governess, had talents that—well, suffice to say, made the DuVal twins a suitable choice as chaperones for children from an aristocratic family with magical powers.

"Jacob!" Henry turned to him just then, his wolfish, gray eyes narrowing in displeasure. "What were you thinking, letting him take the Pigeon out without asking permission first?"

"What, me?" Jake paused, startled and offended that he should have to take Archie's wigging simply because his cousin was out of range.

In truth, he was still not used to having adults tell him what to do after all his years of fending for himself. He still didn't like it, but what could you do. "Do you think I could've stopped 'im?" he mumbled.

"Don't give me your cheek!" Henry barked. "He could've been killed! Don't you understand that? When people don't follow the rules, it's only a matter of time before someone gets hurt!"

"And do you always follow the rules, Monsieur DuVal?" a teasing voice asked from behind them.

Henry looked over his shoulder at the tall, blond lady striding toward them. "Always," he retorted.

She laughed. "What a pity!"

Jake surmised this was Henry's Norwegian archeologist friend and penpal, Miss Astrid Langesund.

Archie had told him Henry spent time with her at every annual science conference, and the two exchanged letters now and then throughout the year.

Miss Langesund assisted her father, the famous archeologist, Professor Langesund, who also taught here at the University. The Langesunds were natives of Norway, and were particularly excited that the conference was taking place in their home city this year.

"That was quite a sprint, sir," Miss Langesund teased as she caught up to Henry. "Have you been training for a marathon?"

Jake liked her accent.

"Sorry, Astrid. I hate to cut our stroll short, but these boys do the dashedest things! That one may be a genius—" he nodded at Archie out on the water, "but sometimes I'd swear he's got no common sense."

"Ah, my father's the same way," she said with a chuckle. "Geniuses usually are."

"Now, now, you're just as much of a genius as anyone else here, and you know how to keep your head on straight!" he protested. "Then there's this one," he added, nodding at Jake. "The rebel."

"Who, me?" Jake asked innocently.

"Yes, you! There's a right way and a wrong way to do things, Jake. If people don't behave in an orderly fashion, everything turns to chaos. Is that what you want?"

"Oh, don't be so strict, Henry. They're just boys." Miss Langesund sent Jake a sympathetic smile, but Henry scowled.

With a huff, he turned back toward the water and folded his arms across his chest, waiting for Archie to bring the Pigeon in to shore.

Miss Langesund turned to Jake. "Since Mr. DuVal has sadly forgotten his manners, I'll introduce myself. I'm Miss Astrid Langesund, and you must be Archie's long-lost cousin, the young Lord Griffon, yes?"

"Just Jake, ma'am," he answered with a slight, respectful bow, just like Henry had taught him. Though the title of Lord Griffon was, indeed, rightfully his, hearing it still made him think of his wicked Uncle Waldrick, who had stolen the title for a number of years, and had nearly succeeded in cheating Jake out of his entire inheritance. Not to mention his life.

"Well, it's nice to meet you, Just Jake." She acknowledged him with a nod. "And welcome to Norway."

"Thank you, Miss Langesund. It's nice to meet you, too."

When she turned back to Henry, the two adults resumed their own conversation; Jake studied her surreptitiously.

Being all of twelve, he was no expert on ladies, but he suspected that with her true Viking blood, the lady scientist could have been a stunner if she weren't such a quiz.

She had the tall, athletic figure, golden hair, and rosy-cheeked beauty of so many Scandinavian girls—Jake had definitely noticed them everywhere since he'd stepped off the ship.

Unfortunately, Miss Langesund had no more fashion sense than the rest of the rumpled geniuses at the convention. Her hairdo was a disaster, two braids wrapped like Danish pastries stuck on each side of her head. Black-rimmed spectacles nearly as thick as Archie's goggles perched on the bridge of her pretty nose.

No doubt the lady scientist was too busy digging up old, dead bones with her famous father to give a fig for female fripperies.

She suddenly turned to Jake. "Has Henry told you about the surprise that my father and I have to show you all?"

"Er, no," Jake said with a curious glance at Henry.

"Miss Langesund and her father recently made a great discovery from the Viking age," Henry informed him. "She has kindly offered to give us a private tour of the exhibit. It's housed right here at the University."

"Brilliant! What did you find?"

"You'll see," she said with a mysterious smile.

"Are you all right, Jake?" Henry asked all of a sudden, giving him a probing glance. "You seem a little... off."

"I do?" Blimey, did he still look rattled after that unsettling episode in the woods? He did his best to shrug it off. "Just a little jolted, I guess, by that earthquake of a bit ago, that's all. Never felt one of those before."

"What earthquake?" Henry asked.

"You didn't feel it?" Jake answered in surprise, glancing from one to the other.

They just looked at him.

"Maybe it wasn't very strong down here by the fjord, but you could certainly feel it up in the mountains," he informed them. "Nearly shook me off m'feet."

Miss Langesund furrowed her brow. "We didn't have an earthquake, Jake."

"Then what was that bang?" he exclaimed, but everyone forgot about him as Archie arrived on the shore.

"Cheerio, everybody!" The beaming boy inventor waved to his audience from the cockpit of his flying machine.

Jake rolled his eyes as the watching scientists gave Archie another round of doting applause. *Here we go again.*

On the voyage over from England, Jake couldn't help but notice that Archie was quite the darling of the scientific world.

About a dozen other scientists and scholars from London had traveled over to Norway on the same ship on which they had sailed, and Jake had been surprised to find that they all knew his cousin.

Apparently, Archie had given his first lecture at one of these annual conferences two years ago, when he was only nine.

That explained it, then. But as Jake had watched Archie being greeted by one brilliant egghead after another, he had begun feeling extremely out of place.

He had nothing to add to the conversation, nothing to offer as he sat in the gilded parlor of the luxury steam-liner, waiting in boredom while Archie talked science with the big-brained adults.

The boy genius had chatted like an old clubman with mathematicians and engineers, inventors and astronomers, physicists who could figure out the weight of the earth, but couldn't seem to manage to brush their hair.

Indeed, crazy hair apparently came with each advanced degree, Jake had irreverently concluded. It seemed a fair gauge: the crazier the hair, the smarter the head beneath it.

In any case, as Archie steered his contraption to shore, Henry went to scold him, and Jake followed to help his cousin pull the Pigeon out of the fjord.

The foreign scientists gathered around, hailing their young mascot on his victory. One gave Archie a hand up from the cockpit.

"You could have killed yourself!" Henry started, but Archie's fellow scientists pooh-poohed his tutor's worries.

Miss Langesund kept the peace. "Why don't you gentlemen come to the Exhibit Hall and get your first look at all the other inventions?" she suggested.

"Good idea. You go on ahead, Arch," Jake said hastily. "I'll put the Pigeon away for you."

"Oh, would you?" Archie exclaimed. "Thanks, coz, if you don't mind. Take good care of her for me!"

Jake nodded, glad to stay out of all that lofty scientific talk. "I'll come and find you when I'm done," he assured him.

"Thanks loads, Jake! See you inside," Archie said, then he went off with his crowd of adult admirers, quite the man of the hour.

Henry could barely get close enough to scold him, which Miss Langesund seemed to find entirely amusing.

As the group headed for the Exhibit Hall, the heart of the Invention Convention, Jake got to work hauling the glider out of the fjord. Once he had it on solid ground, he dried it off with the towel stowed in the boot, then folded down the wings.

Finally, he started wheeling the Pigeon off to the storage room, but he couldn't help glancing back over his shoulder at the distant mountain. He scanned the forests warily, more confused than ever.

If that boom was not an earthquake, then what the blazes had he heard?

CHAPTER THREE
The Invention Convention

When he finished locking up the glider, Jake set off for the Exhibit Hall to find Archie and the others. Walking through the green, leafy grounds of the campus, he wondered if he'd ever go to a university like this. He supposed the place was usually much busier than it was now, in June.

All the students had gone home for the summer. The dormitories and large academic buildings were standing empty, which was why the scientists had decided to hold the conference there.

The campus had plenty of lecture halls like the one where Archie was scheduled to give his speech on aerodynamics later in the week. Plenty of space for the scientists to set up their inventions, so they could show their colleagues what they had been working on.

Archie said this casual exchange of information each year always sent him home with tons of new ideas for things to build and new experiments to play with.

When Jake walked in, the huge Exhibit Hall buzzed with conversation and the noise of the countless strange and wonderful inventions on display.

Everywhere, odd machines were chugging, whirring, hovering, clicking and revolving, burping steam and whooshing out fumes: brass and steel, rivets and engines, pumping pistons, beeps and whistles.

Tables and booths were set up with various displays where the inventors could tell visitors about their gadgets. Jake walked down the aisles between them, gawking at everything that the day's wizards of science from all around the world had dreamed up or discovered.

A woman riding on a dirigible chair floated past, offering a tray of sweetmeats. Jake accepted one and thanked her, marveling at the miniature blimp that kept her chair suspended several feet off the ground.

He wandered on, approaching a cluster of people who were all speaking different languages and laughing at themselves and each other. He furrowed his brow as he read the placard in front of the table.

Professor Stokes' Rosetta Stone Babblegum.

"Free samples! You, young man! Would you like to try a slice of Babblegum?" the inventor offered him, gesturing to various colorful flavors. "Just choose your language—and chew!"

"Do you have Norwegian?"

"Sorry, all out. Would you like to try Swahili?"

He shrugged. "Why not. Thanks!" He accepted a slice of the Swahili-language Babblegum, though he didn't even know where in the world people spoke it.

Moving on, he stepped into an aisle marked Medical Advancements, where he saw an enormous, clumsy fellow with a terrible, ash-gray complexion staring dully into space.

A crazy-haired scientist in a white laboratory coat stood beside the large oaf, speaking to those who had gathered around. "Allow me to demonstrate!" he was saying to his awed-looking audience, then he picked up a violin and began playing a mournful tune.

The melody drew the big, dark-clad oaf out of his reverie. He let out a low, animal moan and began swaying back and forth.

The watchers gasped in amazement and backed away a bit, then applauded as the big oaf began stomping back and forth like he was dancing.

"It's just astonishing, Doctor Frankenstein! What do you call the process?"

"Reanimation!" he replied with a dramatic chord on his violin. "Through the wonders of electricity, we shall unlock the secrets of immortality!"

The people gasped and then applauded, and the scientist put aside his violin to take a modest bow. "I'll be happy to answer all your questions at my lecture tomorrow afternoon..."

A reanimated corpse! Jake shuddered and moved on.

Turning down the next aisle, he spotted Miss Langesund standing in a booth beside an older gent, who was smoking a pipe as he answered questions from the curious. When Jake saw a sign that said ARCHEOLOGY ROW, he realized that must be her father.

But it was not just the Langesunds' Viking artifacts on display in this amazing aisle. The top archeologists from all over Europe had brought their latest finds.

There was a terrifying dinosaur skull with huge teeth and a collection of bones; early tools from cavemen; spooky Egyptian mummies in grave wrappings lay in their opened sarcophagi. But the biggest crowd of all flocked around the booth of a German fellow called Professor Schliemann, who—according to the placard—had just discovered the ancient city of Troy. Security guards stood watch over the solid gold "Mask of Agamemnon."

Whoever that was, Jake thought.

The line to see the ancient Greek mask was too long to bother with for an impatient lad who was more interested in a heaping plate of food at the Welcome Dinner than seeing all this stuff.

Drifting on, hands in pockets, Jake wandered into the AISLE OF INDUSTRY, passing a complicated, noisy heap of metal labeled "Combustion Engine." He did not know what it did or why anyone would want one, so he hurried on, past another massive bulk called a "Freight Elevator," with huge pulleys and powerful hydraulics.

A little farther on, he came to a display of miniature trains where a twangy-voiced American detailed the railways being built across the Wild West, with the help of some new explosive called "Dynamite." It just looked like red sticks to Jake.

Soon, he arrived at the aisle for COMMUNICATIONS. Here he came face to face with the newest wonder from Archie's hero, Mr. Alexander Graham Bell. Proudly displayed on a pedestal sat some weird new contraption called a "Telephone."

Jake wasn't sure how it worked, but rumor had it that it would soon replace the telegraph altogether. He was skeptical. *We'll see.*

Strolling through the IMPROVEMENTS FOR THE HOME aisle, he heard a man demonstrating a brand-new gadget called a "Carpet Sweeper."

"Your chamber maids will no longer need a broom to sweep the floors!" the man promised.

"Amazing!" people raved, staring at the newfangled thing.

That'll put a lot of maids out of work, Jake thought. Next he strolled into a fun row: PHOTOGRAPHY & ENTERTAINMENT.

A man in a top hat was demonstrating something called a

"Cylinder Phonograph" that made music come out of a large horn attached to a rotatey silver thing—and then there was something even stranger.

Jake stopped and stared in shock at the "Moving Pictures." He couldn't believe his eyes as the pictures flashed in continuous motion on the screen.

Blimey, what would they think of next?

Rather overwhelmed by all this Progress, he shook off a disoriented feeling and went looking for his cousin. When he finally spotted Archie with Henry in the aisle labeled PHYSICS & ASTRONOMY, they were surrounded by other geniuses, deep in conversation.

Jake hesitated, not at all sure he wanted to go blundering into the middle of that egghead conversation.

The truth was, he had been feeling self-conscious and defensive about his lack of education ever since they had arrived.

He had plenty of street-smarts after his pickpocket years, but he had only attended the orphanage school long enough to learn the rudiments of math and reading, and he didn't much care for either. He preferred to think of himself a young man of action—more of a doer than a thinker.

Archie, on the other hand, had started solving algebra equations at age four. He took up chemistry by six, and by nine could fix anything mechanical. His favorite hobby was designing amazing bits of gadgetry, and if he could not find the tools he needed to build some new invention, he made the tools, too.

As the tutor for both students, Henry had privately told Jake not to feel bad about his inability to keep up with Archie in their studies. With his world-class intellect, few people on earth could. At age eleven, Archie already held two degrees from Oxford.

And with all the geniuses here, he was right at home.

Jake, on the other hand, felt as dumb in their eyes as Doctor Frankenstein's big, dancing oaf had seemed to the crowd. With that thought, he decided not to join them, but to wait until Archie was through.

Fortunately, he was not left alone for long.

A familiar, high-pitched voice suddenly called his name. "Jake! Jake, look! I almost got everyone on my list! You'll want to see this." Dani O'Dell came striding toward him, all business.

The little redhead had followed him out of the rough-and-tumble rookery neighborhood, where she had been his one true friend through thick and thin.

When his aristocratic relatives had found him, to Jake's relief, Great-Great Aunt Ramona had hired Dani to serve as lady's companion to Cousin Isabelle, Archie's elder sister.

He was thankful because now he didn't have to worry about Dani. She loved her new life as Isabelle's hired companion.

The two girls balanced each other well. Though Dani was only ten, she was rookery-tough, while the fourteen-year-old empath, Isabelle, was a soft and delicate soul.

As Dani marched toward him, her pen and book in hand, Jake decided to play a trick on her and popped the Babblegum into his mouth. "There you are!" she said.

"Jambo!" he answered in greeting.

"What?"

"Nafurahi kukuona. Jina langu ni Jake."

She stared at him, brow furrowed.

He took the gum out of his mouth, laughing. "My name is Jake," he informed her, holding up the chewed gum. "Babblegum. Want to try it?"

She grimaced at his chewed gum, shook her head at him, and muttered "daftling," just as her tiny brown Norwich terrier stuck his head out of the satchel on her shoulder and growled at the "Moving Pictures."

"Calm down, Teddy, they're not real. If you're done speaking whatever language that was—"

"Swahili. Kind of spicy. Cayenne pepper maybe?"

"—I wanted to show you something," she continued, ignoring him. "Have a look at this!" Dani opened the Norway tour book she had bought with her earnings in the shop aboard the massive luxury steam-liner on which they had sailed over from England.

Proudly, she showed him all the famous names scribbled on the overleaf.

Thomas Edison, Nikola Tesla, Jules Verne...

"I'm collecting all their autographs in one book! This is going to be worth a lot o' money someday, you wait and see."

"Brilliant," Jake murmured, glancing at her in surprise.

She lifted her chin, her green eyes glowing with satisfaction. "It is rather brilliant of me, ain't it?"

Clearly, one month in their new, easy life among the aristocrats was not enough to erase from her memory how they had struggled to survive in the rough rookery neighborhood.

Dani had sold apples in Covent Garden Market before both their situations had so drastically improved, and it seemed she still thought like a wee businesswoman. Jake couldn't help but admire her for it, even though Great-Great Aunt Ramona would have sniffed in disdain. Trade, after all, wasn't considered very aristocratic. Nevertheless, the rookery lass was a survivor.

Like him.

"Did you finish unpacking your trunk?" he asked, sparing her the Swahili. A traveling trunk, in itself, was still a novelty to them both, considering this was their first-ever holiday anywhere.

Dani nodded eagerly, tucking her book away. "Miss Helena's still in the dormitory arranging our rooms and pressing our gowns for the Welcome Dinner. She said me and Isabelle could come and have a look at the inventions."

"Where is Isabelle, anyway?" Jake glanced around curiously for his elder cousin.

"Oh, she felt sorry for young Mr. Tesla." Dani gave him an arch look. "Poor thing! He's so shy, he can barely speak to people. You know how Isabelle likes to put others at ease. Well, she got him talkin' about electricity, then nothing could shut 'im up. I couldn't take it anymore, but she couldn't get away. You know our Isabelle. She didn't want to be rude."

Jake laughed heartily, glad he never had that problem.

"Last I saw her, she was letting him rig her up to some contraption that measures the electrical waves comin' out of your head."

"Isabelle's got electricity coming out of her head? Well, that explains a lot," he drawled.

"We all do, you glock-wit." Dani glanced over her shoulder to make sure no one was eavesdropping. "You should let Mr. Tesla measure your brain waves, too, Jake. You really should, considering the *talents* that run in your family—"

"No," he cut her off.

"As a contribution to science! Your brain waves, and maybe the ones from your fingers, too. I've heard you say you think it's some sort of electrical energy that flows out of your hands when you...you know."

"Absolutely not." Jake shook his head stubbornly. "Aunt Ramona warned me not to let these eggheads know what I can do, or they'll take me for a lab rat. Izzy, too, to say nothing of Henry and Helena. If they learn about our abilities, they'll be tryin' to dissect us."

"Oh, I don't think Mr. Tesla would ever do that. He's countin' on Archie to introduce him to Thomas Edison. Did you know Mr. Tesla wants to go to America and work for Mr. Edison someday?"

Before Jake could answer, Dani's little brown dog erupted with angry barking. "Teddy, stop that!" she cried, but the wee Norwich terrier ignored her startled efforts to calm him down.

Eight pounds of pure fury, Teddy squirmed and growled and wriggled, trying to jump out of his satchel on her shoulder—a dangerous height for a little dog to fall. "Teddy, you're going to hurt yourself! Settle down, be quiet! What's wrong with you? Teddy—!"

Dani half-caught the dog as he leaped out of the satchel. She wasn't fast enough to prevent him from escaping, but at least she broke his fall.

Safely on the ground, Teddy bolted, still barking, his leash trailing out behind him. "Teddy! Come back!" Dani yelled.

Jake and she exchanged a look of bewilderment.

Then they both ran after the dog.

CHAPTER FOUR
The Galton Whistle

The little dog dashed ahead, barking as he wove through a forest of legs. Though he nearly got trampled twice, it did not slow him down.

"Where's he going?" Dani cried as they chased.

"I don't know! Let's split up," Jake said. "You go that way to block the exit. I'll head him off here."

She nodded and rushed off, trying to beat the dog to the exits, but Jake sprinted after the tiny terrier directly. His old days as a pickpocket fleeing the London bobbies came in handy as he dodged through the crowd.

"Teddy! Here, boy! Excuse me," he muttered when he bumped into a stout lady blocking the aisle.

Oddly, Teddy seemed to have a very clear idea of where he was going. He bolted around the corner ahead and into the aisle of medical advancements.

Jake was baffled, but saw he had a chance to catch the dog if he jumped aisles. Turning down a parallel row, he vaulted over a display table and landed in the middle of the medical aisle.

Teddy was on his way, thundering straight at him like a furry brown cannonball.

Jake crouched down with his arms spread wide, heart pounding, as Teddy barreled toward him. "Now I've got you," he mumbled, but when Jake dove for him, swiping with both arms to catch the wee rascal, it was no better than his efforts to grab that ghost back in London who had refused to answer his questions.

Teddy almost seemed to laugh at him, leaping nimbly through the circle of his arms.

"Blast it!" Jake landed indecorously on his face in the middle of the floor. At once, he pushed to his feet and was off and running again.

This time, within seconds, he caught up to Teddy. The dog had stopped at one of the booths, as though this had been his destination all along.

The little terrier was standing on his hind legs, tail wagging, his front paws leaning on the knees of a tall gentleman-scientist in a lab coat.

The man leaned down with a chuckle to pat Teddy on the head. A pair of his colleagues standing with him laughed.

"Well, well, what have we here? So sorry, little fellow! Did the noise from my invention disturb you?"

"Arf!" Teddy answered, one ear perked up, the other flopped down.

"Perhaps *we* didn't hear anything, Sir Francis, but here's our proof your whistle really works!" his colleague said with an amiable smile.

"You could never doubt me, could you?" Sir Francis replied. A bald-headed man with mutton-chop whiskers, he picked Teddy up in his arms just as Jake stepped forward to claim the dog for Dani.

"Sorry about that, sir. I'll take him."

"Oh, it's quite all right, young man. I fear I gave him reason to come to me. Is this your dog?" he asked, and when the man glanced at him, Jake was taken aback by the frosty coldness in his deep-set eyes.

It was a chill devoid of cruelty, but made up of unfeeling detachment, as if this Sir Francis fellow were some sort of inhuman machine himself.

What made his dead-eyed stare all the more confusing was that it was so at odds with the cordial smile on his lips.

Unnerved, Jake fairly stammered. "N-no, sir, the dog belongs to my friend—"

"He's mine!" Dani cried, arriving at that moment to snatch her fuzzy babydoll protectively out of the scientist's arms.

The gentlemen standing around laughed at her defensiveness, as though amused that the girl seemed to fear they'd do animal experiments on her pup if they got the chance.

"Apologies, my dear," said Sir Francis with a stiff nod. "I did not mean to upset you or your pet. I was just showing these friends of mine one of my new inventions."

"A whistle that only a dog can hear," one of the other white-coated fellows supplied, hands in pockets.

"Well, cats, too, and most animals can hear it," Sir Francis corrected. "But the sound it creates falls out of the range of human hearing. It's to be used as a training tool for dogs and other animals."

"May I see it?" Jake asked curiously.

Sir Francis nodded with a gesture. "Be my guest."

The other scientist handed it to Jake. Still hugging Teddy close, Dani looked on while he examined it.

The whistle was about four inches long and made of shiny brass. Its design hinted at its purpose: a dog's head adorned the top of it, while a gold chain passed through a ring on the end. "It's hardly meant as jewelry," Sir Francis remarked. "The chain simply makes it more convenient for a dog trainer to wear it around his neck."

"I see," Jake said with a vague nod, wondering if it would work on pet gryphons. He hadn't seen Red since they had left the steamship. The poor, seasick beast had flown off into the forest as soon as they had let him out of his crate in the ship's cargo hold.

Jake smiled to himself at the thought of his strange but extremely loyal and fiercely protective pet, half-eagle, half-lion. He had tried to make Red stay behind in England, but the Gryphon was having none of it. When their party had boarded the steam-liner, Red had run back and forth along the shore roaring so loudly that he had risked being seen by non-magical humans.

That was when Jake had realized that gryphons apparently didn't like flying over the ocean. Maybe because they were half-lion, and lions couldn't swim.

Well, the creatures definitely did *not* enjoy traveling belowdecks in a crate, either, as Jake had also learned.

He had barely managed to coax Red into the large crate marked "DANGER! LIVE ANIMALS" in which the Gryphon had spent the duration of the voyage. Red had been very glad to be released when they arrived, though this, too, had been tricky, keeping the mythical beast from being seen by any of the crew or passengers.

Somehow they had succeeded, and the Gryphon had flown up into the forests to recover from the journey. Why, at this very moment, he was probably gulping down some of those famed

Norwegian salmon from the streams up on the mountain, Jake mused, still examining the whistle.

He handed it back to its inventor with a nod as the other scientists took leave of him.

"Quite ingenious, Galton. Well done!" one said.

"Give our regards to Charles when you see him," the other added.

"I shall, gentlemen. Good day," he said with a nod as his colleagues drifted on to peruse more displays.

"Wait—you're Doctor Galton?" Dani turned suddenly and gaped at him.

"Last I checked," he answered in amusement.

"Sir Francis Galton—the Prince of the Polymaths?" she exclaimed. "Mr. Charles Darwin's cousin?"

"Half cousin," he admitted in a modest tone. He seemed pleased by her recognition and bowed politely. "At your service, young lady."

To Jake's surprise, Dani was ecstatic. "My goodness, I can't believe it's really you!"

"What's a polymath?" Jake mumbled.

"An expert in many different fields of science. Sir Francis Galton is one of Archie's heroes!" she exclaimed.

"Well, bless me," the polymath said with another chilly smile that never quite reached his eyes. "You know young Master Archie?"

"He's my friend," she said.

"And my cousin," Jake replied.

Sir Francis eyed him at once in speculation, as though Jake's being cousins with a genius might make him a genius, too. *Not bloody likely,* he thought, sorry to disappoint the Prince of the Polymaths.

"Of course, the admiration is most heartily returned," Sir Francis said with almost a hint of warmth. "Indeed, I've often said the lad reminds me of myself when I was his age. It's not easy being a child prodigy," he added.

"Sir, if it isn't too much trouble," Dani spoke up, "I wonder, would you sign my book?" Without waiting for an answer, she thrust Teddy into Jake's arms and scrambled to retrieve it from her satchel.

"I'd be honored, young lady," Sir Francis said in surprise. "I don't think anyone's ever asked me for my autograph before!" He accepted her book and set it on the table to sign it.

"So, um, what inspired you to invent a whistle for a dog, Dr. Galton?" she ventured.

"I was studying the range of human hearing, actually."

"Dr. Galton has studied *everything!*" Dani gushed to Jake, no doubt already imagining how the value of her autograph book was climbing as the ink from his signature dried. "Geology. Meteorology—that's the weather—"

"I'm not stupid," Jake retorted.

She ignored him, counting off more subjects. "Anthropology, medicine, all sorts of mathematics. And when he was younger, he went as an explorer to wonderful faraway lands! Isn't that right, sir?"

Sir Francis laughed. "Have you been checking up on me, my dear?"

"Sorry—Archie told me all about you. Between you and your cousin, Mr. Darwin, well, genius obviously runs in your—what do you call 'em—genetics?"

"Yes, my research does suggest that intelligence is a genetic trait. And you are correct, our extended family has always been a science-minded clan, whether doctors or inventors."

"Including inventing weapons of war?" a familiar voice remarked from behind them in a hostile tone.

Jake glanced over his shoulder in shock as his cousin Isabelle joined them, a rare look of loathing on her face.

She folded her arms across her chest. "Wartime profiteering... Rather an odd line of business for a peace-loving Quaker family, isn't it, Dr. Galton?"

Jake and Dani turned to the golden-haired fourteen-year-old in astonishment. Neither of them had ever heard the soft-spoken, sympathetic, usually tenderhearted Isabelle speak to anyone in such a harsh tone before.

Sir Francis also looked taken aback by her unprovoked attack, though the flash of embarrassment on his face revealed her words were true.

Still, Jake was suddenly on guard. He had *never* seen Isabelle be deliberately mean to anyone before. He had not thought her capable of it. She was usually so good and pure that surely her reaction must mean that Dr. Galton was not to be trusted.

Jake glanced darkly at the scientist once more, all the more suspicious.

Isabelle gave the Prince of the Polymaths a glare. "Jake, Dani, come along. Before somebody here should deem us among the Unfit."

She took them each by an elbow and steered them away.

Dani studied her with a worried look, but Jake was baffled. "What on earth did Mr. Tesla do to you? Implant a mean streak in your head?" he asked under his breath.

Staring straight ahead, Isabelle walked them toward the exit. "Stay away from that man, you two. It's bad enough he's befriended my brother. Please, I don't want you going near him."

"Why ever not?" Dani exclaimed.

"That is a deeply wicked man," she said in a hard tone.

"Why?" Jake demanded. "What's he done?"

CHAPTER FIVE
Two Paths

"It's not what he's done, it's what he believes," she replied. "He's the most dangerous sort of person there is. The type who's convinced that everything he does is for the greater good, so how dare anyone question him?"

"Are you sure about this?" Jake murmured.

"I feel like I've got a spike in my head from being near him," she declared. "For me, that's all the proof I need."

They both knew that Isabelle had a sort of allergy to evil. She could sense it even when no one else quite could. It was part of her role as Keeper of the Unicorns; she was responsible for the wellbeing of the protected unicorn herd that roamed the woods of the Bradford family's estate back in England, Bradford Park. She shared telepathy with animals, clearly able to read their thoughts, but she could only sense the emotions of people...and the presence of whatever shadows lurked in their hearts.

"What does Dr. Galton believe that's so bad?" Jake persisted as they walked on through the crowd.

"That some people are worth more than others based on their genetics," she answered.

"Aren't they?" he asked.

"Jake!" She recoiled from the question, then turned and glared at him, appalled. "No!"

"Sorry, I was just asking," he mumbled.

"Well, the answer is no. Not at all. And you must never forget it. Everyone matters, Jake. Every life has value. Not even a genius like the Prince of the Polymaths has the right to play God and decide who deserves to live and who's not good enough. Who's Fit or Unfit. The arrogance of such a notion is obscene."

Dani and Jake exchanged an unsettled look.

"What do you mean, Unfit?" Dani asked worriedly.

Isabelle considered how to say it. "It's almost too cruel to put into words, Dani. Dr. Galton is working on a theory called eugenics that picks up where Mr. Darwin's evolution theory leaves off. He says why not help evolution along by weeding out the weak among us?"

"But we're supposed to protect the weak," Jake said. "That's chivalry."

"That's right. More than chivalry, humanity," she said sharply. "If you asked Dr. Galton and his ilk, he would say that the Unfit include the poor and unfortunate, people who are sick or blind or deaf or simple. Even those whose skin is considered the wrong color. If they had their way, they'd even let unwanted children die."

Dani and Jake gasped simultaneously, thinking of all their dear friends back at the orphanage. Unwanted children, all.

"He would...kill them?" Dani breathed.

"Of course." Isabelle nodded somberly. "What does it matter, if people are only animals, glorified apes? Killing them shouldn't matter any more than exterminating rats or raising chickens for food, should it?"

"But people have a soul!" Dani protested.

"They don't believe that," Isabelle replied.

"But I've seen them," Jake interjected. "Ghosts. The spirits of people who've died. They live on. I know. I've talked to them."

"Say so and they'll put you in a lunatic asylum."

"How horrible," Dani whispered, shaking her head.

But Jake was too furious to comment until he finally managed to growl, "Is Galton one of the Dark Druids? Tell me."

Isabelle put her arm fondly around his shoulders with a sad smile. "No, Jake. He's just a scientist, and sadly, his views are not nearly as uncommon as they should be. I'm afraid, for all their intellect, some of these geniuses are blind to right and wrong. All of their inventions and discoveries, just like your gifts and mine, can be used for either great good or great evil."

She released him from her casual half-hug to point at the Chemistry aisle. "If you want to see the good side, look at Louis Pasteur over there, for contrast with our Dr. Galton. Instead of trying to figure out which diseases classify someone as Unfit, Mr. Pasteur is trying to solve the whole problem of disease by studying this new germ theory. Have you heard of it?"

"A little," Jake replied.

"Some people think that very tiny creatures called microbes, or germs, invade the body and cause us to get sick." Isabelle shrugged. "I would hardly know about that. What I *do* know is that Mr. Pasteur has already saved thousands of people's lives by simply making sure the milk is safe to drink."

Jake stared at the modest-looking man in his fifties greeting people in the Chemistry aisle. Noting how Mr. Pasteur held his left arm at an odd angle and limped a bit, Jake was stunned.

"He's partly paralyzed," he murmured, glancing at Isabelle. "So would Mr. Pasteur be considered Unfit, too, then?"

"He very well might. Heavens, even Thomas Edison might not have made the cut, judging by his boyhood. Everyone knows he failed out of school and had to be taught at home by his mother. Plus, Mr. Edison is somewhat deaf in both ears, so, yes, I daresay Dr. Galton might've tossed him in the trash, too." She shook her head. "I just hope that when my brother grows up, he will choose wisely about which sort of scientist he wants to be."

"You look pale. Are you feeling all right?" Dani asked, taking Isabelle's elbow in concern.

She gave her a grateful smile. "Actually, being around Dr. Galton has given me rather a headache. I could use some air."

"Come on, we'll step outside. I'll go with you," Dani murmured, looking deeply upset by Isabelle's revelations. "Jake, do you want to come along?"

"I think I'll go find Archie," he replied. "Have a word with him about his admiration for the Prince of the Polymaths."

"Good idea." Isabelle nodded. "He'll listen to you more than he ever listens to me."

"Surely Archie doesn't agree with Galton's madness?" Dani exclaimed as they turned to go.

"No, it's not that. You know Archie," Isabelle said. "He just wants to get along with everyone. He makes a lot of excuses for his fellow scientists and falls into the trap, I think, of allowing them to ignore questions of right and wrong in their experiments for the sake of science."

Experiments like, oh, reanimating corpses? Jake wondered wryly, recalling Doctor Frankenstein's dancing dead man. Bloody unnatural.

"I believe the day will come when Archie will have to make a choice and speak out among his colleagues to warn them when they're going too far. At least they might listen to him."

Jake nodded, taking it all in. "Feel better soon, Izzy," he offered.

She cast him a wan smile, then she and Dani left the Exhibit Hall.

Jake, troubled by all he'd heard, turned to look for Archie. As he sauntered back the way he had come, he passed Dr. Galton once more, busy in his booth spreading his warped ideas to more of his fellow scientists. Too bad the man had not stuck to dog whistles and mathematics.

When his stomach rumbled again, Jake glanced down at his pocket watch, wondering how much longer it would be before the Welcome Dinner. He was starved.

But just as he lifted his head again, slipping his watch back into his vest pocket, he glanced up to find a towering, high-wheeled bicycle barreling straight toward him down the aisle.

"Watch out! Move! Move! Out of my way!" the bicyclist yelled, gesturing him aside.

Jake leaped clear just in time to avoid being flattened. The high-wheeler passed so close that the breeze from its spokes fanned his face; its front wheel was nearly as tall as he was.

The lunatic rider zoomed past: a long, lanky man leaning over the handlebars and working the pedals with maniacal speed.

With his opera cloak flapping out behind him, he was humming that famous new song, "The Ride of the Valkyries."

Jake recognized it because he had heard it in London only a week ago, when Great-Great Aunt Ramona had dragged him to the opera for the first time. The tempestuous brass-and-cymbals of the famous Norse-themed song had made quite an impression on him, not the least because the orchestra had played it twice that night— the second time, as an encore.

Aside from that catchy tune, the only thing Jake had learned that night was that he was not a great fan of opera.

But he was even less fond of people who tried to run him over.

Furious at the fool, he stepped back into the center of the aisle and glared after him. Then it was his turn to smirk, for those high-wheelers couldn't make sharp turns.

His eyes narrowed in satisfaction as he watched the fool tip the giant bicycle over, taking the turn at the end of the aisle too fast.

The crazed rider lost control, wrecked the tall bicycle into a pillar, and went flying off the side, landing in a heap of pointy knees and sharp elbows.

But then Jake frowned, for the man got up laughing like a loon-bat, glanced around the Exhibit Hall, and dashed off again, obviously looking for more trouble.

What the—?

When the maniac rushed into another aisle full of delicate inventions, Jake frowned in concern.

Who is this joker?

He followed the stranger with caution. Trailing him from several yards behind, Jake was mystified and a little alarmed by what he saw.

The loon-bat certainly did not behave like a scientist. He wasn't wearing a lab coat, nor did he have particularly crazy hair.

His hair, in fact, was long and jet-black and rather stringy; his face was long and thin, too—almost goatish with his little goatee beard, a dark triangle on his chin. His tall, skinny frame was clad in elegant black clothes and draped in a long black cloak.

As Jake warily approached, the man appeared to be having a grand time, laughing to himself with irreverent delight and playing with all the inventions.

Signs everywhere said *DO NOT TOUCH*, but he ignored them.

He examined one item after another as if they were toys, then tossed them aside.

Jake watched him, taken aback.

Mad as a hatter, the strange man seemed to be in his own world. Then Jake realized that he must be someone important, for everyone else left him alone to do whatever he liked.

The loon-bat dared to put on the thick, padded "Super Strength Gloves" and wiggled his fingers, giggling as he inspected them. He crouched down and tapped the floor, cracking the flagstones with two fingers.

Another hearty chuckle. "Very nice!" Moving on, he paused to try on the "Lie Detector Goggles." Peering through them, he began scanning the Exhibit Hall, and that was when he noticed Jake trailing him.

The man snapped his fingers impatiently. "You, boy! Come here at once!"

"Excuse me?" Jake retorted, offended by the summons.

"Chop-chop, front and center!"

"Why?"

"Because," he said. "I want you to lie to me."

"What?"

CHAPTER SIX
A Loon-bat on the Loose

"Tell me a lie," the odd man commanded. "I want to see if these things work. Go on, hurry. Make it a whopper!"

Jake was not amused. He folded his arms across his chest and tried to look like his stern idol back in England, the warrior Derek Stone. "You shouldn't be touching these inventions."

"Nonsense." The man lowered the Lie Detector Goggles, revealing fiery black eyes that brimmed with mischief and mayhem. "I can do whatever I want. Who's going to stop me? You?"

"If I have to," Jake replied rather more bravely than he had cause for.

The man set the goggles back on the display table. "Boy, you obviously don't know who I am."

Jake shrugged with all his rookery bravado. "Don't really care, either. You're going to break something and it's not right. These people worked really hard on their inventions."

"But that's what I do, my lad. I break things! It's so much more fun than going to all that bother of trying to make stuff. Trust me, you should try it sometime. The real fun's in destruction, not creation. What's your name?"

He eyed him warily. "Jake."

"Take? Ahh, so you take things?"

"No, I said—"

"Excellent—a thief! Ha! I knew I liked you, Take. Rude, too. We shall be great friends. So, what sort of things do you most enjoy stealing?"

Jake gritted his teeth. "My name is not Take."

This was a rather sensitive subject, for Jake had made a very firm break with his criminal past ever since he had spent that night in Newgate Prison. He wondered how the man had homed in on his disreputable history.

Maybe the Lie Detector Goggles had given him a clue. "My name," he forced out, "is *Jake*."

"Oh, dear me. Forgive me, Mr. Lake. So pleased to meet you—"

"Jake."

"Cake? Ah, I'm a huge fan! Nice to finally meet you, Cake. I didn't realize you could appear as a person. Most impressive. Chocolate or vanilla?"

Jake just glared at him.

Even Dani O'Dell had never dreamed of being half this annoying, but Jake gave up on the name joke. Let the glock-wit have his fun. He refused to rise to the bait. "Who are you?"

The man laughed. "A charming, clever, and quick-minded opportunist, misunderstood by all. What do you say to that?"

Jake shook his head. "What are you doing here?" he countered in suspicion.

"Languishing in idleness, I fear."

"What?"

"The age of the gods is past, Cake. It all came to naught, yet here I am, stuck in Midgarth, denied my fearsome destiny. Now? Well, I suppose I'm really just killing time." He let out a long sigh.

"I don't know what you're talking about."

"Never mind. Just dreams."

Jake eyed him warily. "Well, you don't seem like a scientist." He didn't seem as silly now as he had a few minutes ago, either.

"Me? A scientist? Please. I don't have the patience for running experiments. I'm an investor, Cake. It takes a lot of gold to fund all this 'research and development,' as the eggheads call it. Tell me, what do you know of war?"

"War? Nothing, really." Jake shrugged, startled by the rapid change of subjects. It was then that he noticed they had wandered into a shadowy aisle labeled DEFENSE. "Why do you ask?"

"Why, it's a favorite hobby of mine, war. Sport of kings, as they say. That's why I come to these events. Because—here's a secret, Cake. In war, as a general rule, he who has the cleverest toys wins."

"These weapons aren't toys," Jake informed him, stepping in front of the stranger to block his curious stare at a bizarre-looking armored carriage with guns mounted on top. "Is that why you're here? You're thinkin' of starting a war?"

"Always." The man sent him a crafty smile and firmly pushed him aside to stare at the armored carriage again. "That's the greatest mischief there is, after all."

"Who *are* you?" Jake persisted, following him as the man drifted down the aisle to gaze at a new long-range cannon.

He sighed again. "It's complicated, Cake." As the stranger sauntered along, Jake followed.

"Why is that?"

"Because I *change*. Sometimes I'm a salmon. Other times a seal..."

Jake blinked.

"...Or a horse. Bird. Other times a fly, which is more amusing than it sounds. But mostly I'm a prince, Cake, if you really want to know."

Jake scoffed, baffled. "A salmon? A fly? Mad, you are!"

"I prefer 'interesting.' And you may address me as Your Highness."

"Then you can address me as 'my lord,' because I'm more of an earl than you're a prince!" he retorted.

"I *am* a prince, Lord Cake."

"Then where's your land?"

The 'prince' looked askance at him. "Let's just say, I'm not from around here."

Jake shook his head. It did not take a genius to see that this poor mumper was unstable, right nickey in the head. On second thought, maybe he really was royalty, then. The royal families of Europe had been marrying their cousins for so many generations, half of them were born barmy.

"I'm telling the truth," the man protested when he saw Jake's dubious stare. "Ask the Lie Detector Goggles if you don't believe me."

"Maybe I will!" Jake snatched them out of his hand, put them on, then turned to look at the man—and was taken aback by what he saw.

When viewed through the goggles, the 'prince' had strangely elongated ears.

His pointy ears were somewhat hidden by his long, stringy hair, but when he turned his head, Jake could clearly make out the tattoo on the stranger's face.

A dark, intricate swirl of Norse-style knots crossed his cheek and curled up around his left eye like black war-paint.

How had he missed seeing it before? But then he realized: Only the Lie Detector Goggles revealed it.

Baffled, Jake lowered them from his eyes. Lo and behold, the tattoo vanished from the stranger's face.

He peered through them a second time in case his eyes had tricked him, but there it was again. Indeed, a closer look at the tattoo revealed that it did not depict a knotted rope, after all.

It was a tattoo of a serpent.

Jake felt a chill go down his spine at this revelation, but in the next moment, he forgot all about the tattoo, for the madman had just stepped up behind the newly-invented Gatling gun. "Hey-ho, what have we here?"

The multi-barreled weapon was mounted on a two-wheeled gun carriage, like a cannon.

The sign said it could fire over a thousand rounds a minute.

"Hello, gorgeous," the 'prince' murmured heartily as he stepped up behind it and figured out how to load the whole box of bullets. "I must admit, every once in a while, you humans do come up with something fun..."

Not good, Jake thought. Rapid-fire weapon in the hands of a loon-bat. *Not good at all.*

Heart pounding, he set the goggles back on their table and walked slowly, calmly, bravely toward the crazy person. "Um, Your Highness, I don't think you really ought to fool with that."

"Why ever not, Cake?" he asked innocently. "Look what it can do. Angle up, angle down. You can swivel it round from side to side, kill everyone in sight. Lovely! All you have to do to fire is turn this crank..."

"You can't be touching that!"

"Oh, yes I can."

"It's dangerous! Look what it says here." Jake pointed to the sign ominously claiming that Doctor Gatling's intent had been to invent a weapon so invincible that it would make all warfare obsolete.

"Pah! They always say that," the mad prince scoffed. "What rubbish! It's just an excuse. War is in our bones, Cake. They'll never get rid of it. And they'll never get rid of me."

Then he started firing.

Jake clapped his hands over his ears and instinctively ducked his head. Thankfully, the loon-bat aimed the Gatling gun into the shooting gallery set up for weapons tests.

Even with his ears plugged, the bullets sounded to Jake like the loudest popcorn bursting.

Laughing maniacally, the stranger went on cranking and cranking the handle, gleefully unloading. In seconds, empty brass cartridges littered the floor. The Gatling gun roared on, shredding the thick practice target.

Jake knew he had to do something to stop him.

All that madman had to do was swivel the gun in another direction, and people in the Exhibit Hall would be mowed down.

Jake knew the danger of using his powers in front of the public, let alone the scientists, but what choice did he have?

Still holding his ears as the giant machine gun thundered on and on, he let go of his right ear in order to put out his hand.

He summoned up all his concentration, then used his telekinesis to make the cranking mechanism jam.

The Gatling gun abruptly went mute.

The mad prince stopped, making a small sound of disappointment. He shook the weapon. "Piece of junk!"

Jake had already straightened up and was striding toward him, relieved that the stranger hadn't seen him use his hereditary gift.

"It obviously needs more work," the mad prince said in disgust. "I've always said the dwarves make much better weapons than these humans." He started to walk away—only to stop mid-stride.

Jake was still trying to absorb the dwarf remark when the loon-bat held up his hand and froze, as though hearing something in the distance. Then he sniffed the air.

Jake squinted at him in confusion. *What now?*

"Do you smell that, Cake?"

"All I smell is gunpowder," he answered in reproach, his ears still ringing from the din.

"Shh! Quiet! Listen!"

Jake could have sworn that the man's long, tapered ears twitched.

Then the prince started to laugh—slowly, even more wickedly than before. "It can't be..."

He shook his head with a look of surprise, listening to whatever it was he thought he heard. "I don't believe it!" he murmured to himself.

"Believe what?" Jake demanded.

"Tsk, tsk. Somebody's broken the rules. Oh, I love that!"

"Who?"

"Fee, fi, fo, fum... I smell the blood of... but it can't be. That's not allowed, not at all," he whispered gleefully to himself, staring toward the Exhibit Hall doors.

"What are you talking about?" Jake asked in exasperation. But the nonsensical syllables the loon-bat had just uttered sounded familiar. Where had he heard them before?

He suddenly remembered. Of course. The old fairytale, *Jack and the Beanstalk*. The orphanage ladies used to read it to the children.

The mad prince had now forgotten all about him. "I must investigate!" He whirled away abruptly with a flap of his black cloak like a crow's wings.

With the midnight fabric of his cloak streaming out behind him, he rushed out of the Exhibit Hall without another word.

Jake stared after him, confused. *Absolutely bloomin' bonkers.*

Wondering if he should call for campus security, he had barely had a chance to sigh with relief that the lunatic had gone, when he heard Henry furiously calling his name.

"Jake! Get away from that weapon, this instant! How dare you go fooling with that thing? That is not a toy!"

Jake let out a weary sigh. *Here we go again.* Getting the blame for something that wasn't his fault. Typical!

"Jacob Everton, have you lost your mind?" the boys' tutor demanded as he came marching up the aisle. "I told you not to touch *any* of the inventions, let alone the Gatling gun!"

"It wasn't me!"

"Oh, really? You just happened to be standing here beside it? And where did all these casings come from?" Henry gestured toward the empty bullet shells lying all over the floor. "Did they fall out of the sky?"

"It wasn't *me* shooting, it was some lunatic—honest! He was here a moment ago. Didn't you see him?"

"No!" Henry retorted, yanking Jake away from the Gatling gun and bending to pick up all the casings.

"I'm telling the truth! Some loon-bat in an opera cloak. An

investor! He claimed to be a prince."

"Oh, please," Henry retorted. "A prince?"

"He could be telling the truth," Miss Langesund chimed in cautiously as she now joined them in the DEFENSE aisle. "There are a few wealthy investors wandering around here today, and some of them do have royal connections."

"Whoever he was, he was mad as a hatter," Jake mumbled, indignant that he should get in trouble, when he had just saved everyone there from the possibility of a loon-bat on a rampage.

Some thanks!

Henry obviously wasn't impressed. "Look, Jake, the floor is also cracked. Did you do this, too? Were you playing with the Super Strength Gloves? Tell the truth."

"It wasn't me, I tell ye! Put on the Lie Detector Goggles if you don't believe me!"

"Maybe I will!" Henry retorted.

"He's telling the truth!" Isabelle called. She and Dani hurried over to them. Archie wasn't far behind.

"See? I told you so," Jake declared.

With her empathic powers, Isabelle was as good as the Lie Detector Goggles. Still, Henry frowned, unsure what to believe.

"There was some crazy loon-bat running around here messin' with all the inventions," Jake explained, but with Miss Langesund standing there, he couldn't admit he had used his telekinesis to stop him. "When the gun jammed, I guess he just got bored and wandered off. He's gone now."

"Humph," Henry growled. "You'd better watch your step, young man. I have half a mind not to let you come and see the Langesunds' surprise."

"Miss Langesund was just about to take us for a private showing of the big discovery she and her father unearthed," Dani piped up.

"But if this is how you're going to behave—" Henry warned.

"Oh, come, Monsieur DuVal, it's over now, no harm done," Miss Langesund cajoled him. "I'm sure this can be a boring place for a spirited young lad—except for Master Archie, of course. But now I have something to show you children that you are sure to enjoy."

Their tutor was still frowning as the bespectacled lady-archeologist beckoned to them. "Come along, children, this way! Prepare yourselves for a marvel."

"And when we get there, *don't touch anything*," Henry added with a pointed look at Jake.

"I won't!" he said in exasperation.

Then Miss Langesund marched ahead of them; Henry beckoned to the children. With that, they followed her outside and headed across the campus, eager to see the surprise.

CHAPTER SEVEN
Brain Food

A lone in the forest, Snorri sat down to eat a lonely supper. He had trapped a twelve-point buck without much trouble, but for a giant, it was barely an appetizer.

Hungry and grumpy, he sat roasting his venison on the campfire he had made outside the mountain cave he'd chosen for his shelter. He let out a disgruntled sigh, irked at himself. Why was he not happy?

As badly as he had wanted to escape Jugenheim, here he was, far away at last. But he hadn't even been gone twelve hours yet, and he was already feeling homesick.

He couldn't help worrying. Who would feed his dear little sheepies, Zero, Chubs, Maxine, and all the others? Who would keep the nasty, sharp-clawed wolverines away from his chicken coop?

And what if Princess Kaia stopped by for a visit, needing to talk to a friend? Who could she confide in if he wasn't there?

Worst of all, Snorri barely dared wonder what his punishment might be if the gods found out he had crashed down into man-world. What if Thor heard about it and came and bopped him with his hammer?

Still worrying and fretting to himself, Snorri prodded his campfire with a mighty pine branch, when all of a sudden, a crow flapped down onto the log across from him and said, "Hello!"

Snorri was taken aback. "Did you just talk?"

"Of course I did. I was talking to you!"

"Uh, hello." He blinked in confusion. "Sorry, no offense. I just didn't know birds could talk—" *down here in Midgarth,* he had almost added aloud. But fortunately, he had remembered that he wasn't supposed to be here, so he kept quiet.

"Well, we can," the crow replied, giving its wings a small flick like a shrug. "We just don't often choose to. Do you mind if I ask you a question?"

It was Snorri's turn to shrug. Might as well enjoy some company, since he had no one else to talk to in this strange place. "All right."

"I was noticing from my perch on the treetops just a moment ago that you seem out of sorts, and it's just, well, you're awfully large. That is—" The bird cocked its head. "You're not from around here, are you?"

"Uh, um...duh..." Worried over his trespass into the wrong world being discovered, Snorri stammered incoherently. You never knew when Odin might be watching from his white throne up in Valhalla.

The crow hopped closer and lowered its voice. "I'm just going to put it out there, then. You're a giant, aren't you?"

Snorri stifled a gasp. "What gave it away?"

"Don't worry, it's all right! You can trust me," the bird assured him. "I'm not going to tell anyone." It flicked its tail feathers, and when it leaned forward with a mischievous sparkle in its tiny black eyes, Snorri noticed that the crow had a sprinkling of white feathers on one side of its jet-black face. "But how did you get here? I thought Jugenheim was sealed off from Midgarth long ago by the gods! Cruel Odin, and hateful Thor!"

"Shh!" Snorri said anxiously. Only a madman spoke of the scary gods like that.

Of course, a little birdie couldn't be expected to understand that. He cocked his head to the side. "Well, they're the ones that separated the worlds, aren't they? At least that's what I've heard," he added innocently.

"Yes, that's what they say, though it happened long before I was born," Snorri told him. Indeed, the friendly little creature was so easy to talk to that Snorri couldn't help himself.

He heaved a sigh and told the curious bird the whole story of how Prince Gorm had made him miserable back in Jugenheim, how Princess Kaia would never see him as anything more than a friend, and how her father, fierce King Olaf, was probably going to make her marry Gorm the bully, then Gorm would be their next king.

King Olaf didn't have any sons, just a daughter. That was Kaia, and it was not the giants' way to let a lady be the king.

Absorbed in sharing his tale of woe, Snorri recounted to the bird how he had been stewing on all this as he cleared the rocks from his sheep meadow; how he had popped that big boulder out of the ground and accidentally made a hole; and how he had fallen so far out of the great Tree into Midgarth.

As sunset blazed in the west, he poured out his heart about his misery living in Giant Land and his homesick feelings now—how he couldn't win either way, and how back home, everyone thought he was a dunce.

The bird listened in sympathy, hopping about, asking a few thoughtful questions, and listening patiently. Snorri thought him very kind.

Done with his tale at last, he poked the fire despondently. The bird walked back and forth across the log in thought.

It ruffled its feathers as it came to some conclusion, and then it looked straight at him. "Snorri," it said, "I can fix all this. I mean it. I can help you."

"You can?"

"You'd better believe it, friend! Crows are especially clever, you know, and giants, well, it's no secret that giants—aren't. It's not your fault, of course. Odin made you that way. But I can help! In fact, I already have a plan that could change your life forever!"

"Really?" he exclaimed.

"And if you do exactly as I say," the crow informed him, "you can return to Jugenheim a hero!"

"Me? A hero?" Snorri asked in wonder.

"Not just a hero, a king!" the bird declared. "Snorri, you are a giant of destiny! They're wrong to underestimate you, all wrong! You deserve better than this—and if you listen to me, you shall have better. With my help, you can live up to your full potential! Then they'll be sorry."

"You really think so?"

The bird hopped up and down in excitement. "I do! I do! With my help, you'll show them all just how smart you really are! You'll defeat this Gorm fellow, and you'll be the one to marry Princess Kaia, not him. In fact, if you follow my instructions, I can make you the next King of Giant Land!"

"Me...?" Snorri could barely imagine it. "But how?" he asked eagerly.

"Ah, ah, not so fast," the crow warned with a sly gleam in its black button eyes. "If I tell you how to do it, you have to promise me something in return."

"What? Anything!" he said, slightly breathless with excitement and newfound hope.

"Oh, just a little favor," said the crow. "Nothing for now, of course. But later, when you're the King of the Giants, let's just say you'll owe me one. I may need your help one day, and I just need to know that I'll be able to call on you if that day should ever come."

"For what?" he asked.

"Who knows?" the bird replied with another innocent-seeming twitch of its wings. "Hard to say. You never know what might come up. But giants can do things that other people can't. Can't they?"

"That is true," Snorri said proudly. Giants might not be the smartest folk, but they were strong, and most of them were brave to the point of recklessness.

Like Gorm.

Just ask poor Old Smokey, the rather elderly dragon who was continuously pestered by young male giants out to prove their manhood.

Snorri rapped his fist against his chest like Gorm and his bully friends would. "We are a warrior people!"

"Yes, I know," the bird murmured. "And if you ever had a proper leader, you'd be an unstoppable force. So, then, do we have a deal, my friend?"

Snorri was barely paying attention, carried away with heroic imaginings of himself putting Prince Gorm in his place and winning the heart of Princess Kaia.

"Well?"

"Bird, if you can make this happen, certainly! You've got yourself a deal!"

"Good, then. Done! Now, you'd better not forget your promise, Snorri. When someone crosses me, there's a price to be paid. Consequences."

"Yes, yes, of course," he said impatiently, though he wondered what the bird could possibly do to him. Peck him? He brushed the thought aside. "I'll do my part if you'll do yours. So, how do I win Kaia and become king? What's the plan?" he asked eagerly.

The crow's yellow beak almost seemed to curve into a sly smile.

"First, we're going to make you a potion to drink. It has some very specific ingredients that are usually hard to get, but we happen to be in luck. A quantity of this ingredient happens to be nearby. Now, once you drink this potion, then, ha, ha!—you will be transformed into the smartest giant that ever was! A giant *genius!*"

Snorri absorbed this information in awe. "What's the special ingredient?" he asked in a reverent hush.

The crow told him.

Snorri's shaggy eyebrows shot upward in surprise. "Come again?"

"Geniuses," the crow repeated firmly. "Eight or nine of them at least. We need their brains."

Snorri stared at him in shock. "You mean...in their heads?"

"Yes, in their heads, you great goose! The brains must be pureed and stirred with a whisk, then dried to a powder and combined with a few more ingredients, mostly mundane. Feverfew and dewdrops, a little eye of newt. That sort of thing."

"I see..."

"Come now, are you a fearsome warrior giant or not?" the bird asked crossly, seeing his hesitation. "You're supposed to be mighty and ferocious. Can you even roar?"

"Of course I can roar, when I feel like it," he said defensively. "But I didn't really come here to kill anyone."

"Oh, so now you're being judgmental! If you're too much of a goody two-shoes for my plan—"

"I'm not!"

"So, we need some human brains. So what? As a bird, I don't usually like this saying, but if you want to make an omelet, then you've got to break some eggs."

"Or skulls, in this case."

"Genius skulls, exactly. But no worries, if it's not worth a crown to you, along with the heart of your true love, then never mind! I don't want to bother you—"

"No, no, of course I'll do it! I'll catch them, like you said."

"Are you sure?"

"Yes, I'm sure," Snorri muttered. "I was just—a little surprised, that's all."

"All right then. Eight or nine geniuses, as I said." The crow finally seemed satisfied. "Keep them in your traps until it's time. Remember, look for the ones with the crazy hair. If they have spectacles and a bowtie, even better. That's the smartest kind. Especially if they're talking to themselves."

Snorri mumbled the instructions under his breath, doing his best to memorize all the bird's points about where to go to reach the University down the mountain, and what sort of men to grab.

"Have you got all that, Snorri?"

"Yes, bird."

"Good. Now, be careful! And don't let these scientists catch you. You're going to have to be stealthy," the crow warned. "If they get hold of you first, they'll do horrid experiments on you. As much as I might want to help you if that happens, I won't be able to. Or certain gods might find out," the bird added discreetly.

"Uhh, I understand," Snorri rumbled. "Can't have that." The bird sure didn't seem to like the gods.

"No, we can't. So when you catch these men with the big brains, just keep them in their cages until I come back. Once you have the full amount needed, then we'll make the potion. Good luck," the crow added. It spread its jet-black wings and flapped into the air, disappearing among the trees.

Snorri was left standing alone by his campfire, barely able to contain his excitement about his change of fortunes. *King* Snorri...?

That had a nice ring!

His earlier doubts about catching people and turning their brains into powder faded with surprising speed as he let his imagination bask in the glow of his newfound dreams.

Kaia by his side, a crown on his head, and all the other giants finally forced to show him some respect.

That bird better keep up his end of the bargain, Snorri thought as he got to work building wooden cages to hold his future captives. For as anxious as he was to get home to Princess Kaia and his dear sheepies, there was no time to waste.

Gorm was wrong! He wasn't a loser, he was a giant of destiny, and he'd start catching geniuses tonight.

CHAPTER EIGHT
Miss Langesund's Surprise

Miss Langesund led their group across campus and through the university gardens, until they finally approached the little wooden museum that sat all alone at the end of the path.

The building resembled a church, and when Jake asked if it used to be one, she said no. Since her father's big discovery had to do with Norwegian history, they had modeled the building to house the exhibit on a traditional style of architecture that could be seen all over Norway in the small wooden stave churches that dated back to medieval times.

When they reached the little museum, which was presently closed to the public, she unlocked the wooden double doors and then turned to face the group. "Now then, children," she said with a dramatic flair worthy of the ancient Norse bards, "prepare yourselves to step back in time nearly a thousand years to the tenth century—and the golden age of the Vikings!"

Then she opened the door. It swung with a heavy creak.

Though they all were eager to see the surprise, Jake stepped forward first into the shadows.

Inside the hushed space of the museum, the fading light of sunset slanted in through the gothic windows to reveal the long, wooden remnants of a magnificent Viking ship.

The children were awestruck as they filed in, staring at it.

"My father discovered it buried on the shores of Oslo Fjord. The ship is sixty-seven feet long, with twelve pairs of oars, all made of oak."

"This is amazing," Dani murmured.

Miss Langesund smiled. "Indeed. A thousand years ago, these

long-boats were the technological wonder of their time. The Vikings crossed the seas in these boats. But as you can see, the keels are shallow enough that they could travel up rivers, too. No place was safe from their invasions."

"They certainly came to England," Henry said for the benefit of the children. "Stone monuments covered in Viking runes can be found throughout the British Isles. I daresay we've all got some Viking blood in our veins."

"Probably so," Miss Langesund agreed.

Jake homed in on a mysterious, shadowed walkway that led down into the museum floor beneath the ship. He pointed at it. "May we go down there?"

"Of course," Miss Langesund said, gesturing in welcome. "Down there, you can see what the hull looks like from below. This allows us to learn more about the Vikings' shipbuilding methods. Or you can climb up on the catwalk above us, if you want to look down at the inside of the ship."

"But don't touch anything!" Henry warned once again.

The kids scarcely heard, immediately running around to view the ancient ship from all angles. Miss Langesund stepped out of their way and proceeded to explain how her father's team had dug it up painstakingly and moved it bit by bit into this sanctuary, where it would be preserved for future generations of Norwegians to ponder the courage and skill of their seafaring ancestors.

"Any idea who it belonged to?" Henry asked while the children ooh'ed and ahh'ed.

"No, I'm afraid any trace of him is long gone. But it would have been a warlord of some kind, a chief or a nobleman, maybe even a king. If you'd like to step over here and look at the other grave goods we found, you can see by his personal property that he was certainly someone of high rank."

They gathered around a table where the smaller grave goods of the ship's anonymous owner were on display. An incredible sword covered in runes. A drinking horn carved from a massive antler. A cloak brooch, intricately worked in pure silver. A marvelous helmet with a chain-mail tunic, and a round shield whose colors had long since faded. There were jewels, too.

"The Vikings traded with people as far away as the Ottoman Empire," Miss Langesund was explaining.

But Jake was staring at the faint blue glow around some of the grave goods. *Uh-oh...*

Of course, no one else could see what he could.

"Why did they bury their stuff with them when they died?" Dani asked, gazing at the chain mail.

"They thought their dead would need these items in the afterlife. In this warlord's case, no doubt, he went straight to Valhalla."

"Viking heaven?" Jake supplied.

"That's correct."

"I say, did the Vikings also have a bad place, I mean, where bad people went after they died?"

"Oh, yes, indeed! Neiflheim," she replied. "A realm of fire and brimstone beneath the earth."

"Neffle-hime?" Jake echoed.

"That's right. Neiflheim was the realm of the trickster god, Loki."

He furrowed his brow. "The Vikings had a trickster for a god?"

"Loki wasn't their top god," she explained. "That was Odin the Wise, the All-Father, as he was called. Odin was the king of the gods, as well as the patron of warriors, death, wisdom, runes, and prophecy."

"Busy chap," Henry said.

She smiled. "Valhalla means the 'Hall of Odin,' you see. Odin was always said to be wandering around the earth in disguise, looking for great warriors and heroes that he could recruit for Valhalla after their death."

"What, Vikings still have to fight battles even after they're dead?" Dani exclaimed.

"Only one..." Miss Langesund adopted an ominous tone, though she was smiling. "The greatest battle of all, at the end of time. You see, the ancient Viking bards wrote about a final, mighty battle between good and evil that would bring on the end of the world. It was called the Battle of Ragnarok. On one side, Odin would lead his Valhalla army of all the dead great heroes of men to fight on the side of good."

"Who's on the bad side? Thor?" Jake asked, wide-eyed as he tried to imagine it.

"Heavens, no. Thor's the Norse people's favorite." Miss Langesund smiled fondly. "He's Odin's right-hand man and favorite son—the god of thunder. Thor ruled the weather and the sea—two very important concerns for a seafaring people who built ships like this, as you can imagine. No, the leader on the bad side in the Battle of Ragnarok would be our troublemaker Loki, commanding an army of giants."

"Giants?" Dani echoed while the rest of them grinned.

"Oh, my dear, we love our giants and our trolls here in Norway," Miss Langesund said with a chuckle that told them she obviously thought such things were mere legends, like the old Norse gods.

Jake dearly hoped that she was right.

The lady-archeologist folded her arms across her chest and leaned casually against her desk while Henry stood nearby, hands in pockets, gazing at her with a smitten smile.

"Loki was always the troublemaker," she continued. "He loved causing chaos and could change forms at will—"

"A shapeshifter?" Archie blurted out.

When Miss Langesund nodded, all four children tried very hard not to look at Henry.

His smile turned brittle, but he managed not to give his secret away to his lady friend. He cleared his throat, lowered his gaze, and said nothing.

Miss Langesund resumed their lesson on Norse mythology. "Loki was a very interesting fellow—more mischievous than evil—though in some of the old stories, he could be pretty rotten. You didn't want Loki for an enemy, to be sure. But personally, I always saw him more as a free-thinker."

"Why do you say that?" Archie asked as he admired one of the daggers the archeologists had dug up.

She shrugged. "Loki never really followed all the usual Viking rules. He liked to experiment."

"Really?" Archie glanced over in surprise.

She nodded. "Once he turned himself into a woman for a while, just to see what it was like. The ultra-manly Thor was, of course, horrified."

The others laughed, but Jake had gone stock-still, staring past the table. He alone was not surprised when a nearby stack of brochures suddenly flew off the table and fluttered in all directions, strewn across the floor.

"Oh, I'm so clumsy!" the lady-archeologist burst out in embarrassed surprise, since she had been standing nearest to the papers. "I don't know what's the matter with me! I do this sort of thing all the time!"

While she blushed crimson, Henry and Archie instantly stooped to help her pick up the scattered papers. But Jake stood rooted to his spot, staring at the bluish spectral figure looming behind the table. The hairs on his nape stood on end; goosebumps tingled down his arms.

"With all the delicate work we do, have you ever heard of anything so silly as a clumsy archeologist?" poor Miss Langesund was muttering, looking rather humiliated.

"It's all right, Astrid," Henry was saying gently.

"Thank you, gentlemen," she mumbled as he and Archie helped her gather up her things.

Dani glanced at Jake, noticing his sudden stillness. But for his part, he didn't even blink, riveted by the sight of the towering ghost who presently stepped out of the wall wearing a horned helmet.

Blimey.

Ghosts didn't usually scare him, but this one looked terrifying, with his rough beard and tangled long hair with thin braids in front, flowing over his massive shoulders.

Tattoos of Norse knots and Viking runes covered his massive shoulders and arms that bulged like those of a circus strongman.

Scariest of all was the look of his bluish, spectral face—a glare of icy rage.

Jake gulped, rather sure he had just found the original owner of the Viking ship. Indeed, if he were not scared speechless, he could have told Miss Langesund, *You're not clumsy.*

You're haunted.

CHAPTER NINE
The Shield King's Wrath

"*WHO DARES DISTURB MY SLUMBER?*"

The little ship museum reverberated with the booming spectral voice, but nobody reacted. No one else could hear.

That honor belonged to Jake alone, thanks to the unusual talent he had inherited from his mother.

Henry and Archie continued helping Miss Langesund pick up her things while the mighty Viking warrior ghost stormed past them.

Jake watched him warily, unsure what to do. The phantom must have used up most of his energy throwing down Miss Langesund's stack of papers, for thankfully, he didn't have much effect on anything else—which only seemed to frustrate him more.

Isabelle glanced around, as though sensing strong anger from someone in the room.

Unaware of the ghost nearby, she must have assumed it was coming from one of their party. Predictably, she raised her hand to her temple with a slight wince.

The ghost was growing angrier by the minute. The less they paid attention, the more furious the Viking chief became. Jake could barely believe his eyes as he watched the mighty blue spectral figure pick up a ghostly version of his battle axe on display and try to cut Henry in half with it.

Of course, it didn't work. Seeing that his weapon had no effect, the ghost muttered a curse. "By Odin's beard!" He hurled the axe aside and reached this time for his sword, picking up a translucent, bluish copy of it, while the real, solid one remained lying on the table.

Wide-eyed, Jake watched the Viking warlord menace his cousins with the phantom weapon—until he noticed Miss Langesund. He gave her a leer, let out a laugh, and tried to grab the lady-archeologist, as if to carry her off like his stolen brides of centuries ago.

But his giant, muscled arms whooshed right through her, so he whirled away in frustration, only to notice next that Archie was fingering his dagger.

"How dare you trifle with my things, you brazen cub? Put that down or I'll teach you to mind your elders!" The Viking ghost strode over to Archie and tried to smack his hand away from the knife, to no avail.

Archie could neither see nor hear him, nor feel the rap on his knuckles. The ghost was so outraged at being ignored by everyone that he let out a wordless roar, and then flew up onto his ship.

Jake finally snapped out of his daze from watching the ghost. "Er, Henry, a word, please?"

Having just finished helping Miss Astrid pick up her papers, Henry straightened up again. "Yes?"

Jake pulled their tutor aside by his elbow, and, in a hushed tone, hastily explained the situation.

Henry stared at him, absorbing this news. "Oh, dear."

"I can try and talk to him, but you have to get the others out of here. Maybe I can reason with him, find out what he wants. At least let me try. It's either that or he's going to continue raging around these artifacts. He seems furious, and of any ghost I've seen, he looks the most capable of doing serious damage."

Henry frowned, then glanced around the ship museum, as though trying to spot the ghost, but of course, he didn't have that ability.

"What if he does something to harm Miss Langesund or her father when they're in here working alone?" Jake urged. "He could knock the ship down on them when they're underneath studying it or push them off the walkway." He nodded up at the elevated gallery. "If you give me a few minutes alone to talk to him, I'll find out what he wants and try to calm him down."

Henry considered his proposal with a worried glance at his lady friend. He obviously wanted her and her father to be safe when they were in here working.

He looked at Jake again. "You're sure about this?"

Jake nodded.

"Very well," Henry said reluctantly. He started to turn away, then he got an idea. "Maybe you could interview this Viking ghost for Astrid and get more information on the ship. He could be an incredible source of scholarly—"

Jake just looked at him, and Henry's words broke off.

"Right," the tutor mumbled. "Astrid is a scientist. She'll think we're both daft. Never mind." Henry gave Jake a wry smile. "Very well, then. If you're sure you want to do this, I'll make an excuse and get everyone out of here. Then you can slip back in by yourself. But please be careful, Jake. Don't do anything to provoke this Viking ghost. Get out of here if he becomes too threatening, understand? When he was alive, this man was probably a killing machine."

Jake nodded. "Don't worry, I'll be fine."

"Have a care with the artifacts, too. If anything is damaged, I'm afraid we both might get to witness Miss Astrid's inner Valkyrie."

"Huh? What's that?"

"Never mind, I'll tell you later. And Jake, take care to mind your manners. The warrior who owned this ship was likely a king or a chieftain. Be sure and show respect."

"Believe me, I will."

Henry nodded and walked back to the others. Jake followed, but he could not stop staring at the Viking ship, for it had been transformed by the presence of its former master.

With the Viking warrior at the helm, the ship was restored to a bluish, spectral version of its former glory, complete with a single striped sail and a carved dragon figurehead arching off the prow.

Jake was riveted. What a terrifying sight it must have been to peaceful inland farm villages in medieval times—a horde of Viking raiders rowing up the river!

Jake wished the others could have seen it like this, all filled in with faintly-shining spectral energy. He sucked in his breath as the warlord's phantom followers materialized out of the air and picked up their oars. Jake scarcely dared to blink, unwilling to miss a second of it.

Right there in the museum, he could feel the wind and the pitching waves as the Viking chief and his men took to the seas. He could hear their chants as they rowed—though, of course, it was getting them nowhere.

They must all still be attached somehow to the ship, he thought.

Henry announced it was time to go get ready for the Welcome

Dinner and began herding the kids outside, but Jake hung back.

The tutor gave him a private nod and covered his retreat back into the building while the others were distracted.

Jake stepped out of sight behind a display case as Miss Langesund locked the door to the museum. He wasn't sure how long he might have. There was no time to waste.

The Viking warrior was standing at the bow of his ship, looking pleased that the intruders had retreated.

Jake swallowed hard, then steeled his courage and walked cautiously toward the ghost. "Sire! A word with you, if I may?"

The brawny spirit turned and stared at him in shock. "You, boy! You can see me?" The Viking leader came over to the bluish edge of his ship, propping one laced-up boot up on the low bulwark.

"I can," Jake affirmed. "Is this your ship?"

"My ship. My weapons," he growled, nodding at the table with the dagger that Archie had been handling. "My people. My lands! And who are you?"

"Jake Everton, sir. The seventh Earl of Griffon." It still felt awfully strange to him to be twelve years old and a lord. But his title seemed to impress his fellow nobleman, who nodded in begrudging approval.

"*Ves heill.* Health and good luck be to you, young master."

"And to you," Jake answered cautiously. "Might I ask your name, sir?"

"My name?" The Viking warlord threw his head back and laughed. "Oh, that's a good one! As if you don't already know!"

"Er, no. Sorry, sir. No idea."

"Come, what sort of prank is this? You know perfectly well who I am. Kingdoms tremble at my name!"

Jake just looked at him.

The Viking scowled. "Well, that's just insulting. I can tell by your accent that you hail from Angle-land, where I terrorized the eastern coast, and yet you claim you never heard of me? You, boy Earl, must be from a puny, backwater village, indeed, if you have never heard of Ragnor the Punisher, Shield King of the North!"

His crew cheered his announcement of his name with hearty bellows.

"Now, admit you've heard of my glory! Was it not I and my men who plundered all the lands of our enemies? I made all my warriors rich, and gave out gifts like a very son of Odin! It was I who made the

Gauls cower and the Danes beg for mercy, I who sailed to unknown continents, built ships that sea serpents tall as trees could not sink! I who defeated the foul ice grendels—"

His men cheered wildly like the most committed fans at a rugby match.

"That's right!" he vaunted. "And it was I, let it never be forgotten, who wrestled the treacherous Loki to the ground and tattooed his very cheek, so that my people would always know him, no matter what form he took. Then they would never be deceived!"

"Wait—you tattooed Loki's cheek?" Jake exclaimed, startled by this claim, considering he had just met a mad prince with a tattoo on his cheek.

But...no, it couldn't be! Loki was just a legend!

His question went unheard in the general ruckus of the happy warriors cheering and the Viking chief still singing his own praises.

Absently, Jake remembered Dani reading aloud to them from her Norway book about how outrageous bragging had been a major form of entertainment in the old Viking mead halls.

Jake was getting a bit tired of it all.

"Of me, the bards sang tales in every great hall throughout the Norse kingdoms—"

"Sorry, but I've never heard of you," he interrupted impatiently, determined to press on with the business at hand. "Can we get on with it, please—"

"NEVER HEARD OF ME!"

Every Viking warrior ghost aboard threw down his oar and growled, looking ready to pile on Jake.

"I-I'm sorry, sire, I don't mean any insult. It's just that you've been dead for nearly a thousand years!"

This shocked the Viking chieftain into silence.

"Really?" he asked after a long moment. "Has it been that long?"

Jake nodded.

"Hmm. Time flies when you're in Valhalla. Doesn't it, boys?" he muttered to his men, and they all grunted agreement, nodding at each other. But the Shield King of the North was most displeased. "Well, I might be forgotten, but I'm not gone. They have no right to plunder my grave! It's unthinkable, a sacrilege! Why, I will never allow it! Warn them of my fury, boy, for I will drive them out, each and every one of them! I will terrorize them, and *make them pay!*"

More fierce roaring in agreement followed, a general clamor from his henchmen.

"But sire, this place is called a museum. If you allow them to put your treasures on display, there will be a plaque telling of your great deeds and conquests. Then your name will truly be immortal. People will come from everywhere to, er, pay homage to your glory. Far from being an insult, this place will be a monument to all your victories in life!"

"Hmm, well, if you put it that way... You have a smooth tongue. You must have some bardic blood in your veins, Earl of Griffon. One moment." He flew over to confer quietly with his warriors.

Jake waited to see if they would approve.

The Viking ghosts were arguing among themselves, some sounding offended by the opening of the grave, others shrugging, nodding, as though the chance at fame sounded fairly reasonable to them.

Jake recalled something else Dani had read to him, about votes being important to Vikings even back in ancient times. It wasn't such a new invention as everyone thought, he recalled her saying.

Any mighty man of courage who showed enough brains and leadership to win his men's respect could eventually set himself up as a king back then if he tried. You didn't have to be born to it like nowadays.

At last came the verdict.

Ragnor the Punisher returned to the railing of the ghost ship and gave Jake a nod.

"Very well. My men still say it's sacrilege, but for glory's sake, we will stop haunting these grave robbers, provided they tell your world of my, er, *our* great deeds." He glanced over his shoulder at his warriors, then looked at Jake again. "In the meanwhile, we will go in peace for now and return to Valhalla, for we find your world frankly rather bewildering, Earl of Griffon. But," the Viking warned, "I will personally be back from time to time to check on their progress here—and they had better not break my things."

Jake nodded. "Yes, Sire, I will tell them. I'm sure they'll take good care of it all."

"You have put my mind at ease, Earl of Griffon. Farewell."

"Wait! Sir? King Ragnor?" Jake followed him toward the ship.

"What is it, boy?"

"What are ice grendels?" he blurted out, so full of questions he barely knew where to begin.

But Ragnor the Punisher turned around with a hearty laugh. "Ha! Trust me, boy, you don't want to know."

"Pray to Thor you never meet one!" a bearded warrior taunted from the ship, reaching down his arm to help his King up. He had leather armor on and small braids in his long, wild hair.

With his mate's assistance, the Viking leader vaulted back up onto his ghostly vessel.

Jake just stared at them. What a crew they were, this lot! He would not have wanted to be a meek medieval monk living on the English coast nine hundred years ago.

Striding up to the bow of his ship, King Ragnor raised his fist. "Come, men! Back to the Hall of Odin and our beautiful Valkyries!"

They whistled and made rude purring sounds at the mention of the Valkyries.

"Row! Row!" he began chanting at them.

They joined in, their deep, ominous voices reverberating through the Exhibit Hall.

Jake watched in amazement as the ghostly version of the Viking ship moved off the posts where it had been superimposed upon the ancient archeological find.

The bluish, phantom ship whooshed off, just as though it were riding on the water. The chants swelled as the Viking warriors drew on the oars, but faded off when the ghost-ship disappeared through the wall.

Jake remained holding his breath for a long moment after it had disappeared. *Blimey.*

Then he glanced around like someone waking from a dream, still rather dazed by all he had just witnessed.

With the haunting spirits gone, the little museum now had a tranquil atmosphere. He made sure the table display was in its proper order, then hurried to catch up with the others, still amazed.

He let himself out of the building by using his powers; his growing finesse with his telekinesis meant there were few locks he could not master with the right degree of concentration.

Click, pop, turn.

The door opened.

He slipped out of the museum, then locked it behind him again by the same method, not needing a key. In his former life as a London pickpocket, he could have done fantastically well for himself with these abilities, but fortunately for the world, he had sworn off being a thief.

Of course, his stealing skills likely would've won him a hero's reputation if he had been born a Viking, he mused as he slipped off into the darkness, crossing the campus with the stealth of a midnight raider. After all, taking other people's stuff was the main purpose of the Norsemen's social calls to foreign places, from what he understood. Aye, Jake thought wryly, he'd have fit right in with that bold, rowdy lot if his life hadn't changed.

At the moment, however, he'd be satisfied with a large plate of food. With that, he went in search of the long-awaited Welcome Dinner, his stomach rumbling like the distant roar of ice grendels.

Whatever they were.

CHAPTER TEN
Lord of the Shapeshifters

Later at the Welcome Dinner, Jake huddled with Archie and the girls around the kids' side of the table, telling them in hushed tones about his encounter with the Viking ghost.

Meanwhile, on the adults' side of the table, Miss Langesund sat between Henry and his sister Helena, the girls' governess. The ladies all wore richly colored dinner gowns and satin gloves; even Dani and Isabelle were preening in their fancy long dresses.

The boys and all the gentlemen wore formal black and white for the grand dinner officially opening the Invention Convention, welcoming attendees from around the world. The dinner took place in an elegant banquet hall with red carpet, crystal chandeliers, and dozens of large round tables draped in white damask tablecloths and laid with fancy china and ornate silverware, candles and flowers.

Amid this elegant setting, Jake was amused to notice Henry mooning over Miss Langesund. In a gold bustle gown, she *did* look rather magnificent, having changed her awful hairdo and taken off her glasses for the occasion.

Several famous archeologists were also seated at their table, including Doctor Schliemann, who had discovered the ancient city of Troy and the golden Mask of Agamemnon that Jake had seen earlier.

Miss Langesund kept glancing toward the doors of the banquet hall, clearly embarrassed by her father's failure to appear. "I can't imagine what's keeping him," she was saying to their colleagues. "He has been so looking forward to seeing you all again."

"Would you like me to go and knock on his door, Astrid?" Henry offered. "Perhaps he fell asleep."

"Oh, how kind of you. But it's all right, Henry, I'll go. You've got the children to look after. I'm sure he simply lost track of the time. He does that when he's wrapped up in his work."

"Sounds like someone I know," Henry answered with a fond glance at Archie.

"I'll go fetch him," she said. "Hopefully he'll make it here before dessert!"

The gentlemen at the table rose politely as Miss Langesund stood; Jake only remembered to do so after a nudge from Archie.

Absently, he watched the lady-archeologist hurry off, slipping past white-coated waiters, who were now delivering the appetizers. Still on his feet, Jake paused to scan the whole scene in curiosity.

Many people were still coming and going from the banquet hall; others milled about among the tables, reading the place cards to find their assigned seats.

As Jake started to sit down again, he spotted a familiar face in the crowd: the loon-bat in the opera cloak from earlier today. The mad prince—or whatever he was—sauntered casually into the banquet hall, greeting people here and there with lordly smiles and debonair nods.

Jake watched him like a hawk. When the prince turned to bow casually to Mr. Edison and the other American scientists at a nearby table, Jake's gaze homed in on his cheek. He vividly remembered the dark tattoo that he had seen slithering down the side of the stranger's face, but it had only been visible with the Lie Detector Goggles.

He wished he had them now, as he recalled Ragnor the Punisher's boast about tattooing the cheek of Loki.

But surely it was impossible.

Jake shook his head to himself. No, it was too much to believe, even for him. Ghosts, gryphons, fairies—yes, these he knew firsthand were real. But ancient Norse gods?

Then he remembered how Miss Langesund had told them that, according to legend, Loki was a shapeshifter. Maybe Henry and Helena might know something about it.

Jake leaned toward their tutor, seated to his left. "Henry?" he murmured.

The mild-mannered tutor glanced at him in concern. "Something wrong?"

"I'm not sure." Jake beckoned to him to lean closer, then he lowered his voice. "Remember when you found me near the Gatling gun today? And I told you some loon-bat had been playing with it?"

Henry huffed at the reminder and adjusted his waistcoat. "Of course I do, and I'm still waiting for you to come clean about—"

"He's here," Jake interrupted. "The man I was talking about. Any idea who that is?" When he nodded toward the mad prince, Henry followed his gaze and suddenly went very still, staring at the stranger.

"Henry?" Jake asked, but the tutor didn't seem to hear.

Jake could almost see the hackles on Henry's neck rise as his stare locked onto the mad prince; his entire posture changed in a heartbeat.

Henry's face went taut; he barely blinked. Though he did not say a word, Jake wouldn't have been surprised to hear him growl, by the look of him.

His twin sister, Helena, had picked up on the change in his demeanor, too. While Herr Schliemann rambled on about his excavations of the lost city of Troy, she looked at her brother intently.

Henry must have felt her gaze, for he tore his stare away from the mad prince and gave his sister a meaningful glance. "Won't you all excuse me for a moment?" he asked politely. Pushing back from the table, he rose without explanation, taking his dinner napkin off his lap and setting it by his plate.

"Something wrong, Henry?" Archie asked, but Henry didn't bother answering.

"I'm sure he's fine," Miss Helena said brightly, redirecting the kids' attention to Doctor Schliemann's endless story of digging in the dirt.

But Jake knew something was afoot, and it seemed serious.

He watched Henry go right over to the mad prince on the other side of the grand reception room and tap him on the shoulder.

When the stranger turned around, it was obvious they knew each other. Words were exchanged, but it was too far away to make out what the two men were saying.

Jake glanced across the table at Miss Helena to see her reaction. The girls' pretty governess, fair-skinned and black-haired, had paled a bit with shock at the sight of the stranger. She quickly masked her reaction behind an air of calm control. "Children, will you excuse me, please? I must see to my brother. I'll be right back. Isabelle's in charge—she's the eldest."

"What's wrong?" Isabelle immediately asked.

"Not a thing, my dear!" Miss Helena answered brightly as she rose. But you couldn't fool an empath.

Isabelle frowned as her governess hurried off.

Archie turned to his sister with a puzzled look. "What's wrong with her?"

"I don't know, but she was lying." Isabelle paused. "I also sensed fear."

"Miss Helena, scared? I doubt that," Archie muttered.

"Well, something's going on," Dani declared.

Jake nodded. "I'll go find out what it is."

"I'm coming with you," Dani said automatically, starting to get up.

"No, stay here. I'm less likely to be noticed if I go alone." He did not wait for her to argue, but slipped away from his chair and left the table.

Glancing across the banquet hall, he scowled to find that the twins and the stranger had already disappeared. He scanned the vast room, but they were nowhere to be seen.

He decided to go looking for them. They could not have gone far yet. It had only been a moment.

Fairly good at making himself inconspicuous—a vital skill for any former pickpocket—he checked a few different areas off the banquet hall, but when this yielded nothing, he walked outside onto the terrace.

Here many of the men in formal dinner jackets were smoking cigars and pipes and discussing their various fields.

Jake waved off a cloud of smoke and tried the shallow side stairs that led down into the garden. He walked down a few graveled paths among the trees and flowerbeds, looking around here and there. But when he reached the tall green shrubbery maze, he paused, hearing voices.

He crept closer, trying not to let the gravel crunch too loudly underfoot. Then he held his breath, listening to the tense conversation in progress on the other side of the green boxwood wall.

"Those are some interesting children you have sitting at your table."

Jake instantly recognized the mad prince's voice.

"I met the older boy earlier today," he continued. "Telekinesis? Very impressive. What do the others do?"

"So help me, you had better leave all four of them alone," Henry warned.

"Or what?" the stranger taunted. "Do you think there's anything you can possibly do to me? Frankly, I'm disappointed to see you letting yourself be used by lowly humans in this fashion—for what, a guard dog? Lapdog is more like it."

"That's enough, Loki."

Loki? Jake's eyes widened, but he set his astonishment aside for the moment as their tense exchange continued.

"Come, DuVal, you were meant for so much more than this, you and your beautiful sister. Both of you should join me. I always have room in my court for loyal subjects who share my blood."

"We may share your blood, Your Highness." Now it was Miss Helena who spoke. "But we do not share your views about humans, so you'd better keep your distance from our charges."

"Oh, my, my! Aren't you precious! What a cute little threat, my dear. But you should know better than to try giving orders to your superiors. Bad kitty!"

Helena suddenly cried out in pain on the other side of the bushes.

"What have you done to her?" Henry cried while Jake held his breath, wondering if he should attempt to intervene.

"Loki, stop this!" the governess pleaded in a voice filled with pain.

Jake's heart pounded as he listened. It sounded like she was being tortured!

It was all he could do to hold himself back.

Henry was furious. "Leave my sister alone!"

"What? I'm not touching her," Loki said innocently.

"Henry, help!" Helena cried to her brother. "I can't...make it...stop—" Her words broke off into a leopard's roar.

Jake gulped while Loki laughed merrily on the other side of the bushes.

If only Derek Stone were here! The warrior had a particular liking for Miss Helena, and nothing would have stopped *him* from going to her rescue, even if this Loki was the actual Norse god.

"You find this amusing?" Henry snarled at the laughing loon-bat. "Let her change back, Loki! Whatever you've done to her—"

"Oh, shut up. Stop your whining! I've merely freed her true self, DuVal. And now I'll do the same for you!"

When Henry let out a low shout of pain, Jake knew he had to do something. He had no idea what.

He moved his position, peering through the boxwood wall until he could just make out the shape of their tutor dropping to the ground, falling onto his hands and knees.

Loki laughed in delight, watching them. "Isn't it liberating, Henry, to be who you truly are? You've grown much too civilized, the both of you. Her with her corsets, you with your cravats. So tidy, so disciplined! But you don't have to wear a collar, Henry! Both of you can be free if you'll join me! There, now. Doesn't that feel better?"

Jake was already running down the side of the boxwood maze, trying to find an entrance. He did not know quite what he planned to do, but he had to help them somehow.

At last, he found an opening several yards away and flung around the corner.

"Enjoy yourselves!" Loki was saying. "Go and run free for a while! This is a *gift* I've given you both—welcome to Norway! Our lush forests should suit you well in your natural forms. Enjoy the break from all your tedious teaching duties. Take some time to think about my job offer, dear cousins. And don't worry, I'll look after those adorable children for you."

Standing in the opening of the garden maze, Jake froze at the scene unfolding before him.

He had never actually seen Henry turn into a wolf before. He had only seen the end result, never the process.

It looked horrendously painful.

In the moonlight, the grimace of intense concentration on Henry's face seemed to suggest that he was trying with all his might to fight the transformation. To remain himself, their trusty tutor. But it was no use.

"Blast you!" were the last human words Jake heard him say before great claws sprang forth from his fingernails. Fur sprouted from his face. His jaw buckled and began thrusting forward into a pointed snout.

Big, white fangs ripped down from his upper teeth, while his ears tapered into points rising from the sides of his head. He thrashed and let out a dog-like whine of pain.

Meanwhile, Helena's transformation into her other form was already complete. In the sleek, silky form of a powerful black leopard, she was hissing at Loki.

She pounced in between the mad prince—or whatever he was—and her brother, at his most vulnerable in the middle of the changing process.

Henry's cry of anger turned into a brief, canine yelp of pain as the base of his spine shot out into a furry tail.

Jake was aghast, watching it.

Although the change was nothing new to Henry or Helena, both being descended from a proud French shapeshifter lineage that boasted some of the finest bloodlines in Europe, Jake personally never could have imagined having to go through something like that.

As soon as their tutor had fully become a great brownish-gray wolf, he shook himself like a large dog to doff his neat tweed coat. All that was left of his clothes was the cravat tied around his neck like a dog's collar, but he tore free of it with his front paw.

The DuVal twins, usually so civilized, were now in their most savage form, and both of them were furious.

They began circling the smug Loki, the wolf growling, the leopard snarling. Their white fangs gleamed in the moonlight as they warned their mysterious kinsman of his imminent doom.

Just as Henry and Helena lunged at him, Loki turned himself into a swarm of insects; the two big predators leaped harmlessly through the black, buzzing cloud of bottle-flies.

As the wolf and leopard landed and whirled around with angry snarls, Loki reconstituted himself into a man-shaped swarm of flies, laughed at them again, and flew away.

Jake's eyes widened as the cloud of insects whooshed straight toward *him,* standing at the end of the green aisle near the entrance of the boxwood maze.

He tried to jump back around the corner to get out of Loki's way, but he was not fast enough.

"Hullo, Cake," Loki taunted as he rushed toward him, then the flies were upon him.

The bottle-flies swarmed Jake, swirling all around him—disgusting!—trying to get into his ears and his nostrils. All he could hear was the deafening buzz of their wings. Jake thrashed about and waved the insects off madly, but they just kept coming back, crawling through his hair, and trying to wriggle their way down into the collar of his shirt and up the edges of his sleeves.

"Get off o' me!" he finally yelled, spitting out one fly that tried to crawl into his mouth when he spoke.

Having had his fun, the Loki swarm withdrew; the cloud of insects whooshed away.

CHAPTER ELEVEN
Unchaperoned

Jake was left spitting with disgust and brushing off horrid, buggy, tickling sensations, while the trickster god, heading back down the garden path, turned himself back into his usual shape with a low laugh.

Coolly tugging his jacket into place, Loki strode back toward the dining hall.

Jake turned to find Henry and Helena as their respective animals loping toward him down the green boxwood corridor. Even though he knew they meant him no harm, he took an instinctive step back from the two large, wild-looking animals running straight for him. They stopped in front of him, both looking quite distressed.

The black leopard-Helena hissed in the direction Loki had gone, while wolf-Henry looked at Jake and tilted his head with a nervous whine, as if to ask, *"Are you all right?"*

"I'm fine, it's you two I'm worried about! How could this happen?" he cried. "Is that really Loki—the Viking trickster god?"

The wolf and leopard looked at each other, then at him, nodding their furry heads reluctantly.

"He's real? And he's your kinsman? Gadzooks, I don't believe it," Jake breathed, then he shook off his astonishment as best he could. "Never mind—just put yourselves back to normal and let's go after him!"

When both animals made sad noises, Jake began to understand the situation. "What is it? What's wrong? Can't you turn yourselves back?"

The twins nodded.

"No, no, no. You've got to! Try harder! We need you! You can't leave us like this! We're just four kids in a foreign country, with a mad Norse god on the loose! Please!"

The pair exchanged a worried glance, and then proceeded to give it their best.

The wolf braced himself on all four paws and stared at the ground with his furry eyebrows knitted, like a dog trying with all his might to remember where he had buried his bone.

The leopard shut her golden-green eyes and let out a low meow of effort, plainly willing something to happen.

Nothing did.

Jake was getting seriously scared. "I'll go send a message to Great-Great Aunt Ramona. I'm sure she'll have some sort of spell that we can use to undo this..." The wolf suddenly bounded off while Jake was still speaking. "Where's he going?"

His leopard sister turned around and watched Henry run back to his abandoned pile of clothes. The wolf rummaged around in his coat with his snout, then came back a moment later carrying his fob-watch in his mouth.

Henry dropped it by its small gold chain at Jake's feet, much like a dog who had been taught to fetch.

Jake fought the urge to say "good boy," since that was still his tutor in there. Immediately, he bent down to pick up the watch and grimaced as he wiped the canine slobber off it.

Henry let out a low yip.

"Oh! I get it! A watch...Time! Give it some time and maybe the spell will wear off? Is that what you're saying?"

Wolf-Henry wagged his tail.

"Right! Of course. No need to panic yet. He's a trickster god, not *evil* evil, like Miss Astrid said. This is probably just one of Loki's pranks. I knew he was a loon when I met him earlier today in the Exhibit Hall. So, what do you think, then? We give it twenty-four hours, and if the spell hasn't worn off, then send a message to Aunt Ramona?"

Both beasts seemed satisfied with this solution, though no one was happy about Loki's trick. Wolf-Henry huffed as if to say, *"This is very inconvenient!"*

Leopard-Helena let out a low, vexed meow.

"Don't worry, I'll look after the others," Jake assured them. "You two just stay out of sight some place until this wears off. Maybe I'll do some snooping and try to figure out what Loki's up to—"

Both twins growled at him in disapproval.

"Why not?"

Henry bared his teeth while Helena slashed the air with her claws in warning. Their message was obvious: *"Too dangerous!"*

"Fine. Don't worry about Miss Langesund, Henry. I'll tell her that you're, er, sick."

At that moment, Jake heard Loki yelling in distress from the direction of the terrace behind the dining hall.

"Help! Someone, help! Wolf! There's a wolf on the grounds!"

Hang it, Loki was up to more mischief! Jake whipped around to face the terrace with a gasp. "That devil!"

But Loki wasn't finished. Jake could hear him up on the terrace, shouting to the other men. "Somebody, do something! I just saw a wolf in the college gardens menacing a child! Quickly, bring a rifle! Shoot the beast before it eats the poor boy!"

Jake could hear the commotion growing louder as more of the gentlemen who had been smoking out on the terrace harkened to Loki's alarm.

"Where did you see the beast?" one yelled.

"Near the garden maze!" said Loki.

"Call for the campus guard! He carries a gun!" another shouted.

Jake spun back to face Henry and Helena. "You've got to get out of here! Stay out of sight or they'll shoot you. Hurry! Go to the woods! You've got to hide!"

The black leopard shrank into the shadows in fear, but the great wolf hesitated.

"Go, Henry! You're in danger! I'll leave your clothes under these bushes so you can get them later." Jake was already shoving their clothes and shoes under the branches of a towering rhododendron, hiding them away. "If you're not back with us as your regular selves in twenty-four hours, I'll telegraph Aunt Ramona. She'll know what to do—"

The sound of a gunshot interrupted him. The crack of a rifle tore through the night as someone on the terrace fired a shot into the air to scare away the "wolf."

Jake turned to them, aghast. "What are you waiting for? *Run!*"

At once, the twins bounded off through the garden and disappeared into the night.

As they headed for safety, Jake immediately raced back toward the banquet hall to make the men call off this deadly wolf hunt.

Running through the garden, he could hear the commotion on the terrace growing louder. A crowd was gathering. Alarmed guests in formal attire were shouting suggestions at each other about what to do, and of course, there was Loki, right in the middle of the chaos.

"Did you say you saw the beast menacing a youngster in the garden?" one of the scientists cried.

The trickster god nodded earnestly. "Yes, it's probably eaten him already. The poor lad probably never had a chance to scream!"

"How horrid!" a lady gasped.

"I'm fine, I'm right here!" Jake yelled as he pounded up the steps onto the terrace. "I'm the boy he saw, and there's no danger! Everything's all right, people!"

They seemed almost disappointed to lose out on their sport.

"Are you sure?" People gathered around him, while Loki stood back smirking.

"It wasn't a wolf, it was just a dog, and he already ran away. Besides, he was friendly! Perfectly harmless, I assure you. The owner probably lives nearby. Anyway, he's gone now," he told them. "There's no danger! No wolf hunt tonight, everyone!" he declared with as much authority as a boy-earl could muster. "Please, go back inside now. You're going to miss out on your supper!"

This must have sounded reasonable to them, for the crowd dispersed, shuffling back inside to sit down for their meal.

All except for Loki.

He feigned a caring frown. "So, it wasn't really a wolf after all?" the prince mocked him.

"Of course not—as you know perfectly well," Jake shot back with a glare.

Loki glanced at the last of the adults heading into the dining hall, then he eyed Jake warily. "Well, you're rather clever, aren't you, Cakey boy?" he murmured. "But are you clever *enough*? That's the question. After all, you're not exactly a genius like the rest of us here, are you?"

Jake clenched his jaw at the insult, considering it was aimed at the exact weakness about which he already felt self-conscious in this place. He knew he didn't belong here, but no matter, he told himself. He had come for Archie's sake—to cheer on his cousin.

Refusing to be intimidated, he took a bold step forward as Loki drifted toward the shadows. "What have you done to the twins?" he demanded.

But the trickster merely gave him a sly smile, lifted his arms out to his sides, and suddenly, in the blink of an eye, turned himself into a crow as black as night. He let out a raucous caw and went flapping off into the sky.

Jake shuddered to witness such a thing.

As some sort of shapeshifter god, it seemed that Loki did not have to go through any pain to transform himself like Henry and Helena did. He could do it instantly, and unlike the twins, could assume various shapes, based on what he had told Jake earlier in the Exhibit Hall. A salmon, a horse, a fly.

Even a woman.

A chill ran down Jake's spine as it sank in that Loki could be anywhere, turn into anything...

Take on the appearance of anyone.

No wonder Ragnor the Punisher had tattooed the trickster's cheek so he could be identified. Loki must have figured out a way to cover it up most of the time.

I'm going to need those Lie Detector Goggles, Jake thought. He glanced around uneasily, scanning the darkness in case Loki had doubled back.

His expression hardened. There was no telling what the devious fellow was up to, but Jake had not forgotten the mad prince's interest in 'those talented children.'

He had promised Henry and Helena that he'd protect the others in their absence. Without a moment to lose, Jake pivoted and marched back into the banquet hall to make sure Dani and his cousins were still safe. He might not be a genius, but he had guts.

If Loki wanted to harm the girls and Archie, he was going to have to get through *him* first.

CHAPTER TWELVE
Not The End of the World...Or Is It?

"There you are! Finally! I was starting to worry," Archie said when Jake slid back into his seat at their table.

He was relieved to find the boy genius and the two girls just as he had left them, with Professor Schliemann still rattling on about his favorite method for removing dirt from his archeological site.

Jake was glad to see that Miss Langesund had not yet returned from fetching her father. Nice as she was, he was not looking forward to lying to her about Henry.

But it was not as though he could tell her the truth.

"Where are Henry and Helena?" Archie whispered. "What happened out there?"

Isabelle studied Jake with a worried gaze, but Dani frowned at him. "You all right? You look...weird."

Jake did not answer directly. "Everybody, outside. Now. C'mon. We need to go."

At his grim tone, Archie's eyes widened behind his spectacles. "Something wrong?"

"You might say that," Jake muttered.

"What is it?" Dani exclaimed.

"I'll explain later. Come on, you lot." He mumbled a hastily made-up excuse to the adults about why they were leaving the table, though none of these seemed the slightest bit interested. They did not know them, after all.

The four children left the table. Jake hurried the girls and Archie outside. Glancing around, thankfully, he saw no sign of the loon-bat. He gathered them into a corner of the terrace and told them what had happened: that Loki was real, that he'd put Henry and Helena under some sort of spell, and that the twins were now stuck in their animal forms.

All three stared at him in shock.

"Well, what do we do?" Dani cried.

"Do you know where the twins have gone?" Archie prompted.

"They ran off into the woods," Jake replied. "At least there they should be safe for now."

Archie leaned against the brick wall shaking his head. "Loki's real? I can't believe it! What does he want? What is he doing here?"

Jake lowered his head in thought, recalling Loki's fascination with the Gatling gun earlier today. "Maybe..." he started, then quit. "Nah, it can't be."

"What?" Dani prompted.

"Well, you remember what Miss Langesund told us about Loki's final battle against Odin? The ancient prophecy, remember?"

"The Battle of Ragnarok," Dani said. "It's in my Norway book."

"Right. Miss Langesund said Loki wants an army of giants to overthrow the gods. Well, I know it sounds daft, but maybe he's here to buy some weapons or hire some scientists who can design them." Jake shrugged, well aware of how farfetched it sounded. "Loki talks in riddles, but he definitely told me starting wars is his hobby. Maybe he's trying to get his hands on some newfangled kind of gun or cannon that Odin and Thor have never seen."

Dani's eyes widened. "You're saying Odin and Thor are real, too?"

"I don't see why not, if Loki is," Jake replied.

"But this is impossible!" she said. "They're only myths! How can they really exist?"

"Ghosts and gryphons aren't supposed to exist, either. Or fairies, for that matter," Jake said with a pointed look.

Dani gazed at him, crestfallen, for indeed, she had ridden across the sky with him on his gryphon and had held the fairy Gladwin on the palm of her hand.

"We've got to come up with a plan," Jake added impatiently.

"Jake," Isabelle said in a tentative voice, "didn't Miss Langesund say that Loki's great war against Odin was supposed to bring on, um...the end of the world? The Viking version of Armageddon? The apocalypse?"

They stared at each other in renewed dread, for of course, that *was* what the lady-archeologist had claimed.

Archie cleared his throat. "Well, now, logically speaking, if that's what Loki's here to do, he wouldn't have wanted Henry and Helena getting in his way."

"Or us," Jake said grimly, glancing around at the others. "Whatever he's up to, we need to stop him."

"A god?" Archie asked.

"Hold on. You're overlooking one very obvious ingredient," Dani pointed out.

They all looked at her hopefully.

"The Viking prophecy says that Loki needs *giants* to bring on the end of the world! I don't see any giants around here, do you?"

As her always-practical, common-sense observation sank in, looks of relief passed over all their faces.

"That is an excellent point," Archie agreed with a brief chuckle. "If there were giants around here, I think we would've noticed."

"They'd be hard to miss," Isabelle agreed in a cautious murmur.

"There! You see?" Dani said, pleased with herself. She propped her hands on her waist. "This is just Jake being paranoid, as usual. Well, you're always waiting for the worst!" she chided. "The end of the world, on our first-ever holiday? Come *on*."

He scowled at her, but Dani wasn't finished. "Of course, it's a bit of a shock that Loki's real, I admit, but then again, nothing in our lives is exactly normal, is it? You with your ghosts and telekinesis. You talking to animals. You with your big brain," she said to each of them in turn. "Honestly, you lot are lucky to have me 'ere to bring you back down to earth!"

Jake couldn't help smiling ruefully at that. He supposed it was true.

"If we start seeing giants, *then* we panic," Dani declared. "Until then, I vote we concentrate on helping the twins."

"Makes sense to me," Jake conceded after a moment with a nod. "After all, just because Loki *wants* to cause Viking Armageddon, it doesn't mean he *can*."

"True," Archie agreed. "And really, if he hasn't done it yet in all the centuries since Viking times, why should he succeed now?"

Isabelle let out a sigh of relief. "I say we go back to our rooms in the dormitory and wait for Henry and Helena to come back. Somebody's got to be there in case they need our help when they return."

Jake nodded. "We should try to stay out of Loki's way, too, in the meanwhile—just to be safe. Why tempt him?"

They all agreed to this, then started walking back across campus to the dormitory where their party had been assigned four rooms: one for the boys, one for the girls, one for Henry, and one for Helena.

As they went down the stone steps off the terrace onto the graveled path that led across the wide green lawn, they suddenly saw the figure of a lady approaching.

In the darkness, they couldn't tell who it was, so Jake held up his hand, discreetly warning them back. "Remember," he murmured, "Loki can take any shape, look like anyone..."

The footsteps in the darkness grew louder, but when the woman passed beneath one of the iron lampposts that lined the walkway ahead, they saw a golden gown and blond hair, and quickly recognized Miss Langesund.

If it was really she.

Blimey, thought Jake, maybe the carrot-head was right. Maybe he *was* a little paranoid.

With good reason!

As the alleged Miss Langesund approached, Jake studied her suspiciously, ready to use his telekinesis to defend the others in case it turned out to be Loki in disguise.

He could *really* use those Lie Detector Goggles. That would help them see through Loki, no matter his disguise.

But as Miss Langesund hurried toward them, Jake was quickly convinced it really was the lady-archeologist. There was none of Loki's mad, wild humor in her eyes, only worry. "Children, are you leaving already? I'm so sorry I missed dinner! Is Henry with you, by chance?" She glanced around for her gentleman friend.

"Er, no, sorry, Henry's indisposed at the moment," Jake said. "He suddenly started feeling—not quite himself."

"Oh, no! I'm so sorry to hear that! I hope the salmon wasn't bad—"

"No, nothing like that, he'll be fine," Jake assured her.

"Miss Langesund, is something wrong?" Isabelle asked, stepping toward her in concern. "You seem upset."

"Bless you, my dear, well—the truth is, I-I honestly don't know. There may be," she confessed. "I can't find my father anywhere!" she burst out, sounding slightly panicked. "I'm really beginning to worry."

"How now?" Archie murmured, frowning.

"I checked his room. He's not there. I looked in the library, too, but nobody's seen him. I'm going over to check the museum next, and I—well, I hate to be a bother, but I was going to see if Henry would go with me. Sometimes Father has trouble with his heart, and if he's had a medical emergency, I don't really want to be alone when I find him."

"We'll go with you!" Archie volunteered at once.

"Oh, it's all right! I could never impose," she said. "I'm sure I'm just being a worry-wart. He probably got caught up in his work, that's all. Besides, you children must be off to bed soon—"

"We're not babies!" Dani retorted. "It's early yet. We'll go with you."

"Quite right!" Archie said. Though he was only eleven, he was a true English gentleman down to his fingertips and could never resist the chance to aid a damsel in distress. "Don't fret, dear lady! We'll be glad to help you find your father," the boy genius assured her.

Chivalrous pipsqueak, thought Jake, slightly annoyed to be taken away from their own worries, which were bad enough.

Miss Langesund forced a smile, but the fear in her eyes told a different story. "You're all very kind."

"Archie and I will help you look for your father," Jake quickly intervened. "The girls should probably go back to the rooms in case the twins, um, need any help. Since they're not feeling well."

"Oh, right!" Dani answered, catching on. "They might need us to help take care of them."

"Helena's feeling poorly, too?" Miss Langesund echoed in surprise.

"You know how it is with twins," Archie said, thinking fast. "One can't get sick without the other feeling the same symptoms. It always happens that way with the two of them. But don't worry, I'm sure they'll both be fine soon."

"Till then, you'll just have to make do with us," Jake said with forced cheer, reassuring her with a nod.

"Very well, then, if you don't mind coming along. If Father's had an attack of some sort, I may need one of you to run for a doctor," she said with a grateful smile.

But as soon as she turned away, Jake leaned toward Dani. "Stay sharp and get to safety," he whispered. "I don't want that loon-bat anywhere near you girls."

With a firm nod in answer, Dani took hold of Isabelle's arm, then the girls headed back toward the dormitory buildings, following the lighted path.

The boys turned again to Miss Langesund.

"Shall we?" Archie asked.

She nodded, then the boys followed her back to the little museum. It dawned on Jake as they went that this was the perfect chance to speak to Ragnor the Punisher again—if his spirit was back, hanging about in the ethers.

The fierce Viking ghost might be able to tell him more about the trickster god and his devilish ways. Perhaps he'd have a few tips on how to manage Loki.

Unfortunately, when Miss Langesund unlocked the door, they quickly found that her father was not there.

Nor was the phantom warlord.

While Archie checked beneath the boat and up across the catwalk, Jake glanced around the darkened museum with a frown. *Blast.* It seemed he had done too good a job of convincing Ragnor the Punisher to quit haunting the museum and return to Valhalla.

Miss Langesund headed for the back door of the little ship museum. "Maybe Father's outside. Sometimes he likes to step out back for a break and smoke his pipe on the park bench near the edge of the woods."

When she opened the door, Archie picked up a lantern and followed her out. Jake drifted out a few steps after them, still warily eyeing the Viking ship over his shoulder. But as soon as he stepped outside, he saw Miss Langesund ahead.

Holding up the hem of her long dinner gown, she left the trail of stepping stones that led away from the museum toward the woods. "Master Archie, bring the light, would you?" she called.

"Have you found something?" he asked, hurrying toward her to shine his lantern on the grass.

Miss Langesund bent down with a stricken look and stared at an object on the ground. "Oh, no..."

"What is it?" Jake rushed over as she picked it up, in a daze.

By the light of Archie's lantern, he saw Miss Langesund's hand begin shaking as she lifted what she had found up to the light.

She never did answer his question, nor did she have to.

The answer was self-evident.

Jake and Archie exchanged a dark glance.

"Father's tobacco pipe," she forced out. "He always keeps it in his pocket."

As they stood there in dread, scanning the black, shadowed woods that loomed just a few yards away, there was no sign of Professor Langesund.

"Miss Astrid," Jake said calmly. "You should probably put that down in the same spot where you found it."

"Why?" she choked out.

"It's evidence," he answered in a grim tone, and Archie steadied her as she let out a shocked sob. "We need to call the police."

PART II

CHAPTER THIRTEEN
Misunderstood

Bow tie, crazy hair, spectacles: check, check, check. The three geniuses Snorri had caught so far fit all the crow's specifications.

The first was a mathematician who had been playing his violin between equations, as if the music helped him jar his ideas loose. Snorri had heard the haunting tune and had been drawn to it, tiptoeing up to the edge of the woods.

Seeing a man sitting alone who fit the right description, he had snatched him from right off the park bench by the fjord where he had been relaxing.

The second dupe had been just as easy prey. Lost in their thoughts, these geniuses weren't very good at sensing danger, Snorri thought with a scoff. He had found the second one studying plants in the forest.

The rumpled fellow had seemed particularly interested in the little black dots that grew on the underside of fern leaves. He had been so absorbed in his work that Snorri, as large as he was, had crept up on him completely unnoticed.

The third had been a bit more of a challenge. He had stepped out behind a small wooden building on the edge of the campus to take a few puffs on his tobacco pipe.

Snorri had smelled the piquant smoke wafting through the woods and followed his nose toward it; in moments, he had peered out of the leafy shadows at the smoking professor, whose back was turned.

The stalking giant had noted all the details. Neat beard, tweed vest, shirtsleeves rolled up.

No bowtie, but his spectacles and the ink-stains on his fingers gave him away. He was some sort of scientist all right, and after

Snorri grabbed him, he soon learned that the third professor was a digger of old, dead bones.

What mad ideas these humans took into their heads! Even the dullest-witted giant knew it was terrible bad luck to go digging up dead men's graves.

Well, the bad luck that the grave-digging scientist must've long had coming caught up with him in the form of Snorri. He had grabbed Professor Langesund just as the absent-minded archeology professor remembered that he was missing the Welcome Dinner.

Professor Langesund barely knew what hit him as Snorri snatched him off his feet, covered his mouth to shut him up, and dashed back into the woods again, carrying his prize under his arm.

Snorri had run all the way back to his mountaintop cave, where he had tossed Professor Langesund into another cage made of branches tied together with vines. He had strung the cage up high over the cavern floor so his captives couldn't escape.

Since then, well, Snorri was not sure *what* he had expected from these fellows. They didn't have scientists back in Giant Land, but from his dealings with them so far, he was rather glad of that.

Geniuses, Snorri had decided, could be nasty little creatures. Honestly, they were beyond rude! Not even Gorm, with all his boasting and his insults, had ever referred to Snorri as an "it," for example.

He clenched his jaw as he heard them talking and kept his back turned to them, sitting before his campfire and doing his best to ignore them. They hadn't stopped discussing him since he'd put them in their cages.

"Splendid mutant! Magnificent specimen!"

"Incredible! It must be over twenty feet tall! How is this possible?"

"I don't know, Albert. It's obviously a hominid of some kind, but at this point, impossible to say. We'll need years to study this creature before we'll understand it properly. By Jove, this is going to rewrite everything we know of evolution!"

"If we could show this creature to the world, we'll be more famous than Mr. Darwin!"

"Yes, but how do we get it back to the university? The beast is dangerous!"

Snorri was very close to losing his otherwise nonexistent temper.

"Have you tried communicating with it, Gunther? Does it speak?"

"I've heard some grunting sounds that seem to have some meaning, but it's hard to be sure if it understands. It barely responds."

"Yes, well, its language is no doubt primitive."

"But look, it's mastered the use of fire! It wears clothes and it even has a few rudimentary tools."

"You think it has a name?"

Snorri rolled his eyes.

These geniuses were so daft and so consumed with the hope of studying him that they barely spared a thought for the danger they were in.

Not that Snorri cared.

Such rude boors deserved to have their brains turned into powder and made into a potion for someone more deserving.

Thank goodness, the crow showed up at last, a flap of motion silhouetted before the moon. Finally, someone with common sense!

"Well!" his glossy, black-feathered friend greeted him, fluttering down onto the log across from the fire. "I see you're making excellent progress, Snorri! Or should I say King Snorri? You'd better get used to hearing it. Soon!" the bird promised.

The reminder of their bargain cheered Snorri up considerably after his captives' abuse. In truth, though he was too shy to say so, it was not the crown itself he cared about, but winning Princess Kaia. Whoever married her would be the next king, and oh, how he loved her! Always had. A hopeless case.

Hopeless—until now.

The fire popped and the bird bobbed its head to escape a small shower of tiny sparks that arced up from the flames. "So, how many brains have you collected, my friend?"

Snorri nodded over his shoulder with a brusque grunt.

"Three! Very good."

"Nasty little vermin," Snorri grumbled. "How many more will you need to make the smart potion for me?"

The bird considered for a moment. "Five more should do quite nicely."

"Five...?" Snorri echoed uncertainly.

"Your whole hand." The bird pointed with his wing.

"Oh! Five. Right. I knew that," Snorri muttered. "In that case, I should only need another day or so to catch the rest."

"Excellent! I'll be back to check on you tomorrow, then. As soon as you have the full number of geniuses, I will make the smart potion. And then you'll be as intelligent as all of these brains combined," the bird reminded him with a jaunty wink.

Not that he needed reminding. Indeed, it was all he had been thinking of. Why, when he was an *intellectual* giant, then Gorm wouldn't have any reason to make fun of him anymore.

More importantly, Kaia was sure to find the new-and-improved Snorri the most suave, sophisty-cated, fascinating fellow she had ever met. She would almost positively fall in love with him.

She just had to.

"Remember," the crow interrupted his little daydream. "Bow tie, crazy hair, spectacles."

"Right, right, right."

"And don't let anybody see you, except the ones you catch."

"I know. Or they'll dissect me."

"Yes," the crow said sympathetically. "I'm glad you understand the risks. Well, until tomorrow, then! Good luck, Snorri, you giant of destiny!" The bird flew off again, circling higher into the sky.

As it disappeared into a cloud bank, Snorri suddenly realized that the three smarty-pantses in the cages had fallen absolutely silent. Not a single rude word came from the direction of the cave.

Snorri glanced slowly, cautiously, over his shoulder and saw them gripping the bars of their cage and staring at him in shock.

"You understand us?" the mathematician blurted out, staring at him.

"Th-th-that bird," the bone-digger stammered. "It, it talked?!"

Snorri gave them a sarcastic "primitive" growl in answer. Why enlighten them with facts?

They obviously thought he was dumb as a rock and more of a thing than a person.

Besides, he had no desire to make conversation with people whose brains he was going to drink in a powdery potion, if he understood the bird's plans correctly.

He turned away and broke another huge branch over his knee, ignoring the bewildered questions of the scientists. Then he took out his knife and cut a length of twine. Firmly tying two branches together, he got to work on building another cage for the five remaining geniuses that he had yet to catch.

It kept his mind off feeling homesick and a peculiar twinge of guilt already taking shape in his big, dumb heart. For as he worked, sitting beside his fire, a dark question passed like a shadow over the landscape of his mind...

For the smart brew to be made, these annoying little scientists were going to have to die. *That crow doesn't expect me to kill them, does he?*

He paused, mulling it over. A very disturbing question.

Falling into Midgarth was bad enough—against Odin's rules—though he had done it by accident. Drinking people's brains in powdered form or otherwise was considerably worse, and sure to be frowned upon—even though Odin, who *made* the rules, was rather bloodthirsty himself, being the god of war and all.

Moreover, though Snorri might be the village idiot of Jugenheim, he was not at all sure he was even *capable* of carrying out eight cold-blooded murders.

That sort of thing was Gorm's expertise.

Snorri shuddered despite the warmth from his fire. But his mind was made up. He didn't mind catching them, but when it came time to kill those annoying little geniuses, the crow was just going to have do it himself. Peck them to death or something.

For his part, he was not that kind of giant.

And come to think of it, maybe that was why he had never quite fit in back home.

CHAPTER FOURTEEN
Once A Thief

When the boys returned to the dormitory later that night, Dani and Isabelle knew at once by their grim expressions that something bad had happened.

For their part, the girls had nothing to report yet—no sign of Henry or Helena.

"Did you find Professor Langesund?" Dani asked as they all gathered in the missing governess's room.

"No," Jake said, "we only found his pipe."

Then Archie explained how they had stayed with Miss Langesund until the authorities had arrived. "But she sent us away as soon as the police wagon rolled up. She didn't want us getting dragged into this mess."

"Criminy," Dani breathed. "What do you think happened to the professor?"

Jake shook his head, at a loss. "I have no idea. But something obviously did."

Teddy let out a low whine and laid his head down on his paws.

"Meanwhile, we four are on our own." He glanced around at them. "We're going to have to be extra careful and look out for each other. There's something very weird going on around here."

"Well, let's hope for the best," Isabelle said in a comforting tone. "It'll sort itself out. I'm sure everything will be fine. Maybe Professor Langesund simply wandered off for a moonlight stroll in the forest. Maybe he dropped his pipe and didn't even realize it.

"As for Henry and Helena," she continued, "you needn't worry about them. Even as animals, they're clever enough to stay out of sight until they're able to come back to us. We just have to wait for them. With any luck, they'll be back by tomorrow morning."

The others exchanged a dubious look, though they appreciated her attempt to make them feel better.

Then Jake suggested they all take turns waiting up throughout the night, in case Henry and Helena showed up needing help.

Of course, if the twins returned, still stuck in their animal forms, Jake wasn't sure how they were going to sneak two wild animals into the college dorm, unseen. They would just have to cross that bridge when they came to it. He'd think of something.

Archie volunteered for the first watch, from eleven P.M. to two o'clock in the morning, but Dani told him to go to bed—she would do it. Since it was already quite late, they would only need three shifts.

The others agreed that Archie should be the one to get a full night's sleep, since he had to participate in a science panel discussion in the morning with a Chinese physicist and a Scottish engineer.

He would need a good night's sleep to be sharp enough to answer the audience's questions.

"You've got your genius reputation to keep up, after all," Dani told him. "Just go to bed. Teddy will sit up with me."

Jake said he'd take the hardest shift, from two till five A.M., and then Isabelle would watch from five in the morning until full daylight.

Dani and Jake said goodnight to his cousins.

Archie went into the boys' room, while Isabelle withdrew into the room for the girls across the hallway.

"I'll sit up with Teddy in Miss Helena's room," Dani said, nodding toward the next door beside the girls' room.

Henry's chamber was next door to the boys' quarters. Jake nodded and stepped into the governess's room with her.

"Aren't you going to bed?" Dani asked.

"Just want to make sure you're all settled," he mumbled.

She eyed him with a frown. "You're more worried about all this than you're letting on."

"Well, we *are* up against a Norse god, you carrot-head," he whispered with a scowl. "I can't help feeling that Loki is behind all this somehow. Not just with Henry and Helena, but Professor Langesund, too. But why?" He shrugged, having no answers and no clear idea of what was really going on.

All he had was a simple plan to get a hold of those Lie Detector Goggles. He had a feeling they were going to need them.

Dani studied him suspiciously. "I know that look. You're planning something, aren't you?"

"There's a device in the Exhibit Hall that'll help us identify Loki no matter what shape he takes. I'm going to go steal it," he whispered.

Her green eyes flew open wide. "Jake, you said there are policemen all over the campus now looking for the professor!"

"Aye, they're distracted with their search," he countered in a reasonable tone. "With him gone, nobody's going to be paying attention to the inventions right now. I can get in and out of the Exhibit Hall before anyone even notices me."

"But you swore off stealing, remember?"

"This is different. Our safety's on the line! What choice do we have?"

"Ugh." Dani dropped her face into her hands for a moment. "If you get caught, I don't know you."

"I'm not goin' to get caught. I haven't lost my touch."

She lifted her head and stared at him in disapproval.

"I'll put the goggles back when we're done using them, all right?"

"All right," she grumbled, scooping up her dog. She carried Teddy with her to the armchair beside the window, then sat down to keep watch. "Jake," Dani said as he headed for the door.

He glanced over his shoulder in question.

"Be careful," she offered. "And good luck."

He sent her a cocky smile. "Who needs luck when you're as talented as me?"

She rolled her eyes, but Jake flashed a grin.

Leaving her and Teddy to their sentry duty, he stepped out into the corridor and pulled the door shut quietly behind him. He glanced both ways, making sure none of the other conference-goers were wandering the halls. Fortunately, he found himself alone.

The dormitory full of student bedrooms was quiet; all the doors down the long hallway remained closed.

Right, he thought, with a small nod of determination. Then he moved off stealthily to carry out his mission. He just hoped his thieving skills weren't getting rusty.

It had been a while.

CHAPTER FIFTEEN
The Not-So-Lucky Bowtie

By breakfast the next morning, Jake was groggy from the night's adventure, and a bit nervous about the risk of getting caught with the stolen Lie Detector Goggles.

This, of course, did not dull his appetite.

Dani and Archie sat across from him at their table once more in the banquet hall, staring at him like he was more of a wolf than Henry.

He paused in the middle of shoveling a forkful of scrambled eggs into his mouth. "What?"

"How can you gorge your face at a time like this?" Dani asked, meaning of course that Henry and Helena still had not returned.

He just shrugged and went on eating.

"Maybe he's right," Archie said with a sigh. "If today's anything like yesterday, we'll need to keep up our strength."

Dani pushed her fruit salad around her plate unhappily. "I can't believe they're not back yet. I was sure I'd wake up and find them here and everything back to normal."

"Don't worry," Jake ordered, having swallowed his last bite. "We'll get it all sorted soon. First order of business is Archie's panel. Finish eating, Arch, then I'll walk you to your classroom. Dani can stay with Isabelle. I don't want any of you wandering around alone."

Archie took off his spectacles and rubbed his eyes. "Blimey, I've got a headache coming on."

Jake and Dani exchanged an amused look to hear him use their Cockney street slang.

But the boy genius forced himself to brighten up. "Guess I've got to act normal in front of the crowd, though, what?"

"Are you nervous to speak in front of all those geniuses?" Dani asked.

"Nah, I've got my lucky bowtie on for the occasion!"

They laughed even though he was serious.

"I'm going to go fix a plate of food for Isabelle," Dani announced, rising from her chair.

Archie leaned closer across the table after she had gone. "Do you see Loki anywhere in here?" he whispered.

"No, but that doesn't mean he's not here in some other form."

"Too bad you can't pull out the you-know-whats."

"Right," Jake wearily agreed. As much as he wanted to look around the busy cafeteria to see if Loki was present in some new disguise, he did not want to be seen using the Lie Detector Goggles— which he had stolen last night without too much difficulty.

On an impulse, he had also swiped Sir Francis Galton's dog whistle. If it worked on ordinary dogs and cats, he hoped that maybe they could use it to summon the wolf and leopard back to campus.

After sneaking away from the Exhibit Hall last night with his contraband, he had run to the edge of the woods and blown the whistle several times. It made no sound that he could hear, but maybe it got the twins' attention, wherever they were, out in the forest.

When Dani returned with Isabelle's breakfast, the boys accompanied her back to their rooms. When they arrived, Isabelle shook her head sadly: still no sign of Henry and Helena. Then Archie collected his notes and papers for his discussion panel, and the boys left.

Jake walked Archie across the campus into one of the big university buildings full of lecture halls and classrooms. When they found the classroom where the panel was to take place, there were already dozens of scientists sitting in the rows of desks, waiting for the talk to begin.

With one thumb hooked in his vest pocket, Archie nodded cordially to his fellow panelist, the large, redheaded Scottish engineer.

Dr. Wu, the Chinese physicist, their third panel member, had not yet arrived.

Archie turned to Jake. "Don't worry, you don't have to stay for this."

He nodded in relief. It was not like he would understand a word of it, anyway. Besides, he had to check on Miss Langesund this morning and see if the local police had made any progress on finding her father. "Good luck," he told Archie, giving him a firm clap on the shoulder. "I'll come and meet you in the hallway after."

Archie nodded, then Jake went on his way, privately in awe of his younger cousin. The boy genius took it all in stride, but if it were him having to give a speech to a bunch of world-class geniuses—well, that was worse than facing Loki.

As he walked across the campus toward the Viking ship museum, he hoped Miss Langesund did not ask too many questions about how Henry and Helena were feeling this morning, if they had recovered yet from last night's sudden illness.

Jake was wondering the same thing himself. For all he knew, Henry might have turned back into a person out there in the woods somewhere, and might be making his way back to the campus right now. Helena, too. *Blimey, I hope no one sees them before they can get to their clothes.*

Awkward! But apparently this sort of mishap was a regular occurrence in the lives of shapeshifters.

Jake did not envy them as a species.

Reaching the Viking ship museum, he pushed open the heavy wooden door once again and went in trying to look innocent—the place was bustling with policemen. And there sat Miss Langesund at her desk, red-eyed and disheveled, still in her golden dinner gown, but with her spectacles on once more.

Poor woman, she looked like she hadn't slept a wink. A horrible thought stopped Jake in his tracks halfway to her. *I hope they haven't found him dead.* His heart started pounding at the prospect of receiving much more terrible news than he had expected.

Only one way to find out. He swallowed hard and forced himself to keep walking forward.

"Oh, hullo, Jacob," the lady-archeologist said, perking up slightly when she saw him. "Is Henry better today? Will he be coming? And Helena, too, of course?"

"No, I'm afraid they're even sicker today. Maybe by tomorrow. Any news?"

"Some." She closed her eyes with a dire look then blew her nose in her handkerchief. "I'm afraid the situation is even worse than we thought yesterday."

"Have they found him?" he asked in a low tone, bending down on one knee beside her desk in concern.

She shook her head. "Not a trace. But at least he's not the only one."

"What?" he exclaimed.

"In a way, I'm relieved about it. If they've been taken for their knowledge, they must still be alive."

"What do you mean?"

"The police have been interviewing people all morning." Miss Langesund glanced around with a sniffle, as though not sure how much she was allowed to tell him. Then she lowered her voice and confided, "My father's not the only scientist who's gone missing. There are five more scientists unaccounted for this morning."

"You mean—?" he whispered in shock.

She nodded. "Somebody's kidnapping geniuses."

* * *

Hands in pockets, Archie frowned as the last of his panel attendees left the classroom, as disappointed as he was. Dash it all, they'd had to postpone their presentation because Dr. Wu had never showed up.

Physicists! There was no living with them. Had the dolt forgotten to ask his assistant to wake him up on time?

In any case, everyone had left early. The panel had been rescheduled for four o'clock this afternoon.

Archie told himself that was for the best. That way, he'd get another shot to dazzle his colleagues with his latest thoughts on aerodynamics and still be back to the rooms by tea-time. Hopefully, by then, Henry and Helena would have returned, and everything would be fine.

As much as it sometimes bothered him to have to go through life chaperoned all the time, never roaming free like Jake, he was gnawed with continuous worry about the twins. They were like family members after all these years.

Their running off like this was unheard-of. He was trying his best to act brave in front of Jake, but in truth, he was really scared.

Cold fear was giving him a stomachache. Realizing he needed a distraction to take his mind off it all, naturally, his first thought was of the Pigeon. Working on his inventions always made him feel better, calmer, more like his usual self.

So, he headed for the warehouse where she was safely stored, tossed his trusty bag of tools into the cockpit, then rolled her back down the graveled path and out to the water's edge, the same spot where he had steered her ashore yesterday after his test flight.

It was a beautiful view, and it cheered him.

The day was bright, the surrounding forest swaying back and forth in the cool, lively wind.

The breeze drove the white-capped waves across the fjord and ran riot through Archie's dark hair, rumpling it every which way. The peaceful setting made him smile.

He loosened his lucky bowtie, then took his safety goggles out of his leather tool-bag and strapped them onto his head. He took a deep breath and let it out, feeling better already.

Time to get to work.

Absorbed in his tinkering, Archie was unaware of two large eyes watching him from the cover of the woods.

Crazy hair, bowtie, spectacles...

Check, check, check.

But that's a puny one. Must be the runt of the litter, thought Snorri. Still, the little one fit all the bird's specifications, and the opportunity was too good to pass up. Besides, he might be on the small side, Snorri thought, but maybe his brain was extra-large.

He looked around, saw the coast was clear, and made his move with impressive stealth for a person of his size.

Boom-boom, boom-boom...

Archie let out a startled yelp as the ground began to shake and rattle and pound violently enough to break his concentration on his work. Egads.

Earthquake!

But as he steadied himself, he frowned, for the slams came at regular intervals; it had a rhythm, and earthquakes didn't do that.

The sound was getting louder. Coming up behind him?

"What the—?"

Squinting with confusion, Archie turned around...looked up...and stared for a second in disbelief.

Then he screamed.

CHAPTER SIXTEEN
Put Me Down!

The moment Miss Langesund told him someone was abducting scientists, Jake bolted out of the Viking ship museum.

His first thought was of Archie.

Cursing himself for being paranoid, he nevertheless raced back across campus to the building where he had left his cousin half an hour ago.

Though Archie's panel discussion would still be in progress, he decided he would just sit in the back of the classroom and wait until it was over. Whoever was kidnapping scientists wasn't going to get anywhere near his cousin, he vowed. But striding down the hallway, Jake saw the door to Archie's classroom hanging open ahead, and when he leaned in, nobody was there.

A wave of panic started to wash through him until he read the announcement scrawled across the chalkboard.

Archie's handwriting: *Aerodynamics panel rescheduled for 4:00 this afternoon.*

Relief made him clutch his chest and lean against the doorframe. Well! Something must have come up, Jake concluded.

He immediately wondered if one of the scientists on Archie's panel had failed to appear. Might he be one of the missing? This made the danger seem closer than ever.

He stepped out into the hallway, wondering if Archie would have returned to their rooms for safety's sake, or would he instead have gone to work on his experiments, simply out of habit?

Hesitating for a second, Jake realized Archie might've decided to sit in on one of the other lectures currently in progress. He walked down a few of the empty hallways, glancing into the other classrooms to see if his cousin had taken a seat inside any of them.

He passed an old janitor pushing a mop around, but paid him no mind—until the old man spoke after Jake had passed him.

"Looking for someone?"

Jake paused, arrested by that deep, gravelly voice with its rich Norwegian accent.

He turned around, surprised that a humble janitor could speak to him in English. "Yes, actually, I am," he answered with wary gratitude.

As he walked back toward the old man, he couldn't help but sense the force of character in his steely gray eyes—or rather, eye. He only had one; the other was covered with an eye-patch.

The janitor wore faded coveralls and old, battered boots. He was a large-framed man with a shock of pewter hair and a sun-browned face like a weathered hunk of wood, as if he had spent most of his life outdoors.

Must be an old soldier, Jake thought, judging by the missing eye and the way the janitor grasped his mop.

He held it like a weapon.

As Jake approached, the old man's single eye searched him with a probing, piercing stare, as though he were taking his measure, testing his mettle.

Jake shook off a vague uneasiness about the old man. "I'm trying to find my cousin, Archie Bradford. He's about my age and would've been the only other boy in the building besides me. He has dark hair and freckles—"

"That way," the janitor interrupted gruffly, nodding toward the exit at the end of the hallway. "I'd check down by the fjord if I were you. Better hurry," he added in a low rumble.

"Why?" Jake asked in alarm.

The janitor ignored the question and simply went back to pushing his mop.

But when Jake rushed off at his warning, the mysterious old janitor watched him with a close eye and a faint, speculative smile.

Jake burst out of the classroom building a moment later and raced down the winding path to the water's edge.

He could have kicked himself for not realizing sooner that, of course, there was only one place Archie would have gone when his panel was postponed: to tinker with the Pigeon!

Creature of habit that he was, Archie would have likely gone back to the same spot where he'd landed his flying machine yesterday in boat mode.

Jake ran down the path toward the water's edge, still a bit puzzled about how that strange old janitor could have known where Archie went. But even before the fjord came into view, he suddenly stopped in his tracks.

Boom-boom, boom-boom...

There it was again!

That same dull, deep, pounding noise that he had heard yesterday in the forest and had mistaken for an earthquake.

He still had no idea what it was, but if he could catch up to Archie before it faded, he had no doubt the boy genius would know.

In motion once more, this time he ran even faster, barreling down the graveled path.

Jake rounded the bend and came to the bottom of the hill where the campus path joined the waterside Promenade. But upon arriving, he skidded to a halt and gasped in shock.

The pounding sound continued in the distance as Jake stared in horror at the shore.

There, at the water's edge, lay the Pigeon—broken, floating on her side, bobbing like a dead thing in the waves.

"Archie!" he yelled. His heart in his throat, he sprinted toward it. "Archie?!"

As he splashed out into the shallows and grasped the wing, he didn't know if Archie had had an accident or what.

Taking hold of the Pigeon, he heaved it over, terrified he was going to find his cousin pinned underneath it, drowned.

But, no. As the Pigeon splashed upright onto its canoe bottom, water running off its sides, there was still no sign of Archie, and somehow, this was almost worse.

Jake waded out deeper into the cold, swirling waves in a panic, diving in to search the water for his cousin. "Archie?! Where are you? Archie!" he screamed.

"Help!" A thin cry reached him from the distance.

Jake whirled around just in time to see the trees shaking in one part of the forest. He brushed the icy water out of his eyes and squinted in confusion.

It was as though some large creature had just shoved the

branches aside and was hurrying through the woods. The pounding noise seemed to be coming from that direction, too.

Instantly, Jake slogged out of the water. Dripping wet, he bolted across the pebbled beach, racing toward the woods.

Boom-boom, boom-boom! The noise grew louder as he followed Archie's cry for help. It sounded like gigantic footsteps, but that didn't make any sense.

Jake didn't know *what* to think or what was going on, but that did not stop him from following. He dashed into the green, shadowy woods—not his favorite place to start with—and paused, glancing in each direction, unsure which way to go.

The booming was so loud now it seemed to be coming from everywhere at once, reverberating through the very ground.

How could it be anything *but* an earthquake? he thought. But when he saw the treetops shaking up ahead, he immediately followed.

"Hold on, Arch, I'm coming!" he shouted, though he doubted his cousin could hear him over the clamor.

Jake ran, tearing through the underbrush, until a wall of bramble-bushes blocked his path. Protecting himself as best he could, he charged through the mass of thorn-tipped branches.

Woody needles pulled his hair and scratched him through his clothes, but he was undeterred, until finally, he burst out into a clearing on the other side.

Unfortunately, he was too late.

As he stood panting in the grove, it was impossible to say which way Archie had been taken. The pounding sound was fading in the distance.

"Archie!" Jake screamed, his hands cupped around his mouth. He took another breath to yell his cousin's name in the other direction, but that was when he saw it, and the shout died on his tongue.

There in the grove before him, smashed into the soft brown soil, was the most enormous footprint he had ever seen.

He walked over to it in a daze. "Impossible," he whispered.

The footprint was about five feet long, heel to toe, and made an indentation six inches deep in the forest turf.

Stepping down into the footprint, Jake turned around slowly in a circle, staring at it in disbelief. Miss Langesund's tales of the old Norse legends echoed through his mind. *"Oh, we love our Norse giants and our trolls here in Norway..."*

Giants? Then came a darker thought. *Loki!*

Impossible as it seemed, in a flash, Jake was fairly sure that a giant had taken his cousin. And that meant that Loki was further ahead in his plans than anyone had guessed.

Heart pounding, Jake flipped his wet hair out of his eyes, trying to think of what to do next. But he was at a loss. Even if he could somehow catch up to Archie's kidnapper, what could he possibly do to stop a giant?

He was just a twelve-year-old kid.

But then, all of a sudden, a familiar war-cry like an eagle's screech from above signaled that help was on the way.

"Caw!"

"Red!" Jake drew in his breath, looking skyward. "I'm down here, boy!" He waved his arms so that his fierce, feathered pet would quickly find him. But with his sharp eyes, the Gryphon had already spotted his young master.

The large, dangerous creature depicted on Jake's family's coat-of-arms came diving out of the blue sky, angled through the trees, and swooped down into the clearing.

Red's powerful, scarlet wings fluttered until his lion-paws touched down on a sun-dappled boulder.

"Am I glad to see you! Perfect timing." Jake ran toward the not-so-mythical beast and instantly noticed Red looked agitated.

No wonder.

The Gryphon's sole mission in life seemed to be to protect him, and danger was obviously near.

But with the arrival of his fearless pet, Jake's dismay turned almost magically into determination. "Someone's taken Archie. I think it was a giant!"

"Caw!" A war-like glow filled the Gryphon's golden eyes, as if he already knew.

"Did you see who took him, boy? Do you know where they went?"

The Gryphon tossed his head and whipped his tufted tail from side-to-side with anger.

"I'll take that for a yes," Jake mumbled, climbing onto Red's back, where he took hold of the beast's sturdy collar. "Right! Let's go save our genius."

"Caw!" Red agreed. Then the Gryphon jumped off the boulder and took a few running steps across the clearing, his broad, lion-paws silent over the forest floor.

Leaping into the air, Red unfolded his wings with a whoosh, then they were spiraling upward into the treetops. Jake held on tightly to the collar, his knees hooked in front of the Gryphon's wing joints.

Within seconds, they were above the forest, gliding toward the summit of the hills.

Dense woods that could have hidden any number of unexpected creatures covered the dramatic contours of the Norwegian landscape; in the distance, the fjord was a deep, dazzling blue.

The Gryphon soared higher so they could see farther in every direction. The breeze grew chillier as they ascended. Red's head moved back and forth as he scanned the landscape with his eagle eyes.

Jake searched as well. A flock of birds passed under them, flying in the opposite direction. Down on the water, countless boats meandered this way and that. Tiny people promenaded along the path or teetered along on high-wheeler bicycles like the one Loki had crashed in the Exhibit Hall.

On the hunt for Archie, Jake and Red skimmed across the brushy, greenish-blue tops of another stand of towering Norway spruces. They passed the plunging cascade of the mountain waterfall so close that they felt the cold spray of the plume fleck their faces.

Then Red took him higher, over the cliff at the top of the waterfall. Beyond that were more rugged hills.

Jake was beginning to despair of ever finding them in this thick wilderness, when suddenly he noticed that the trees ahead were shaking. He pointed. "What's that?"

Red made a small, uncertain noise and headed in that direction. Mighty conifers and massive oaks and elms were being pushed aside as something passed below.

Something big.

Their trunks swayed as if they were no more than blades of tall grass that shook when a badger hurried through the underbrush.

Obviously, this was no badger.

Jake murmured to Red not to get too close. He wanted to see for himself exactly who or what they were dealing with before they allowed themselves to be spotted.

His pulse pounded with half-terrified excitement. He had seen a lot of strange things ever since his twelfth birthday, when his supernatural abilities had started to appear. Still, a real, live giant was certainly something new. As they got closer, he heard once more the echo of that by-now familiar rhythm.

Boom-boom, boom-boom, boom-boom.

A giant's footsteps? That mystery was on the verge of being solved...

Flying low enough that they could easily duck behind the treetops if they had to hide, Jake and the Gryphon followed. Branches creaked and treetops crackled, and all of a sudden, a towering shape emerged from the forest.

Archie's kidnapper walked through a clearing, and Jake found himself looking down at the top of a bald head.

He blinked rapidly, making sure his eyes did not deceive him. He leaned low against the Gryphon's neck. "Do you see that, too, or am I losing my marbles?"

Red's answer was a low, lion growl.

The bald head sat atop enormous shoulders and a huge broad back, clad in a plain brown coat. That was a giant, all right—a big, lumpy lurch of a fellow, about five times the size of an ordinary man.

Jake shook his head to clear it, and wished with all his might that someone would've told him before he came here that Norway had giants, for he'd have just as soon stayed home.

Instead, he urged the Gryphon onward, and as they got a little closer, he could hear Archie yelling at the giant at top of his lungs. "Put me down, you big oaf! You've got no business kidnapping me! It's bad enough you broke my Pigeon after years of work and testing—"

"Stop squirming!" the giant rumbled at him in annoyance. "You complain a lot for such a little thing."

"I'm not little, you're ridiculously large! You're not going to get away with this, you know. They're going to come looking for me. Not to brag, but I happen to be a very important boy!"

This was the angriest Jake had ever heard his cheerful cousin sound, not that he could blame him. *Keep yelling, Archie.* It helped reassure him that he was more or less all right for now.

Though it was a great shock to see his cousin being carried off by a giant in broad daylight, at least now he knew for sure that Archie was alive. When the giant disappeared into the trees again, Jake and Red swooped after him.

Now that they had seen the towering kidnapper for themselves and had at least an inkling of what they were dealing with, it was easy to track the giant by the din of his pounding footsteps and the shaking of the trees as he passed through the forest.

At length, the giant climbed out of the woods and lumbered across a bare section of rocky ground. He seemed to be heading for the high, arched entrance of a cave set into the mountaintop.

When Jake noted the remains of a huge campfire outside the cave's entrance, terrible fairytales about giants instantly came to mind.

Fee, fi, fo, fum, indeed. *He'd better not even think about roasting Archie.*

Jake watched intensely as the giant disappeared into the tall, yawning entrance of his lair; he murmured to Red to land somewhere in the woods where they'd be able to see the cave without being seen, themselves.

As the Gryphon descended, Jake felt much better knowing his cousin was nearby, still relatively safe. Now it was just a matter of sneaking into that cave and getting Archie out of there.

Maybe the other missing scientists were in there, too.

But why? he wondered. What did the giant want with them?

Considering the Viking prophecy about the Battle of Ragnarok, he wondered if the huge fellow was actually doing Loki's bidding.

In the Exhibit Hall, Jake had seen for himself how interested Loki was in all the new gadgets—especially weapons, or as he'd called them, toys. Maybe Loki wanted to force the kidnapped geniuses to invent dangerous things for him to help him wage his long-awaited war against the gods.

As Archie's huge kidnapper disappeared into the cave, Jake wondered how many *other* giants might be in there. What if there were more, the beginnings of Loki's army of giants?

That would make rescuing Archie considerably more difficult.

When Red's paws touched down on the forest floor, Jake slipped off his back, then they both crouched down behind a fallen log with a good view of the cave.

"Becaw," Red said unhappily.

"I know, boy. Don't worry, I'll get him out of there. You did a good job finding him."

Red pushed his feathered head affectionately against Jake's

shoulder, rather like a giant cat. The beast did not know his own strength, however, and only succeeded in knocking Jake over.

"Red! Not now! Stop fooling around. Yes, yes, you're a good Gryphon, but we've got to save Archie. I don't know... I don't see or hear any more giants around here, do you?"

Red scanned the area, then sniffed the air through the nostril holes high on his leathery, golden beak. He snuffled and shook his head in the negative.

"As I thought," Jake murmured, crouching behind the mossy log. He studied the situation before him, then nodded slowly. "I think I've got a plan."

Red cocked his head to the side and looked at Jake for his instructions.

"You fly around outside the cave and make some noise," Jake whispered. "See if you can get the giant to chase you. Stay high enough that he can't get hold of you, but try to lead him off a-ways. While you've got him distracted, I'll slip into the cave and rescue Archie. I'm betting the other missing scientists are in there, too. I'll free them all—if they're still alive," he added grimly.

"Caw," Red confirmed with a nod, getting a serious look in his golden eyes again.

But as the Gryphon pushed up onto all fours, ready to lift off for his part of their rescue mission, the giant suddenly reappeared, stepping out of his cave.

"Get down!" Jake whispered. He and Red instantly ducked down behind the log again and listened.

They could hear the giant singing to himself. "More brains, more brains, I'm gonna git me two more brains!"

Jake furrowed his brow and slowly peered up over the top of the log. "He's leaving! Well, that's odd. It looks like he's heading back down the mountain. Wonder why."

There wasn't time to ponder it. He turned to Red. "I'm going in." There was no time to waste. He cast his fears aside with a mental heave of effort. "You stay here and keep watch," he instructed. "Caw to warn me if you see the giant coming back. Otherwise, save your strength. Once I get Archie out of there, you'll have to carry two of us back down the mountain instead of just me."

"Becaw," Red answered fretfully.

"Don't worry, I'll be careful," Jake mumbled. "You do the same.

Those missing scientists are probably here, so it's important that you stay out of sight. If they were to see you, well, I don't trust that bunch not to try to capture you—or worse."

Red's eagle eyes gleamed like he'd like to see them try it.

Jake nodded to him, their plan confirmed. Then he stole off through the woods, while the *boom-boom* of the giant's footsteps faded down the mountain.

CHAPTER SEVENTEEN
The Giant's Lair

Jake stayed low, crouching as he hurried toward the tall, tapered entrance of the cave.

It was times like this, when stealth was needed, that he was glad of his years of experience as a pickpocket.

Sneaking up to the edge of the cave, he stole a quick glance over his shoulder to make sure the giant was still nowhere in sight. Then he braced himself and ventured in.

Drip, drip...

Water fell from the stalactites that hung overhead like dragon's teeth. He wiped a droplet off his forehead with a nervous scowl. His eyes adjusted slowly to the darkness.

The cave was extraordinarily quiet. It opened before him into a narrow tunnel, pitch-black.

He did *not* want to go in there.

A shiver of awful memories from his brief stint as a coalmine boy at age nine sent a wave of queasy coldness through him.

The orphanage had sent him off to several different apprentice masters, factories, and such, before he had finally run away for good to fend for himself on the streets of London. But between the coffin-black darkness underground, the constant threat of exploding gases, and most of all, the cruelty of the older boys with their initiation pranks, the coalmine had been his worst experience by far. Worse than fighting Fionnula Coralbroom.

In short, Jake did not like caves or underground places. But if that blasted giant had stashed Archie in there, then so be it. He had to rescue his cousin and the other scientists as well, if they were in there.

Somehow he forced himself to take another step, and another. He did not dare call out to Archie for fear his cousin would yell back; the giant might hear them and return.

Jake crept deeper into the rough, black tunnel, choosing every step carefully, ducking and biting back a shriek when a bat swooped overhead. "Charming," he muttered, his heart pounding, his hands clammy.

But he thought first of Derek Stone, and then of Red waiting faithfully outside—the two bravest beings he knew—and he kept going.

At last, some thirty yards into the cave, he saw a faint, flickering glow ahead. Light! *Thank goodness.*

As he went closer, he found that the tunnel opened up into a large limestone cavern, tall and round.

A perfect hideout for a giant.

The cavern was dimly lit by a few torches, and Jake's eyes widened at the sight of the gigantic woolen cloak spread out like a makeshift bedroll over by the wall.

"Boy! Psst! Over here!" someone whispered as he stepped fully into the cavern.

He whirled around and didn't see anyone at first.

But then came Archie's voice.

"Jake! Up here!"

He tilted his head back and gasped. The giant had put them in man-sized birdcages!

"Hurrah, coz! I knew you'd come! Didn't I tell you fellows he'd find us?" Archie asked the other scientists in his usual cheerful tones.

The flickering torchlight revealed the geniuses locked up in four wooden cages crudely fashioned from branches and twine.

They were suspended from the ceiling at rooftop height, some twenty or thirty feet above the cavern floor. No doubt that would ensure the captives broke their necks if they tried to escape. The giant had left them with no way down.

As Jake's stunned gaze traveled over the scene, assessing the situation, he realized that the giant had jammed a slender tree-trunk between two rocky outcroppings high above the cavern floor.

This he had used as a beam off which to hang the cages like so many Christmas ornaments, stringing them up with forest vines for rope. There were two captured scientists in each of the three lower cages, while Archie hung from the highest one, imprisoned by himself for now.

Right. Between the welcome light from the torches and the presence of people who needed his help, Jake forgot all about his hatred of underground places. Instead, he shook off his astonishment and got right to work. "Hang on, everyone!" he called, careful not to speak too loudly. "I'm going to get you out of here! Is anyone injured? Archie, are you all right?"

"Not happy," he answered in a flat tone. "That big idiot broke my Pigeon *and* I got a gash on my leg when he dropped me. But it's not too bad. I'm all right. At least I also found Dr. Wu!"

"Ni hao," the Chinese physicist greeted him with a polite bow from another cage. "Thank you to come for save us!"

"Don't mention it," Jake answered.

"A giant, Jake! An actual Norse giant!" Archie exclaimed.

"I noticed."

All the geniuses, some still wearing their white lab coats, started talking excitedly at once. Jake heard them referring to their kidnapper as a "spectacular find," but he hushed them, bewildered at how they could be so smart and yet fail to miss the point entirely. For example, that they could die a gruesome death, become this giant's supper.

"Quiet, you lot! Is anyone else hurt?" Broken bones would make getting them down even more difficult.

The scientists shook their heads. "No, no."

Whew. "Are any of you Professor Langesund, by chance?"

"Here!" A bearded man with spectacles peered through the bars of the middle cage, to Jake's relief.

"Glad to see you, sir. Your daughter's very worried." Then he glanced back to his cousin. "Archie, how bad's your leg? Can you walk?"

"Affirmative!" he answered, pulling off his jacket. "I was able to grab my tool-bag when he caught me, so I have my pocketknife. I'm making a bandage now." He unfolded the blade out of the knife's handle and then sliced off the sleeve of his coat to wrap around his hurt leg.

"Good." Jake nodded. "When you're done with that, cut the ropes holding your cage door shut. Then pass the knife on to the next; you gentlemen will have to do the same. First order of business, everyone needs to work on getting their cage doors open while I figure out a way to get you down."

Hopefully without having to use my telekinesis, Jake added silently as he hurried around the dark, shadowy cave searching for something to use as a ladder. Great-Great Aunt Ramona's warning not to let the scientists find out about his abilities was still ringing in his ears.

Heaven forbid they decide that he was a "find," like the giant—to say nothing of what they might do to his gryphon.

Just then, Jake spotted another half-finished cage over by the cavern wall. Beside it lay a coiled length of the vine that the giant had been using as rope. He ran to get it, gathering it up while the geniuses used various methods of getting their cage doors open.

Archie sawed away at the vines with his knife; Professor Langesund struck a lucifer match that he must have carried at all times to light his tobacco pipe. He used the match to burn away a small spot of the rope, severing it with the little flame. Then he pushed his door open.

Dr. Wu and the man locked up with him worked on plucking the knot free as Archie pushed his door open.

Folding his pocketknife again to tuck the blade safely into the handle, Archie began shifting his weight to make his cage swing back and forth, until he was safely able to hand off the pocketknife to the men in the next cage.

They, in turn, began hacking away the knots.

Jake ran to the cavern floor beneath Archie's cage and hurled one end of the vine up to him. His first throw didn't go high enough. The vine-rope fell back to earth; he gathered it up and threw it again.

This time Archie caught it.

"Don't tie it," Jake instructed. "Just loop it over one of the bars of the cage. That way, we can pull it back down and use it again after you climb down."

Archie did as Jake had said, feeding one end of the vine-rope through the bars, creating a double strand. Jake twisted the two strands into a single, coiled cord then stood at the bottom, holding it steady, as Archie carefully climbed down.

When his feet touched down on the cavern floor, Jake immediately noticed his cousin was limping a bit. "You'd better head out of here now," he advised. "No need to wait for us. You'll take longer than we will, walking on that hurt leg."

Archie clapped him on the shoulder. "Thanks, Jake. I knew you'd come."

"Of course! By the way, our ride is waiting outside in the forest."

"The Red kind?"

"Exactly."

Archie nodded and started the trek back up the tunnel alone while Jake untwisted the vine-rope and pulled it back down. When he had retrieved it, he ran to toss the end of it up to the two men in the next cage.

One by one, the captured scientists shimmied down the vine in the same manner.

Professor Langesund gave Jake a hearty pat on the back when he had reached the ground. "Well done, lad."

"Thanks. Now get out of here, you lot!" he ordered. A few of the freed geniuses were wandering around the cave marveling over the giant's personal effects. "Go on! He could be back at any moment!"

"Oh! Yes, yes, of course." They snapped out of their scholarly daze and hurried up the long, black tunnel toward safety.

Jake waited tensely for the last captive genius to climb down the vine-rope from his cage. But just as the fellow's feet touched the ground, Jake heard a desperate eagle-cry echoing frantically from the far end of the tunnel.

"Caw! Caw! Caw!"

"What was that?" the scientist cried.

A warning from Red. Jake paled, pushing the scientist toward the tunnel. "Hurry! The giant's coming back! Everybody, *run!*" he hollered up the tunnel at the top of his lungs.

But it was too late.

Boom-boom-boom-boom!

As they raced up the rocky tunnel, stumbling on the jagged, slippery rocks, the giant's pounding footfalls shook the earth.

In the next heartbeat, the light at the end of the tunnel was blocked by a gigantic, man-shaped silhouette.

Too late.

They were trapped.

The giant had returned.

And he was blocking the only exit.

CHAPTER EIGHTEEN
Blockhead

Everyone in the tunnel screamed.

The giant roared back, his hot, stinky breath whooshing down the tunnel to riffle their hair and fleck them all with spit.

As Jake grimaced in disgust, the giant ducked his head and charged.

Archie had the good sense to fling himself behind a stalagmite jutting up from the cave floor. For once, his smaller size worked in his favor, helping him to hide. Still, Jake was desperate to reach his cousin so he could protect him. With Archie slowed down by a hurt leg, Jake knew his cousin would need his help if they were going to make a run for it.

As he ventured forward, he could see the white-coated scientists ahead of him in the tunnel running to and fro around the giant's legs. They were trying to dart past the towering beast to freedom, but no one had succeeded in getting very far yet.

Their shouts of terror echoed off the stone walls of the cave as the great hulk swiped at them with his mighty arms.

Jake looked on, aghast, as the giant scooped up Professor Langesund; another scientist, thankfully, came to his aid, poking and beating the creature in the back of the leg with a large stick he had found lying near the cave's mouth.

Distracted by the whacks on his calf, the giant must have loosened his grip; Professor Langesund managed to pry back the massive fingers wrapped around his waist. The professor sprang away free, then the scientists started throwing rocks at the giant from all directions, confusing him.

The chaos gave Jake cover as he crept up the dark tunnel to join

Archie, who was still leaning with his back against the stalagmite. Having lent his pocketknife to the other men to get their cages open, he had resorted to wielding a screwdriver from his tool-bag for protection. He offered Jake a wrench for the same purpose, but Jake shook his head, staring toward the cave's mouth. "Look! The fight is moving outside!"

Some of the scientists had reached the clearing outside the cave's entrance. The giant had turned to chase them. Others were still running every which way.

"C'mon, we can slip out while they've got him distracted," Jake said. "All we have to do is get to Red. Can you stand up? Here, lean on me."

"Thanks." Archie stood with a slight wince and slung his arm around Jake's neck, leaning on his shoulder.

The two cousins hurried up the tunnel as fast as Archie was able to hobble, with Jake supporting him. As the boys neared the mouth of the cave, they had a clearer view of what was happening just beyond the arched stone entrance.

"Back in your cages, you brains!" the giant boomed. "Get back here, I say!"

The geniuses were running around trying to escape the giant, but none attempted to leave the scene.

"Why won't they go?" Jake asked in worry. "Are they waiting for us?"

"I doubt it," Archie said. "Before you arrived, some of them were discussing how to capture the creature."

"Are you joking?"

"No! They said a real, live giant would be one of the greatest scientific discoveries of the age."

"Perfect," Jake muttered. Why was nothing ever easy?

At least Red had obeyed him, staying out of sight—except for his lion tail, twitching angrily from behind a nearby boulder. Thankfully, the Gryphon continued to heed his warning.

Meanwhile, the earth shook as the giant ran to and fro, chasing the scattered scientists. The grown men were only up to his knees, but they moved much faster than the lumbering giant.

"Just a bit farther," Jake urged Archie. "Almost there…"

The giant, frustrated with his inability to catch all the little scientists running around him, twisted around, waving his arms wildly trying to grab them.

That was when he turned and spotted the boys, lagging behind, but nearing the mouth of the tunnel.

Jake and Archie froze as his stare homed in on them.

The giant seemed to realize that while the men might be too fast to catch, the boys, slowed by Archie's injury, should be easy prey. He came stomping toward them down the tunnel.

The boys were only as tall as his shins. They backed away as the giant approached, but there was nowhere to hide.

"Where do you think you're going?" the giant thundered as he ducked his head, coming back into the tunnel.

"Ah, Jake?" Archie sent him a panicked glance. "Any ideas?"

"You're the genius!" he retorted as they backed against the rocky wall in dread.

"I've still got my tool-bag, but–*whooooa!*"

"*Nooooo!*" Jake yelled in unison with him as the giant angrily grabbed the boys, catching one in each hand.

"Jake!"

"Archie!"

"Bad brains! Back in your cages!" their towering captor scolded.

Feeling the iron grip around him, Jake realized that all the giant had to do to kill them both was *squeeze*.

Archie was yelling his head off in a most ungentlemanly fashion, but Jake was already plotting his next move.

"He's taken the boys!" one of the scientists yelled to the others who had managed to get out.

Jake was racking his brains for a solution.

His options seemed limited as the giant marched back down the tunnel to the cavern. There, he shoved both boys into the cage where Archie had previously been trapped by himself.

"You are very, very bad!" the giant scolded them. "Stay in your cage now!"

"I don't wanna stay in the cage!" Jake yelled back in the giant's face. This was now possible because the cage was suspended at about the creature's eye-level.

"No talking back!" The giant squinted at him. "Wait! Who is this one? I didn't catch you! You're no genius! Crazy hair, but no bowtie, no spectacles! What are you doing here?"

"I came to rescue my cousin and the others from you, you

oversized bully!" Jake held onto the bars for dear life as the cage swung back and forth from the boys being tossed into it. "You have no right to go around kidnapping people!" Even as he forced himself to look the cretin in the eyes, he could not believe he was face to face with a real Norse giant.

Archie's kidnapper was one terrifying individual. He had a heavy build, with a thick enormous neck, and a big round belly. He had weathered skin, as though he spent most of his time outdoors, and he wore simple brown clothes rather like a medieval peasant's garb—a belted tunic and baggy, woolen breeches in drab, earthy colors. His huge feet were encased in a pair of the most enormous boots Jake had ever seen. Most of all, he smelled dreadful.

Jake wasn't sure if it was his breath or a lack of bathing, but the giant smelled like onions, feet, and moldy sheep. His eyes were dark and deep-set in his head, and he had a bit of an under-bite, with a pair of dull-tipped up-fangs jutting from his lower jaw.

Suddenly, Archie elbowed Jake discreetly. The other geniuses had come sneaking back into the cave, apparently to stage a rescue of the boys.

Heroic fellows, they crept back into the cavern, some carrying sticks, others stones. They tiptoed into the cavern, split up, and began surrounding the giant.

They obviously had a plan, and though Jake was not quite sure what they intended, he kept the giant talking to distract him. If his attention stayed fixed on the boys, the big brute wouldn't notice the men closing in.

"Where did you come from?" Jake demanded. "Why have you been abducting all these people?"

"None of your beeswax!" the giant retorted in his deep, rumbling voice.

Jake frowned. It was hardly the terrifying sort of answer he had expected. "Well, you must have a reason!" he persisted.

"Maybe I do and maybe I don't," the giant answered warily, then all of a sudden, from the corner of his eye, he glimpsed his returning captives. "Hey!"

The scientists attacked.

The giant whirled around to defend himself, accidentally bumping Jake and Archie's cage with his shoulder. The nudge sent it swinging wildly again.

The boys shouted and held on for dear life, struggling to close the door so they would not fall out. Meanwhile, the fight that erupted below them was far more chaotic than the previous one outside.

All at once, the yelling scientists hurled their stones and charged the giant with their sticks, beating him about the knees.

The giant roared back at them and swatted away three men at once. A single backhand sent them flying.

Seeing this, Archie glanced fearfully at Jake.

The boys had only just brought their cage under control, and both were slightly queasy from all the wild swinging. Archie yelped when he saw Dr. Wu nearly get stepped on. "Jake, do something! You've got to help them!"

Jake hesitated.

"What are you waiting for?" Archie cried.

"It's just that Aunt Ramona warned me not to—"

"Jake, he's going to kill someone!"

"All right, all right, never mind." Jake closed his eyes for a moment, settling his mind, trying to calm his seething thoughts and fears.

He gathered up all his mental focus, then lifted his right hand, concentrating intensely.

Blocking out all notice of the fight below, he opened his eyes and stared at the jagged rock formations hanging from the dark, dank roof of the cavern. He took a deep breath, then flung a bolt of crackling magical energy from his fingertips toward the stalactites.

A few cracked off the rocky dome and plunged down onto the giant's head.

"Ow!"

One stuck in his scalp like a thorn for a second before it tumbled to the ground. Jake made more stalactites crash down onto the giant, though these were smaller, not as sharp.

The massive brute made sounds of pain and ducked his head, putting up his arms to try to ward off still more falling rocks.

"Take cover!" Archie shouted to his colleagues while Jake kept at it. He did feel slightly guilty making rocks fall on the giant, however. That had to hurt, and he didn't like using his telekinesis to hurt someone.

Besides, the giant surely could've killed the scientists by now if that had been his goal. Instead, he had only caged them. Still, something had to be done to get the great blockhead under control.

As Jake's outstretched hand and even his arm vibrated with his concentrated effort, more chunks of stone cracked off the ceiling and fell on the giant's thick head and shoulders, pelting him with rock.

"Take cover!" the scientists were still yelling to each other, running toward the edges of the cavern.

"We need to get out of here! The cave is coming down!" Professor Langesund shouted.

"No, no! The boy is causing it somehow!" another exclaimed. "Look up there!"

"How on earth is he doing that?" a third asked in amazement.

Jake could dimly hear the scientists' exchange, but he refused to pay attention. He would deal with them later; for now, he kept all his focus fixed on his task of knocking the giant out.

His pulse pounded as he concentrated on a particularly bulbous chunk of stone hanging down among the rock formations.

Break off. Fall, he mentally commanded it, and it began to vibrate a little and creak. Jake could already feel a massive headache coming on from using his powers to this level of intensity, but he did not relent.

Suddenly, from above, there came a mighty crack, followed by a grinding noise of stone on stone as it came down.

The giant looked up and saw the boulder plummeting toward him. "Uh-oh," he rumbled, then it landed on his head. They could almost see the stars in his eyes as he lost his balance, swaying before he crumpled.

BOOM!

When he hit the ground, out cold, all the scientists flew up into the air, literally bounced off their feet by the earth-shaking impact of his fall.

"Yes!" Archie cheered as both boys watched from their suspended cage. "Jake, you did it!"

Jake sagged against the bars, drained. "Aye," he mumbled, his head already throbbing. *Let's just hope I don't soon regret it.*

CHAPTER NINETEEN
The Oubliette Spell

The moment the giant crashed to the floor, several scientists jumped on him at once to hold him down.

This was quite unnecessary, as the creature was unconscious, but no one was taking any chances.

"Tie him up before he comes to!" Jake yelled. "Use those vines! Hurry!"

While the others hurried to restrain the giant with as many of the rope-vines as they could find, Professor Langesund held a sharp stick to the snoring giant's throat.

"Don't move, monster!" he yelled.

"Er, would somebody throw one of those vines up here before you use them all on him?" Archie requested, holding up one finger politely. "We'd like to get down."

"Of course, Master Archie!"

"Thanks, Dr. Wu!" he called back a moment later, when the Chinese physicist hurled one end of a vine up to them.

Archie fed it quickly through the branch-bars. Jake nodded at him to go first, and the boy genius climbed back down the vine-rope as before.

Meanwhile, some of the scientists were tying the giant's ankles together using the creature's own huge cloak coiled into a rope. Others were bravely securing his huge wrists with the lengths of vine that the giant had been using to fashion cages.

When Archie reached the bottom, he waved up to Jake, who then followed. It was a little tricky getting onto the double strand of coiled rope from the relative safety of the cage, but he gripped it with his hands, ankles, and knees, and began inching down.

As soon as his feet touched the cavern floor, Jake let go of the rope, dusted off his hands, turned around, and suddenly saw he was in trouble.

Having tied up the giant, the scientists were now free to turn their attention to him. They started crowding around him with fascinated looks.

Uh-oh.

"Young man, how did you do that?"

"Huh? Do what?" he asked innocently.

Archie sent him a nervous glance.

"*How* did you dislodge the stalactites from the roof of the cave?"

Jake smiled, though his heart started pounding. "I'm sorry, I don't know what you're talking about."

"Come, come, lad! We saw you!" a crazy-haired fellow in a white lab coat insisted.

"Me? I didn't do anything," he replied with great conviction, and indeed, anyone who knew him could confirm he was very good at being obtuse.

"You were holding out your hand, like so, and somehow causing those stones to dislodge from the ceiling!"

"Which was jolly good of you, by the way," a bespectacled fellow in a bowtie added, clapping him on the back. But instead of letting go, the smiling scientist gripped his shoulder, as though sensing Jake's growing need to flee.

He did not like being grasped like that. It took him straight back to his days of dodging the bobbies. And occasionally getting arrested. Another fellow whipped out a magnifying glass and leaned nearer, studying his face.

"Excuse me!" Jake retorted, pulling back, but the man ignored his protest and went right on scrutinizing him.

"Forgive our curiosity, dear lad," another said, "but we'd really like to know just how you did it! What's the trick?"

"The trick?" Growing more nervous by the second, Jake realized a good lie was in order.

Thankfully, he remembered a topic he had overheard Archie and his egghead friends discussing in the parlor aboard the luxury-liner.

"Very well. I wasn't supposed to talk about it. But Archie's been fiddling around with a, er, a little ray gun. Whatcha-ma-call-it? An aether gun. That's right. That's how I did it," Jake said sincerely.

The gentlemen-scientists turned to the boy genius in surprise. "Egads, Archimedes!"

"You've made progress with your aether gun design and never mentioned it?"

"Let us see the device, by all means!"

Archie blanched, then sent Jake a private, panicked look.

Jake glared at him. *Say something!*

"Oh, um, I," Archie said, and Jake quickly saw the flaw in his plan. Easygoing Archie was the world's worst liar. He froze like a rabbit in sight of a wolf. "Uh, er, rrrright..."

I am going to throttle him, thought Jake. "Gentlemen, don't you think we have bigger things to worry about right now?" he reminded them, hooking a thumb over his shoulder at the sleeping giant.

"Oh, never mind him, he's out cold," one of the scientists assured him. "Come, let us help you find this aether gun. Did you drop it? I hope it isn't broken. We all want to see it."

"Well, you can't," Jake countered, suddenly inspired. "The truth is, it's...it's implanted in my body!"

"How now?"

"Don't be preposterous."

"It's very small!" he insisted.

"*Where* in your body?" another man demanded.

"My hand!" Jake said innocently, holding up his right hand.

But Professor Langesund took off his spectacles and shined them, eyeing him with a look of disapproval. "Gentlemen, I daresay these boys are having a bit of fun at our expense."

"Never!" Archie cried, scandalized at the thought of being caught lying to adults. "Jake?"

The Italian mathematician waved off the others' mumblings. "Even if ze device ees implanted in your hand, a-can you to use it to transport ze giant a-back to ze University?"

"Why would I want to do that?" Jake shot back. "So you can all do experiments on him?"

"Precisely," said Professor Langesund, putting his spectacles back on.

Jake blinked at his frank confession, but another scientist folded his arms across his chest, scowling at the boys.

"Aether gun, my foot!" he said to the others. "I don't know what these boys are trying to pull, but enough of these tall tales. Explain yourselves! Master Archie, what is going on?"

Jake glanced desperately at Archie.

"This lad has just performed an extraordinary feat, one that we have a duty to understand!" the scientist continued. "He manipulated solid matter without even touching it! Don't you see what this means? Not only are we standing in the presence of a real, living giant, we could be looking at the first true case of telekinesis on record!"

"*Not* on record!" Jake suddenly yelled, pulling away from them. "All of you, leave me alone!"

"How did you do it?" the scientist demanded.

"I don't know, I was born this way!" Jake burst out.

Archie lowered his head with a groan. "Jake."

"Then you admit it was you?"

"Can you feel the static electricity in the air?" one of them asked his colleagues excitedly. "It must be some form of electromagnetic energy that he is somehow able to harness and control. We should tell Tesla about this..."

Indeed, the electricity in the air left over from Jake's use of his powers had left their hair looking crazier than ever.

The geniuses pressed around him once more. As they loomed on all sides, Jake realized he was more afraid of them than he was of the giant. That large, dull-witted oaf seemed relatively harmless compared to this pack of wild-eyed geniuses, who did not seem to care that he was a person, not a lab rat.

"When we get back, you must allow us to run some tests—"

"No!"

"Everyone, please!" Archie cried, suddenly pushing his way among them. "My cousin rescued us today. Isn't that enough? He may have secrets, but sometimes it's better not to know!"

"How unscientific of you, Master Archie!"

"Don't you want to further the Progress of Man? Make the world a better place?"

Another nodded earnestly. "It's for the good of humanity!"

"*Pah, they always say that,*" Loki himself had opined, as Jake recalled. "*It's just an excuse.*"

"Get back, you barmy lot!" he yelled. "Bunch of ingrates, you! I just freed you from captivity, and this is my thanks? Now you'd make *me* a prisoner?"

"Not a prisoner," the magnifying-glass man said in annoyance.

"Don't be so dramatic."

They weren't listening.

"Right," Jake growled. "Archie, plug your ears."

It was time to resort to the Oubliette spell, which Great-Great Aunt Ramona had taught him to use in case of emergencies.

At his warning, Archie realized what he meant to do. "No, Jake, you mustn't! We daren't risk it, not with them!"

Jake glanced at him in exasperation.

"Please! These are some of the greatest intellects on earth. If you Oubliette them, some of their discoveries could be lost forever!"

"Too bad. They've left me no choice. They're not turning me into a guinea pig. *Now*, Archie!" he warned.

Archie quit arguing. "Very well. Twelve hours ought to do it." With a worried frown, he lifted his hands to cover his ears.

Jake stepped back, beginning to whisper Great-Great Aunt Ramona's forgetfulness spell under his breath. You had to repeat the words three times.

"From memory, unwind the spool,
And walk away a happy fool.
The past twelve hours you now forget,
Cast into the oubliette!
OBLIVIOS!*"

"What's this nonsense?" one of the scientists muttered, but Jake merely repeated the chant. They started looking a little confused during the second repetition. On the third, the puzzled scientists suddenly went from scoffing to stupefied.

They stood around motionless, staring into space.

He nodded at Archie to let him know it was safe to uncover his ears. Jake turned back to the scientists, for the next step was to give them instructions of some sort. Fill in the blank space that he had just created in their overactive minds.

He cast about, first of all, to give them a simple explanation for the circumstances in which they found themselves: "You went out on a pleasant nature walk," he told them. "But then you became lost in the woods. It's all right, though—you're quite safe. You've even found your friends along the way. Oh, you've been having a grand time," he informed them, "chatting about your work. You're all quite happy and safe. It was just a little absentminded mishap. You lost track of the time."

Archie looked askance at Jake, who continued. "Now you will walk back to campus and carry on with the Invention Convention as usual," he commanded. "You will tell the police and anyone else who asks that nothing out of the ordinary happened. Everything's normal, everything's fine. Have you got that?"

"Everything's normal...fine," they repeated, a mumbling choir of mesmerized geniuses.

"Excellent! You've been enjoying yourselves, but now it's time to get back to the campus. This way, now! Everybody, follow me! Watch your step! Up the tunnel we go and back to campus."

"Back to campus..." they echoed.

Keeping his fingers crossed that this would really work, Jake led the enchanted scientists back toward the cave's mouth. Carefully guiding them over the uneven, rocky floor of the cave, he wasn't sure exactly how much time he had to get them pointed in the right direction. If he recalled correctly, Great-Great Aunt Ramona had said it took about five minutes for the Oubliette spell to fully 'set,' but it was hard to be sure. This was the first time he'd ever actually had to use it.

Archie followed, still limping a little. He was bringing up the rear to make sure none of the mesmerized scientists wandered off alone.

Jake glanced nervously over his shoulder as they passed the snoring giant. Though the massive creature was securely hog-tied, he did not intend to leave him unsupervised for long. He had many questions to ask the oversized lout, and he fully intended to get some answers.

When they stepped outside, all of them squinting in the sunlight, Jake stood aside, waving the scientists past. "Move along, gentlemen! Come now, careful on the rocks. Mind your footing. There's the path you want." He pointed toward the woods. "That will take you back to campus. Just head down the mountain. You'll find your way."

From the corner of his eye, Jake noticed a familiar lion tail twitching impatiently from behind a nearby boulder. Thankfully, the rest of the Gryphon remained hidden.

Still, they could not get rid of the geniuses fast enough for him. If the scientists caught a glimpse of Red, then Jake feared he might have to give them a double dose of the Oubliette spell—and who could say what *other* information he might accidentally wipe from their minds?

He had no desire to harm them. He just wanted to be left alone. Standing near the giant's extinguished campfire, he continued to shoo them away. "Off you go! That's right, enjoy your nature walk. Head that way, and with any luck, you'll be back at the banquet hall in time for supper. Go on."

"Nature walk," they echoed as the whole group shuffled off toward the trailhead.

"Back for supper..."

"Beautiful woods, trees..."

"Lovely day..."

"Pleasant..."

At last, they disappeared into the pine forest, and Jake exchanged a dire glance with Archie.

Both boys let out huge sighs of relief.

Of course, there was still a giant to deal with in the cave, but at least Jake no longer had to worry about being dissected.

With the scientists gone, Red bounded out from behind the boulder and landed in front of him with a low growl of disapproval. He pecked the ground in front of Jake's feet in reproach. "I know, boy. Don't worry, I'm fine," he assured his irritated Gryphon.

"What's wrong with him?" Archie asked.

"He's just being overprotective, as usual. He's got his beak in a twist that I ordered him to stay out of the fight when he knew I was in danger. But you still obeyed me like a good boy!" Jake patted the Gryphon's scarlet head—which only insulted the beast's dignity more.

Red ruffled his feathers indignantly and turned away with a snuffle.

"So what do we do now?" Archie asked.

"Interrogate the prisoner. We've got to assume he's working with Loki. Remember, Miss Langesund told us Loki's goal was to build an army of giants. Looks like he's already started. I'm going to try to get some details out of him about whatever Loki's planning."

Archie frowned. "I'm not sure he'll know much. He didn't seem very bright."

"Leave it to me," Jake replied with sturdy confidence, pivoting toward the cave. But then he paused. "Say, do you have your collapsible mess-kit with you?"

"Always." Archie dug into his trusty tool-bag and pulled out a round piece of metal gear. "What do you need? Fork, spoon, knife?

Cup, saucer?"

"As big a pot as you can make it."

"No problem." Archie flipped away the metal clamp, twisted the tin lid until it came free, unfolded one piece then another, and after a few more neat, efficient twists and pops, handed Jake a serviceable pot for boiling water or cooking beans over a campfire.

"Thanks." Jake strode over and filled the pot with cold water from the stream, then carried it back into the cave. "This should wake him up."

Archie followed. "Good idea!"

"Why do they call it the Oubliette spell, anyway?" Jake asked his cousin as he carried the water carefully into the black, uneven tunnel.

"Oubliette comes from the French word *'oublier'* meaning 'to forget,'" Archie said absently as they groped their way through the darkness. "In medieval times, the oubliette was the worst, deepest, nastiest, underground cell in a castle dungeon. Just a hole, really, where they used to throw prisoners into solitary confinement, then 'forget' about them. Leave 'em to rot, I guess."

"Well, that's cheerful," Jake muttered.

"Rather!" Archie agreed. "The important thing is, the Oubliette spell works. I've seen Aunt Ramona use it loads of times to protect the secrecy of the Order."

"Good. Let's just hope our absentminded professors don't get lost on their way back to campus," Jake said dryly.

Archie chuckled. "With all the police and search parties out looking for them, somebody's sure to find them sooner or later."

Red caught up to the boys, landing between them with a pounce. His golden eyes gleamed in the darkness as he prowled along with them through the dark tunnel.

Before long, they reached the wide, torch-lit cavern, where their oversized captive still snoozed.

Jake carried the pot of water closer. "Stand back, Arch. Let's see what this big oaf has to say for himself, shall we?"

Archie nodded, keeping his distance while Red looked on.

"Brace yourselves," Jake warned. Then he threw the pot of cold water in the sleeping giant's face.

CHAPTER TWENTY
Big Questions

The giant spluttered as he awoke, blinking away the water that ran down his broad cheeks in dusty rivulets.

His deep-set eyes flew open, then his bushy brows knitted together in wrath. A great, rumbling roar started low in his chest, growing louder as it made its way up his throat to burst out of his mouth: *"Arrrr!"*

Jake jumped back as the giant began thrashing.

"Let me go!"

"Not very fun being held captive, is it?" Archie yelled, but Jake bent down and seized the big sharpened stick that Professor Langesund had been using as a spear.

He threatened the giant's eyeball with it. "Explain yourself, monster, or I'll blind ye!"

"Monster?" the giant asked abruptly, pausing in his rage. "Well, I hardly think I deserved *that.*"

The relatively mild response threw Jake off his stride, but he refused to ease up on the brute. "Are you alone?" he demanded in his meanest voice.

The giant stared at him as if he were an idiot. "You're here."

"That's not what I meant!" Jake said impatiently. "Are you here with friends? Are there other giants in the area?"

"Oh—no." The giant quit struggling against the many loops of rope holding him down and sighed. "Just me."

"Where did you come from?" he demanded.

The giant looked at him like he was daft. "Uh, Jugenheim. Where else?"

"Yoo-gan-hime?" Jake echoed.

"That's the old Norse name for Giant Land," Archie discreetly informed him. "It starts with J, but you don't pronounce it—like *Johann* Sebastian Bach."

"How long have you been here?" Jake continued, turning back to the giant.

"Got 'ere yesterday," he said.

Jake eyed his massive prisoner in suspicion. "I don't suppose you've got a name?"

"Of course I've got a name! Who hasn't got a name?"

"All right, then. I'm Jake. That's Archie. What do we call you?"

"Snorri. Snorri the Shepherd. Because I keep sheep back home."

"I figured that," Jake muttered.

"They're probably starving right now, poor little things," Snorri added.

Jake furrowed his brow. This giant was looking less and less frightening by the moment. "What are you doing in Norway?"

"What? Norway?" he said in alarm. "I thought I was in Midgarth!"

"Norway is a *part* of Midgarth," Archie explained in a longsuffering tone.

"Midgarth?" Jake asked.

"The old Viking name for earth. The world of humans."

Jake snorted and turned back to the giant. "Very well, so what are you doing here in *Midgarth?*" he repeated impatiently.

"I don't know! I never meant to come here!" Snorri the Shepherd burst out defensively. "It was an accident."

"An accident?" Jake echoed. "Right."

"It's true!" The giant heaved a sigh, then, sounding a little disgusted with himself, he explained: "I accidentally made a hole in the crust of the earth up in Jugenheim, then I fell through it. Go on, laugh! Laugh all you like! Everyone does. I'm used to it," he said glumly. "That sort of thing *always* happens to me. I'm a loser."

Jake and Archie exchanged a puzzled glance. Snorri's answers were nothing like the fearsome words the boys had been expecting. Was this an act? Some sort of sad sack routine to make them lower their guard?

Jake wasn't sure what to believe, but he pressed on, determined to get his interrogation back on track. "Why did you kidnap all those scientists?"

The giant looked a bit nervous at this question.

"Explain yourself!" Archie chimed in angrily. "You had no right to do that, you know! You broke my invention that I've been working on all year! You're lucky I didn't have my real aether gun with me or you'd be sorry!"

"But I am sorry," the giant said in dismay. He lowered his head. "I didn't mean any harm, really." He hesitated. "The bird made me do it."

"What?"

"The little talking crow," Snorri said.

They stared at him.

"Talking crow?" Jake asked.

"Aye, he flew right down onto the log beside my campfire just when I was feeling awfully homesick. We got to talking, and he was very kind when I told him all that had happened to me—about the hole and all, I mean, and Princess Kaia."

"Who's that?" Jake asked warily.

The giant stared at him like he was a complete ignoramus. Then he scoffed. "Only the most beautiful lady in all the Nine Worlds!"

Jake and Archie exchanged a dubious glance.

"The crow said he could help me win Princess Kaia's hand in marriage. He said he could brew up a potion to make me the smartest giant that ever was! That's why I snatched those men, and this little runt, too."

"Excuse me!" Archie retorted.

"How's a crow going to stir anything, anyway? He hasn't got any hands," Jake pointed out.

"With his beak—probably," Snorri shot back, though it was clear he, too, had been troubled by this question.

"Please, go on," Jake urged, his suspicions already taking shape.

"The bird said if I drank the potion then I'd become smart and charming and turn into a fascinating fellow. Then Kaia would fall in love with me and we could be happy-ever-after." The big, fierce lug let out a lovelorn sigh, much to Jake's bemusement. "But it was all just a dream, I suppose."

"You can't be serious!" Archie burst out. "You caused all this havoc over a *girl*?"

Jake couldn't hide his amusement, either. "A girl giant," he drawled with a wry glance at his cousin.

"I can't help it. She's *byooootiful* and I love her!" Snorri cried.

"The crow said we needed to catch some geniuses so we could crush their brains into powder for the potion—"

Archie stopped laughing abruptly. "What? You were going to turn my *brain* into a powder? My brain?"

"Well, I couldn't go back to Jugenheim being the same old loser as I was when I left. Everyone back home thinks I'm just a joke," Snorri confessed. "That bird said he could make me clever—clever enough to win the princess and even become the next king of Giant Land! Can you imagine? Me? King Snorri!" Then he sighed again. "Well, I guess all that's over now. A stupid dream. No hope for a new life. Same old, boring, dummy me."

Jake had to admit he felt a bit sorry for him. But he furrowed his brow as he mulled the giant's tale. "This crow promised to make you king of Jugenheim?"

"That's right," Snorri said.

"What did he want in exchange? There had to be a catch."

"Well, now that you mention it…" Snorri glanced around the cave uneasily, as though he expected the bird to return at any moment. "He said he might need to ask me for a favor in the future sometime, when I was king. He said I'd owe him one."

"I see." Jake narrowed his eyes, certain of it now. *Loki.* "Tell us more about this bird. What did he look like, exactly?"

Snorri half-shrugged against the vine-ropes still binding him. "Just a little black crow with shiny wings like polished coal, and he had…yes, a little dappling of odd white feathers on his cheek."

Jake shook his head. *Just as I suspected.* "Snorri, you were deceived," he said grimly. "That crow was Loki in disguise."

"What?" Snorri started to bolt upward, but the ropes held him down. He looked so appalled that Jake was immediately convinced that the giant had had no idea who he had been dealing with. "Loki? But y-you must be wrong! That would be terrible!"

"I know. If he would've made you king, you soon would've found yourself having to answer to him."

"Like a puppet ruler," Archie chimed in, nodding sagely.

"But I don't want to be a puppet! I'm just an ordinary shepherd!" The giant stared at the boys in dread. "I hope you're wrong. I'd get in so much trouble if this was true! I'm not even supposed to be here, not even by accident! Giants aren't allowed in Midgarth! That's why the gods made a seal between the different worlds." Then Snorri gasped as a new thought struck him. "Oh, please don't tell me Thor found out I broke the earth! If Odin knows, too, then I'm doomed!"

"Never mind them. Loki's the one you have to worry about, that trickster," Jake growled. "He's been all over this place causing trouble."

"You should see what he did to our tutor and our governess!" Archie agreed with a nod.

Snorri's eyes widened.

As Jake considered the situation, folding his arms over his chest and tapping his fingers on his opposite biceps, he brooded on it. Something had to be done.

It seemed that he and Archie had successfully disrupted Loki's plan to trick Snorri into becoming his puppet ruler over the giants.

But if this seal between the worlds was broken, then the trickster god might still manage to slip into Jugenheim and find some *other* giant to work with.

Even without Snorri, Loki might still find a way to amass his army of giants, just like in the ancient Viking prophecy.

Jake knew he couldn't let that happen.

Considering that his sole purpose in life was to follow in his murdered parents' footsteps and become one day a Lightrider like them—sworn to helping magical creatures in distress—he had to do something.

Archie, meanwhile, was shaking his head. "You know, Snorri, if something sounds too good to be true, it usually is. You mustn't be so gullible."

"He's right," Jake agreed. "We're all going to have to be on our toes, because I'm fairly sure that Loki is the one behind all this..."

Then Snorri listened, motionless with dread, while Jake told him about the Viking prophecy that Miss Langesund had revealed, how Loki would try to marshal up an army of giants to war against Odin and Thor.

"You mean that devil nearly tricked me into causing *the end of the world?*" Snorri whispered hoarsely when Jake had concluded with the Battle of Ragnarok.

"Afraid so."

Snorri was so upset that he lifted his head just enough to bang it on the rocky ground a few times. "Oh, how could I be so stupid? Dumb, dumb, oaf!"

"Get a hold of yourself!" Archie chided.

"You don't understand, Master Archie!" the giant cried. "Nobody back home knows anything about this terrible prophecy! The gods must've kept it from us to try to prevent it from coming true. Now everyone's in danger—even my sweet Kaia and her father, King Olaf!"

Jake weighed their options, staring at their captive. "Snorri, if we set you free, you must promise to go back to Jugenheim at once and warn your people what Loki is scheming. The giant folk will have to be on their guard to avoid his trickery; Loki is crafty. He can make himself look like anyone."

"That's just it," Snorri said miserably. "They'll never listen to me! All they do is laugh at me. That's why I wanted so much to be smart. Because Prince Gorm makes fun of me and everyone thinks I'm a joke!"

Jake frowned as pity for the big lug pulled upon his heartstrings. Hesitating only for a second, he made his decision. "Well, then. If that's how it is, there's only one solution. We'll go with you."

"What?" Archie cried.

"We'll escort him home to Giant Land and vouch for him in front of the giant king, that the threat from Loki is real."

"Oh, would you, really? Thank you, thank you, Master Jake! That will certainly help, but...on second thought, I'm afraid it won't fix our Loki problem for long," Snorri said with a ponderous frown.

"Why is that?"

"Because Princess Kaia is supposed to marry Prince Gorm. It's not official yet, but it's what her father wants. King Olaf says Prince Gorm is everything a giant should be. Loud, bossy, rough. And a great warrior," Snorri added with a glum look. "Just a big bully if you ask me—but he's Mr. Popular."

"Sounds charming," Archie mumbled. Being a smallish lad himself, he had plenty of experience with bullies, at least until Jake had come along.

"If you could hear the way Gorm talks to the other warriors, always wanting more—more gold, more lands, more power—well, I think he's just the sort of giant who'd be glad to make a deal with Loki. Knowing Gorm," Snorri added, "he'd probably *enjoy* fighting the Battle of Ragnarok."

"Then we'd better make sure he doesn't inherit the throne." Jake paused as his plan became clear. "You must have it, Snorri. You must marry Princess Kaia and be the next king of the giants, just as you had hoped. After all that's happened, I trust you've learned your lesson that Loki can't be trusted. If you were to become the next king of Jugenheim, I feel certain that you would know better than anyone to stay on the lookout for Loki's tricks from now on. If you were king, you could actually block the prophecy from coming true by refusing to cooperate with him, ever."

"Oh, yes! I would do anything to keep Jugenheim and Kaia safe—but there's just one problem!"

"What's that?"

"Whoever marries the princess becomes the next king, and Kaia would never want to marry dumb old me, not the way I am. I'm nowhere near good enough for her."

"Don't say that! Come now, don't worry," Jake encouraged him. "We'll help you win this princess for your bride!"

"Hold on," Archie broke in, staring at Jake like he feared he'd lost his mind.

Jake glanced over at him in surprise. "What's the matter?"

"I am not going to Giant Land! This is daft."

"What? Archie! How could you stand to miss a chance like this? Giant Land!" Jake exclaimed.

But Archie shook his head, looking more stubborn by the minute. "My panel's been rescheduled for four o'clock this afternoon, and my big speech is in three days." He cast an indignant glance at Snorri. "I was set to unveil the Pigeon to the world before this brute came and wrecked her. Now you want me to help him? Let him help himself! I'm busy! I'm going to need every free minute until my speech to fix the mess he made of my poor girl. *If* she can be fixed," he added in reproach. "Besides, how can you even think of gadding off to Giant Land when Henry and Helena are still out there somewhere, stuck as animals?"

"Why do you think Loki did that to them?" Jake countered. "To keep them from interfering in his plans! Archie, if we don't go and warn the giants what Loki's up to, it could mean the end of the world!"

"That's a lot of hokum," Archie said, dismissing it with a wave of his hand. "There's no such thing. The world has been around for millions of years and will continue on for many millions more. Nothing you or I or even Loki does is ever going to change that."

Jake was taken aback by his narrow-minded remark. "You're starting to sound like those arrogant scientists."

"And you sound like a harebrain!" Archie declared, losing all patience. "You can't just jump on your Gryphon's back and go flying off to Jugenheim."

"You have a Gryphon?" Snorri asked, but both boys ignored him.

Red had been sitting out of sight from where the giant was tied down.

Jake was upset that Archie was even considering not coming along. "How boring can you be? Mr. Responsible! Is it really so important?"

"You would say that," Archie retorted.

"Come on! You go to these conventions every year! So what if you miss this one? The Pigeon's already broken, anyway. Just postpone your speech till next year!"

"I've been preparing for this for months!" Archie said angrily.

"You know what I think?" Jake retorted. "You just like the attention."

"This is very important to me!"

"More important than seeing Giant Land?" Jake asked eagerly, already excited at the prospect of what he knew would be an unparalleled adventure. "Oh, come on! You know you want to."

"What if this brute is lying to us, eh?" Archie countered. "Did you consider that? Use your head for once! Why would you possibly trust him? He was going to eat my brain, Jake. My brain."

"Well, he said he was sorry."

Snorri nodded sincerely and repeated his apology. "Very sorry, Master Archie. I was tricked. Er, will somebody please untie me?"

"Don't push your luck," Archie growled at the giant, then gave Jake a dirty look. "Unlike *some* people, I don't back out on my responsibilities. I gave my word that I'd make my presentation, and that's that."

"Pfft," Jake retorted. "Don't come, then. If you're too scared, I'll bring the girls instead!"

"Oh, no, you won't!" Archie stepped closer. "It's too dangerous for young ladies!"

Jake snorted, more rattled by his cousin's refusal to join him on the adventure than he let on.

But Snorri, meanwhile, was full of questions. "Master Jake, do you really think I have a chance with Princess Kaia? I mean, I know she likes me better than Gorm. We're friends, like. But she's a princess! So pretty. And smart! She can even *read*, and that's something not many giants can do, I can tell you. The truth is, she could have anyone. Without the potion, I don't see why she'd ever pick me."

"Great, a giant who's insecure," Archie muttered.

Jake looked at Snorri, unsure what to say. He was probably right. No female in her right mind would fall in love with him. "Well, maybe we could just...clean you up a little," he suggested, though he didn't have the foggiest idea where to start.

"I see. So you're going to transform this giant toad into a prince?" Archie folded his arms across his chest and looked at him wryly. "What, maybe you can have him spout a little poetry for the princess? Bring her giant flowers?"

"I don't know!" Then inspiration struck. "I've got it! We'll bring Isabelle! She'll know what to do. Isabelle's fourteen—practically a grown-up lady," he told Snorri. "Main thing is, she's a girl, so she'll know all about that mushy, romantic junk that girls like. I'm sure she'll be able to give us some tips on how you can charm the princess—assuming giant girls are more or less like, er, regular ones?"

"I should think so," Snorri said eagerly.

"You are not dragging my sister into a kingdom full of these oversized barbarians! It's too dangerous! She's delicate!"

"Oh, I have a feeling Izzy's tougher than she looks," Jake remarked.

"Can this Isabelle of yours really help me?" Snorri asked, sounding breathless at the possibility that he might have a chance.

"Of course," Jake declared.

Still hogtied, the dusty, homely giant was suddenly beaming with newfound hope for winning his ladylove.

"This is insane, Jake. You're as mad as Loki. How's this poor soul going to win a princess? He's a mess. He smells like a volcano that shoots off cow manure instead of lava."

"He just needs a bit of spit and polish, and a little advice from the girls."

"Have you ever seen my sister when she gets around boys her own age? She turns beet-red and practically dives under the furniture to hide! She doesn't know anything about courtship. She's still two years away from her debut in Society. But even if you had an expert governess like Miss Helena to guide you, I mean, look at him. He's hopeless!"

"Aw, he's not so bad." Jake leaned closer and added confidentially, "Between you and me, I doubt this giant princess is much of a prize herself."

"Hey!" Snorri yelled, overhearing.

"Well, you're not bringing Isabelle and Dani into danger. I forbid it." Archie folded his arms across his chest. "It is my duty as a gentleman to protect our girls—especially Dani, since she's only ten!"

"You've never been properly punched in the nose by Dani O'Dell, have you? Not yet. But you will one day, I'm sure."

"You just want to see Giant World!" Archie thundered at him.

"And you just want to stay back on the campus where all those people treat you like a brainy little god! You're just the darling of the scientific world, aren't you? Well, fine! Enjoy your fame! Stay back and bask in all the adulation."

"My, that's a big word for you!"

Jake scowled at him, insulted past patience. "Do as you like. *I'm* going on an adventure. Red! Give us a ride back to civilization." He whistled to his pet.

"What's that thing?" Snorri exclaimed as Red pounced into view and flexed his feathered wings.

"That's my Gryphon," Jake replied. "His name is Red, and if you cause any trouble once we're on the road to Jugenheim, I'll sic him on you and let him eat your liver."

"Why would I want to cause trouble?" Snorri cried.

"'Cause you're a giant," Archie growled. "And giants are bad. That's probably why the gods sealed off your world, you know."

Snorri thought this over for a moment. "We're not all bad, and besides, maybe Odin sealed off *your* world, not ours. Did you ever think of that?"

"Enough!" Jake interrupted. "Never mind my cousin, Snorri. Some of us believe in giving people a chance, even if they're a little different from us. Some of us have been there and know what it's like when others treat you like a joke." He gave his brainy cousin a dirty look. "Let's get out of here. I may not be a genius, but I'm smart enough to know we need to be gone before Loki comes back to check on Snorri's progress in rounding up the geniuses. When Loki sees them back on campus, he's going to know something's up. We don't have much time till then, so let's get going."

"Gladly," Archie shot back, throwing his tool-bag angrily over his shoulder.

As the two boys scowled at each other and headed for the Gryphon, Jake was quite upset. It was the first time he and Archie had ever argued.

It didn't feel very good. Worse, the prospect of his adventure to Giant Land did not sound near as fun with only the girls along. They were the best girls he knew, but still.

It wasn't the same.

"Wait! You can't leave me here like this!" Snorri yelled after them as the boys walked toward the Gryphon, who waited for them to climb onto his back. "Aren't you going to untie me? Please?"

Jake paused and glanced back uncertainly over his shoulder.

"Don't leave me here defenseless!" Snorri pleaded. "What if Loki comes back and tries to punish me for letting the brains escape? At least untie my hands so I can defend myself!"

With a frown, Jake walked back cautiously toward the giant. "If I set you free, do I have your word I can trust you? You promise not to go causing trouble? Better yet, don't even leave this cave."

"Snorri gives his word," the giant answered with a solemn nod.

"Very well. But remember, if you break your promise, no one's going to help you win Princess Kaia's love. And that'll hurt even worse than Archie's aether gun."

Snorri shuddered. "I want to marry her more than anything! You'll understand when you see her."

Ugh, thought Jake. Falling in love made people look so silly. He was very sure he would never fall prey to such nonsense.

"Let me borrow your knife," he muttered to Archie, who handed it to him in spite of their quarrel.

"You're lucky I remembered to ask for it back from Dr. Wu before they left," his cousin remarked with a huff.

Thrusting off his doubts about the wisdom of freeing the giant, Jake sawed away the knotted ropes holding him captive. "I'm trusting you," he warned. "Don't make me regret it."

Snorri thanked him profusely as he sat up rubbing his wrists. He stretched his neck this way and that, then rubbed his bald pate where the stalactites had whacked him. "Ow," he mumbled.

"Sorry about that, but you did bring it on yourself."

"It's all right," Snorri said with a sigh.

"Now then." Jake tilted his head back to look the giant sternly in the eyes, pointing at him. "Wait here and stay out of sight," he ordered. "Use the time to gather up your things and get ready for our journey. So help me, Snorri," he added, trying to look as threatening as possible despite the fact that even sitting down, the giant still towered over him. "You'd better be here waiting in this cave when I come back, or I'll let Red hunt you down and have at you."

Red growled on cue and slashed the air with his front claws to intimidate the giant into complying.

Snorri eyed the Gryphon meekly. "I'll be right here the whole time, I swear."

"Good. I should be back in less than an hour with the girls."

"No, you're not," Archie said.

"With Isabelle?" Snorri asked.

"That's right, and another one called Dani. And I say we leave the decision up to them, whatever the girls choose to do," he added in a crisp tone, handing his cousin back his folded knife.

"Fine!" Archie retorted, tossing the knife back into his tool-bag.

But he did not take his eyes off the giant for a second now that Jake had untied him. Instead, Archie backed steadily toward the Gryphon.

Jake could understand why his cousin didn't trust the giant after being kidnapped by him. But to Jake, now that their interrogation was complete, the only frightening thing about Snorri was his breath.

The smell was awful as the giant let out another lovelorn sigh.

Coughing slightly, both boys climbed onto the Gryphon's back. Red, too, retched a bit at the odor, gagging through his beak.

"Do you really think this Isabelle of yours might be willing to help me?" the giant asked hopefully.

"No doubt about it. Isabelle's just a big softie," Jake assured him. "She could never say no to a charity case like you."

CHAPTER TWENTY-ONE
A Great Quest

"**A**bsolutely not," said Isabelle. She shook her head stubbornly. "I'm sorry, Jake. As much as I'd like to help, I need to stay here to wait for Henry and Helena. They're more important."

"More important than stopping the end of the world?" Jake exclaimed.

"I'm the only one here who can talk to animals," she countered, "and since that's the form they're stuck in, what if they need me? They're like family, Jake. After all they've done for us, I can't run off with you and abandon them."

Jake scowled, but he could understand her feelings. "All right," he grumbled. Snorri was going to be disappointed, but there was still Dani, who was technically a girl. He turned to her. "What about you, carrot?"

Dani shook her head in regret. "I hate to miss it, I really do, but if you're not going to be here, and Loki's on the loose, then I'd better stay here to protect Isabelle and Archie."

"I beg your pardon!" the boy genius said indignantly.

Dani shrugged. "No offense."

Archie scowled, pushing his spectacles up higher onto his nose. But Dani was right. The little rookery redhead was much tougher than the two sheltered aristocrat children. Somebody had better stay behind who wouldn't freeze up in a fight.

"Looks like it's just me and Red, then," Jake mumbled. As the realization sank in, the prospect of going to Giant Land suddenly sounded considerably more scary. It was somehow much easier to act brave when the others were there, if only for his pride's sake.

Without them, he'd have to face his fears alone.

"Right," he said, slightly dry-mouthed, but he gathered his resolve. "We'll go it alone, then—me and Red. You keep the Lie Detector Goggles so you can watch for Loki. Don't trust anyone unless you check them out through the goggles first. You never know what form Loki might take to try to trick you. Also, the Galton whistle," Jake added, reaching into his pocket. "You can keep using it to try to summon Henry and Helena. If they're still in animal form, they should be able to hear it." Then he frowned. "Where the devil did I...?"

Feeling in one pocket, then the next, he checked his coat; his vest; again, his trouser pockets. He glanced at Archie. "Did I give the dog whistle to you?"

"No."

They checked all the rooms, but it was nowhere.

"Blimey, I can't believe I lost it. Would you just check your tool-bag?" Jake persisted, turning to Archie again.

"You didn't give it to me! But all right, if it makes you happy," the young inventor muttered, obviously still annoyed with him over their quarrel.

But the Galton whistle wasn't in Archie's pocket or his tool-bag or anywhere. Jake shook his head in frustration. He could have kicked himself. "Blast it, I must've dropped it somewhere along the way. Maybe flying over the forest or somewhere in the cave. It's so dark in there, I'll never find it."

"Don't worry, we can manage without it," Isabelle said. "I'm sure the Prince of the Polymaths can make more. Besides, Henry and Helena know where to find us if they want us."

"She's right," Dani said. "We'll be fine here. You just concentrate on what you have to do and get back here in one piece, all right?"

He nodded.

"Here, Jake." Isabelle gave him a satchel of supplies and two canteens of water.

"Thanks. I don't expect this to take more than a few days," he added as he pulled the leather knapsack up onto one shoulder. "You lot keep your wits about you." He glanced at Dani. "Somebody should go and check on Miss Langesund later. She's going to be very happy to see her father again. He and the other scientists should be wandering back onto campus any minute now, if they haven't already arrived."

They nodded.

"Good luck, Jake." Dani startled him with a quick hug. "Be careful in Giant Land. Don't get stepped on."

He gave her a lopsided grin. "I won't. Good luck to you all, too. I'll see you soon." He turned to go.

"Oh—fine then, you win!" Archie burst out.

"What?" Jake glanced at him in surprise.

"Hang on, let me get my things. I'm coming with you!"

Jake turned around, brightening. "You are?"

"I can't let you go and do this by yourself. You're going to need at least one intelligent person on hand. But I'll only come on two conditions!"

"Yes?"

"First, you have to promise me we'll be back here in three days so I can give my big speech, as scheduled. Second, I'll need time along the way to fix the Pigeon. We're bringing her with us."

"We are?"

"Your giant can carry her for me—as he jolly well should, since he's the one who broke her. She's not heavy. I'm sure Snorri can carry her easily. We'll strap her across his back. That way, I can work on her and get her ready for my speech while you're doing...whatever it is you plan to do."

"Anything else?" Jake asked in amusement while Archie, still annoyed, threw some extra supplies into his tool-bag.

"Yes, in fact. You promise not to interfere while I go about collecting some data on the giants and their world."

"Ah, I knew there'd be a catch."

"It's called field work. It's not just for fun, it's for science!" Archie retorted defensively as he put his Super Subminiature Box Camera into his tool-bag, along with some pencils, and of course, an extra notebook. "It seems a fair exchange. You save the world while I do some research on the giant race."

"Done," Jake said with a chuckle.

Isabelle and Dani smiled gratefully at Archie, looking relieved that Jake wouldn't have to go it alone after all.

It seemed they all had their jobs to do.

"Don't forget a hat and coat," Dani warned, and of course, the boys obeyed. Jugenheim was part of Scandinavian legend, after all. It was likely cold where they were going.

Archie wrote a hurried note canceling the four o'clock panel discussion that had already been rescheduled. Considering that Dr. Wu would probably not be back in time for it either, this seemed the only sensible thing to do. Dani promised to take the note to the office for him.

Saying their final goodbyes, Jake suddenly remembered to consult the girls for any helpful tips they might have about how Snorri might win the heart of his princess. When he asked their advice, they rattled off a whole list of bewildering pointers, which Jake memorized to tell to Snorri later.

With that, Archie and he set out, their first stop the edge of the fjord to collect the Pigeon. There, they hauled the poor, half-mangled flying machine out of the water and set her on her wheels.

As the water poured off her wings, the boys gathered up the broken bits of flying machine strewn around the beach and stowed them in the cockpit.

At last, with the Pigeon limping along on her bent wheels—much as her young inventor was still limping from being accidentally dropped by the giant during his abduction—the boys began pulling the flying machine back up the mountain, where Snorri awaited their return.

* * *

Snorri sat inside the darkened cave, anxious to get out of Midgarth and home before certain gods found out about his trespass.

Of course, Odin was technically retired now, and had been ever since the monks had first come over from Ireland to convert the Vikings to the Cross. But still, the old, one-eyed former god of war remained someone only a fool would trifle with.

Loki must be truly mad to think of going up against Odin and Thor. Snorri shuddered at the thought of incurring their wrath himself. He hadn't meant any harm. Breaking the seal had been an accident—and just his luck.

Nothing ever goes right for me. He heaved a lonely sigh in the darkness, hoping he wasn't being stupid again for trusting those two boys just like he had trusted that lying little crow. He hoped they could help him.

With his boots freshly laced, his cloak fastened around his neck, and everything in him longing to go home, he got up and paced toward the mouth of the cave to see if the boys were coming. He couldn't wait to be on the road.

Back to Kaia...

Snorri was eager to meet the Isabelle-and-Dani girls that the boys were bringing to help give him advice.

Suddenly, halfway up the pitch-black tunnel, a glint of gold shining on the cavern floor caught his eye.

He bent down and picked up the small, unusual object.

"Hullo, what are you, then?" His bushy eyebrows shot upward as he lifted it up to his face for a closer look. A tiny, shiny cylinder of gold sparkled between his fingers.

"Ohh, look what I found," he murmured to himself in wonder. "Byoootiful...jewelry!"

With a tiny sculpted dog's head on the top!

Kaia loved dogs, and therefore, he instantly knew what to do with it. He'd give it to her for a present.

Princesses loved presents. Everybody knew that.

The shiny thing had a small ring at the top of it; he would string it through some ribbon and she could wear it round her neck.

With a grin, he tucked the golden jewelry into his pocket to give to her when the time was right. Best to keep it secret until then, he thought. He didn't want anyone trying to steal it or ruining his surprise.

Why, he quite believed he'd turn out to have a knack for this romance business, once he got the hang of it.

Then he heard the boys calling from outside.

* * *

Jake and Archie were a little winded from hauling the Pigeon back up the mountain. Thankfully, Red had helped once they met up with the Gryphon inside the forest.

The noble beast had lowered his dignity to allow the boys to harness him with the ropes, then he had pulled Archie's flying machine behind him like a horse hitched to a wagon.

Snorri was disappointed when he saw that the girls had not come with them, but Jake assured him that Isabelle had sent him with good advice, which he would soon share once they were underway.

But first he told the giant he would have to carry the Pigeon. Snorri felt guilty for breaking it, so he gladly agreed. Jake slipped the harness off of Red, then tied the ropes into a huge loop so Snorri could sling it over his shoulder. This the giant did, lifting the flying machine easily onto his back.

"All right, then. Everyone ready?" Jake asked, glancing around at his companions. "We have to be back in three days for Archie's speech, so we'd better get going." He turned to Snorri. "Which way?"

"Uhh..."

The giant went and stood on a boulder to get a better view of the surrounding landscape. Lifting his hand to visor his eyes, he turned this way and that, hesitating.

"Snorri," Archie mumbled in exasperation. "Have you forgotten the way back to Jugenheim?"

"There!" the giant suddenly said, pointing as the misty clouds parted. "Look! Yggdrasil," he said in a tone of awe.

There, on a distant mountaintop, a gigantic tree trunk as thick as a Norman tower rose from the crest of the mountain, up, up, into the gray clouds.

The boys stared at it, then looked at each other in amazement. Jake had never even heard of a tree that big.

"Jugenheim is up there somewhere in its branches," Snorri said. "Home."

"You mean we have to climb that thing?" Archie asked.

Snorri nodded. "C'mon."

The giant started marching off with his usual enormous paces. *Boom-boom, boom-boom.*

"Wait up!" Jake hollered.

"Huh?" Snorri stopped and turned around, then smiled sheepishly when he saw that he had nearly left them a quarter-mile behind. "Sorry," he rumbled when they finally caught up to him.

"We have to stick together!" Jake chided, panting after running to catch up.

"Sorry, I'm just eager to go home. But don't worry, I can walk slower."

"Good," Archie muttered, giving Jake a reproachful glance—as if every mishap along the way was already his fault.

Jake was too excited about the adventure before them to care. His eyes were shining and his steps were light as the four of them set out—together this time—for the first leg of their journey, to reach the legendary Tree of the Universe.

Snorri led the way with the Pigeon slung across his back. Jake and Archie followed, but they soon found that walking directly *behind* Snorri meant having to cross through each of his giant footprints, jumping down into the foot-shaped depression, climbing up the other side.

Since this was a waste of energy for the long journey ahead, they moved up to walk beside him, one on either side. Red prowled along beside Jake, who, for his part, could not have been happier, to be heading out on an adventure.

It was a great day: This was what he had been born to do, Jake thought, following in his parents' footsteps.

He might never have known them, torn away from them as a baby by the wicked schemes of Uncle Waldrick and the sea-witch, Fionnula Coralbroom, but in acting as a Lightrider, like they had been, Jake almost felt as if he knew them.

Marching through the tall grass of a high, mountain meadow, he was invigorated for the quest ahead. The breeze tousled his blond forelock; beneath it, his eyes gleamed with anticipation.

He could barely wait to see Giant Land.

PART III

CHAPTER TWENTY-TWO
The Enchanted Wood

Hiking through the forest, the travelers glimpsed the azure sky now and then through the branches. Along the path, they passed fascinating rock formations like trolls turned to stone.

Occasionally, the trail broke into sweeping views of distant emerald valleys and the sapphire fjord, where a whale breached with the simple joy of being alive. They shouted in amazement to see it splashing up into the air and crashing back down into the deep. When its great gray tail slipped below the water for the last time, they trekked on, through tranquil woods perfumed with the piney scent of Christmas trees.

To be sure, Jake was many miles now from the grimy streets of London, coated in coal soot. But as much as he could appreciate spending a beautiful summer's day roaming through the green mountains of Norway, he was impatient to get there, reach their destination.

Besides, he was still a city kid at heart, and every now and then, he could not help feeling as though *things* in the forest were watching him.

Then they set foot on the base of the next mountain, and Jake grew nearly certain of it. Indeed, he could almost pinpoint the exact moment they crossed the border leaving the normal world and entered into magic-ruled territory.

He could feel it in his bones, and he became uneasy.

This second mountain was the one at whose summit Snorri had spotted the mysterious Tree they'd have to climb to get to Giant Land.

As they started up the slope with Snorri in the lead, he recalled the odd rock formations they had passed and tried not to think about

Miss Langesund's earlier mention of trolls. Giants were obviously real, so why should trolls be any different?

He didn't mention this concern aloud, though. He didn't want to scare Archie. If trolls were real, maybe they were afraid of giants, he reasoned. Maybe, seeing Snorri, the trolls would keep their distance, and if all else failed, at least they still had Red.

Recalling how vicious the Gryphon could be—when the occasion called—helped to put his mind at ease.

Up the mountain path they marched. His knapsack started to feel like twice its weight hanging off his shoulders. Jake was glad he'd worn good boots.

At least there was plenty of time to discuss Isabelle's tips for Snorri about how to woo the princess.

Snorri was as shocked as Jake had been when he'd first heard her strange advice. "Listen to her?" he echoed. "Make her laugh?"

"I know. Weird, huh? But that's what she said." Jake wiped the sweat off his brow with a pass of his forearm, then stepped over a mossy log.

"But I already do all that!" Snorri replied.

"Then maybe she already likes you, and you just didn't know it yet," Archie chimed in from several feet behind them.

This shocked Snorri even more. The giant paused in astonishment and turned around to gape at him. "Already likes me?" He abruptly frowned. "Say, little master, are you all right?"

"My leg's bleeding again," he admitted.

Hearing this, Jake also stopped and turned around in concern, only to find his cousin limping along and lagging farther behind on the trail than he had realized.

Blast it, he had forgotten all about Archie's hurt leg. He frowned and went back to him, thrusting away a flitter of fear as he hoped that nothing with fangs in the forest smelled the blood oozing through Archie's bandage.

Wolves. Bears. *Trolls?*

"Why don't you ride on Red for a while?"

"I'll be fine." Archie picked up a suitable walking stick from among the fallen branches lying around. It split into a natural Y shape at the top, so he used it for a crutch. "There. Right as rain."

"Honestly, Red doesn't mind—"

"I don't need to be carried! I can pull my own weight," the smaller boy said defensively.

Jake suspected Archie's pride was still smarting from Dani O'Dell's offer to protect him. Somehow Dani's opinion on most things seemed to matter an awful lot to Archie, Jake had noticed.

"Suit yourself," he mumbled. "Just don't overdo it, Arch. We've still got a long way to go."

"Actually, I think we're almost there!" Snorri pointed in excitement. "I see a clearing. It's not far!"

All Jake could see was the dense forest surrounding them and the angled ground before them, covered in its uniform blanket of old brown pine needles and dead leaves.

Snorri could see farther than they could from his vantage point, however, being five or six times taller than the boys. "Another mile at the most and we should be there, at the Tree," the giant promised.

"Well, that's good news," Archie murmured. Red pounced over to walk beside the boy genius the rest of the way in case he stumbled. Jake gave his Gryphon a discreet nod of gratitude for looking after his cousin.

They labored on.

But with every step closer to the summit and the Tree of legend, Yggdrasil, the more Jake's sense of eeriness intensified. The forest shadows seemed to grow darker. The path became more difficult, a steep, rocky scrabble.

At one point, a rush of stones rolled down the trail at them, as if the mountain itself were trying to drive them off. Fortunately, Snorri was at the front of the line and these were no more than pebbles to him. The giant quickly turned his back, put his feet together, and shielded the boys and Red from the brief rockslide.

"Whoa! Avalanche," Jake exclaimed as the stones bounced past them on both sides.

"You two pips all right?" Snorri asked after the rocks had passed. The boys nodded and asked him the same. Snorri said he was quite unscathed, so they thanked him for his quick thinking and pressed on.

Then Jake noticed that the Gryphon also looked on full alert. Red's small tufted ears were cocked, his golden eagle-eyes scanning the surrounding trees for any sign of a threat. It seemed he wasn't the only one who sensed something strange about this mountain.

Red let out a low, unhappy growl.

"I know, boy," Jake murmured to his pet. "I feel it, too. We're not welcome here. Unfortunately, we've got no choice. It's the only way to Yoo-gan-hime."

The Gryphon snorted skeptically through his leathery beak.

Then Jake noticed that his cousin was wearing a look of perplexity, like he was pondering some equation. "What is it, Arch?"

"Oh, I was just thinking about the rockslide."

"What about it?"

"Why it might've happened."

"Something doesn't want us here."

"Nonsense. There's obviously a logical explanation."

"Oh?"

"Given the time of year, the melting snows and spring rains must have loosened the turf and freed the stones," he mused aloud. "Then gravity takes over and the stones fall away from their places, following the path of least resistance—"

"Ow!" Jake suddenly cried as an acorn beaned him in the head.

He looked up into the branches above him with a scowl while Archie started laughing.

"Good shot, squirrel!"

"I didn't see any squirrel," Jake muttered, rubbing his noggin indignantly. "Did you see it?"

"No." Archie shook his head. "But what else could it be? Maybe the wind..."

"There is no wind," Jake replied.

Archie frowned, then they pressed on, until a moment later, another acorn struck—this time hitting Archie on the shoulder, while a third thunked Snorri in the back.

"What is this? Somebody's throwing acorns at us!"

"What kind of squirrel has that good of aim?" Jake demanded.

Snorri stopped and turned around, eyeing the boys as though he suspected them of playing a prank on him. "Was that you doing that?"

"No!" they exclaimed in unison.

Then a shower of acorns came down on them all at once.

They were too busy protecting their heads to see who or how or where it was coming from, but it would have taken an army of trained squirrels to unload on them like that.

Fortunately, the deluge of acorns pelting them was brief. When it had passed, they looked at each other in bafflement.

"Honestly," Archie murmured, frowning as he scanned the woods. "My weird-o-meter is going off."

"You have a weird-o-meter?" Jake asked in surprise. "Now there's a useful invention!"

Archie just looked at him. "It was a joke."

"Too bad. Maybe you should invent one. It would probably come in handy, given the lives we lead," Jake muttered, then he shivered a little. "Is it getting colder?"

Archie nodded. "Because of our elevation."

"Ah." It was a fine thing, having a logical, science-minded person on hand under such circumstances, Jake reflected. But as they soldiered on toward the clearing that Snorri had seen ahead, things got even weirder, until not even Archie could explain the strange sounds the forest was making.

They moved into the gloomy shadow of the mountain, where the trees seemed to moan at them like spirits in a cemetery, creaking their branches and rattling bony twig-fingers as though trying to scare them away.

Just the breeze, just the breeze, Jake assured himself over and over as he glanced around.

He could have sworn some of those trees got up and walked a few steps, writhing on their roots somehow.

The vines seemed to slither over the thick boughs. The thorny brambles here and there seemed to reach for them to tear their skin, and from the corner of his eye, Jake kept seeing threatening faces in the gnarled bark of the old oak trees.

They passed strange, knee-high mushrooms with polka-dotted umbrellas and smooth boulders covered in rich moss, like cozy little resting places made just for them.

But Jake knew a magical trap when he saw one, and none of them dared even pause.

All the while, as they labored on up the steep path, an abnormally large wood moth followed them, wavering after them from tree to tree.

Each time it landed on a tree-trunk to rest, the white markings on its ragged brown wings spied on them like big, strange eyes.

Stupid bug, Jake thought, resolving to ignore it—and to stick to cities from now on. Determined to ignore the eeriness of this forest, he concentrated on putting one foot after the other.

They were almost there.

"I really should see about buying one of those dirigible hover chairs," Archie jested in the tense silence, panting with exertion.

"That would come in handy right about now," Jake agreed. "I'll take one, too."

"Aw, gnats!" Ahead of them, Snorri suddenly began swatting at a cloud of gnats hovering over their path. "Ugh, I walked right into them. Didn't—even—see them!" He was spitting them away from his mouth and blinking them out of his eyes and waving his arms around like a wind-mill come to life.

Jake and Archie looked at each other, both suppressing a laugh—until the huge colony of gnats drifted lower and enveloped them, too.

They tried to hurry forward through the cloud of insects, but the gnats followed them, drawn to their body heat and the moisture of their sweat.

Red tried flapping his wings to shoo the tiny insects away from himself and the boys, but this, too, proved useless.

They kept trying to get past them until the tiny creatures' assault halted all their progress. They couldn't see, could barely breathe.

They had to shut their eyes and mouths and cup their hands over their noses to block the curious insects from flying up their nostrils.

"What do we do?" Archie cried, quickly shutting his mouth again.

"I think I have an idea!" Snorri answered just as briefly. "But you have to hold your nose!"

Without any other options, they did as he said. Jake had no idea what Snorri intended as he leaned forward from the waist, his homely face bunched up with a look of intense concentration.

All of a sudden, the giant let out the mightiest fart the boys had ever heard.

The deep, long note reverberated through the mountains like an Alpine horn calling the shepherds home.

The whole cloud of gnats instantly fell dead. Jake and Archie nearly did, too, when laughter made them gasp for air.

Big mistake.

"Run for your life!" Jake choked out, already bolting up the path to escape the stink.

Archie, gagging, reached for the Gryphon and climbed onto his back. Red launched away at top speed, coughing.

When they had reached the top of the slope, both boys applauded loudly for Snorri, who came trudging up after them with a grin from ear to ear.

Even Archie approved. "Most impressive, sir!"

"Told you I had talents," the giant said brightly.

"Probably best not to show off *that* one to the princess," Archie advised.

"Guess what?" Jake exclaimed. "Besides being able to fart like a flugelhorn, our giant friend here is an excellent navigator!" He gestured to the clearing ahead of them. "Look, Snorri! You've found the Tree."

CHAPTER TWENTY-THREE
The Secret Meadow

"Great Euclid!" Archie whispered as they stepped up to the shadowed edge of the forest and stared into the sun-dappled glade.

There, in the flowery meadow, hidden by miles of wild woods, stood the towering base of the Tree of Viking legend, Yggdrasil. Even its gnarled roots were gigantic, as big as houses and covered in velvety green moss. Yggdrasil was so huge that not even its lowest branch was in sight.

Tilting their heads back to stare up at it, all they could see was the towering wooden pillar of its trunk, disappearing into the clouds.

Then Archie looked at him and grinned. "Jake, meet beanstalk. Beanstalk, Jake."

Red snorted at his quip, but Jake just looked at him.

"Well, we *are* two Englishmen sneaking into Giant Land! You have to admit the story fits." Archie elbowed Snorri in the side of his knee. "Go on. 'Fee, fi, fo, fum.' Please?"

"We don't really say that," Snorri mumbled, casting the boy genius a frown. Then he gazed reverently into the clearing again. "Isn't it beautiful?"

"And creepy," Jake muttered. "Stay on your guard, everyone."

"Look at the swans!" Snorri pointed with a dreamy smile at the pair of swans swimming in a tranquil stone pool beside the Tree. "And the flowers! I've never seen colors like that before, so pretty and bright."

"They *sparkle*," Archie agreed. "They almost look like blown glass or crystal...or sugarplum candy!" He pointed to an otherworldly orange trumpet flower in fascination. "I wonder if you can eat them!"

"I wouldn't advise it," Jake said, suddenly more uneasy here than he had been in the woods.

None of them seemed too eager to take the first step into the meadow, content to enjoy its beauty from the edges. Red was glancing around with an aquiline scowl, his tufted lion-tail thrashing back and forth in agitation.

"Do you think I should pick one of those flowers for Kaia?" Snorri asked the boys.

"Don't even touch them. These flowers might contain some magic poison, and even if they don't, if you pick one, it'll be dead by the time we get there," Jake replied. "Besides, you'd have to explain where you got it. And that could cause some problems, considering you're forbidden to come to Midgarth."

"Oh, right." Snorri craned his neck to look up at the tree again. "So how in the Nine Worlds are we going to climb this thing?"

"No idea," Jake murmured. "There must be some sort of trick to it. Come on, Arch. Let's put that big brain of yours to work. Help me figure this out."

"Let me get a picture of the tree." Archie set down his tool-bag and reached into it, pulling out his camera.

"What's that?" Snorri asked.

Archie grinned proudly. "That's my Super Subminiature Box Camera! It's only two by three inches, the smallest camera money can buy, favored by private detectives—"

"Arch, we don't have time for this!"

"You said I could!" he belted back at once. "That's the main reason I'm here, Jake! Field work! Remember?"

Jake scowled, but Archie tossed him a measuring tape. "Here. Go take a circumference of the trunk for me," he ordered as he began setting up his camera. "I need exact measurements, or my colleagues will never believe it's real."

"You can't tell them about this!"

"Why not?"

"That barmy lot will come and chop it down so they can count the tree rings!"

Snorri glanced at Archie in alarm, but he waved off Jake's claim.

Jake tossed his knapsack onto the ground. He was glad to be rid of the burden for a while, anyway.

Snorri did the same, taking the stopper off his huge canteen.

"Maybe we could just stay here and rest awhile. It's awfully nice and peaceful. Maybe a snack before we climb?"

Jake's stomach grumbled in agreement with this suggestion, but for once he ignored it. "Don't be daft. We have to press on." *I am not getting stuck in this strange forest after dark.* With Archie's measuring tape dutifully in hand, he took two steps into the meadow to go measure the trunk of Yggdrasil, only to freeze in his tracks when all the brilliant, crystalline flowers snapped shut.

"Ah, crud," he whispered.

"What did you do?" Archie cried.

Not daring to move his feet another inch, Jake looked around for an explanation. "Not... quite... sure. I think when I stepped past those orange flowers..."

Archie gasped with understanding. "Crystals! The flowers mark out a perimeter. You've tripped off some sort of magical alarm!"

Then a clap of thunder sounded right above them.

They all jumped. The two swans floating in the stream flew away, spiraling upward around the tree. Black clouds rolled in with astonishing speed, darkening the glade.

Red leaped forward to stand by Jake's side, snarling at unseen forces in the air.

All of a sudden, a disembodied voice boomed at them from all directions: *"Turn back!"*

"Blimey," Jake said with a gulp. "I knew those stupid woods were enchanted."

"None shall pass," the voice said. *"Leave this place! This is your only warning!"*

A bolt of lightning split the air above Jake's head. He ducked; Red roared at the invisible person behind these tricks.

Then a piercing screech from above split the air. Jake looked up as two winged, coal-black shapes dove toward them from the sky.

Red instantly went into full battle-mode, unfurling his wings, unsheathing his lion-claws. He reared up onto his back legs and slashed at the air with his front paws.

Jake stared, incredulous, at the incoming creatures, monstrous, reptilian birds arrowing straight toward them.

"What are they?" Snorri cried.

"They almost look like pterodactyls! But that's impossible," Archie said.

"Tera-whats?"

"Dinosaur birds! They found them in the fossils."

But studying them again, Jake shook his head. "No, I think those are the swans."

"They've changed," Snorri rumbled.

"Duck!" Jake hit the ground, covering his head with his hands as the black swan-things swooped low. He felt the breeze as they passed inches above him, one after the other.

The second scratched Jake's back with sharp talons as it whooshed by. He yelled out in pain, but managed to lift his head for a better view of what in blazes was attacking them.

The birds had long necks with large, toothed beaks, shiny black scales in place of feathers, and red, glowing eyes. They circled the glade and headed back for a second pass, hurling straight toward the intruders like two black, nasty javelins.

Still lying on his stomach flat on the ground, Jake tried to gather his wits enough to use his telekinesis on the creatures. But before he could throw a bolt of energy at them, Red launched into the air to battle them.

Jake watched in something of a panic as his brave pet clashed with the creatures, fighting them in midair. With Red keeping the swan-things busy, Jake shot to his feet and retreated a bit.

Archie had the presence of mind to snap a picture, but Snorri just stood there with his mouth hanging open. When the Gryphon sent one of the evil black swans crashing to the ground with a hiss, there was another flash of lightning, another disembodied voice.

"Turn back now or you shall die!"

"Who's there?" Jake demanded.

The voice sounded female. Actually, it sounded like several voices layered into one, all speaking at once. Weird. *"Who dares trespass in this place?"*

"Show yourself!" he commanded boldly.

"Oh, you don't want that, child, believe me." Only one voice offered that response, along with a hag-like snicker.

Then, again, all three voices boomed together: *"Do not try our patience. In the name of Odin, go now, or you shall pay!"*

Jake could not tell which direction the sound was coming from. The ominous warning seemed to emanate from everywhere at once. He glanced meaningfully at Archie to see if the boy genius had any thoughts.

Whoever was behind those voices, Jake was sure they were somewhere close, watching, but unseen. Archie shook his head and shrugged, at a loss, while Red battled on, flying and slashing in midair as he fought the second monstrous black bird.

The first, which the Gryphon had already knocked down, struggled to its feet again, shook itself off, and returned to the fight.

Jake winced, his heart pounding in fear for his big, feathered friend. As strong as he was, the outnumbered Gryphon couldn't go on like this forever.

"Give me your walking stick!" he called to Archie. When his cousin threw it to him, Jake held it like a cricket bat. He gathered his courage, then charged into the fray, taking a whack at one of the black creatures attacking Red. "Leave him alone!"

More lightning.

"How dare you attack our birds?" the voice shouted at him.

"Call them off or I'll smash 'em in the head!" he yelled, but the only reply he received was a lightning bolt that landed near his feet.

He jumped away with a yelp and fell on the flowers, which snapped at him like angry Venus flytraps.

He felt a massive hand pull him up by the back of his collar. A moment later, Snorri set him on his feet back near his cousin.

Jake dusted himself off. "Thanks, Snorri—but why are you just standing here! You're a giant! Can't you do something? Please! Go help Red before they kill him! Those birds are small enough that you could grab them—"

"Listen to me!" he interrupted. "There's something I have to tell you!"

"What is it?" Jake asked impatiently.

"I think I know who's here," the giant mumbled, nodding toward the meadow.

"You do?" both boys exclaimed.

"I remembered." The giant nodded with a look of dread. "It's the Norns," he whispered.

"The what?"

"Who?" the boys exclaimed.

"Three terrible witches who guard Yggdrasil."

"Witches!" Jake said in alarm.

"You might've mentioned that earlier!" Archie retorted.

"I'm sorry, I forgot!" Snorri said defensively. "I never paid much attention in school."

"There's a shock," Archie muttered.

"Great." Jake harrumphed. *Witches!* He'd had enough of their kind back in London with Fionnula Coralbroom.

He glanced around the glade for any sign of them, but the witches preferred to remain invisible.

"Quickly, Snorri, what can you tell us about them?"

"Well, they're called the Norns, also known as the Wyrd Sisters."

"Like in Shakespeare?" Archie exclaimed. "Macbeth?"

"Huh?" Snorri grunted.

"Never mind," Jake said. "Just tell us how we defeat 'em."

"You don't. They're too ancient, too powerful. They're like, like the Fates," Snorri said, weighing each word as though it hurt to search his brain for pertinent details. "They weave the cloth of destiny. There's three of them: past, present, future. They guard the Tree... Oh, yes, and the stream there. Of course! It's all coming back to me now. The water, there! You see?" He pointed to the pool where the swans had been floating when they had arrived. "The Norns water the tree Yggdrasil from the Well of Wisdom."

"Maybe we could get *you* a nice big drink of that, too," Archie muttered.

"How did you deal with them last time?" Jake asked hurriedly. "When you landed here before?"

"I never saw them! When I fell out of Jugenheim, I landed way over there on the next mountain."

"Well, what do we do?" Jake asked impatiently.

The invisible Norn answered the question for him: *"Flee or die!"*

Archie turned on his heel. "Cheerio, then."

"Get back here!" Jake laid a hold of Archie's shoulder and turned him around. "We've got to stick together! If we go off separately, they can pick us off one by one."

"How can we fight what we can't even see?" Archie threw up his hands in exasperation.

"Don't you have a gadget for this or something?"

"What, my Invisible Witch Slayer? Sorry, I left it at home. With my weird-o-meter."

"You don't have to be sarcastic," Jake said in frustration. His usually polite cousin really must be hanging around *him* too much.

Jake turned back to face the clearing. "Maybe the Norns will just...listen to reason. Don't go anywhere, you two. I'm going to try and talk to them."

"Jake!"

He ignored Archie's protest, his heart was pounding with fear that he hoped did not show on his face. He took a brave step into the glade. "Hullo, anyone home? Please, ma'am, er, ladies? Norns, whatever you are—we mean you no harm!"

"Get out!" A lightning bolt came with their reply.

Archie dove out of the way. "Please don't kill us! We're too young to die!" he yelped from the nice, soft patch of moss where he had landed. "I'm sure you're very nice Norns. I-I loved you in Macbeth."

"None shall pass!"

"Yes, you already mentioned that." Jake was losing patience.

He cast about for some way to make the Norns listen. Then inspiration struck as he suddenly realized something that they had in common.

Trees!

Of course. The Norns served Yggdrasil, and Jake and Archie were hereditary members of the Order of the Yew Tree.

He hesitated to mention it, though, for it was taking a bit of a risk. If the Wyrd Sisters were bad witches, friends of the Dark Druids, then claiming a connection to the Order of the Yew Tree would only make things worse.

But when one of the black swan-things bit Red on the shoulder, Jake had had enough. This had to stop.

"We're not a threat!" he repeated. "We come in the name of the Order of the Yew Tree!"

"Jake!?" Archie whispered, hearing this.

But suddenly, to the boys' amazement, a huge head appeared, floating in the air, in the middle of the glade. "The Order, you say?"

It was a female head, peering down at them.

It flickered a little like the moving pictures he had seen in the Exhibit Hall. This tipped Jake off that the head, like the voices, was probably just an illusion being projected somehow from somewhere nearby.

"You're a little young to be agents of the Order," the Norn head said, looking unconvinced.

"He meant our parents," Archie corrected. "Mine are diplomats;

his were Lightriders. Of course, they're dead now," he added helpfully.

The head rotated to face Jake, hovering closer. "Is that so? The son of a Lightrider coming to see us? Well, now, that is something. What do you want with Yggdrasil?"

"We only wish to see our friend home safely. He's got to get back to Jugenheim." Jake pointed at Snorri.

The head rotated once again to face the giant. "So, you're the one who broke the seal. Naughty, naughty."

Snorri blanched. "It was an accident, ma'am! I'm very sorry."

The Norn pursed her lips in knowing disapproval. "Giants," she said with a humph. "Very well! You may enter the sacred grove. Then we shall see if Yggdrasil will accept you." The Norn gave a terse command that caused her vicious black swan-things to stop attacking Red.

With that, the head vanished, and at once, the darkness cleared.

CHAPTER TWENTY-FOUR
The Norns

Jake immediately hurried over to check on Red. In the few seconds it took him to reach the Gryphon, the little meadow returned to its previous perfection: golden sunshine; brilliant flowers; emerald moss. The swans looked a little worse for wear, honking unhappily as they returned to their pool to smooth their rumpled feathers, snow-white once again.

To Jake's relief, Red was more or less unscathed. The scratch on his shoulder healed in seconds, and the great beast shook himself like a dog. It helped to settle him down after his fight.

"Good show, Red. You were grand." Jake reached into his pocket and gave him one of Dani's pilfered dog biscuits usually reserved for Teddy. It wasn't much, but it was the thought that counted; the Gryphon gulped down the treat with gratitude.

Jake patted his pet's scarlet-feathered head, then turned around and was astonished anew to see a girl on a tree swing slowly being lowered from the cloud-swathed branches of Yggdrasil.

He leaned to whisper in Archie's ear, "That can't be one of the Norns?"

"Who else would it be?" Archie whispered back.

"But she's only our age!"

Archie shrugged. "She looks it, but if the Vikings knew the Norns, that means she's ancient. You heard what Snorri said. Past, present, future. This one must guard the future, since she's still a kid."

Sure enough, the girl-witch sitting prettily on her tree swing had not come alone. A wooden platform now began descending from the mists high above them.

They could hear the creaking of pulleys and, oddly enough, the rattling of fine china and glassware as the platform approached the ground.

When the platform came near enough for them to get a better look, Jake noted that it was suspended by thick, hairy vines at each of the four corners. It had a little railing around it to prevent anybody falling off, and as it came to earth, settling on the grass before them with a loud noise, he was delighted to find that the two older Norns had come prepared to offer the weary travelers hospitality.

They had a pretty table and chairs set up for an elaborate tea party, right there on the platform in the heart of the beautiful meadow.

The girl-witch hopped off her swing and skipped over to the table, where a sweet old lady with white hair was sewing in a rocking chair, and a smiling middle aged woman who looked like the perfect mother beckoned to them. "Anyone hungry?"

Jake frowned. Witches. They knew just how to tempt you.

The table was arrayed with little sandwiches and cakes and tea and chocolate, and his stomach was already grumbling.

But he stopped himself. That smiling mother-witch looked familiar. He was fairly sure she was the one behind the giant head.

He sent his cousin an uncertain glance. "What do you think?" he whispered confidentially. "They don't look so bad to me. Is this how they were in Macbeth?"

"Not at all," Archie whispered back. "Shakespeare showed them as warty old hags who danced around a cauldron. Mad as hatters, very nasty."

"No giant heads?" Jake frowned. "Maybe they're a different set of Wyrd Sisters."

"Or maybe the Bard used poetic license—"

"We can appear to you gentlemen as we did to your silly Bard, if you prefer," the mother-witch called in amusement. "But since you are friends of the Yew Tree, we thought this would be nicer for you."

"How did she hear us?" Jake breathed, baffled.

"I don't know, but we'd better not be rude. That might not be...healthy."

"Right," Jake said. With that, they ventured over to the table.

Jake was glad to let Archie take the lead in this matter. His aristocratic cousin had much more experience than he did in the art of how to conduct oneself in polite company. "This is very kind of you, ladies." Archie offered the Norns a gentlemanly bow; Jake quickly followed suit.

The mother-witch beamed with approval. "Join us." She beckoned them over. "Would you like some tea and sandwiches?"

"No," the boys said in unison while Snorri gave an enthusiastic "Yes!"

"Never eat magic food," Archie whispered angrily to him.

"Oh! Er, sorry, I mean no," Snorri said in disappointment. "Thank you, ma'am, Norns."

As the boys approached the platform, Jake remained on his guard. This was all much better than lightning bolts and a giant floating head, but even in their nice aspect, all three of the witches still had a devious look in their eyes.

"Oh, look at the little Lightriders!" the granny Norn cooed. "Aren't you adorable? Come here you two little cherubs and let me pinch your cheeks!"

Jake halted, bristling. "She cannot be talking to me."

"I think she's talking to both of us," Archie whispered.

Criminy, they were on a mission, a quest! Heroes on an adventure did not, as a rule, have grannies doting on them.

Both boys pretended not to hear.

"You can at least sit down, can't you? Unless you're always rude?" the pretty young girl-witch challenged Jake.

"He is," Archie jested.

Jake scowled at him, but the boys cautiously sat down at the table.

Snorri lowered his bulk onto the ground nearby. Red sat on his haunches between the boys' chairs, eyeing up the food.

"Beautiful gryphon you've got there. I haven't seen one of them in ages. Wherever did you get him?" the mother asked as she poured some tea for granny.

"I inherited him," Jake replied. "So, um, if you don't mind, could you please tell us how to get up the tree to Jugenheim? We're in a bit of a hurry."

"Why is that?" the granny asked, stirring her tea.

Jake got distracted watching the girl slather strawberry jam all over a piece of freshly baked bread.

It was torture, all this lovely food.

Archie elbowed him.

"Huh? Oh. Right, we just don't want to get caught in the forest after dark."

"Very sensible of you. The trolls are restless this time of year. Hungry, too, just waking up after their winter's hibernation."

"Trolls?" Archie's eyes widened. He turned to Jake. "Did she say trolls?"

Jake tried to look calm about it and cleared his throat. "Ahem. So what's the trick to how we climb this tree of yours?"

They all three laughed.

"What a silly fool!" the girl burst out merrily.

"Skuld, don't be rude," the mother chided the girl. "The truth is, you can't climb it, and it's certainly not *our* tree. Nobody owns Yggdrasil. The water, darling," she reminded her daughter, or youngest sister, or whatever they were to each other.

"Yes, Verdandi." The girl rose and went to fill a watering can that sat beside the stone pool where the spring water was loosely captured.

When her watering can was full, Skuld went and poured it on the roots here and there, which caused a remarkable reaction in the tree.

Yggdrasil gurgled greedily and almost seemed to breathe, expanding and contracting like a person's chest when taking a deep breath. The roots moved a bit like giant toes wriggling in contentment.

Skuld went and got more water, pouring it on another part. "There you are. That should keep you for a while." Then she noticed the boys watching her curiously. "One of us always has to water the tree," she explained, "and one of us always has to be sewing, too. We trade off. It's easier that way."

"But enough about us and our boring lives," the mother witch said, pooh-poohing her. "So! You're with the Order. How exciting! Do tell us any news of our friend, the Old Yew. How is he?"

"He?" Jake turned to Archie in startled confusion. "What does she mean, he?"

His cousin ignored him. "Oh, he's fine, ma'am. There was a bit of the shoestring root rot fungus going around last autumn—"

"Oh, no!"

"But the Old Yew and his children came through it just fine," he assured her.

"Well, that's a relief."

"Wait," Jake said. "The Yew Tree from the Order of the Yew Tree is a person? That has children?"

"He's a tree spirit, obviously. The oldest in England. What did you think he was?" Archie replied.

"They say he takes up several acres nowadays, down there on the grounds at Merlin Hall. Oh, I haven't been there in years," the granny Norn remarked with a chuckle, busily pulling the needle and thread through on her embroidery hoop.

Jake saw she was working on a section of an incredibly intricate tapestry that showed Yggdrasil.

"I should think so," the mother-witch agreed. "He must be going on what, nine-thousand years now, wouldn't you say, Granny Wyrd?"

The elderly Norn nodded with a happy sigh. "Oh, such times! He was such an adorable little sapling in those days. Barely a twig!"

"Give him our best when you see him. And do please tell him that Cousin Yggdrasil sends his regards."

"Certainly," Archie replied with another polite nod.

"The Yew Tree is a *person*?" Jake repeated, still astonished. "Why didn't anyone tell me that?"

Even Red seemed amused at his confusion.

"You must excuse my cousin," Archie said to the Norns. "He was missing for eleven years, and we only just got him back. I'm afraid there's lots he still doesn't know. Yes, Jake. The Old Yew is obviously a tree-person. Who do you think was the judge at Uncle Waldrick's trial? That's why they call it the Yew Court."

"A tree was the judge that sent my uncle to prison? You've got to be joking."

"Oh, trees are much more complex than most of you humans give them credit for," the mother-witch, Verdandi, replied. "At least the Vikings understood their glory."

Archie pushed his spectacles up higher on his nose. "I believe that's why every Viking chief built his great hall around a massive oak tree, if I'm not mistaken?"

"You are correct." Verdandi seemed pleased. "Either they built their halls around a real tree, or they constructed an artificial one indoors as a way of honoring the oak groves."

"King Olaf's great hall has a live tree!" Snorri chimed in.

Verdandi nodded with a look of appreciation. "The giants still know how to honor the old ways. You humans, though—"

"Mother! Don't get her started," the girl-witch warned with a roll of her eyes. "All that happened *long* before their time."

"I suppose," the mother Norn said begrudgingly.

"Verdandi's still peeved that the monks persuaded the Vikings to abandon pagan worship."

"Ahem, well, I see." Though Jake was still slightly baffled, he shook off his confusion and got down to business. "So, perhaps now, if you don't mind, you might tell us how to get to Jugenheim, if one can't climb Yggdrasil?"

"Of course. Forgive our chattiness, boys." Granny Norn smiled indulgently. "We don't get many visitors up here."

It didn't really seem like you wanted any, what with the lightning bolts and all, Jake thought, but he kept this opinion to himself.

"Very well, on to business, then. Enough of the pleasantries." Verdandi stirred a lump of sugar into her tea. "To take your friend back to Jugenheim, you will have to make an offering to Yggdrasil. You'll throw it in the Well." She pointed to the stone pool where the swans floated tranquilly once more. "If Yggdrasil is satisfied, then you may pass. If not, you can't. It's that simple."

Jake and Archie exchanged a worried look. They hadn't brought anything in their gear but the essentials.

While both boys immediately began pondering what they could spare from their supplies, Snorri asked the obvious question. "What sort of offering does the Tree like?"

"Gold?" Jake asked. He had plenty of that, thanks to the goldmine in Wales that his parents had left him.

Only a few weeks into his aristocratic new life, Jake had not yet had a chance to go and see it, but he hoped to soon. Red had originally discovered it back in the Middle Ages, for, as Aunt Ramona had explained, that's what gryphons did.

They could find veins of gold in the earth, which was why they had been hunted nearly to extinction. Jake was also excited to meet the crew of dwarves who worked in his goldmine. He had never seen a dwarf, but he was told they were honest, hard workers, with excellent singing voices.

In any case, gold coins were heavy to carry, so he hadn't brought much with him on their journey.

Archie, meanwhile, was worried that the Norns might want him to give up one of his beloved gadgets as an offering, and certainly not his tiny, new-fangled camera. "Yes, what sorts of things?" he echoed Snorri's question. "Personal effects?"

"No, no. Yggdrasil doesn't care about those things. What matters to him is how much the offering matters to *you*. Take Odin, for example," the mother Norn explained, glancing toward the water. "When Odin came here as a young warrior-god wanting to drink from our Well of Wisdom, even he had to make a sacrifice."

"Really? What did Odin give?" Archie asked.

"His eye," she said.

Their mouths fell open.

"I'm going to need both of mine," Jake blurted out.

"You can give whatever you like, it's up to you. But it has to be in equal measure to whatever you want in return." Verdandi shrugged. "Odin wanted enough wisdom to become a worthy king of the gods. To him, his eye was a fair trade. Though it was rather bloody when he stood here and gouged it out with his dagger. Not a pleasant thing to witness, I can tell you."

Jake shuddered. "We just want to get to Jugenheim."

"Quite so," she answered with a smile. "An eyeball seems excessive." She paused. "You know, we have noticed over the years that our dear Yggdrasil does have certain preferences."

"Like what?" Jake asked.

"Secrets, dreams, hopes. Ambitions. Things like...oh, your unspoken heartaches. Or your worst fear."

They stared at her.

"Or a kiss!" the girl-witch suggested with a flirtatious little smile at Jake.

He blanched.

While Verdandi scolded her for being forward, wise old Granny Wyrd leaned closer. "Listen to me, young heroes. What Yggdrasil likes most of all for an offering is your greatest sorrow. Either your worst mistake, for example, or the worst thing that has ever happened to you."

They absorbed this dire revelation in wonder.

"W-why is that?" Archie stammered.

"Because those are the things that usually teach people the most about life, if they're willing to learn from them. Don't forget, your offering will be added to the Well of Wisdom, from which we draw the water for the tree. Nothing adds to wisdom like suffering. That's why your biggest mistakes, if you learn from them, are some of the most precious things you possess. Yggdrasil would appreciate that."

"How...?" Jake asked, mystified, but he should have known the answer was, of course, by magic.

Granny Wyrd handed them each a tiny silk sack tied with ribbons. "You must whisper your chosen secret into one of my little notions bags."

As he accepted one of the tiny pastel-colored bags, Jake recalled that 'notions' did not just mean ideas. It was also the term that ladies used for their sewing equipment, like buttons and bits of lace and things.

He knew this because he had made the mistake of knocking over Great-Great Aunt Ramona's notions basket once and having to clean up everything he had spilled.

Archie accepted one of the dainty little notions bags from Granny Wyrd, too. His was yellow. Jake's was light blue, and Snorri's was green.

"So you just...talk into it?" Jake murmured uneasily.

Granny Wyrd nodded. "No one else need hear. It's between you and Yggdrasil. Whisper your secret into the bag, then tie the ribbons tightly, and throw it in the well." She nodded toward the water where the swans floated.

The boys looked at each other uncertainly.

So far, Jake thought, this adventure was not at all going the way he had imagined. Sitting here having tea with some ladies was not exactly the stuff of warriors and heroes, but, oh-bloody-well.

He got up from the table and walked away to be alone so he could reflect on which of his sorrows to use. There were certainly plenty to choose from.

While Jake, Archie, and Snorri pondered it, Red had no trouble deciding on what *his* offering should be, so he, too, would be allowed to pass. He reached around with his beak and plucked a crimson feather from one of his wings, then dropped it on the table in front of the mother-witch.

His feathers were very precious; each one contained powerful magic.

Verdandi took it and admired it for a moment while the boys were still thinking. "Thank you, Gryphon." She put his feather in a notions bag, too.

The mood in the meadow had changed as they contemplated the worst, saddest, most fearful moments of their lives.

Jake finally decided which one to sacrifice. It was no eyeball, but hopefully, it would satisfy the mysterious Tree. He turned away from the others, lifted the silk bag up to his mouth, and whispered his secret into it.

He quickly tied the ribbons to keep it shut, then brought it back uncertainly toward the table.

"Now, go and throw it in the pool," Granny Wyrd instructed.

Jake nodded and headed for it. The girl-witch, Skuld, fell into step beside him. Archie and Snorri weren't far behind as they, too, finished the same process.

When he came to the edge of the tranquil stone pool, he listened for a moment to the babbling music of the stream feeding into it on one side and flowing out the other in a little waterfall.

Then Jake glanced at Skuld. "What's going to happen when I throw it in?"

"You'll see."

"Should I be worried?"

She just smiled. "Don't hit the swans. Go on, unless you lack the courage?"

That was all she needed to say. He frowned in answer to her impertinent challenge, then hoping for the best, tossed the dainty fabric sack into the Well of Wisdom.

It plopped in with a splash and, to Jake's surprise, instantly sank like a stone, even though it was empty.

Archie and the giant looked on, having joined him.

The swans honked as the water began to bubble and fizz.

"Ohh, you must've picked a good one," Skuld murmured. "Lots of bubbles!"

The two older Norns had remained at the table but had turned in their chairs to watch the proceedings.

"Now," the girl-witch ordered one of the swans, gesturing toward the pool. The bird dove in and disappeared under the water.

"What's he doing?" Archie asked.

She didn't answer, staring over the edge of the pool into the deepest part of the well. They all peered in, waiting for they-knew-not-what.

"Here he comes!" Jake exclaimed when the white outline of the swan became visible through the water. As the bird glided closer, they could see he was holding something in his beak.

A moment later, the swan burst up to the surface again, carrying the blue notions bag that Jake had thrown in.

This time, the bag held a small bulge that told him obviously something was inside it. How strange! Jake thought. The swan flew over to the railing of the platform, where Granny Wyrd took the notions bag from his beak. The swan and Red exchanged a hiss as the boys ran over to see what had materialized inside the bag.

Lo and behold, Granny Wyrd lifted a spool of peculiar-colored thread out of the bag. "Ahh, yes!" she murmured to herself, lifting it up. "This should do nicely."

When she held up her embroidery needle, the end of the magical thread flew out from the spool and darted through the eye of the needle, threading itself. Granny Wyrd didn't even have to touch the enchanted sewing needle; she merely held up her embroidery hoop and it did all the work.

Jake could hardly believe what he was seeing. By some mysterious enchantment, his whispered pain had turned into thread and was now busily weaving itself into the Norns' endless Tapestry of Fate.

He watched the needle duck and fly through the cloth, pulling the magical colored thread with it, filling in more of the picture.

Skuld looked askance at him. "That wasn't so bad, was it?"

"I guess not," he mumbled, though he did feel strangely exposed by having his secret sorrow—being separated from his parents—turned into a thread that everyone could see.

"Sorrows and mistakes make wisdom for the well," Verdandi explained. "It turns to thread, which we weave into the tapestry, where it can help others face their fates with what you've learned through *your* experience. Hopefully, as time moves on and wisdom gets absorbed, humanity will grow smarter."

"Progress?" Archie echoed, a favorite word among the scientists.

"There's more to intelligence than building new inventions," the Norn replied. She looked askance at Snorri. "Your turn."

The giant followed suit, then Archie concluded the same process. The pool bubbled; the swans retrieved the notions bags; and the magical thread popped out to weave itself into the ever-expanding Tapestry of Fate.

Soon, the three travelers all were feeling the same vague embarrassment at having their secrets exposed, even if no one looking at the tapestry could easily tell what they had whispered into the bags. But the mother-witch glanced at them with a knowing eye.

"If it didn't hurt a little, it wouldn't be a sacrifice," she said. "Just ask Odin."

Red's offering was the last to go into the Well of Wisdom, and when the thread came out, it was especially magnificent: scarlet with a sheen of golden sparkles to it, just like his feathers.

"There," Granny Wyrd whispered when the magical needle stopped. No sooner had she held up the tapestry to admire the newly filled-in sections of the picture, than all of a sudden, they heard a loud click from the direction of the Tree.

The mother-witch smiled broadly, and the girl-witch laughed. "There you go!" She pointed to Yggdrasil.

The travelers turned to look. Jake's eyes widened as a large door popped open at the ground level of the mighty tree-trunk.

Verdandi nodded toward it. "Go on. Yggdrasil has accepted your offerings. You may pass."

"Farewell, young heroes," Granny Wyrd said. "May Thor grant you a fair wind and safe travels."

"Goodbye," they said. "And thank you."

Skuld walked them over to the tree-trunk. Jake and Archie peered through the opening. "Go on. What are you waiting for? Step in. The giant will have to duck his head down," she added with a dubious glance at Snorri.

Jake and Archie exchanged a look of astonishment, but they shrugged their knapsacks back onto their shoulders and stepped into the creaky brass-and-iron elevator hidden inside the Tree.

"Come on, Red," Jake called. The Gryphon ran to him, prowling in to huddle by Jake's side. Red let out an unhappy sound, glancing around inside the dark hollow of the Tree.

"Am I going to fit in there?" Snorri asked, still outside the trunk.

"Sure. It's as big as a freight elevator in here," Archie reported.

But Snorri was still nervous. "I hope it can carry my weight."

"You're not the first giant to pass through here, you know," Skuld replied. "Though, of course, it's been centuries since the last time a giant stood on Midgarth soil... Never mind, you'll be fine."

Snorri bent down, ducking his head under the doorway in the

tree-trunk to step gingerly into the massive cylindrical elevator, a handsome cage of steel and brass.

"How do you Norns know about hydraulics, anyway?" Archie asked, looking around at it.

"Oh, you'd be surprised at the things we can see through the eye Odin left behind for us." Granny Norn reached into her sewing basket with a ruthless little smile and held up a blue human eye.

As the boys shrieked and grimaced at this gruesome prop, the girl-witch laughed and rolled the iron grate of the elevator's door closed. "Going up!"

She pressed a button made to resemble a knot in the wood, and the wooden tree-trunk door slammed shut.

Robbed of daylight, they could barely see one another, and at once, a deep, mechanical rumbling sounded from nearby—as if the elevator's working parts were hidden in the roots.

"Hold on!" Archie warned.

Jake clutched the iron bars of the cage-like door before him.

Then they all shrieked as the elevator rocketed straight upward into the dark hollow of the giant tree-trunk.

CHAPTER TWENTY-FIVE
In the Arms of Yggdrasil

Up and up the elevator shot through the darkness at top speed. They were still screaming when it finally reached the top and wrenched to a halt.

A bell went *bing!* Again, the tree-trunk door slid open.

Snorri let out a queasy groan while Jake and Archie scrambled to find the latch on the iron door-grate. At last, they hauled it back and stumbled out to freedom.

They found themselves on a huge, broad balcony made of polished planks with an intricate railing of branches around the edges. The platform itself hugged the trunk of Yggdrasil, encircling it like the crow's nest high up on the mast of an old pirate ship.

"Sweet cerebellum," Archie murmured in shock. He glanced at Snorri. "Is this Jugenheim?"

The giant shook his head dazedly, staring at the view. "No."

"Then where are we?"

Snorri shrugged. "Yggdrasil."

Jake slowly took a few steps forward, turning to look in every direction. He saw that the platform was built right beneath the tree's central junction, where the immeasurable trunk of Yggdrasil split into its two main branches, each as wide as roads.

Both had endless steps carved right into the bark of the tree; mossy, wooden arrow-signs pointed the way to the nine different worlds of Norse lore. Most of their names Jake couldn't hope to pronounce, but there was one he recognized: *Jugenheim.*

He pointed to the sign. "Look! Simple enough. We go that way."

The others turned to confirm it for themselves and were relieved by his discovery. Meanwhile, Red had crossed the balcony to the railing and summoned them over with an eager "Caw!"

They followed.

As Jake went to stand beside the Gryphon, he gripped the rough wooden railing in awe. *What a view.* From up here, you could see everything, almost to the edges of the earth. Gold skies and violet, both the sun and the moon were visible—one coming up, the other going down. Beneath them, the kingly Atlantic embraced the earth's blue curve.

Jake stared in wonder as the others stood beside him. Closer beneath them, the fjords and the forests were veiled by floating wisps of clouds. To the west, in the middle distance, they could see the familiar craggy coastline of Scotland and the Hebrides. To the southeast loomed the mighty Alps. "It's like we're sitting on the roof of the world."

"Can you imagine the flight I'd have if I launched off from here in the Pigeon?" Archie asked, staring rapturously at the horizon.

Jake frowned at him. "Don't even think about it."

The young inventor took out his telescope and they took turns peering through it for a while, until finally, it was time to go.

Between the viewing platform and tea-time with the Norns, they all agreed they'd had enough of a rest from their hike. The boys gathered up their gear once again, while Snorri shouldered the Pigeon. Red padded along after them as they followed the sign to Jugenheim and began their long march up the steps carved into the giant branch.

Jake held on tightly to the vine handrail as he climbed. Going higher into the canopy of Yggdrasil was fascinating. The grayish-brown bark armoring the tree looked as strong as slabs of stone.

Every green leaf was as big as the jib sail on a schooner, and the higher they went, the more the leaves rustled in the fair wind that blew in off the ocean.

The playful breeze made the boys nervous about being knocked off their feet and whirling to earth like giant winged seeds.

Fortunately, their gear helped weigh them down. Occasional glances through Archie's telescope revealed huge gates at the far ends of the main branches they passed; they realized the towering gates of stone and iron were the formal front entrances to the respective Nine Worlds.

Amazing, Jake thought. They labored on.

After a time, Jake noticed that Archie had started limping again, but no one suggested taking a break. Time was ever on the move, even for the Tree of legend; the light below was changing. The sun stretched its golden rays westward, and as it sank into the sea, the moon rose higher, shedding a romantic glimmer over the windswept coasts far below. Jake could see the stars sparkling like fairy lights among the branches, and rather regretted that Dani wasn't there to see it.

"I suppose all the scientists have made it back to the university by now," Archie remarked. He sounded slightly out of breath.

Jake felt pretty winded, too. The air was thin at this elevation. "I should think so," he answered. "Let's hope they haven't remembered anything they should've forgotten."

"And that the girls remembered to check on Miss Langesund."

"They won't forget," Jake replied. The carrot-head was reliable when it came to such matters.

They pressed on, and still, none of them mentioned the incident with the Norns. Clearly, no one wanted to talk about what they had whispered into Granny Wyrd's little notions bags.

Jake wondered about the others, but their secrets were safe from him. Fair was fair; he had no desire to share his own.

At last, they came to a small landing where the main bough split again into two slightly smaller branches. More stairs stretched up before them in either direction, but unlike the road-sized branch they had traveled so far, the two paths ahead were each only about as wide as alleys. Just two worlds were listed on the mossy finger-sign now: Asgard to the left, Jugenheim to the right.

"Now we're making progress!" Jake said, wiping the sweat from his brow. "Look at that!"

"Asgard!" Panting with exertion, Archie turned to Snorri. "Isn't that the home of the gods?"

"Don't *you* have posh neighbors," Jake teased.

Snorri nodded and craned his neck, peering upward. "Their world's up there in the highest branches of the Tree. I hear it's very nice, indeed."

"I suppose it would be." Jake paused to swig some water from his canteen, and the others followed suit.

When Red opened his beak expectantly, Jake spilled out some water into his pet's open mouth. Red gulped it down, then sat and waited for them in contentment. The Gryphon was the only one who did not look the least bit tired from their all-day hike.

Jake took a drink himself then wiped off his wet mouth with the back of his sleeve. "Looks like we're almost at Jugenheim." He gestured to the next bough, which tapered off into the distance.

"We don't need to go as far as the gates," Snorri said. "The hole I accidentally made should be right around here somewhere."

Jake nodded. "We'll keep an eye out for it, then."

"I hope this branch can hold me," Snorri said anxiously, peering ahead.

The alley-wide branch did look rather precarious for a person of his size, especially with the added weight of the Pigeon slung across his back. But Jake somehow managed a nonchalant shrug. "You should be fine," he said with more assurance than he felt.

If all else failed and the branch snapped under Snorri's weight, he vowed to himself he'd be ready to catch the giant by using his telekinesis. He hoped his powers were strong enough for that. He had never tried lifting anything so large. Hopefully, it wouldn't come to that. "Let's go. Er, after you," he said to Snorri.

If the branch broke under the giant, he did not intend to join him in his fall. Snorri blanched, understanding Jake's worry, then set one foot gingerly on the thinner bough.

It held without so much as a creak.

"Well, that's reassuring," Archie murmured to Jake.

A while later, the boys exchanged a grim glance when the branch tapered to the size of an ordinary footbridge.

"Don't worry, it'll hold," Jake repeated to calm the nervous giant, though he watched from behind with a wince as Snorri tiptoed forward.

So far, so good. Jake glanced back at Archie to see how he was faring; the boy genius adjusted the bandage around his leg, then trudged after him, leaning on his makeshift crutch.

Thankfully, they proceeded without disaster, though the night was growing darker by the minute.

And then—at long last—they saw a strange sight that heralded their arrival.

A distinct circle of sunshine lay across their path ahead.

Snorri pointed in excitement. "That's it! The hole I made when I pulled the boulder out of my meadow! This is where I fell!"

"You fell all this way and lived?" Jake asked incredulously.

Snorri crept out cautiously onto the branch to stand under the empty hole. With his face turned skyward, he soaked up the sunshine spilling down from his homeland.

Apparently, it was already daytime up in Jugenheim.

"Won't we *ever* get any sleep?" Archie asked, covering a yawn.

"Soon," Jake said.

Red crowed eagerly, pouncing into the circle of sunshine that broke the gloom. "Why don't you fly up there and have a look around, boy?" Jake said to the Gryphon. "Scout it out. Make sure it's safe and that nobody's coming."

"It should be quiet up there," Snorri said. "I live quite a ways from the village. They made me move farther out from everyone else because they say I snore too loud." He paused. "Sometimes it gets lonely. That's what I told the Norns."

Jake wasn't sure what to say to that. He nodded sympathetically. "Still, let Red go up first, just to make sure the coast is clear. We don't want to be seen sneaking in. Hopefully no one up there has found out yet about the seal between the worlds being broken. Go on, boy. Then come back and tell us what you see."

Red bobbed his head in agreement, then launched off the branch. He flew up through the hole in the earthen crust many yards above them and disappeared into Jugenheim.

They all waited anxiously until he returned a few minutes later, peering over the edge of the hole with a happy "Caw, caw!"

Jake nodded. "Looks like it's safe to go!" he told the others. "Come on back down here, Red! Archie and I need a ride up."

As the Gryphon flew back down and landed nimbly on the branch, Jake turned to Snorri. "Do you think you'll be able to pull yourself up there?"

The giant nodded. "You two go first."

"Good luck," Jake said, then he and Archie climbed on Red's back, exchanging a glance of excitement.

Then the Gryphon stretched his scarlet wings and took flight once more, carrying his breathless passengers up through the gaping hole into the kingdom of the giants.

CHAPTER TWENTY-SIX
The Rock In Question

Jake's heart pounded as Red burst through the hole in the rocky crust of the ground. As they shot toward the blue sky, the boys looked around in amazement at the landscape of Jugenheim below.

Snorri's farm sprawled beneath them—a pasture ringed by a gigantic post-and-rail fence. Everything they saw was about five times larger than in their world, so that Snorri's humble cottage was almost as big as Griffon Castle, the home Jake had inherited from his parents back in England.

"Look at the garden!" Archie cried, pointing.

The boys laughed incredulously at the size of the vegetables growing in the burgeoning garden beside the giant's cottage. The turnips were big enough that if one were hollowed out, it could have indeed served as Cinderella's carriage with no other magic needed.

"And the orchard!" Jake chimed in.

Apples as big as watermelons hung from the trees.

Meanwhile Snorri had gathered up his courage to leap off the branch of Yggdrasil, catching himself on the broken part of the earth's crust, where he dangled for a moment.

Jake looked over his shoulder and was relieved to see the giant puffing and straining, but successfully heaving his great bulk up through the hole.

Snorri hooked his elbows over the edge, and then carefully swung his right leg up onto solid ground. Jake grinned as the giant flopped safely onto his back in the grassy meadow from which he had originally fallen.

"Oh, it's *sooo* good to be home!" Snorri groaned in relief.

The boys laughed, then Archie pointed to the huge, rounded

boulder not far from the spot where Snorri lay. "I'll bet that's the stone he told us about!"

It was huge.

"You think he actually moved that thing?" Jake exclaimed.

"Sure looks like it," Archie said with a shrug, and he was right. The rugged, rounded shape of the boulder was a perfect fit for the outline of the hole in the ground.

The sooner Snorri got that hole plugged up again, the better— preferably before Loki found out about it and realized he could finally get into Jugenheim to start causing havoc.

Jake guided Red to land on top of the boulder in question. Snorri was lying inert in the tall grass, a dopey grin of exhaustion on his face.

For someone who had wanted to get as far away from home as possible, he certainly looked happy to be back.

"Up, you! No rest for the wicked!" Jake hollered down to him with a smile. "You need to roll that rock back into place!"

"Don't press it in too firmly, though!" Archie added. "We'll still have to get out of here soon."

"How soon?" Jake asked his cousin while Snorri let out a weary sigh before slowly lumbering to his feet.

Archie shrugged. "After we've had a look round, I guess. I told you, I've got to be back in three days."

Snorri set all his gear down and shrugged off the shoulder-strap by which he had been carrying the Pigeon.

He took a deep breath, rubbed his hands together as he approached the big rock, and furrowed his brow with a look of concentration. "Shoo," he ordered the boys, waving them off the boulder. "I don't need any extra weight on here."

"This I've got to see," Jake taunted the giant merrily. "Set us down over there, Red."

"How in the world did you move this thing in the first place?" Archie exclaimed as Red lifted off again, hovering nearby. "It must weigh ten, eleven tons! Did you use any tools for leverage? A spade or something?"

"Nope." The giant shook his head. "I was just angry. At Gorm."

"Whew! I don't think I ever want to see you angry, mate," Jake vowed.

"Don't worry," Snorri said with a chastened look. "It doesn't

178   E.G. FOLEY

happen very often. I'm usually quite calm."

The Gryphon flew down into the field and the boys got off his back.

The giant stared at the rock, sizing it up.

Jake and Archie stood in grass up to their chins while Snorri shrugged his shoulders to warm them up for his mighty task. He flexed his wrists, then he stretched his neck from side to side—at which it let out a series of ear-splitting pops.

The boys hollered in alarm at the noises, but the giant showed no signs of serious damage.

The boys began to cheer him on, chanting: "Go, go, go!"

The giant let out a loud grunt as he hurled his bulk against the ten-ton boulder.

It rocked. They shouted in astonishment, then whooped at their dull-witted companion's show of strength.

"Come on, Snorri! You can do it!"

"Do it for Jugenheim!" Archie yelled. "Keep your people safe from Loki!"

"Do it for Princess Kaia!" Jake teased.

Sweat burst out on Snorri's face, which had gone beet-red; his arms shook with exertion; strange grunts of effort escaped him; his boots dug deep into the turf as he drove all his weight against the boulder.

All of a sudden, it slammed into place.

Snorri sighed and fell into the grass again in exhausted relief. The boys applauded madly.

When the dust cleared around the spot where the boulder had rocked back into place, Jake nodded to his cousin to go and have a closer look with him.

Archie followed, shaking his head in wonder as the boys approached the towering stone. "I can see why Loki wants an army of these big boys," he remarked to Jake with a discreet nod at Snorri.

"Aye." Jake tossed his forelock out of his eyes. "You'd need them, going up against the god of war."

"And the god of thunder," Archie agreed. "Not just one god, but two. Father and son team, remember? Jake, do you think Odin and Thor are real, too?"

He shrugged. "I never would've thought Loki was, but I talked to him myself, so who knows? I don't think we can rule it out."

"I hope we don't run into them," Archie mumbled.

"Why not? Aren't they supposed to be the good guys?"

"Well, compared to Loki, yes. But that's not saying much, is it? I mean, any god such as Odin who welcomed human sacrifice is not one that I'm too keen to meet."

"Wait, what? The Vikings had human sacrifices?" Jake exclaimed, turning to him in shock.

"Oh, sure! Why do you think our poor ancestors in England were so terrified of them? Even what was left of the Roman Empire cowered from the Norsemen—and the Romans weren't exactly sweethearts themselves, what with throwing people to the lions and all. Didn't you see it in Dani's Norway book? The Vikings used to hang prisoners of war from their sacred oak trees once a year as an offering to Odin—to say nothing of their special punishment, known as the Blood Eagle."

"Blood Eagle? That sounds neat."

Archie looked askance at him. "You would say that."

Jake grinned. "Why? What's a Blood Eagle?"

"Oh, only the name of this nice little torture the Vikings used to save for their most valued prisoners. Captured enemy kings and such."

Jake lifted his eyebrow in question.

Archie leaned closer while Snorri continued recovering in the grass. "They'd take a knife, see," the boy genius confided in ominous tones, "and make two slits across the prisoner's back. Then they'd pull his lungs out through the slits—"

"*What?!*"

"As the prisoner took his last breaths, his lungs, still partly attached, would pump like bloody wings sprouting from his back."

Jake had stopped in his tracks and stared at him in horror.

"Well, you asked!" Archie said.

"That is disgusting!" he cried. "Who ever thought of that?"

Archie shrugged. "Just be glad the Irish monks rowed over to convert them and made them stop doing that sort of thing."

"Blimey."

"You can say that again."

Jake paused as a frightening thought struck him. "Didn't the Norns say the giants still live like the Vikings did, under the old ways? You don't think that means Blood Eagles, do you? Because if so, I'm thinkin' we should probably be, er, kinda careful around them. Not make them angry," he said uneasily.

"You think?" Archie drawled.

Jake scowled at him, but blazes. No wonder Snorri had wanted out of here. Shaking off the gruesome image of the Blood Eagle as best he could, Jake crouched down to inspect the seal of the earth around the bottom of the boulder.

Little chinks and crevices spiderwebbed the dry dirt around the base of the rock. When he knelt down to peer through a few of these tiny cracks, he could still see Yggdrasil and the starry sky below.

He straightened up again with a thoughtful frown. The seal wasn't perfect, but it was good enough for now, considering that he and Archie would still have to get out of here once they had warned the giant folk about Loki's scheme.

But after what his cousin had just told him about the Blood Eagle, Jake was suddenly not as eager about visiting the Norse giants as he had been before. He was rather annoyed with himself, actually. Why did he never look before he leaped?

As much as he longed to follow in his noble parents' footsteps, becoming a Lightrider, he was still only twelve, after all, whether he liked to admit it or not. He was still new at helping magical creatures in distress, but he scowled at the thought that he *did* seem to have a talent for getting in over his head.

This was remarkably easy to do in Giant Land, where everything was huge and tall. In fact, Jake realized he had just lost the short boy genius somewhere in the tall grass. He cupped his hands around his mouth and hollered, "Archie?"

"I'm here!" The giant blades of grass rustled and then parted. His cousin stepped back into view, much to Jake's relief. "I wonder if this is how Gladwin feels when she's spending time with us," Archie remarked as he rejoined him.

"Hmm, it's probably worse for her," he replied, considering that the average fairy was only about five inches tall.

Gladwin Lightwing, a royal garden fairy, had helped to reunite Jake with his relatives. She was small enough to hitch a ride, as she often did, in his breast pocket. It would have been funny to see her here in Giant Land, he mused. She would have seemed as small as a speck.

All of a sudden, the boys heard a deep, swift drumming that made the ground begin to vibrate, shaking them off balance.

"What's that?" Archie cried.

As Jake looked up, his eyes widened. "Move, we're going to get squashed!"

He yanked his cousin toward the boulder just as their first glimpse of the approaching animals loomed above the tall grass.

The boys dove aside, terrified, as a herd of sheep as big as elephants came running.

Woolly legs and enormous hoofs were everywhere. The boys pressed back against the boulder to avoid being trampled. But a moment later, Red flew down to rescue them, having seen the danger.

The boys scrambled onto his back, and the Gryphon instantly lifted away, angling clear of another massive sheep.

"Look at them all! They're huge!" Archie exclaimed as the trusty Gryphon flew them up to safety on top of the boulder.

Meanwhile, some distance away, Snorri had sat up from where he had sprawled happily in the grass. "Sheepies?" He shot to his feet to greet them. "My babies!"

The sheep crowded joyfully around their master, bleating and baaa-ing. The Jugenheim sheep were, of course, proportional to the giant.

"Chubs! Zero! Maxine!" He greeted them by name, petting and doting on them. "Oh, it's so good to see you! I missed you, too, poor little lambkins! I'm back now. Don't worry, Daddy's home..."

From their safe perch atop the boulder, Jake and Archie exchanged a startled glance.

"There, there," the giant continued, soothing his panicked flock. "It's all right. I'm back now, and I will give you carrots for a treat!"

"Poor Snorri!" Archie murmured as they watched the fierce-looking giant doting on his fluffy pets. "No wonder he wanted to leave Jugenheim."

Jake nodded in amusement. "He probably doesn't fit in here at all."

But on second thought, if Blood Eagles and general Viking ferocity were the norm around here, then maybe, Jake mused, they should be grateful for that.

CHAPTER TWENTY-SEVEN
Casa De Snorri

"**H**ome sweet home! Come in, little masters! Welcome to my humble abode." A few minutes after his joyful reunion with his sheep, Snorri flung open the huge front door to his turf-roofed cottage and beckoned his visitors in.

"Would you care for brambleberry tea?" he offered. "It's very refreshing."

"Why, thank you, that would be fine," said the gentlemanly Archie. He was satisfied with the spot where Snorri had stowed the broken Pigeon before they had come in. The flying machine awaited repairs in the garden shed outside.

"Brambleberry tea, Master Jake? I grew the brambleberries myself, grafted from wild ones. I admit I've got a bit of a green thumb," Snorri said cheerfully. He was obviously delighted to be home.

"Er, sure, I'll try it." Jake couldn't stop gawking at the gigantic furniture. The simple wooden table was easily fifteen feet high.

Before them stretched a braided yarn rug as wide as a lake. To the left loomed a massive stone fireplace, its rustic mantel as tall as an ordinary rooftop.

As Snorri shut the door carefully behind them, Jake shook his head at the huge boots tucked against the wall. They were nearly as tall as he was.

Stepping over the boys, Snorri hastened to put away a few bits of clutter lying here and there. "Pardon the mess. I'm not used to having visitors," he apologized. "Just an old bachelor, me."

Soon they had the brambleberry tea with a gob of Snorri's homegrown honey from his own beehive in the back.

Jake didn't even want to think about giant bees.

They were all exhausted from the day's long journey, in any case, and everyone was starved. Though the boys had their supplies to draw from, Snorri did not want to be seen as lax in his hospitality, for this was a point of honor with all the Norse people. He went outside and picked one of the apples as big as soup-pots from his orchard, and cut it up into pieces for the boys.

With his guests settled, Snorri bustled about preparing his own meal. It seemed the average giant required prodigious amounts of food for his dinner.

So, while Snorri cooked, humming to himself in front of his roaring hearth fire, the boys climbed up onto the footstool. Then, one by one, they took a daring leap across the gap, bouncing onto the cushion of the massive armchair.

The seat of the chair had about the same dimensions as their shared dorm room back at the University. It looked like the perfect place to get some sleep, as long as Snorri didn't forget they were there and accidentally sit on them.

Archie took off his coat and draped it over himself as he lay down on his side. "Nice and comfortable," he said, letting out a large sigh. "It feels so good to shut my eyes..."

With a yawn, Jake finally closed his eyes, as well. Red lay down protectively beside him, his eagle beak resting on his crossed lion-paws, his wings tucked against his sides, his tufted tail wrapped around his haunches.

As tired as Jake was, though, he found he couldn't fall asleep, pondering all the astonishing things that had happened today.

"I wonder if the girls have seen Henry and Helena yet," he remarked after a few minutes, but there was no answer from Archie.

He looked over and saw that the freckled boy genius was already fast asleep. He smiled wryly, but a few minutes later, he drifted off, as well.

About two hours later, voices from outside awoke him.

Blinking against the light of the evening sunset, Jake found that Red had not left his side. The Gryphon was awake, though, and listening; his small tufted ears were pricked up toward the window. Archie was still sleeping.

Before Jake could decide whether to ignore the noise and go back to sleep, the door to the other room opened and Snorri poked his head out, looking groggy and more rumpled than usual.

Having finished cooking and eating alone, the giant must have decided to get some sleep, too. Snorri noticed that Jake was awake, also, and nodded to him as he stepped out of his bedroom. The giant shuffled past the armchair where the boys were resting and crossed to the window. He moved the curtain aside and peered out.

"What's going on out there?" Jake whispered.

"Not sure," Snorri whispered back over his shoulder. "Bunch of my neighbors are standing out along the road. Looks like they're watching a parade or something."

"Maybe we'd better go see what's going on. Make sure this has nothing to do with Loki," Jake said.

Snorri glanced grimly at him. "Aye, maybe you're right."

Archie sat up rubbing his eyes. "What's going on, fellows?"

"Get up. We're leaving," Jake said, and relayed to him what Snorri had just reported. Both boys hurried to put their boots and coats back on.

Snorri returned to his bedroom and did the same.

He seemed worried when they rushed out of his cottage a few minutes later. "When you see my neighbors, be careful what you tell them," he advised. "If anyone figures out that you two are from Midgarth, that could be trouble for me."

"Well, what are we going to tell them?" Jake asked.

"It's obvious we're not giants!" Archie agreed as he threw his tool-bag over his shoulder and ran to keep up.

Snorri mulled the question. "Why don't we just tell them you're dwarves?" he suggested as they hurried across the fields toward the road.

"Dwarves?!" the boys exclaimed in unison.

The giant nodded earnestly. "We don't often see them in these parts, but at least dwarves are allowed in Jugenheim."

Before this matter was quite decided, they reached the country road that wound past Snorri's farm, and Jake and Archie stared in amazement at what they saw.

It *was* a sort of parade. Giant peasants watched, applauding, as towering giant warriors rode past on gigantic horses, heading for the vast Viking great hall in the distance.

The sunlight glinted on the passing riders' helmets or crowns. Seated on their gigantic steeds, with extra horses carrying their gear, they wore chain mail and rugged riding gauntlets. They looked like giant princes or royal knights on their way to a jousting tournament.

"Who are they?" Jake yelled to Snorri over the thunderous applause of the gathered crowd.

"I don't know. I'll see what I can learn," Snorri mumbled, then he shuffled off to consult his neighbors.

The 'dwarves' and the Gryphon followed warily. With all of the commotion of this impressive caravan arriving, nobody paid attention to such small creatures.

"Hullo, Petunia," Snorri greeted a massive, homely lump of a peasant giantess who was carrying a fat white goose in a basket. She wore drab, shapeless clothes in a vaguely medieval style. "What's all the excitement?" he asked her.

"Why, Snorri! There you are!" Petunia greeted him with a rap on the shoulder that would have been enough to knock down a tower back in Midgarth.

"She's a dainty thing," Archie whispered to Jake.

"Where've you been, boy? Nobody's seen you in days!" Petunia bellowed.

Snorri quickly feigned a cough. "Been a bit under the weather. Summer cold. The worst."

"Oh, sorry to hear that. Better now?"

"Aye. Used the chamomile growing in my garden."

"Just as you should!" she agreed. Then she cackled. "Why, poor thing! We all thought the reason nobody's seen you was because you'd heard the news and were in your cottage sulking!"

"I don't sulk," he said indignantly. "What news?"

"Oh, dear." Big Petunia hesitated. "If you haven't already heard, I'm not sure I should be the one to tell you, then."

"Tell me what?" he asked in alarm.

"You're not going to like it. I'm afraid it's Princess Kaia—"

He gasped aloud in horror. "Is she all right?"

"Of course, she's fine, lad! Though she's none too happy, I'd imagine. She's a headstrong one, that girl. Mind of her own, which always leads to trouble. I reckon now she knows what defying her father will get her."

Snorri stared at his neighbor lady in confusion. "Defying her father? W-what did she do?"

"Well, she refused to—" The giantess suddenly stopped herself with a guarded frown.

"Refused to what?" Snorri cried in alarm.

"No." Petunia clammed up with a stubborn shake of her head. "I'm keepin' my mouth shut. Only a fool would get in the middle of this. Nobody likes a gossip—especially when the talk involves Prince Gorm," Petunia added in a whisper.

"Gorm?" Snorri echoed, paling.

Petunia nodded shrewdly. "You were always a friend to the princess, ever since you two was babies. You should go and talk to her yourself."

Snorri had turned three shades of white at this cryptic news.

"What are you doin' with them dwarves?" the giantess suddenly asked him, eyeing Jake and Archie in suspicion.

"Oh—they're just visiting," he forced out.

Petunia squinted at Red. "What's that thing they got with 'em?"

"He's a gryphon, ma'am," Jake ventured.

She nodded, still looking rather skeptical about the strangers. "Dwarves, eh? Big feast tonight to welcome the visiting princes. Whole village is invited. You dwarves should come up to the great hall and sing us a few of your famous dwarf songs."

Jake and Archie stared at her, then exchanged a startled glance.

Fortunately, she lost interest and wandered off, now that the parade had passed.

When the boys turned to Snorri, he looked on the verge of panic. "I've got to go and see if Kaia's all right!"

"Are *you*?" Jake inquired.

"If anything's happened to her—"

"Now, now, calm down," Jake ordered. "Your neighbor said the princess is fine."

"Yes, it's just—I have this terrible feeling," Snorri forced out. He turned to face the distant great hall. "King Olaf has been badgering her to marry Gorm for months, like I told you. But Kaia doesn't like him. The King kept saying Gorm would be the best leader for the people after him, so she was sort of willing to go along with it. But then I went and told her she shouldn't have to marry that bully if she don't like him."

"Did you?" Jake asked, bemused.

"Aye, she don't need no Gorm. I said when her father dies that she could lead the people by herself. Well, she *could!*" he added pugnaciously. "She's smarter than ten Gorms and a whole lot braver than me. Brave as any warrior. She can fight—she can even read!"

"Yes, you mentioned that," Jake muttered.

"When I stood up in the great hall and told everyone that she could be Queen all by herself, everyone laughed at me. That's why I was so angry the day I pulled the boulder out of the sheep meadow and broke the earth." Snorri shook his head, looking slightly dazed. "What if she actually took my advice while I was gone and told her father that she's refusing Gorm? Now all those princes coming here...what if I've only made everything worse for her with my advice? Oh, why would anyone ever take my advice?"

"Now, now, let's not jump to conclusions before we have the facts," Archie chided.

"You're right." Snorri took a deep breath to calm himself down, nodding. "I must go and see her. Find out what's really going on." He turned toward the great hall. "Come on, dwarves."

"Hold on!" Jake called as Snorri turned to go.

The giant turned.

"You are *not* going to see the princess lookin' like that," Jake declared.

Snorri glanced down at himself in surprise. "Why not? What's wrong with me?"

"You're a mess!" He gestured impatiently at Snorri's dirty clothes. "She's a royal princess, man! You're going to have to do better than that. Especially now," he added. "Hate to say it, but I'm afraid you just got more competition for your princess than Gorm alone." Jake hooked a thumb toward the knights and princes who had ridden past.

Archie nodded in agreement. "At least wash your face so you don't show up smelling like a musk-ox."

Snorri looked taken aback at the boys' simple advice. "Kaia don't care about that stuff."

"Maybe she's just too polite to tell you," Archie said pointedly.

Jake gave a sage nod. "No girl likes a stinker, my large friend. Remember Isabelle's advice. Clean yourself up first, then you can go and see her. Trust us."

Snorri frowned, then sniffed his armpit and grimaced. "Maybe you're right."

The boys nodded, coughing at the cloud of odor that came down like a fog. Even the Gryphon looked revolted; Red covered his beak with the edge of his wing and gagged.

Snorri knew he was fortunate. Only a real friend would tell you the truth about something so indelicate.

The boys did not allow the gentle giant to leave his cottage until he had washed his face in his hands, changed into clean clothes, and brushed his teeth.

They told him to munch on a peppermint leaf to freshen his breath. He took a comb and a little scented oil and used it to smash his wiry few hairs down neatly onto his head.

In a much more presentable state, he now received their approval. So, at last, they all rushed off to King Olaf's great hall.

It was time to find out what exactly had happened here in Jugenheim while Snorri had been away in Midgarth.

CHAPTER TWENTY-EIGHT
A Little Madness

Meanwhile back in Midgarth, Dani sat with Isabelle at dinner that night in the banquet hall, watching people ribbing the "absentminded" scientists who had returned safely to the conference earlier that day.

Miss Langesund in particular held onto her father's arm as if to make certain the professor did not "wander off" like that ever again.

"Oh, I don't know what got into me!" he was saying. "It was such a beautiful evening last night, I suppose I got carried away and just strolled off into the woods!"

"He got carried away, all right," Dani remarked to Isabelle under her breath. "How can he not remember getting kidnapped by a giant?"

"The Oubliette spell is very powerful," Isabelle whispered back.

"Well, as it turned out, I wasn't the only one who had wandered off," the professor continued with a chuckle. "Lo and behold, there were all the others—just as lost as I."

"Ah, sounds like a fairytale to me!" Professor Schliemann teased his old friend, now that the two famous archeologists were finally reunited. "I'll bet the group of you were meeting out there in secret over some great new discovery you don't want the rest of us to know about yet!"

"Never!" he answered. "Honestly, we all just wandered off somehow." He patted his belly. "Fortunately our stomachs led us back to this fine dinner!"

"I can't believe you are making light of it after all you put me through!" Miss Langesund chided him. "Father, you have no idea what a fright you gave us all."

"Oh, come, daughter, you are a scientist as well. You know how easy it is to get wrapped up in your thoughts. Or perhaps you feared the trolls from your childhood bedtime stories had captured me in the forest and eaten me, eh?"

"Oh, Father!" she scolded while the other adults laughed. "I'll have you know the existence of trolls has never been *dis*proved," she added archly.

It was good to see her happy again.

Nevertheless, the girls stayed on their guard, scanning the huge dining hall for anyone who fit Jake's description of Loki in his mad prince form.

Of course, the Lord of the Shapeshifters could appear in any form he liked, but fortunately, Dani had the Lie Detector Goggles tucked away in the satchel with Teddy on her lap.

Admittedly, it was not good manners to bring a terrier to the dinner table. But she dared not risk leaving Teddy alone back in the room, for what if Henry and Helena returned to the dorm in their wild beast forms, forgot themselves, and accidentally ate her dog?

That would never do. Safer to keep her furry little friend with her. For now, however, there was still no sign of the twins, though the girls had watched and waited all day.

As for the boys, Dani knew she had to account for their absence somehow, so she told Miss Langesund that Jake and Archie had caught the same illness Henry and Helena had.

It wasn't as though she could tell the woman the truth: *"The twins have turned into animals and the boys are off on a mission to Giant World."* They'd lock her in the loony bin.

Well, she didn't like lying. But sadly, judging by what she saw through the Lie Detector Goggles, it seemed like everyone did it. She took them out for a quick, furtive glance around the room, on the hunt for Loki.

As she scanned the banquet hall, it was rather depressing to see the lies coming out of the mouths of so many adults around them. The majority of the lies were quite small and harmless, such as: "Oh, yes, I think your invention shows great promise," or "What a lovely dress!"

Isabelle suddenly nudged her. "What about that man over there? He looks rather shifty."

At once, Dani raised the Lie Detector Goggles to her eyes, praying no one noticed her in possession of a stolen artifact. She made a quick assessment of the beady-eyed man that Isabelle had pointed out. Then she shook her head.

"No tattoo," she reported, but just as she hid the goggles again, Teddy let out a growl.

The little brown terrier tensed. Dani followed her dog's gaze to a black-haired man in an opera cloak who had just come sauntering into the crowded banquet hall.

The mad prince!

Dani grabbed the Lie Detector Goggles, lifted them to her eyes, and peered at the man. She gasped when she saw the dark tattoo scrolled along his cheek.

At that moment, as if he felt her stare, he turned his head slowly and looked straight at her.

In a second, through the goggles' magnifying lenses, she saw his coal-black eyes turn as frosty as an arctic winter night.

Dani lowered the goggles in sudden terror. "He saw me." The one thing Jake had said was not to let Loki realize they were on to him. "Isabelle," she forced out, trying to sound calm. "We have to get out of here. Now."

"Is it Loki?"

"Yes. He looked right at me."

Teddy started barking madly as the girls shot to their feet. The dog's clamor earned Dani several disapproving looks and scowls from the adults at the surrounding tables.

"Bringing a dog to the table! Where does she think she is? Paris?"

Loki pivoted, tossing one side of his scarlet-lined opera cloak behind his shoulder, he started toward the girls with a look of wrath.

"Go!" Dani cried.

Isabelle was on her feet, rushing for the door, reaching back to grab Dani's hand to make sure they didn't lose each other. But when Dani glanced back over her shoulder, she saw that Loki had stopped chasing them.

The trickster god had halted in his tracks, staring at Professor Langesund.

Slowly he scanned the other returned scientists, a look of rage passing over his sharp features.

"Hold on," Dani murmured to Isabelle. "Something else has got his attention."

Isabelle paused.

The girls watched as Loki seemed to put it together in his mind, recognizing the scientists that the giant had abducted.

With a final warning glare at the girls, he seemed to decide they were not his top priority after all.

Though his cold look promised dire punishment to come, he abandoned the chase for now. Turning around, he headed for the row of doors on the other side of the banquet hall.

"Come on!" Dani tugged on Isabelle's arm. "Let's go see what he's up to!"

"Follow him? Dani! I'm not sure that's such a good idea—"

"Right. You stay here. You'll be safer inside. I'm going after him." Not waiting for her to protest, Dani followed Loki cautiously from several yards behind.

The trickster god marched toward the doors that led out onto the terrace overlooking the garden. When he disappeared outside into the night, Dani crept up to the edge of the doorway to spy on him.

Then she witnessed something she never expected to see.

There were a few adults out on the terrace chatting in small groups under the stars. Gentlemen smoking, ladies sipping wine. Loki strode out, ignoring them all, as if he was past caring who saw him. Halfway across the terrace, he turned himself into a crow right before their eyes and flew away with a piercing caw like an angry, mocking laugh.

Dani was left staring at the dark sky, slack-jawed and dreading to wonder where he was off to now.

* * *

Fool! That oversized nincompoop!

Loki could hardly wait to hear what excuses the bumbling boob Snorri would make to explain how the "brains" had escaped.

As the crow flies, it was only a few minutes up the mountain to the cave, and as he winged his way through the night, the annoyed god entertained several possibilities of what he might turn Snorri into to punish him for his incompetence.

Not permanently, of course. Just long enough to make himself feel better. Vent his frustration with his hapless henchman.

If this was a foretaste of what it was going to be like working with giants, he was not sure he had the patience. He was going to have to learn how to speak *slooooowly* and simplify all of his instructions until they were foolproof. Surely not all giants could be this thick, he mused. Unfortunately, for now, Snorri the Shepherd was the only giant available, so he supposed he'd just have to make do with the dunderhead.

But when Loki reached the rocky mountaintop where Snorri had made camp, he found the place deserted. The extinguished campfire was not a good sign. The ashes were long cold.

Landing on the mountain, Loki turned himself back into his usual human form, smoothed his clothes, and didn't miss a step, marching directly into the dark cave.

He held up his hand and caused a bright flame to appear on his fingertip, lighting his way into the pitch-dark tunnel.

But by the time Loki stepped into the large, rounded cavern, he confirmed in a glance that the place had indeed been abandoned.

Empty cages. No sign of Snorri.

He turned with eyes full of flaming rage, then tipped his head back and roared in frustration.

"By Fenrir's claws and the deepest depths of Neiflheim!" he cursed under his breath, and finally got his temper under control.

Snorri must have run away in terror after his failure.

So, where did he go? Loki mused as he sauntered back outside and stared up thoughtfully at the starry sky.

The answer came to him at once. No great mystery, really.

The frightened giant would've most likely gone running home to Jugenheim.

A cunning gleam came into Loki's dark eyes as he considered his next move. If he could catch up to the giant on his way home and follow him, then Snorri would unwittingly lead him to the place where Odin's seal between the worlds was broken—the hole where the big, lovesick dunce had fallen through. For if Snorri could get out, then that meant *he* could get in.

A sly smile curved his lips. Why, he might soon have his army of giants yet!

Of course, Odin and Thor would rage if they found out about his forbidden trespass into Jugenheim. But by then, it would be too late for them to do anything about it.

Yes...

Loki made up his mind. *Forget that idiot shepherd. I'll sneak into*

Jugenheim and find some other giant who'll cooperate with me. And it'll be a proper giant this time—the normal sort of giant—who appreciates a good brawl with mayhem and destruction.

With that, Loki turned himself into a falcon and soared through the air, heading for Yggdrasil.

Under the cover of darkness, he flew higher and higher; as a falcon, he could reach much greater altitudes than he could as a crow.

At the next mountain, he saw the Norns far below, weaving their tedious Tapestry of Fate by candlelight. The Wyrd sisters didn't see him. Even if they had, they didn't worry him. He outranked them. They were only witches, after all. Hardly a problem for a mighty Norse god.

Up and up he circled, finally passing the huge trunk of Yggdrasil and flying up into the canopy, weaving through the branches. His wings were growing tired as he passed the gates of world after world, following signs for Jugenheim.

Finally, when he was so exhausted that he could barely flap his sleek brown wings anymore, in the distance, he saw tiny pinpricks of light coming down from above, sprinkling the wide branch ahead of him.

With his last ounce of strength, he flew toward it.

He landed on the branch, panting through his little hooked beak.

What he saw when he looked up filled him with excitement. Little cracks and crevices surrounded the underside of a massive boulder.

So that's where the dunderhead fell out, he mused. *Then that's where I'll get in!*

One minor problem. The tiny cracks in the earthen crust around the boulder were much too small for a falcon to fly through.

Thankfully, this was no great obstacle for the Lord of the Shapeshifters.

Loki simply turned himself into a dung beetle and flew up to the spot where Snorri had broken Odin's seal between the worlds.

With his tiny insect feet, Loki-as-beetle gripped on upside-down to the crust of Jugenheim. Then he crawled over to the edge of one of the cracks around the rock.

Using his little black pincers as shovels, he got to work digging a way in. He couldn't wait to see the look on Odin's face on that sweet day of his long-prophesied victory, Ragnarok!

The day he, Loki, stormed Valhalla with his army of giants, cut off Thor's head, Blood Eagled the old man Odin, and burned the All-Father's white palace to the ground.

Oh, that day was coming.

At this very moment, he was closer than ever to bringing it into being.

When his destiny came to fruition, then *he* would rule as king of the gods in Odin's place. And instead of law and order, all the Nine Worlds would learn to enjoy...a little madness.

CHAPTER TWENTY-NINE
Princess Kaia-of-the-Yellow-Braids

King Olaf's rustic great hall stood at the center of the giants' medieval village. Made of mighty oak logs over stone foundations, it reminded Jake of a massive mountain ski lodge.

Archie discreetly clicked a photograph as Snorri led them through the village toward it. Along the way, the boys stared in amazement at all the towering peasants going about their business.

The place was bustling with activity as giant servants hurried to and fro, helping the arriving knights and princes get settled; they showed them to their quarters and led their towering horses to the giant stable.

Others—plainer folk—paid little mind to the visiting noblemen, but went on with life as usual: craftsmen and artisans, aproned butchers and blacksmiths going about their work, a farmer taking his vegetables to market in a huge cart pulled by two enormous oxen. A giantess with a cloth wrapped around her head was fetching water from the well. She cranked the handle, raising a bucket nearly as big as a bathtub.

Passing through the village, the boys felt in danger of getting stepped on by some careless passerby. With the constant earthquakes from so many giants' footsteps all around them, it was all they could do to keep their balance as they walked. Just when they were finally getting the hang of how to stay upright amidst all the shaking, a pack of giant children ran by, laughing and kicking a rounded boulder for a ball.

Once more, Jake and Archie climbed wearily to their feet from where they had sprawled on the ground, dusted themselves off, and hurried after their guide.

Snorri was already marching up the few front steps to the doorway of the great hall. The ironclad door was decorated with all sorts of interesting runes, knots, and old Norse designs that Jake was sure Miss Langesund would have loved to study.

A pair of giant Viking guards on duty flanked the door with spears like cedar trees in their hands, and shiny, horned helmets on their heads.

"Hurry up!" Snorri called back, waving the boys on.

Apparently, the guards were used to seeing him here, for they waved him through and nodded at his explanation of bringing the visiting 'dwarves' to meet the princess.

Archie gazed up at the steps they had to climb and sighed.

Jake smiled wryly. "Come on, I'll give you a boost," he told his shorter cousin.

The boys hurried to climb the steps. It would have been easier to fly up them on the Gryphon, but Jake had left Red back at Snorri's cottage for now, in the hopes of drawing less attention.

When they reached the top of the steps, they had to run to catch up to Snorri, who was already striding eagerly into the great hall ahead of them. He was obviously impatient to see the princess again.

Inside the great hall, the boys marveled at the manly, Viking space. Under a high, vaulted ceiling, the vast main room stood empty. Rows of long wooden tables and benches awaited the next meal. A huge stone fireplace yawned near the king's raised dais at the front of the room. Around them, the wood-planked walls were hung with all the round, decorated shields of the local warriors.

But the boys marveled most at the living oak tree growing up right through the center of the room. King Olaf had obviously built his great hall around it, just like the Norns had said—but there was no time to gawk at it.

Snorri beckoned them into a smaller room off the back, where Princess Kaia was working on her spinning wheel.

She hummed absently to herself while the wheel whirred and the wool yarn flew, spun finer and finer with each revolution.

When the boys arrived in the doorway, Jake studied the giant lady, bemused.

After hearing so much about her, he wasn't sure what he had been expecting from a Norse giant princess. Certainly, it was no surprise that she was, as they say, big-boned.

Very big-boned.

Sturdy and strong, muscular—the warrior daughter of a warrior king.

Instead of the yellow braids Snorri had told them about, however, she wore her long blond hair flowing rather wildly over her shoulders. Jake also noticed that, for some fine princess, she wasn't dressed all that differently from the Viking-styled peasant women outside. Just a little nicer.

The white long sleeves of her nightgown-like under-garment showed beneath her sleeveless blue wool kirtle—a gown of the same basic shape as the jumper-dresses Dani liked to wear.

The blue kirtle was pinned in place with a fine metal brooch at Princess Kaia's shoulder. Several layers of bright, beaded necklaces adorned her neck and chest, while the belt around her waist was hung with various items, including a mean-looking knife and a bunch of keys.

But despite the nasty weapon at her side, when their shepherd friend tapped on the side of the open doorway, the princess let out a girly gasp and jumped up from her spinning wheel. "Snorri! Where have you been?" she cried at once. "Oh, I was so worried about you! Come in, come in!"

As she rushed toward them, the boys backed away to avoid being crushed under her soft leather boots. Their lacings were as thick as Jake's arm.

Princess Kaia hadn't even noticed the 'dwarves.' She stopped and tilted her head, studying Snorri. "You look...odd."

"What?" Snorri turned bright red and glanced self-consciously at his clean, spiffy reflection in the square glass mirror on the opposite wall. "Uh, I do?"

"Did you fall in the river? You look...clean. Hmm! Well, never mind." She shook off the puzzle of his strange, sudden cleanliness. "I went to see you, and you weren't at your cottage!"

"You came to see me?" Snorri quite lit up.

"Where did you go?" she exclaimed. "No one was watching your sheep!"

Before he could manage to answer, she suddenly noticed Jake and Archie. "Oh, Snorri!" She turned back to her friend, clapping her hands with excitement. "You brought me dolls!"

"We're not dolls!" Jake said indignantly.

"You're not?" She bent down with an indulgent, knowing smile, as if the boys were two years old, not heroes sent to save the giant race. "Well, what are you, then, cute little thing?"

Jake's scowl deepened. This was too insulting.

"We're, er, we're dwarves, Your Highness," Archie spoke up. But as usual, he was the world's worst liar.

Princess Kaia narrowed her blue eyes and leaned closer, looming over them. She studied Jake and then Archie, in turn. "Oh, yes, you are dolls," she said. "I've seen dwarves and you don't look anything like them."

"We're dwarves," Jake replied.

"Then where are your beards? Dwarves always have beards."

"Uh, they're child dwarves. Just boys," Snorri said, but when she eyed him skeptically, he faltered. "Their beards haven't grown yet."

"I see. But then...where are your axes? Even a young dwarf ought to have an ax."

"We lost them?" Archie suggested.

Jake glared at him.

She frowned, rose to her full height, and folded her arms across her giant bosom. "Snorri, you had *better* tell me right now what is going on. You might be able to fool the others, but you can't fool me. If they're not dwarves, and they're not dolls, then what in Thor's name are they?"

"Snorri," Jake warned.

Snorri stammered helplessly. "I, um, well, y'see, it's just—"

"Oh, bother!" Princess Kaia lost patience and picked Archie up by the back of his jacket, holding him up toward her face to inspect him. "Now then," she said. "Who are you?"

"Please don't eat me, ma'am!"

"Eat you?" she echoed, suddenly glowering at him. "Are you calling me a troll?"

"Sorry-no—please, put me down!"

"Put him down!" Jake agreed, though it wasn't much good to yell at someone when you only came up to their knee.

"We're humans!" Archie blurted out.

She gasped and turned to Snorri. "Humans? From Midgarth?" she whispered, wide-eyed. "Is that where you went? The world of men? Snorri, how did you—how *could* you?" she stammered. "It's forbidden!"

"It was an accident, I swear! Please, you mustn't tell anyone!" he begged her. "Don't tell your father. I didn't mean to, honest!"

She put Archie down and shut the door quietly. "Tell me everything," she ordered.

And he did.

"...No one can find out about any of this. Especially not the breach between the worlds until it's fixed," Snorri finally concluded after explaining all that had happened since his disappearance. "Most of all, don't tell Gorm."

"You're right about that," she agreed. "Knowing him, he'll want to take his followers on a raid down to Midgarth straightaway."

"That's why we all have to say the boys are dwarves, so nobody will realize they're from Midgarth. Of course," Snorri added with a penitent look, "I didn't want to lie to you."

"For all the good it did you! I'm not a fool, you know," she retorted.

"Please, won't you help us, Kaia? If *you* say they're dwarves, then everyone else will believe it automatically, since you're the princess. Everyone always does as she says," Snorri told the boys.

"But why did you bring them here?" she asked.

"These boys are no ordinary humans!" Snorri answered. "They're wizards back in Midgarth—"

"No, we're not!" the two exclaimed in unison.

Jake scoffed. "Wizards!"

"Well, you are, of a sort. You can both do very unusual things." He turned to Kaia again. "I brought them here to help us fend off Loki. They're here to vouch for me, that everything I've said is true."

"Well, I believe you, Snorri."

He smiled bashfully. "Thank you, but we both know it's your father who's got to be convinced. So, now we've told you everything. Your turn. Tell us what's been going on around here. Who were all those warriors arriving on the horses?"

Princess Kaia sighed. "Perhaps you'd better sit down."

They did.

"Remember a few days ago in the great hall, when Father announced my betrothal to Prince Gorm, and you stood up for me and said I shouldn't have to?" The giant princess smiled at the boys. "You should've seen him. He was so brave! He told the whole village I shouldn't have to marry *anyone* against my will. He even said it to my father's face—which could have got him killed."

"Well, you shouldn't," Snorri grumbled.

"My father's heart nearly stopped at such defiance. And poor Snorri, all the warriors howled with laughter at him for saying such a thing. But you know," she added, "those words got me thinking… That's why I came to your cottage to talk to you, Snorri."

He ventured a glance at her.

"You were right! Why should I have to marry Gorm, just because he's been kissing up to my father? That boor! He doesn't care about me. He just wants to be king. So," she continued, "I talked to my father about my feelings, and for a moment, I almost thought he was listening." She let out a large sigh. "But instead of letting me inherit the crown by myself, Father came up with this horrible idea of a contest."

"A contest?" Jake echoed.

"For my hand in marriage!" she burst out angrily. Then she jumped up and paced. "Have you ever heard of anything so humiliating? Now I'm even worse off than before! Just a *prize* in this stupid competition for feats of strength and daring!" She shook her head, rolled her eyes, and pushed her hair behind her ear. "That's why all the foreign knights and princes have come. And my father will be lucky if I ever *speak* to him again," she finished with a huff.

Snorri's face had gone ashen.

"Uh, maybe we could talk to him for you. Your father, that is," Archie offered. "After all, our country back home is ruled by a woman. Queen Victoria!"

"That won't work. We're supposed to be from Dwarf Land, remember?" Jake reminded him.

"Oh, right…"

"Whatever happens, Your Highness," Jake said somberly, "you need to be aware that Loki's out to gain control over your people. That's the main reason I wanted to come here and personally warn the giants that the threat from the trickster is real."

"Don't worry. I will protect my people," she replied, a fierce Viking gleam came into her eyes. "No matter who I'm forced to marry, that Loki with his dirty tricks will never get through me."

"What a woman," Snorri breathed. Then he froze, as if he had not intended to say it out loud.

When the boys laughed at him, the lovelorn giant turned red and stared at his toes.

Princess Kaia chuckled.

"Come on, Snorri!" Jake stood up and clapped his hands together, inspired. "Time to go."

"Where?"

"We've got to get you signed up for this contest, of course!"

"*What?*" The giant shepherd sat bolt upright, his eyes widening. "Me?"

"You heard me," Jake replied. "You must enter this contest, Snorri, and it's imperative you win. I don't want Loki getting a crack at any of those mighty warriors, or it'll be doomsday for us all."

Snorri broke out into a sweat, nervously glancing back and forth from Jake to Kaia.

In truth, the great oaf was the last person in the world that the fate of the world should ever have to rest on, Jake reflected. But Snorri was too caught up in embarrassment over what this could mean for his friendship with Kaia to remember what was at stake.

No big thing, just the end of the world.

"Y-y-you wouldn't have to marry me i-if I won, of course," he stammered. "I would never make you. That is, y-y-you could be free." He suddenly turned away. "Oh, this is the stupidest idea!"

"Why?" Archie asked.

"Me, win? Against all those shiny knights and princes?" Snorri threw up his hands in dismay and only managed to knock a decorative shield off the wall. "Sorry." He bent down to pick it up, fumbling as he hung it up again. "Never happen! Not in a million, chillion years."

"There's no such thing as chillion," Archie said.

"You could win, with our help," Jake declared, while Kaia kept mysteriously quiet. "We could be your coaches, like. All those warriors brought helpers and advisers."

"But I'll be a laughingstock! It'd be the joke of the year! Stinky old musk-ox me against all those heroes?" Poor Snorri was practically hyperventilating at what they were asking him to do.

"We all make fools of ourselves over something," Jake said in a philosophical tone. "Might as well be for a good cause."

"He's right, Snorri," Archie encouraged him. "Do you want Her Highness to be forced to marry someone else?"

Princess Kaia gazed at her devotee with her big, blue eyes. Snorri stared back.

"W-w-well, of course not," he said with a gulp.

She smiled. "You're awfully brave, Snorri. You'd really do that—risk yourself—for me?" the princess asked softly, and if there was any doubt, at that moment, Snorri was a goner.

He gave her a miserable look like a doomed man, but nodded. "Why not," he said with a sigh.

"Excellent! Come on, then, you big oaf," Jake ordered. "Let's get you signed up for the contest and figure out how you're going to win this thing."

"You heard the dwarves." Kaia sent her hapless friend a pitying smile. "Thank you, Snorri," she added as they headed for the door. "See you at the feast tonight?"

He nodded again, forcing a smile. But as the boys led him off to sign up for the contest, Snorri walked out like a prisoner headed for the gallows.

CHAPTER THIRTY
The Giants' Feast

Later that night, a gigantic pig turned on a spit over a raging bonfire. King Olaf himself hosted the feast to welcome all the visiting knights and princes before kicking off the great tournament tomorrow morning.

The whole village had turned out to join in the festivities, and the boys marveled at everything they saw.

The music was deafening, and the earth shook as numbers of the giants danced in rings. Everywhere the warriors drank mead and boasted back and forth. In one corner, the visiting princes arm-wrestled. In another, brawny knights took turns sharpening their weapons on an iron rod. Sparks flew as metal honed metal.

The giant children, each as tall as pillars, listened to a giant bard telling stories about the gods. Jake and Archie exchanged a wry glance to hear him tell of the rollicking adventures of the on-again, off-again pair of friends/enemies, Thor and Loki. It was no mystery which was the favorite of the populace.

Jake wondered if Loki might be motivated in part by jealousy of the red-haired thunder god. Thor was everyone's hero, but the children booed when Loki's name was mentioned.

Archie snapped pictures here and there with his miniature camera. They spotted Princess Kaia dancing with the others—and Snorri trying hard not to stare at her.

They also got their first look at King Olaf, an extremely manly Norse chief with a snowy beard and a shock of white hair beneath his rugged iron crown. A dragon brooch clasped the ends of his red cloak at the shoulder.

An imposing figure, he was accepting the compliments of the

visiting princes, who lifted their drinking horns to him with many a toast. The boys heard him telling the foreign visitors a little about the contest ahead. "There will be three parts to our tournament: a test of strength; a test of courage; and a test of wits."

"That last one should be interesting, under the circumstances," Archie mumbled.

Jake smiled wryly at him.

"The last man standing after all these deadly challenges will have proved himself worthy to marry my daughter and inherit my crown," King Olaf declared. "Not that I'm in any great hurry to be rid of either!"

The princes laughed at his jest, and the boys moved on, taking care to avoid getting stepped on. Archie was nearly drenched when one of the giant knights sloshed mead from his drinking horn above them. Jake saw it coming and yanked him out of the way just in time, otherwise, his cousin might have drowned under the cascade.

Snorri must have seen the near-miss, too, for he came running over. "Are you all right, Master Archie? I can't have anything happen to my coaches!"

"I'm all right, thanks." Archie nodded and dried his spectacles.

Jake was about to challenge Snorri to ask Princess Kaia to dance when a fierce-looking, dark-haired giant came swaggering over to them.

His eyes shone aggressively, and Jake suspected he had already had too much ale to drink. "Well, if it isn't the village idiot! So, shepherd—" The towering warrior paused to let out a mighty burp, punching himself in the chest to force it out. "I hear you've entered our contest."

Snorri backed away from him a little. "Hello, Gorm," he said warily.

Gorm propped one huge fist on his waist and clapped Snorri as hard as possible on the back in what was supposed to look like a friendly greeting. "You do realize, dolt, that I'm going to crush you, right? To be honest, I'm really looking forward to it."

"Leave him alone, Gorm!" Kaia came marching over and stood between the two. She must have seen the trouble brewing. "Snorri can enter the contest if he wants to!"

Gorm scoffed. "He has no chance of winning, but just suppose he did. Think of your future, married to this buffoon!"

"You're the buffoon!" Snorri answered.

"What did you say?" Gorm demanded, moving toward him.

Kaia stopped him, planting her hand on his armored breastplate. Gorm glanced down at her in warning. "It's cruel of you, letting your stooge do this for you, Kaia. He's just going to get humiliated again and probably killed. All the feats are dangerous. But perhaps our fearsome shepherd isn't worried about dragons?" Gorm taunted, staring past her at his rival.

Archie looked at Jake, wide-eyed. "Dragons?"

"Blimey," Jake whispered in anticipation.

"Even I don't relish going into those woods," Gorm said in an ominous tone, gazing at Kaia. "But I shan't hesitate, my love. Because you're worth it."

"Ugh," she muttered.

Gorm flashed a smarmy grin. "I know you think I'm angry about your refusal to marry me and your father's notion of this silly contest, but you're wrong. I don't mind a bit. I'm not afraid to *earn* you. By the time it's over, you'll come to your senses and realize I'm what's best for you *and* for Jugenheim."

"No, you're not," Snorri said with that same pugnacious look on his homely face that Jake remembered from the cave.

Once more, Gorm reacted accordingly. "What did you—"

"Gorm—save it," Kaia ordered. "Snorri, don't bait him."

Snorri glared and stayed silent, while Gorm managed a wolfish smile. "As you wish, milady," the warrior said, flicking a derisive glance at his foe. "I suppose you're right. There's no real harm in letting him participate. We could always use some comic relief."

As Gorm swaggered away, Kaia grabbed Snorri's arm. "Don't let him get under your skin. Come, dance with me!"

Snorri looked terrified of this order, but there was nothing the boys could do to save him as she cheerfully dragged him away for a dance.

Meanwhile, Jake and Archie could hear Gorm talking to his wild Viking henchmen in the corner. "Now, tomorrow, when the contest starts, I want to hear you cheer for me. It's important the people see that I'm the clear favorite. We need to get the people on my side against the others. It's a mental advantage." He pointed shrewdly to his temple, and the big brute warriors all nodded with dawning understanding.

"All right, Gorm, we'll cheer!"

"Good," he said, looking around at all of them with a cold nod. "After all, why should we let one of these foreign strangers come in and marry our chieftain's daughter? Become our next king? I think not."

The warriors shouted agreement, pounding on the table.

"She belongs with one of us," Gorm said, "and I'm the obvious choice."

"Aye!" they said again.

"Why would the king insult you like this, Gorm?" one of his followers said cautiously.

"Ahh, it's not the old man's fault. It's Kaia's doing, but don't worry. She'll learn to do as she's told and mind her place when she's my wife. As for His Majesty, why, he probably went along with it just to test my mettle. See if I'm really worthy. But I know I am, so I don't mind. I enjoy the challenge. So great a prize should not be won too easily. Believe me, if I was angry about it, you'd know," he added with an ominous laugh.

"Right, Gorm, nobody wants to see you angry, Gorm!" his followers nervously assured him.

Jake and Archie exchanged a worried glance while Prince Gorm held out his cup for someone to go and refill it.

"Let's just get this contest over with, and later, once I'm king, we'll see about expanding our people's territory. This land is getting too small for us. Why should we not lay claim to other kingdoms? It will be like the old days of our ancestors, sailing off to distant lands— plunder and pillage!"

"Good times," they said.

"That's right! Stick with me, lads, I'll make you rich!" he promised. His followers let out a hearty cheer, and Prince Gorm lifted his chin proudly.

As the boys watched from a safe distance, Jake knew in his bones that Gorm would do whatever it took to win.

He was mulling over how to make sure Gorm didn't cheat during the tournament, when all of a sudden, Jake was lifted off his feet without warning.

"Look! Dollies!"

He let out a yelp as a giant little girl lifted him high in delight. "Hello, nice doll! What's your name?"

"Put me down!" He kicked and struggled to no avail as the ten-foot-tall six-year-old giggled happily and hugged him.

"Help! Archie, do something!" he bellowed, muffled against her shoulder as he kicked. "Put me down!"

Archie, curse him, was trying not to laugh.

But then, the wee girl's big (very big) sister ran over to investigate. She was slightly older, maybe eight or nine.

She bent down a little, resting her hands on her knees as she beamed at Archie. "Oh, look at the cute little gnomes!" the second giant girl cried.

Archie backed away.

"Don't be afraid! I won't hurt you, little gnome!" she said sweetly.

"I'm sorry, miss, we're not gnomes and we're not dolls, either. Would you please tell her to put my cousin down?"

"But what are you, then?" the older one asked.

"Obviously, we're *dwarves!*" Jake bellowed when the smaller one let him up for air.

"Did someone say dwarves?" A third giant youngster joined them presently—a boy this time, about Jake's age—probably their brother, judging by the family resemblance.

The minute Jake saw the mischievous gleam in the giant boy's eyes, he knew this one was trouble.

"Look, everyone!" the giant boy called to the other children. "Dwarves! Ho, ho, you know what that means?"

"*Dwarf tossing!*" the other children cried. "C'mon!" they shouted to each other. "Peter's found a dwarf!"

Peter laughed heartily, lifting Archie off the ground.

"Help!" he cried.

"Put him down!" Jake warned, pushing against the giant girl's two-handed grip around his waist to free himself.

"Don't worry, you'll be next!" Peter boomed merrily as his friends ran over to join the fun.

"Higher, higher!" the children chanted as Peter began tossing Archie into the air like a ball and catching him again.

"Noooooo!" his cousin pleaded.

They ignored him.

Well, Arch, Jake thought, watching in dismay, *you wanted to fly. Here's your chance.*

"Go over there!" Peter waved one of his friends a few yards off. "I'll throw him, you catch."

"You'll kill him!" Jake protested.

"No, we won't," Peter said while his chum ran off, laughing, and got into position to catch Archie.

"Please don't do this," Archie was begging them.

"Ready?" the giant boy called to his friend.

The friend waved. "All set!"

Peter began swinging Archie. "One... two..."

Thankfully, Kaia heard the "dwarves" screaming, for she was already running toward them, leaving Snorri dancing by himself. "Children! Stop that at once!" she ordered—but she was too late.

For at that precise moment, Peter let go of Archie, hurling him into the air.

"Ahhhhhh!" he screamed, his arms and legs pin-wheeling as he soared through empty space, this time, without the help of any flying machine. *"Hellllp!"*

He landed abruptly in a soft place: Princess Kaia's bosom, where he bounced once, then fell, vanishing with a yelp down the front of her giant dress, through no fault of his own, of course. The princess also shrieked as if a spider had dropped into her clothes.

She had meant to catch him, but not like that!

A moment later, Archie's head popped up like a baby bird in a nest. "Jake?" he whimpered, gasping for air. "Help?"

The giant children roared with hilarity and even Jake had to hold back laughter. The proper young English gentleman was perfectly mortified. Poor Archie didn't know where to look. He held up his hand to shade his eyes from things he ought not to see. "Oh, I'm so sorry, Your Highness!" he stammered.

Princess Kaia plucked him out of the front of her dress, frowning sternly at the giant children. "It's all right, Master Archie. It wasn't your fault," she said, striving to regain her royal dignity.

She set him back down gently on the ground, then pointed sternly at the giant little girl, Jake's captor. "Anna, put him down! Children, that was most uncalled for. Peter, all of you, leave the dwarves alone. They are our guests! We must treat them with respect. If you bother them again, I'll have your parents take you home to bed."

Jake and Archie huddled together mistrustfully as the giant children mumbled their apologies.

"That's better," Kaia said, hands on hips. "Now run along and stay out of trouble!"

"Thank you," Jake said to the princess while Archie leaned against him like he might pass out. "Are you all right, coz?"

Archie just looked at him like he might never get over it.

To make things even more humiliating, the boys now realized that the king himself had seen the whole thing and had gotten a good, merry laugh out of it.

King Olaf came sauntering over, still chuckling. "You must forgive our children, master dwarves. Giant younglings are known to be especially high-spirited."

The boys managed to bow to him, though they were barely up to the mighty giant's knee. "It's all right, Your Majesty," Jake offered. "No harm done."

Archie's low whimper told a different story, but only Jake heard it. He elbowed his cousin and muttered out of the corner of his mouth, "Pull yourself together! It's the King of the Giants!"

"They were huge. They were all around me," he croaked.

"Shrug it off! You'll be fine," Jake whispered.

"We are honored to have you for our guests!" King Olaf continued. "Perhaps you would favor us with some dwarven music? Your people are renowned singers. Would you do us the honor of sharing some of your songs from your land with our guests?"

Jake and Archie froze at this request.

"Sing? In front of all these people?" Archie blurted out, still traumatized by the dwarf-tossing incident.

Jake was even more eloquent. "Uh…"

When King Olaf's shaggy white eyebrows drew together at the boys' hesitation, they realized it wasn't *really* a request. More like an order.

"Right," Jake forced out with dire thoughts of being Blood Eagled for such disobedience. "Of course, sire. Of course we'll be glad to sing for you. It would be an honor."

The towering king of the giants looked satisfied. He nodded to a servant, who picked the boys up one by one much more respectfully than the children had and set them on one of the picnic tables.

Surrounded by their Norse giant audience, the boys looked at each other in absolute terror.

Jake's mouth was so bone-dry with fear he could hardly speak, let alone carry a tune. "Can you start?"

Archie shook his head, his eyes stark and wide. "I have a terrible voice. It cracks."

"Me, too." Jake swallowed hard, his heart pounding. "But we have to, or we're dead. We have to make them think we're dwarves. Humans aren't allowed here, remember?"

Both breaking out in a cold sweat, the boys glanced at each other in panic.

Jake gulped and looked back at the king. "We're not really very good singers, sire, c-compared to our, our countrymen back home."

"No matter. You will find us a tolerant audience." The king sat down and waited for them to sing.

Blimey. Jake couldn't think of a single song.

His mind was a blank.

The king tapped his jeweled fingers impatiently on the arm of his massive wooden throne.

"I can't do it," Jake breathed, totally frozen with stage-fright.

Archie somehow found the courage to come to the rescue. He took a small step forward and cleared his throat.

Jake turned to him in desperation.

"Ahem." He began rather pitifully, his voice quavering and thin as he attempted an all-too-familiar song. "Row, row, row your boat gently down the stream. Merrily, merrily, merrily, merrily, life is but a dream."

Jake closed his eyes for a second in soul-deep relief. It was better than nothing. Apparently, it was the only song Archie was able to think of under the pressure. It seemed new to the giants, who listened intently.

Jake forced himself to join in on the second repetition.

Gorm let out a rude snort of laughter when Archie's voice cracked, but now the two cousins were determined. Joining forces, they sang louder.

On the fourth time through, the king began to clap in time with the song, and all the princes quickly followed suit, hoping to win the King's favor.

Encouraged—or at least able to breathe again—Jake suddenly remembered it was customary to sing this nursery song as a round.

As Archie continued singing the main line, Jake paused, waiting to come in on the second phrase of the song. The giants ooh'ed and ahh'ed at the tune sung in round form by the two boys, and applauded as the song continued.

Jake gave Archie a meaningful nod, then he walked down the table waving his arms at the left half of the audience, signaling to them to join in.

Even Snorri had quickly memorized the words—easy enough for a giant. Once the shepherd started singing, all the giants on the left began to sing along.

Archie had realized Jake's intent, and pleased with the notion, likewise, moved down the table and motioned to the giants on the right.

Kaia helped him, leading the other group in singing. Her half caught on and joined in, carrying the second line of the round.

"Row, row, row your boat, gently down the stream..."

"Row, row, row your boat, gently down the stream..."

"Merrily, merrily..."

"Merrily, merrily..."

"Life is but a dream."

"...Dream. Row, row..."

All the giants were singing now. The children had leaped up and were holding hands, dancing around in a ring.

The night boomed with the happy tune, until finally, the laughing audience exploded in thunderous applause. The noise reverberated so loudly that the other Eight Worlds all probably thought a storm was coming.

Which it was, Jake thought, with Loki's scheme never far from his mind.

Now that he had gotten to know the giants a little better, he was all the more determined to stop the trickster god from manipulating these large but simple folk into helping him bring on the end of the world.

And the best way to do that was to make sure Snorri won this tournament, married the princess, and inherited the crown.

All their worlds depended on it.

PART IV

CHAPTER THIRTY-ONE
The Boulder Contest

The next morning, the tournament began with a test of strength. Colorful pennants snapped on the breeze and drums rumbled, adding to the excitement. All the giant peasant folk came out to watch. They gathered in the fields outside the village around the biggest hill nearby—a great, green mound known as Jotmar's Head.

Along the bottom of this hill, the ten contestants lined up, each with a large, rounded boulder placed in front of him.

On the top of the hill stood Kaia, holding up a flag.

The Master of Ceremonies, a balding, pompous official in long robes, explained the details to the contestants. "You must carry your boulder up the hill. It's a race, gentlemen! Whoever is the first to reach Her Highness at the top and take the flag wins this challenge. Whoever comes in last will be eliminated before the next test. Secondly!" he continued. "You must retain control of your boulder at all times! If you drop it, you must start over again at the bottom of the hill. And furthermore, any player who does not have his boulder in his arms when the contest ends will also be eliminated from the tournament. Those are the rules of our first challenge. Simple enough, I trust. Any questions?"

There were none.

The giant knights and princes each turned to consult briefly with their coaches and advisers. Snorri, likewise, turned to the boys.

Archie squinted against the morning sun, studying the angle of the hill. "Watch out for those gopher holes. There are a few patches of mud around the bottom of the hill, too, where your footing could get tricky. And you're going to have the sun in your eyes."

"Is it just me, or does my boulder look bigger than everyone else's?" Snorri asked in dismay.

Jake hesitated, not wanting to upset him, but it did seem true. "Don't worry about it. You can do this," he assured him. "Just make sure to keep a good grip."

"Slow and steady wins the day," Archie added.

"He's right. Don't pay any attention to what anyone else is doing," Jake advised. "Just focus on your own race."

Snorri absorbed all their advice with a nod, then tried a few different holds on his massive rock to find the best way to pick it up.

Other giants all down the row were doing the same.

Gorm was glancing around at his competition with a cunning smirk. He seemed to be planning something.

Then the Master of Ceremonies blew the horn, calling the contestants to attention.

It was time to begin.

"Good luck, Snorri!" the boys called, backing away. Snorri gave them a resolute nod.

"On your mark," the Master of Ceremonies intoned. "Get set...!"

The giants picked up their boulders.

"Go!"

A loud horn blew and, suddenly, all the giants were in motion.

The ground shook as they rushed across the green field in a pack. The boys struggled to stay upright in the earthquake of their pounding footsteps.

As the pack moved farther away, Archie took his telescope out of his tool-bag and held it up to his eye, then passed it to Jake.

Snorri had a good grip on his boulder, Jake observed, but unfortunately their large friend was already behind.

The boys watched in concern, realizing only now that they had failed to warn him about how the *other* giants might behave.

For example, if the contestants could manage to knock each other out of the competition by making one another drop their boulders, that was perfectly allowable within the rules.

Snorri *was* going a bit slower than his rivals, but maybe, Jake thought, that was for the best. His lagging behind spared him from getting caught up in the melee of giants trying to bash each other out of the competition as they ran.

The giants in the lead were ramming each other with their shoulders, tripping each other along the way as they heaved their huge stones up the hill.

The peasants cheered wildly for their favorites. King Olaf was clapping and hooting for Gorm; in fact, rumor had it the King had wagered a fine sum of gold on Gorm to win.

As the hill grew steeper, each contestant had to work harder. The competitive knights and princes were growing desperate to win.

Jake could just imagine how all this must look from Princess Kaia's viewpoint. A dozen red-faced, heaving giants marching up the hill carrying boulders as big as carriages. Seeing them all rushing toward her must have been a slightly terrifying sight.

Prince Gorm was in the lead, but Jake peered through the telescope and saw one of the visiting knights pull even with him. The two were neck and neck.

Gorm glanced over angrily. Of course, he was not about to let anyone get ahead of him, so when his rival started to inch into the lead, Gorm stuck out his foot and tripped him.

The other giant roared and went down with a crash, dropping his boulder.

Jake and Archie gasped as the great rock began rolling back down the hill, plowing into other contestants, knocking them aside like gigantic bowling pins, and causing them to drop their stones, in turn.

Snorri was still marching along at the back, slow and steady, as Archie had advised. But in the confusion of loose rocks rolling by, and angry knights and princes chasing after them, he managed to pass several of his rivals.

The boys cheered to see he was no longer in last place.

The giants who had dropped their boulders in the chaos had to chase their escaping rocks downhill and start over again from the beginning.

But suddenly, catastrophe loomed.

A massive boulder that had gotten away from one of the players was rushing down the hill, heading straight for the group of giant children.

The giant boy, Peter, and his friends and his little sisters were off playing apart from the main crowd of spectators. Engrossed in having their own junior version of the contest, they were not paying the slightest attention to the danger barreling down on them.

Directly in the path of the oncoming boulder, they were going to be smashed!

Jake saw Snorri hesitate as he, too, noticed the danger. The path ahead of him to the hilltop and a possible victory was finally clear. From being in last place, he suddenly had a shot at winning!

But as Snorri looked over at the giant children in jeopardy, he couldn't help himself.

One of the giant mothers screamed, spotting the disaster about to take place—but she was too far away to help.

Her scream jarred Snorri into action.

Jake and Archie stared in amazement as Snorri turned and ran, carrying his boulder sideways across the hill rather than straight up the slope toward Kaia.

He ran faster than they ever would've thought he was able to; and *because* he was in the back, he was able to block the path of the approaching boulder before it struck the giant kids.

He arrived just in time a few feet in front of the rolling rock to plant his own boulder squarely in front of the oncoming one.

The two rocks collided, and the impact was so great that it shattered both of the great stones. Snorri threw up his arm to shield his face from the hail of gravel.

Pebbles rained down over him—all that was left of his boulder—plus a few fist-sized chunks.

"He saved them!" Archie exclaimed. "But what's he going to do now? How can he finish the contest?"

Jake shook his head grimly. "I don't know," he murmured.

"He's going to be eliminated," Archie said in worry.

Snorri seemed nonplussed. He looked at the ground, unsure of how to proceed, nor did he seem to hear the villagers cheering for him. He started picking up the pebbles and chunks and putting them in his hand so he could at least *try* to continue the contest.

Unfortunately, it was already over. Gorm had won.

Setting his boulder down at the top of the hill, Gorm snatched the flag out of Kaia's hand and held it high, waving it back and forth like a proper champion.

But because of the wind's direction and his distance up the hill, it took a few seconds for him to hear the villagers booing him.

His arrogant grin faded as the sound reached him.

"Boo! Cheater! Look what you did, look at the trouble you caused!"

"We all saw you! Those children could have died!"

"This was your fault!"

"Snorri should be the winner!" yelled one of the giant mothers, whose child he had saved.

Snorri looked over in surprise.

"He saved our lives!" Peter shouted. The other kids joined in, yelling their agreement.

"I'm sorry, but rules are rules!" the Master of Ceremonies said. "All those who lost their boulders during the race are eliminated, including Snorri the Shepherd!"

"No fair!" people yelled.

"Let Snorri stay in the tournament!"

"His rock is shattered! He didn't complete the competition, therefore, he is disqualified!" the Master of Ceremonies insisted.

"Boo!"

The whole village began booing the Master of Ceremonies, and Gorm was beginning to look concerned.

Jake could understand why. Based on what he'd overheard Gorm telling his followers at the feast last night, his sole reason for participating in the tournament was to become the next king. But Gorm desired the admiration of the people; he did not wish to start out his future reign by being despised by his own subjects.

"Snorri! Snorri! Snorri!" the people were now chanting.

Snorri looked around at them, rather dazed.

Gorm tried to hide the worried look on his face as he carried the flag back down the hill. The closer he came to the people, the more they jeered at him, making faces and blowing raspberries at him.

"Boo, Gorm! Cheater! We want Snorri! Let Snorri back in the contest!"

Gorm did his best to ignore them and approached King Olaf, who was sitting in the shade of a striped canvas canopy. "Well done, champion," said the king.

Gorm bowed in respect. "Thank you, sire."

King Olaf's gaze trailed across the booing crowd. "Our people don't sound happy."

"Sire," Prince Gorm said loudly, making sure the people heard him and realized how generous he was. "As the winner of the first round, I would like to request that the shepherd be allowed to continue in the contest—even though he ought to be disqualified, according to the rules. Perhaps we can show mercy, under the circumstances," Gorm said with a grand flourish.

The people stopped booing to hear the king's response.

"Snorri did have a good reason for his failure," the king admitted. "But perhaps now the shepherd sees that this is a contest for warriors! Now that he's seen for himself the deadly seriousness of our endeavor, maybe he would be glad to be freed from it. Round Two will be even worse than this—the test of courage does involve a dragon, after all." King Olaf looked skeptically at Snorri, expecting cowardice, perhaps. "Shepherd, you have done a noble thing today. But do you really wish to continue?"

Snorri had a hapless look on his face, a crestfallen slump to his shoulders. He did not look at all enthusiastic about facing down a dragon.

Surely he was tempted to seize this dignified out he had been offered and flee back to the safety of his farm.

But then he glanced at the people who were cheering for him, probably for the first time in his life. He frowned mistrustfully at Gorm and glanced up the hill at Princess Kaia. "Yes, Your Majesty," he answered bravely. "I'll continue, if you will allow me."

The crowd cheered.

"Done! And you may thank Prince Gorm for his magnanimity," King Olaf added, nodding at his favorite.

Snorri did not appear to have the least idea what magnanimity meant, and for that matter, neither did Jake.

If Dani were here, she could've told him. He rather wished she were, for the carrot head would not have believed her eyes at all this. Meanwhile, Princess Kaia beamed to hear that Snorri was still in the running. The first round of the contest for her hand in marriage was over, and against all odds, her one true ally had at least managed not to get himself killed.

The Master of Ceremonies ordered the field to be cleared. Everyone would take a break for lunch, and then the second round of the tournament would continue in the afternoon.

The test of courage—against the dragon.

CHAPTER THIRTY-TWO
Old Smokey

"**N**ow, as we all know, dragons are great hoarders of gold and treasure," the Master of Ceremonies announced to the six remaining contestants, who were all rather sleepy after a heavy lunch.

With the afternoon sun climbing into the sky, they had gathered in a clearing in the woods, well beyond the village and its surrounding fields.

Of course, there was no audience for the second round. It was much too dangerous to allow spectators this close to a dragon's den.

Aside from the contestants and their coaches, the village elders had come to serve as witnesses, and of course, King Olaf and Princess Kaia, surrounded by their giant Viking guards.

Of the ten players who had started out in the tournament, six now remained—one of which had only been invited back in by the skin of his teeth.

Jake had no doubt Gorm was still angry about that.

The Master of Ceremonies smoothed his long, official robes and continued with his explanation. "The object of this challenge is to prove your courage as a possible future leader of our people. To do so, you must go through these woods—" He pointed at the trail into the forest. "Find the mouth of the dragon's cave, and sneak inside. It's still daylight, so Old Smokey *should* be sleeping. Obviously, you don't want to wake him.

"Sneak past the dragon, find his hoard of gold," he continued, "and from his treasures, choose a special gift for Princess Kaia. Whoever brings back the best gift for Her Highness wins. But be warned, anyone returning empty-handed will be eliminated.

"Those who remain will advance to the third and final round of the tournament tonight—the test of wits. Good luck, gentlemen," he added. "And remember, if anyone should wake the dragon, follow the evacuation procedures we discussed earlier. Unless you wish to be barbecued."

The other knights and warriors turned to discuss these instructions with their coaches. They seemed awfully cool about it all. Most of them must have already had some experience with dragons, Jake thought.

Snorri, on the other hand, was looking rather green around the gills. "I shouldn't have had that second helping at lunch," he rumbled, rubbing his round stomach. "I don't feel so good."

"It's only nerves," Archie said. "Try not to worry."

"I wish I was home taking care of my sheep. If anything happens to me, who will look after them?"

"I'm sure Princess Kaia will see they're well kept, but look on the bright side," Jake offered. "This is your chance to really impress her, show her how much you care!"

"If you say so."

The Master of Ceremonies came along, holding up a handful of straws. "Pick one," he told Snorri.

Snorri pulled a long piece of straw out of his grasp.

As the Master of Ceremonies walked away, Jake realized the players were drawing straws to see who would have the bad luck to go first, and in what order the rest of them would take their turns to sneak into the cave.

While the others drew their straws, Jake and Archie discussed strategy. Earlier contestants had a clear advantage: There was more treasure to choose from, and with each new player who ventured into the cave, the chances went up that someone would make a noise that would bring the dragon fully awake.

But while going second or third or even fourth would be desirable, nobody wanted to go first, for there was no telling what sort of mood in which they might find the dragon. Yes, it was daylight, but what if the beast was only dozing?

The first player would be the one to find out.

The only worse position had to be last place, for by then, with so many intruders traipsing in and out of the cave, the last man to go surely had the highest chances of getting eaten.

When all the rivals' straws were compared, they found that Snorri would go fifth.

"Not too bad!" Jake assured him. Second or third would have been better, but at least he didn't have to go either first or last.

Prince Gorm, unluckily, had drawn the longest straw: sixth place.

Dead last.

But Gorm, if he was anything, was brave, and according to the tales he liked to tell, he was an expert on dragons.

They would soon find out if this was only idle boasting, but he seemed to welcome the challenge. He went around grinning at his rivals and holding his straw up proudly, then sticking it between his teeth like a farmer, as if this brush with doom was just a lark.

Snorri shook his head at the daredevil. For his part, the poor shepherd looked scared to death.

In any case, with everyone's turns decided, there was no more putting it off. One of the visiting princes had drawn the shortest straw and so, had the unfortunate honor of going first. He put on his helmet, lifted his shield, took a deep breath, and marched off into the woods alone.

Kaia covered her eyes with both hands and put her head down.

Jake could tell she wanted to scream to see men being forced to risk their lives all because of her. Not that any of this was her idea. When she lowered her hands from her face and forced herself to watch, she glanced at her father in obvious fury for putting these men through this. But King Olaf was just enjoying the show.

Everyone waited in pulse-pounding suspense to find out if the dragon would come charging out of the forest or if the first prince might make it back alive.

Irritatingly, as mere 'dwarves,' Jake and Archie could not see anything behind all the towering giants.

Jake tapped Archie on the shoulder, then gestured toward a nearby tree. His cousin nodded eagerly and they both began climbing a massive spruce tree nearby.

When Archie's footing slipped and left him dangling several yards above the ground, Snorri quickly came to his aid, giving him an easy boost up onto the thick branch, where Jake joined him.

The boys made themselves comfortable and immediately Archie took his telescope out of his tool-bag again and lifted it to his eye.

"What can you see?" Jake prompted.

"He's almost to the mouth of the cave..." Archie paused, scanning. Then he suddenly gasped. "I can see the dragon! He's sleeping! I can see his snout, just inside the cave. Great Euclid, Jake... he's *huge*."

"Can I see?" Jake asked eagerly.

Archie looked a little shaken as he handed him the spyglass. "I've never actually seen one before. Egads."

"Too bad your precious Mr. Darwin isn't here."

"You're right. I should take a picture of this to show him." Archie reached again for his tool-bag to get his camera.

"Why bother? He'd only think it's a fake." Jake brought the telescope up to his eyes and searched the woods until he found the cave.

When he spotted the sleeping dragon, he nearly laughed aloud in amazement, so shocked by the sight that he could've fallen out of the tree. He had never seen anything like the beast before.

Magnificent and terrifying.

He couldn't see much of the creature shadowed in its cave, but its snout was resting on its crossed front feet, and clouds of smoke or steam rose from its nostrils with each peaceful snore.

The dragon's scaly hide was a greenish black, the color of moss and forest shadows, perfect for helping the huge beast blend into its environment. Jake stared in awe at the claws as big as threshing sickles protruding from each knuckle on the sleeping dragon's front feet.

That's right, have a nice dream, Smokey, old boy, Jake thought with a shiver. He could see why his mentor, Guardian Derek Stone, had a particular fondness for dragons.

The creatures were spectacular. Of course, if that thing woke up, Jake mused, they were all probably doomed. Then, through the circle of the telescope, he saw the first contestant creeping towards the cave.

Jake held his breath. How the giant prince forced himself to keep going *toward* the dragon instead of running away from it, he could not fathom.

Kaia had to be impressed by this show of courage.

"He's in!" Jake reported to the others in excitement.

King Olaf turned curiously. "How can you see so far?"

"The dwarves have a device," Snorri said.

"What of the dragon?" someone asked.

"Sound asleep."

The other warriors sighed with relief.

Barely a bird sang in a tree. The woods were deathly silent as they all waited for the first prince to return.

"C'mon, Jake, it's my telescope, let me have a turn! Quit hogging it."

As he handed Archie back his spyglass, an object in the sky caught Jake's attention. He looked up and saw the Gryphon soaring toward them, circling lower.

He frowned but dared not risk waking Old Smokey by shouting at Red to go back to Snorri's cottage, where he had left him.

With his eagle-eyes, Red quickly spotted his master, and a moment later, glided down onto the branch beside him.

"Be-caw," he complained at being excluded.

"What are you doing here?" Jake exclaimed in a whisper. "I told you to stay put!"

The Gryphon lowered his head a little at the scolding, but Jake suspected that, left alone at Snorri's cottage, Red had been tempted to eat one of their host's beloved sheep.

That would not have gone over very well.

Still, recalling something Derek had told him once, Jake was worried about having Red so near a dragon's cave.

Gryphons and dragons hated each other, according to Derek.

It had to do with both mythical beasts' connection to gold.

Gryphons could locate veins of gold in the earth, and on rare occasions, when certain people earned their trust, they would show their human friends where these precious mineral deposits could be found.

That was how Jake's family had come to own their goldmine in Wales centuries ago. One of his medieval ancestors, a humble young squire called Reginald Everton, training to be a knight, had chanced to save a large, mysterious, golden egg from destruction.

The egg turned out to belong to a mother gryphon, and inside it, waiting to be born, was baby Red. Whether Reginald knew it or not, gryphon eggs were extraordinarily rare and quite priceless, but he did not hesitate to give the egg back to its parent.

Because the young squire had proved he was pure of heart and could be trusted, Red's mother, in gratitude, had shown the lad to the location of a glittery vein of gold in the rugged mountains of Wales.

Young Reginald had rushed home to tell his father about it—at that time, the one-day powerful Earls of Griffon were but humble yeomen farmers. The boy's father journeyed to confirm his son's tale, then raced back home and sold the family farm in order to buy the land on which the otherwise-secret stash of gold awaited.

That was how the Everton family became rich, and stayed that way, when most other wealthy families lost their fortunes within a few generations due to foolishness.

In any case, because of the people they occasionally befriended, gryphons could appreciate the backbreaking work that went into mining the gold, the craft and care that went into melting it down to purify it, and molding it into something beautiful, and above all, the wisdom it took to own it without becoming corrupted.

Dragons on the other hand...

Well, after all that effort by humans, dragons had no qualms about swooping down out of the sky and stealing the finished golden objects, just to horde them in moldy old caves, where they were of no use to anyone. Dragons never shared; they always kept accumulating more as if by compulsion; and they'd kill anyone who tried to take their trinkets.

Dragons, in short, went against everything gryphons stood for.

Which explained why Red was scowling in the direction of Old Smokey's cave, having caught the giant reptile's scent. That warlike gleam sprang back into his golden eyes, and his feathers began to bristle, especially around his neck.

"No," Jake ordered, laying a firm hand on his shoulder. "You need to keep calm. You're not even supposed to be here."

Red growled low in his throat, but obeyed, sitting on his lion haunches on the branch beside the boys.

"That's better. Thank you, Red. I know you hate him, but we'll be done here soon." Jake patted his agitated pet on the withers, then turned to Archie. "Any sign of the prince yet?"

"No... wait, yes. There he is! I see him! He's coming!" the young inventor announced. "He's made it out alive!"

And sure enough, he had.

The first prince returned, ashen-faced and soaked in a cold sweat, but unscathed. He put his offering for Kaia—a jeweled necklace—on the table by the Master of Ceremonies, and then went to pass out after his ordeal.

The second fellow went, then the third, and the fourth, and each brought back gifts of gold for the princess. The second, a magnificent goblet. The third, a beautiful dagger. The fourth, a jeweled shield fit for the daughter of a warrior king.

And now it was number five's turn: Snorri.

He put on his horned helmet with a resolute look. As he buckled the strap under his chin, he fumbled with it a little, his giant fingers trembling with fear.

Watching him, Jake thought back to his first sighting of Snorri and how terrified he had been of him.

There was a lesson here, he thought in a philosophical mood. Things were not always what they appeared.

Always good to keep that in mind when dealing with Loki the Shapeshifter, too, he decided.

"Dear Odin, don't let me get eaten," Snorri mumbled.

"You'll be fine. If these blokes can do it, so can you," Jake assured him.

"You can do it, Snorri!" Archie chimed in.

"Just remember, this is for Princess Kaia and your people. Fix your mind on what's at stake."

"Right." Snorri nodded firmly and gathered up his courage.

Then the boys watched anxiously as their unlikely champion trudged off into the woods.

CHAPTER THIRTY-THREE
One False Move

Princess Kaia wrapped her arms around herself, looking frightened, as Snorri disappeared into the trees.

But thanks to Archie's spyglass, the boys were able to watch their friend's progress at least as far as the cave's mouth. Snorri's movements in the woods grew stealthy. He darted from tree to tree, hiding as he moved closer.

Maybe the tension was making him giddy, but Jake found it just a wee bit hilarious watching a giant, of all creatures, try to sneak.

"Dragon's still asleep," Archie reported.

Jake listened for all he was worth, but a moment later, he couldn't take it anymore. "I can't stand it, let me look!" He snatched the spyglass from his smaller cousin.

"Hey!" Archie protested. "You see this, Red? The way your master behaves?"

Red pecked Jake as if to say, *Give it back.*

"I will, just a second..." Jake's heart pounded as he held the spyglass to his eye. He could see Snorri tiptoeing towards the entrance of the cave, just like the others had. *Come on, come on, just pick something and get out of there, you lump...*

Snorri disappeared into the cave, and to Jake's relief, still, that dragon showed no signs of waking.

A minute passed.

Two.

Five.

"What's taking so long?" Archie whispered. "Do you see him coming back yet?"

"No."

"You know Snorri. Probably got lost somewhere in the dark," Gorm joked while they all waited.

Princess Kaia glared at him, then clasped her hands in prayer, and gazed desperately at the sky. "Oh, Father Odin, please don't let him die. He shouldn't have been forced into this in the first place. He's just a gentle giant."

The warriors snickered at her prayer, but just then, Jake saw Snorri through the spyglass. He held his breath as the shepherd tiptoed past the sleeping dragon's huge snout. Old Smokey's head alone was nearly as tall as Snorri's shoulder.

As soon as the shepherd was a few feet past the mouth of the cave, he broke into a run, barreling toward them.

The boys cheered as loudly as they dared when Snorri was back safe. Kaia looked so relieved that Jake wondered if a mighty Norse giantess could ever faint.

"Well?" Gorm sauntered over to the gift table with his usual obnoxious smile. "Let's see what you brought back for Her Highness. Took you long enough."

Gasping for breath, Snorri presented his offering. "I had to find the right gift."

When he laid it reverently on the table, Gorm's bushy eyebrows shot upward. "What. Is. *That?*"

The knights and princes stared at Snorri's gift in shocked silence, and then suddenly, they all burst out in uproarious laughter.

The Master of Ceremonies tried to shush them. "Quiet! Are you mad? You're going to wake Old Smokey!"

But they couldn't help themselves.

"A book! By Loki's beard, what is she going to do with that?!" the first prince bellowed with humor.

Gorm wiped away a tear of laughter. "Oh, Snorri, this time you have really outdone yourself. A book, of all things!"

"It's not even a nice one! It's old and moldy from the damp of the dragon's cave!" another warrior mocked him. "It's practically falling apart!"

"Might as well use it for toilet paper!"

Snorri hung his head.

The handsomest of the knights, with long golden hair, turned arrogantly to Kaia. "Oh, Princess, this so-called present is practically an insult. Shall I thrash him for you?"

Kaia's blue eyes were as icy as the North Sea when she glanced up from the book, which she had opened carefully, though it looked like a miniature in her hands. "For your information, you fools, this is an illuminated manuscript, and I am very happy to have it."

"Aw, what a lady she is to tell this pretty lie," Gorm drawled.

"Kindhearted of you, Highness," the handsome one said with a patronizing smile.

"It's all right," Snorri mumbled to Kaia. "You don't have to pretend you like it. I just thought—"

"Shut up, Snorri," she ordered. Sweeping them all with an angry, regal stare, she fluffed her cape over one shoulder, pivoted, and went to sit down grandly in her chair.

Gorm, of course, was not about to be outdone, especially not by Snorri. He bowed to the princess. "Your Highness, we all know you are too much of a lady to show your disappointment in this buffoon. But it's my turn now, and I will make it up to you, bring you back a present worthy of you. You'll see. Back in a trice!" He drew his sword and turned to face the woods, pausing to pose like a proper hero, glancing about dramatically before striding off into the shadows.

"I hope he gets eaten," Archie muttered.

"I don't think he'd taste very good, even to a dragon. Don't let him get to you, Snorri," Jake added.

Their exhausted friend went to sit down on the grass. Snorri took off his horned helmet and downed a swig of water from his canteen, still looking a bit like he had just seen his whole life flash before his eyes.

Judging by his expression, Jake could tell that Snorri was still feeling embarrassed about his choice of gifts and the way the other giants had made fun of him.

But he shouldn't have worried. While King Olaf, the Master of Ceremonies, the other contestants, and the boys waited anxiously to see what would happen to Gorm, Kaia was examining the ancient book in fascination.

It must have belonged to a human, Jake thought, for although it was a large tome as thick as a Bible, it looked tiny in her hands. Delicate patterns of gold and silver filigree sparkled in its old leather binding as she opened the cover. Using only her fingertips, she carefully turned the miniature-seeming pages, yellowed with age.

Archie, meanwhile, monitored Gorm's progress through his

telescope. "There he is," he murmured. "That was fast. Goes to show how much thought he put into it, just grabbed any old thing. Wait..." Archie paused. "What's he doing?" he murmured to himself.

"Can I see?" Jake asked.

"I'm not sure what he's up to. See what you think," Archie said, sharing his spyglass with him once more.

Jake lifted it to his eye while Red scratched an itch behind his ear with his hind foot. "Hold still, you're shaking the branch! I'm trying to look, you glocky feathered mumper!"

"Caw," Red apologized and stopped.

As Jake studied the situation, it only took a moment to figure out what Gorm was doing.

Naturally, he was showing off, as usual.

Out to prove himself superior, Gorm had gathered an *armload* of presents for the princess.

It didn't seem to matter *what* he took. Instead, he was grabbing everything in sight—all the shiny stolen treasures he could pile into his arms from the dragon's horde.

Gorm even bent to pick up one of Old Smokey's shed dragon scales.

Jake recalled Derek mentioning that dragon scales were wonderfully useful raw materials. They could be cut and shaped into deadly bladed weapons or formed into pieces of body armor.

Unfortunately, as Gorm bent to pick up a greenish scale the size of a dinner platter, he was carrying so many prizes and pieces of stolen treasure, that one of the golden cups fell from his grasp and crashed to the cave floor right beside the dragon's head.

Its golden eye opened.

Jake gasped. "It's awake!" he shouted while Gorm broke into a sprint, fleeing the cave, racing back toward them.

King Olaf jumped to his feet. *"Readyyyy!"* he shouted to his mighty Viking warriors, who drew out their lances.

Both Kaia and Snorri also rose. The knights and princes drew their swords.

Jake was riveted. Still gazing through the telescope, he did not notice the Gryphon's response. Frozen, he could not stop staring in horrid fascination at the waking monster.

While Gorm came racing back to the rest of them, Old Smokey stood up on all fours in his cave. He shook himself awake like a dog, his scales clattering together softly with the movement. Then he sniffed the air through his big, round nostrils.

He must have smelled the lingering scent of intruders in his lair, for he suddenly blasted out a furious screech that echoed for miles around.

Then he came charging through the woods, straight at their party.

CHAPTER THIRTY-FOUR
Battling the Dragon

With the angry dragon on his way, Jake and Archie cowered in the spruce tree, while the king's men and all the knights and princes got into position to fend off the beast.

All except for Snorri.

"He's running away!" Archie cried.

"No. He's taking the princess to safety!" Jake corrected.

Sure enough, Snorri grabbed Kaia by her wrist and started dragging her up the forest path.

"Well, what about us?" Archie exclaimed. "He forgot to put us down!"

"Don't worry, we've got Red. He'll fly us out of here," Jake said absently, watching as Kaia dug in her heels, resisting Snorri's efforts to protect her.

It seemed the warrior princess preferred to stay behind and fight the dragon, too.

Gorm burst into the clearing only a few yards ahead of the dragon, still carrying his armful of gold. "I win! I brought back the most!" he shouted as he dropped his stash of treasure on the prize table. "Now the fun begins! Ha, ha!" Gorm barely had time to turn and grab a weapon before the dragon was upon them.

Jake and Archie stared in open-mouthed shock when the beast arrived in all its terrible glory: fangs gleaming, nostrils steaming, a wicked glitter of sun on its greenish-black hide.

Old Smokey paused at the edge of the clearing, as though startled to find a bristling phalanx of armed giants waiting for him.

The warriors were as still as statues, holding their position. Jake's heart pounded.

"It's as big as a Tyrannosaurus Rex," Archie breathed.

"A what?"

"I really need to take you to the museum when we get back to London!"

"You mean if we don't get eaten here?" Jake muttered.

The dragon hesitated; spread its leathery wings and roared, as if it might just let them off with a warning.

Jake could not take his eyes off the terrifying thing. Red growled beside him, but Jake held him back.

"No, boy. This enemy's too big for you," he whispered. Not even Red could defeat that thing, Jake was very sure.

Nevertheless, Derek had assured him that while dragons were indeed territorial, they were not the mindless killing machines that legend claimed. Some were even rather friendly, he had said. The one exception was when anyone touched their treasure.

And so, as the dragon's fiery eyes swept the scene before him, he spotted the table piled with gold from his horde, and that was that.

The beast attacked. It launched into the clearing and began to do battle against the giant knights.

The dragon promptly devoured four of the visiting knights and princes. It swatted the royal guards away with a mighty flick of its spiked tail, then breathed a shot of fire at the king, who leaped behind a boulder.

Arrows bounced off its scales without effect.

Gorm yelled to get its attention, banging on his shield. Old Smokey turned to him, eager to continue his rampage.

"Come on, you great lizard! Let's have some fun!" Gorm lunged at the dragon: Old Smokey bit down on his lance.

Gorm kept hold of the weapon, and the dragon shook his head like a dog with a toy in its mouth. It threw the lance with Gorm still holding onto it. When it released him, Gorm and his spear went flying off into the woods.

In a frenzy, Old Smokey turned to search for more people to destroy. For a second, Jake thought he and Archie were doomed. They held perfectly still on the high branch where Snorri had put them—practically on eye-level with the monster.

But instead, the dragon's fiery gaze homed in on Snorri and Kaia; they were running away, and their movement must have roused his instincts to chase.

It raced off after them.

"Oh, no! Snorri can't fight, and all that Kaia was carrying was that book. They're defenseless!"

Jake knew he had to help them, but how? His mind raced.

Suddenly, he had an idea. He focused his attention on the prize table, where all the golden treasures lay abandoned.

Stretching out his hand, he summoned up his telekinesis to levitate the largest gold cup into the air.

Concentrating carefully, he sent it hurtling toward the dragon and then slowed it down, making sure the gleaming goblet passed right before the dragon's eyes.

Old Smokey got distracted by the shiny golden object floating by. He snapped his jaws to grab it, but Jake made it dance just beyond his reach.

"It's working!" Archie exclaimed.

Heart pounding, Jake used his telekinesis to make the cup fly through the air in the other direction, away from Snorri and Kaia.

The dragon followed as though mesmerized by the shiny treasure. Old Smokey forgot all about his battle as he kept trying to catch the flying goblet.

Jake was relieved to have captured the beast's attention.

All that remained now was to get rid of him.

"Go...*fetch!*" Jake hurled a bolt of energy that sent the cup sailing over the forest, far away.

The dragon bounded away after it, spreading his wings as he chased it away over the trees.

Archie turned to Jake in excitement. "He's gone! Let's get out of here before he comes back!"

"Red, fly us down." The boys climbed on the Gryphon's back.

Red was still seething over the nearness of his traditional enemy, but he brought them safely to earth just as Kaia and Snorri came running back into the clearing.

"Jake, you are a wizard, indeed!" said the princess.

"At your service," he replied with a bow.

Snorri looked shaken. "I thought we were two dead ducks."

"Father!" Kaia rushed to King Olaf, who now came out from behind the rocky mound, where he and the Master of Ceremonies had taken cover from the dragon's fire.

"I'm all right," the king assured his daughter.

Gorm came marching out of the woods, still holding his spear. "Ah, good! I see we're all still alive."

"Not all of us," Jake muttered, glancing around at the dead guards and what was left of the knights and princes.

"Huh," Gorm grunted. But suddenly inspired with how to turn the grim moment to his advantage, he gave the king his most heroic stare. "Sire, allow me to avenge our fallen comrades by assembling a war party to come back and destroy the beast."

"Excellent idea—" the king started.

"Father, no! Don't you dare!" Kaia thundered without warning. "If you let him kill Old Smokey, I swear I'll never speak to you again!"

"What?" her father uttered.

"This isn't the dragon's fault! He's just an animal, following his instincts. Oh, I knew this stupid contest was a terrible idea! Please. Old Smokey has never bothered us as long as we leave him alone."

Jake now realized why the princess had been resisting Snorri's efforts to drag her to safety. It was not that she wanted to come back to help fight the dragon. She had wanted to keep her father's men from killing it.

"The dragon only attacked because they went into his lair! What else did you expect?" she demanded. "To slay him now would be most unjust! Besides, what would Odin say?"

King Olaf frowned, glancing from Kaia to Gorm and back again. "Perhaps my daughter is right. We'd better leave the beast alive. After all, there's no telling what sort of curse the gods might send down on us if we kill it."

"But sire, it ate these warriors!"

"And so they have gone to Valhalla, Gorm. They died a noble death," the king replied.

"We need to get out of here before the dragon comes back!" Jake pointed out.

"He's right. Come, Snorri," Kaia ordered while the boys got back on the Gryphon. "Let's go back to the great hall."

"But wait, milady, don't you want to see your gift from me?" Gorm asked with another smarmy smile.

"Leave the dragon's gold," the king said with a wave of his hand.

"But I must give her a token of my affection to fulfill this leg of the tournament. Here." Gorm reached into his moose-skin breeches and pulled out a sweaty jeweled tiara.

It did not smell very good, considering where he had stashed it. He offered it to Kaia.

She took one look at it, then at him, and grimaced in disgust. She turned around and started walking. "Get me out of here."

"But Your Highness, you haven't told us which present you like best!" the Master of Ceremonies called after her.

She just shook her head as she walked away, too revolted to reply.

Gorm grinned at the Master of Ceremonies. "As if she's really going to pick a book."

CHAPTER THIRTY-FIVE
Wild At Heart

Meanwhile back in Midgarth, the long, lonely notes of a wolf's howl summoned Dani and Isabelle out to the moonlit forest beyond the university.

Twigs cracked under their careful footsteps as the girls ventured into the woods.

"Henry? Is that you?" Isabelle whispered.

"It had better be him," Dani muttered. She did *not* want to be out here with a *regular* hungry wolf on the prowl.

Isabelle scanned the darkness nervously. "Miss Helena? Are you here?"

Two large animal shapes stepped silently into view, their furry silhouettes silvered by moonlight.

"It's them!" Dani pointed.

"Oh, thank goodness!"

The girls stepped forward into the clearing where their shapeshifting tutor and governess awaited.

Dani did not want to admit it, but she felt an instinctual wariness about getting too close to them right now. Even though she knew it was the twins, they were rather terrifying in this form. With Henry's fangs and Helena's claws, two such animals could have torn the girls apart.

Isabelle showed no such hesitation. She rushed straight over to Helena, bent down, and hugged her. Henry wagged his tail. She hugged him next. "Oh, I'm so relieved to see you both!"

Dani ventured closer, seeing it was safe, after all.

"How are you? Is there anything you need? Anything we can do to help?" Isabelle knelt down and looked into the leopard's glowing eyes.

She always got a particular, thoughtful expression on her face when she was reading an animal's mind. But whatever leopard-Helena communicated to her, it obviously upset her.

Isabelle stared at the graceful big cat with a stricken look. "No, no!" she whispered, shaking her head.

Leopard-Helena gave her a little lick on the forehead, as she might have done to one of her kittens.

Dani looked on worriedly. "What is it?"

Isabelle had gone pale as she turned to Dani. She looked like someone who had just been punched in the stomach. "I'm afraid...they've only come to say goodbye."

"What?"

Softly, Isabelle gave voice to the thoughts and feelings she perceived in their shapeshifting governess's mind. "It's been years since they've spent this much time in their animal forms. The lure of the wild is calling them away."

"Away? What do you mean? They can't just run off and leave us!" Dani said, aghast. She turned to the twins. "We need you! Lady Bradford left you in charge of us! You can't abandon us—what are we supposed to do?"

"They can't help it," Izzy murmured. "They're reverting back to nature. That's why they needed to come and see us now. Before long, they fear they'll be too dangerous and wild to come around us anymore. They say their human side is...fading."

Dani refused to accept this. "Surely something can be done! We'll contact Lady Bradford like we should have done from the start. She must have a spell to bring them back—"

"That's just it," Izzy said, glancing over at her with tears in her eyes. "They don't want to come back anymore."

Dani stared at Isabelle in shock.

Isabelle gazed at the shapeshifters. "It's hard for them, they're telling me. They try at all times to be so diligent and disciplined and conscientious about everything for our sakes—all the rules of etiquette, our lessons and activities, our food, clothes, schedules—all their responsibilities in taking care of us. But now that they've had a taste of the wild, they just want to be free."

Dani barely knew what to say. It was one thing for a student to be sick of rules and lessons, but a teacher? Henry and Helena, of all people?! They were always so proper, so correct. She never would have guessed that they sometimes longed for a freer life.

Wolf-Henry walked over to Isabelle, sat down, and offered his front paw to her like a trained dog doing a trick.

Isabelle took his massive paw gently in her hand, but tears filled her eyes. "Do you really have to go?"

Wolf-Henry whined in regret and licked his snout.

"All right, then," she whispered.

"No, it's not all right!" Dani exclaimed abruptly, turning to the fierce, gray wolf. "You can't do this! Archie will be lost without you, Henry. Lady Bradford's never going to find us new teachers we like half as well as you. Don't you see?" Her lower lip quivered. "We love you!"

"And that's why we have to let them go," Isabelle said softly. "We have no right to chain them." Then she stood up.

Wolf-Henry whined and leopard-Helena let out a mournful meow.

"You can come back to us anytime you want. Promise you'll be careful out there. Look after each other."

Wolf-Henry let out another painful whimper.

Isabelle nodded. "I will."

"Will what?" Dani asked her, wiping away a tear, but it was quickly replaced by another.

This was too awful. It reminded her all over again of losing her Ma to yellow fever.

Isabelle was fighting not to cry. "He wants me to tell Archie and Jake how much they mean to him, and that he's sorry, and he'll miss them."

With a sad purr, leopard-Helena rubbed her feline body alongside the girls like an oversized housecat doling out her affections. But with a final tickle of her whiskers, she rejoined her brother the wolf, and they gazed one last time at their former charges.

Dani took another step, following them, as they turned away. "Please, don't go! Come back!"

But it was no use. They ran away and disappeared into the shadows. The girls were left standing there in silence, until a distant, forlorn howl of farewell reduced them both to tears.

CHAPTER THIRTY-SIX
A Match of Wits

At the giants' feast that night, Jake sat alone out of the way, eating his giant food, and thinking about the day's events.

After returning from the woods and the bloody second challenge of the tournament, the boys and Red had gone back to Snorri's cottage with their host. All of them had needed to regroup and catch their breath after that ordeal.

The third and final challenge, the test of wits, was to come soon—tonight—at this very feast. But Snorri barely seemed to care.

He was still ashamed about his choice of gifts for Princess Kaia. Somehow it would not sink into his thick skull that she had loved the illuminated manuscript.

When they had returned to his cottage, he kept mumbling that he had something better to give her, a proper present, made of gold, but he refused to show it to the boys.

"It's private, just between her and me!" he had insisted. "Besides, if I show you first, you'll ruin the surprise. Kaia deserves to see her present first!"

"All right, all right!"

The boys had backed off. Jake suspected that Snorri didn't want to show them his other present for Kaia out of worry that someone might make fun of that, too.

So the gift remained a mystery.

Meanwhile, Archie went out to the shed to work on the Pigeon for a while, and Jake made sure that Red got something to eat.

He called the Gryphon out to the babbling stream that wrapped around Snorri's farm. There, Red had pounced into the water and caught a baby salmon nearly as big as himself. Seeing his fierce feathered friend devouring the fish, Jake was satisfied the meal would keep Red's mind off Snorri's sheep for a while longer.

Still, he hoped his sometimes-unpredictable pet did not get a craving for lamb chops when their backs were turned.

When it was time for the feast, Archie and Red had stayed behind while Jake and Snorri walked up to the village together. Even as far away as the farm, they could smell the mouth-watering scent of the giant roasted bull smoking on the open fire.

The tantalizing smell of barbecue doubled Jake's desire to gorge himself, as usual.

Snorri, for his part, mumbled that he was too nervous about giving Kaia her mystery gift to even think about food. "I got butterflies in my stomach," he admitted.

"Ah, don't worry, whatever it is, I'm sure she'll love it," Jake said to humor him.

"I hope so. She always liked dogs."

"You're giving her a dog?"

"No! Don't ask me!" he warned. "I won't tell. You'll see later. I'm sure she'll show you, if you ask."

They parted ways at the feast. Jake wished him luck; Snorri nodded his thanks, then marched off in a cold sweat to present his mystery gift to his ladylove.

Rather amused by the lovesick giant's discomfiture, Jake turned around and followed his nose in the direction of the food.

Before long, he had found an out-of-the-way perch on a giant handrail, where he proceeded to gnaw on his giant food as best he could. It was delicious. The roast beef just fell apart. Finally, a helping of adequate size for a growing lad! Giants knew how to eat. He'd give them that. Jake chewed and smiled, smiled and chewed, and washed it down with a gulp of cider, watching everything.

He kept one eye on the road, expecting at any minute to see his cousin coming along to get some dinner, with Red in tow.

As Jake lifted his giant biscuit with both hands and took a bite, he wondered how the girls were faring back in Midgarth, and if there was any word yet of the twins.

Or of Loki, for that matter.

Then he scanned the feast full of laughing, eating, talking, bragging giants. No one seemed overly concerned about the deaths of the visiting knights and princes. Life went on as usual. He found that curious. But, as the Norns had said, the giants followed the old ways, and the Viking peoples were great believers in Fate.

If Fate decreed those blokes were supposed to get eaten by a dragon today, then that was that. So be it. No use crying over spilt milk, seemed to be their opinion. They shrugged it off and moved on with their lives.

For Jake, it wasn't that easy, having been there and witnessed the whole thing. Of course, loudmouth Gorm did not show any sign of regret over all the people he'd gotten killed today by his blunder.

Jake shook his head. Maybe Gorm had woken the dragon up on purpose, knowing the beast would attack and hoping it might help him get rid of a few of his rivals.

Presently, Gorm was holding court as usual in one corner of the feast, surrounded by his followers, telling tales of the day's adventures, and exaggerating about everything.

The important thing was, the contest was now down to only two: Gorm versus Snorri.

No doubt, behind his bragging, Gorm was humiliated by that fact in itself, Jake mused. It must have chafed his giant ego that against all odds, the lowly shepherd, the village idiot, was keeping pace with him.

As for Snorri, he was giving Kaia his mystery gift even now.

Jake could see them sitting together on a bench at the far edge of the feast. He did not have Archie's telescope on hand, or he would have spied on them to see the object Snorri was offering her, some small trinket that he had set in the palm of her hand.

It can't be a ring! Jake thought in surprise. No, there was no way Snorri would go proposing marriage now, when the whole point of this tournament was to determine whom the princess would marry. Besides, Snorri had mentioned the present had something to do with a dog. *Hmm...*

Whatever it was, Kaia seemed to like it. She was all smiles as she marveled over it, then Snorri seemed to go into shock when she leaned near and kissed his cheek.

"Ha!" Looking on from a distance, Jake lifted his glass of cider and sent them a private toast, then laughed and took a swig.

At last, Archie arrived, reporting that he'd made good progress on the Pigeon's repairs. When he went up to get some food, Jake accompanied his cousin. After all, Great-Great Aunt Ramona wasn't here to disapprove of him taking seconds.

Twilight was fading into darkness, and the boys were just finishing their oversized meal when the Master of Ceremonies climbed the torch-lit platform where the royals sat.

He banged his baton and called for everyone's attention. While the whole village gathered around, King Olaf and Princess Kaia took their seats.

"Ladies and gentlemen," the Master of Ceremonies began, "it is time for the third and final test in our tournament for the future kingship of our people and the hand of Princess Kaia of Jugenheim. Will the two remaining contestants please come forward?"

The crowd cheered and booed variously, depending on their preferences, as Snorri and Gorm went to stand at the foot of the platform.

Jake wasn't sure how many in the audience were truly for Snorri, but it seemed quite a few were against Gorm. The prince's brawny followers did their best to silence his detractors, shoving and roughing up people in the crowd who booed him.

Snorri stood by, meanwhile, stiffly waiting for the Master of Ceremonies to continue.

As for Jake and Archie, their seat on the nearby handrail gave them a good view of all the proceedings.

"Hear ye, hear ye!" the robed official resumed when the crowd's noise quieted down. "For this final test of the rivals' cunning, the Ice Wizard will join us to present the contestants with a riddle. You will then have twelve hours to solve this puzzle, gentlemen. It is now nine o'clock at night. At nine in the morning, you will give your answers. The first to give the correct answer wins the tournament. Let the warlock appear!"

On cue, he did—in a sudden puff of smoke and a shower of colored sparks.

All the giants gasped to find the mysterious, robed figure of the Ice Wizard suddenly standing on the platform in their midst.

"Blimey!" Jake stared, wide-eyed.

The enchanter was an imposing yet bizarre figure in scruffy, hanging robes and horned headgear.

He wore a kind of skullcap adorned with curled antlers. His cloak was trimmed with gray fur and he carried a tall oak staff with a gemstone in its gnarled end. His long gray beard was braided in two thin strands, but the most startling aspect of his appearance was that his face was covered in tattoos: intricate swirls of indigo and black, runes and arcane symbols of mystic power.

These, above all, gave Jake a start.

He knew by now that tattoos were popular among all the Viking folk. But the only person he'd seen with ink on his face before was Loki.

It can't be, he thought, his heart pounding. Loki was still back on earth causing trouble at the campus.

Wasn't he?

The Master of Ceremonies stepped out of the way with a polite gesture, presenting the shaman to the crowd.

The old Ice Wizard shuffled to the edge of the platform, looming over the two contestants.

The whole village waited, holding their breath, as the warlock delivered his riddle in a weird, singsong voice: "What has four wings but doesn't fly, stands twelve feet above the pool, but never swims, and though surrounded by wisdom, is often vacant?"

You could have heard a pin drop as these words were uttered.

For a long moment afterward, no one said a word, pondering the mystery.

"Now you have my riddle!" the Ice Wizard proclaimed with a cackle. "If neither of you can solve it by this time tomorrow morning, then you both lose, and I win the princess and the crown!"

"What?" Kaia breathed, starting forward in her chair.

The wizard simply floated down from the platform and began hobbling away.

Kaia had gone ashen. The boys glanced at each other, appalled.

Even the king looked shaken. "What is the meaning of this? I never approved this," he exclaimed to the Master of Ceremonies, who stammered with shock.

"I-I didn't know he was going to say that, sire! Honestly! I only called him in because I-I thought he'd be a n-neutral third party!"

"Well, call him back and tell him no," the king ordered. "I don't care about his magical powers. That weirdo will never marry my daughter nor take my crown—not under any circumstances! How could you let this happen? He's too bizarre, living out there in an ice cave by himself. It isn't natural!"

"But sire!" The Master of Ceremonies blanched. "Y-you want me to cross the Ice Wizard?"

"You heard me," King Olaf answered in a steely tone.

The Master of Ceremonies was starting to panic. This was even worse than a dragon on the loose. "But what if he gets angry and casts a curse on the village? Or turns us all into something dreadful? Please, sire, I beg you! Let's just give Prince Gorm a chance to solve the riddle fair and square before we risk angering someone as dangerous as a warlock!"

King Olaf glowered at him, then glanced over at his favorite. "Gorm?" he said ominously. "Do not let me down."

"I won't, sire." Prince Gorm marched away.

Meanwhile, Kaia glared at her father for ignoring Snorri altogether. "There's another person in this contest, Father!"

"For a test of wits? Please," the king retorted.

She gave him a truculent look while Gorm hurried after the warlock. "Pray, good enchanter!"

"What do you want?" the Ice Wizard snapped.

"Can't you give us one more clue?"

When the sorcerer glanced over his shoulder in surprise, Jake felt there was something familiar about the scornful twinkle in his eyes.

"I should think not! You're just going to have to use your brains! Don't cry, I know it's difficult for you," the warlock taunted. "Just do your best."

Gorm glowered at the insult, but even he did not dare risk angering this mysterious outsider.

"Come on," Kaia muttered, gathering Snorri and the boys. With Red in tow, she led them into the back room of her father's great hall, where she'd been spinning on her loom the first time they had met her.

There, in privacy, they put their heads together to work on solving the riddle. Archie had quickly written it down so they wouldn't forget the question.

Snorri stared at the ground, looking slightly queasy, but he still attempted to reassure her. "Don't worry, Your Highness. You won't have to marry him. Better Gorm should win you than that weirdo."

"You won't have to marry either of them," Jake insisted. "Between the four of us, I know we can figure this out. You've got my cousin here, who's a bona fide genius—"

"And Jake's got the street-smarts to have survived all those years as a London pickpocket!" Archie countered, perhaps not wanting *all* the pressure to solve the riddle on his own head. "You'd have to be pretty clever to stay a step ahead of the bobbies."

Jake didn't want to be the main person responsible for solving the thing, either. "Yes, but I never invented a robot! Archie has."

Meanwhile, Red sat on his haunches and watched the boys serenely as they both tried to dodge all the headaches that came with being the leader.

Princess Kaia took a deep breath and nodded, her hands planted on her thick waist. "Let's just all calm down here and think about this logically."

"Why don't we try and take it bit by bit?" Archie suggested, looking reassured by her managing tone.

To be sure, the boy genius had the most experience of all of them in formal problem-solving. Jake was awfully glad at this moment that Archie had come.

The young inventor rose to his feet and paced, stroking his chin as he read the slip of paper with the riddle, puzzling over the first line. "What has four wings...but doesn't fly. That could mean certain birds that can't fly. Like ostriches or—"

"Penguins!" Snorri yelled out suddenly.

"Right. Or, it could be referring to a statue of a bird. Because a statue cannot fly, either. Or...conversely, it might be relying on another use of the word...wings, meaning, say, the different blocks of a large building. Like a hospital has different wings..."

"Or a palace," Kaia offered softly.

Jake's skull was beginning to hurt already. "What about that next part?" he asked impatiently. He strode over to Archie and read the slip of paper over his shoulder. "What stands twelve feet above the pool, but never swims... Dash my wig, I have no idea."

"And is surrounded by wisdom, yet often vacant?" Archie finished.

They stood in silence for several moments more, pondering it until their brains began to throb. *This is impossible.* Jake shoved the fearful thought away. Each of them mumbled the riddle again and again under their breath, confusion on all their faces.

"Perhaps this bit about the pool is the best place to start," Archie said at length. "At least it seems to be a solid clue. If we could find the pool in question, then we could simply look at whatever stands twelve feet above it. When we find *that* object, it should give us another clue to follow."

"Sounds logical to me," Kaia answered warily.

"Agreed." Jake paused, but they still didn't know where to start. "What if you put the pool thing together with the part about wisdom?" he asked after a minute of puzzling it over in vain. "Are there any pools or ponds or wells around here that might be associated with wisdom somehow? Knowledge? Learning?"

"Well..." Snorri and the princess both racked their brains. For Snorri, this looked particularly painful. "Actually," Kaia spoke up, "there is a magical pool I know of, that's supposed to have healing waters. It's said to be sacred to the goddess, Freya."

"Excellent! That could be it!" Archie exclaimed.

"Who's Freya?" Jake asked.

"Odin's wife, the queen of the gods."

Jake stopped. "Isn't Odin the god of wisdom?"

"Yes!" Kaia suddenly jumped to her feet. "I think we're onto something! This really could be it!"

"Do you know where to find this pool?" Archie asked.

She nodded, already reaching for her cloak. "Let's go!"

They went.

CHAPTER THIRTY-SEVEN
The Unsolvable Riddle

This hunch had better be right, Jake thought, for they used up the first hour and a half of the twelve permitted just to *find* Freya's magical pool in the moonlit woods.

Holding up their lanterns as they moved along the path, they finally came upon it, tucked away in a lush valley among the sprawling forests of Jugenheim.

Arriving at last, they stood around looking at the beautiful still waters. The pool was crystal-bright and very peaceful in the silver moonlight, with a small waterfall dancing down into it.

But as far as clues went, they were disappointed. *Nothing* stood twelve feet above this pool, as the riddle specified. No tree with a branch hanging down. No decorative arch or fountain. Not even a bird flying by.

"I guess we're stuck," Archie said with a sigh. "There's nothing here."

"Don't lose heart," Jake told the others sternly. "Let's not give up too soon. Never mind the part about 'twelve feet above' for now. What about the line that says 'four wings but doesn't fly'? Look around for anything that might fit that description. Maybe there's a bird statue around here or something."

"Well, it would have to be a pair of birds for four wings," Kaia reminded them. "Two birds, two wings each."

"Right."

They all looked around the pond and even climbed up to the little waterfall to check there, too.

Again, nothing.

Half an hour later, they angrily gave up on this lead and hurried back to the village, reaching it at midnight. Ultimately, they had wasted three hours total in the excursion, all for naught.

Nine more hours to go—and it was clear they were going to be up all night trying to figure it out.

"I wonder what approach Gorm and his coaches are taking," Archie murmured.

Snorri said nothing. Studying him, Jake could almost see the giant berating himself for ever attempting to participate in this contest. He looked like he was already defeated, and that in itself set Jake's teeth on edge. He could not stand when people gave up without a fight. How could a huge, mighty giant, of all people, let fear get the best of him?

"Nine hours left," Kaia said wearily as they returned to the great hall.

"We've got to come up with something fast," Archie said.

"What if it's not an actual pool, but only something that resembles one? Like a mirror or something?" Jake suggested.

Kaia turned sharply to stare at him, then suddenly ran out of the room.

"Was it something I said?"

Snorri followed her. It was all the boys could do to keep up with the two giants as they ran outside to the king's private garden behind the great hall.

"Look!" Kaia rushed over to a stone birdbath on a pedestal. "See? It's like a pool! And here—" She pointed excitedly to the pair of small, stone, dove statues perched on opposite edges of the birdbath. "Four wings!"

"She's right!" Snorri exclaimed. "They have four wings, they never swim, and they're above the pool!"

With frowns and furrowed brows, they all stared at the birdbath for a long moment, wanting this to be the answer.

But Archie slowly shook his head. "No. Not good enough. I'm sorry, but we're not there yet. For one thing, the birds are just a few inches above the pool, not twelve feet, and besides, what's this birdbath got to do with wisdom?"

"Oh, right," Jake echoed, remembering the other elements in the riddle. "It's supposed to be surrounded by wisdom." He didn't notice anything particularly wise about this garden, though it was pretty enough, especially when lit with a few lanterns on a balmy June night.

"Well, yes..." Kaia could hardly hide her disappointment. "But the garden is often vacant!"

"Yes, but why would the Ice Wizard bother to make the riddle about a birdbath? Surely it's got to be something more meaningful than that. Something significant, important...oh, I don't know." Archie let out a sigh, took off his glasses, and massaged his eyes with his fingertips. "I'm getting a headache." He put his glasses back on. "Time to take a break."

"We don't have time for a break!" the princess cried.

"Sometimes, Your Highness, the quickest way to find an answer is to stop thinking about it so hard for a while," the boy genius said. "Then the answer simply pops into your head."

"Yes, but what if it doesn't pop in time?" Kaia demanded, her cheeks flushing with anger. "You're not the one who'll have to marry that old horn-headed weirdo!"

"Maybe there's something useful in that book that Snorri brought back from the dragon's cave," Jake said.

They all looked at him.

Snorri lifted his eyebrows. "Maybe it's got a clue in it."

"Now there's an idea," Archie said.

"Yes, but I can't read it very well," Kaia said in dismay. "It's all in Latin."

"Archie knows Latin." Jake nodded at his cousin. "Would you give it a try?"

"Absolutely," he said, abandoning the hope of taking a small break.

Back inside, Princess Kaia fetched the illuminated manuscript and gave it to Archie. As he started poring over it, translating the old Latin, Jake yawned, stretched, and walked outside to try to clear his head before diving back into the mind-twisting riddle.

Archie was right, his brain needed a break.

Better yet, the feast was still going on. He could always do with a snack. Yes, he thought, brightening. That was just the thing to restore his flagging energy—especially since they'd probably be putting out the sweets right about now.

Jake left the great hall and walked back to the feast in the center of the village. It seemed the party would be going on all night as the villagers waited to find out which of the two contestants would come back with the correct answer and thus become their next king.

That was when Jake spotted the dessert table in the square. *Ahh.* Sweet pastries! They awaited him on a long table near the base of the royal platform.

He made a beeline for the desserts, but was careful as he went not to get stepped on, for by now, most the giant warriors were silly from drinking mead since nightfall. Too many cups of the stuff made the giants clumsy. Jake was careful to steer clear of them.

He recognized several of Gorm's followers among the bunch telling crude jokes, but as he glanced around the square, he did not see Gorm himself anywhere. No doubt the prince and his coaches were off trying to solve the riddle, too.

Arriving at the dessert table, Jake was in a hurry to get back to his teammates, but he had to stand in line. To his surprise, waiting in line a few people ahead him was the Ice Wizard.

This gave him a chance to observe the sorcerer furtively without being noticed in return. As the line shuffled forward, Jake recalled his earlier suspicions about the wizard. He leaned in discreetly to get another look at the tattoos painted all over the sorcerer's wizened face.

As fierce and strange looking as he was, the Ice Wizard was obviously delighted by the pastries. He could barely make up his mind whether to try the ones with almond or apricot. Leaning on his gnarled staff, the wizard inspected the array of sweets before him.

"Ah! Hullo, you...and you..." he mumbled as he collected a few treats.

There was something so familiar about him as he lifted the pastry he desired. Wriggling his long, tapered fingers happily, he reached for another, humming to himself.

It took Jake a second to recognize the tune, but when he did, he froze.

He'd heard that song before—most recently in the Exhibit Hall, from somebody who had nearly run him over with a high-wheeler bicycle.

A tune that nobody from Jugenheim should know.

"The Ride of the Valkyries."

Jake abandoned his place in line and ran.

Dodging giant feet, he raced back to the great hall. Moments later, he burst into the back room, gasping for breath.

The others looked over in surprise.

"Jake? What's wrong?" Kaia exclaimed.

Archie jumped to his feet. "You're as white as a sheet! What's happened?"

"Becaw?"

"It's Loki!" Jake gasped for breath, his heart pounding. His mind reeled as he managed to shake his head. "The Ice Wizard is Loki. He's here."

"*What?*"

"Are you sure?"

"I'm sure. The riddle is a trick. It doesn't have an answer. At least, no answer we'll ever be able to find by using ordinary logic." He shut the door behind him. "He's the trickster; that means the riddle's a trick question."

"How do you know it's him?" Archie asked gravely.

As Jake told the others what had just happened, they glanced at each other in shock.

"It's the same song he was humming the first day I saw him in the Exhibit Hall, when he was riding that ridiculous high-wheeler. I'm certain it's him. The way he acted, barmy in the head, slightly twisted. It's Loki, all right." He shook his head angrily. "I should have known! He must've covered the rest of his face in ink to mask the tattoo that Ragnor the Punisher gave him all those centuries ago."

"Very clever," Archie murmured.

"The point is, we've been going about this all wrong. No wonder we haven't made any progress! We need to look at this riddle from a totally different angle. He *is* the trickster god, but there has to be an answer that actually fits. His victory wouldn't count if the answer turned out to be nonsense. At least now that we know we're dealing with Loki, we can assume he won't play fair. So, where do we start?"

"Well...we did find something about a pool in this ancient manuscript from the dragon's cave," Archie said warily. "But I don't see how..."

"Let's hear it," Jake said.

Archie tapped a paragraph of bold Latin script on the open page. "The Irish monk who wrote this manuscript claims to have baptized Odin himself in a pool that lies within Valaskjalf."

"Inside *what?*" Jake asked.

"Valaskjalf," Archie repeated.

"What the deuce is that?"

Archie glanced at Kaia.

She gave the boys a skeptical look. "Valaskjalf is said to be a white marble castle, Odin's palace. In Valhalla."

Jake sat down abruptly. "Valhalla?"

She nodded.

Archie picked up where she had left off. "According to the manuscript, the monk baptized the Norse god privately inside his castle, so as not to throw the whole pagan world into a tizzy. Apparently there's some sort of indoor pool inside the palace."

Kaia folded her arms over her chest in silence while Snorri looked around worriedly at all of them.

"Well," Jake said with caution, "that would certainly qualify as 'surrounded by wisdom,' since Odin is the god of wisdom, right?"

"Yes. And his home is often vacant, when he's out wandering the world in search of heroes—warriors that he can recruit for Valhalla," Kaia added. "He's also the god of war, so when there's a battle, he's usually there."

They all were silent, digesting the ramifications of all this.

"So, is that the answer, then?" Jake said at last. "Odin's castle—how ever you say it?"

"Valaskjalf," Snorri repeated.

"Not sure if the castle itself is the answer, or some particular part of it..." Archie's words trailed off as he met Jake's stare.

Without a word, both cousins reached the same conclusion.

Jake was the one who said it out loud. "We're not going to know for certain unless we go and see it for ourselves."

"But how can we go to Valhalla?" Snorri asked. "It's the land of the dead! We're alive—and I for one intend to stay that way."

"Well, we have to be sure! We can't just throw an answer out there," Archie said. "Not if Loki's already here among us, impersonating the Ice Wizard."

"Archie's right," Jake backed him up. "We have to know for sure. We dare not get the answer wrong. So how do we get to Valhalla?"

"There are...many gates," Kaia said slowly. "Some say as many as five hundred different portals. I only know of one. I could take you there, but whether you'll be able to get in once we reach the gates, I do not know."

Jake nodded darkly. "We have to try."

"Is there time, Your Highness?" Archie checked his fob watch. "It's one A.M. We've only got eight hours left."

"If we're going, we need to leave now," she replied. "It's a good three hours there and back."

"But Your Highness!" Snorri insisted. "If they're wrong, all is lost!"

"Do you have any better ideas?" Jake exclaimed.

Snorri gave him a blank look, but Archie tried to intervene.

"You must admit it does sound highly dangerous, Jake. Not to mention a little insane. To have us go to the gates of Valhalla, enter the land of the dead, and then break into Odin's palace, all in the vague hopes of finding some pool?" Archie shook his head, paling now that he had spoken the steps of their daunting task out loud. "We'll be lucky if we don't get Blood-Eagled."

Jake winced at the reminder of that nasty Viking punishment. "You don't have to come if you don't want to. I'll go myself. Me and Red. Right, boy?"

"Caw!"

"Jake," Archie chided.

"Look, I know this is a gamble," he said, "but if somebody doesn't come back with the right answer, and Loki gets control of Giant World, it's Ragnarok for all of us."

"He's right. Enough talk. Come on," Kaia ordered, grabbing her cloak and heading for the door. "I'll take you on my ship. If Thor smiles, we'll have the winds at our backs."

Jake called his Gryphon to his side; Kaia gave them extra gear to keep them warm, and off they went.

To sail to the land of the dead.

CHAPTER THIRTY-EIGHT
Valkyries

As Kaia's royal Viking ship glided through the swirling mists, Jake shrugged deeper into his coat. It was too bad Miss Langesund couldn't be here, he thought. The lady-archeologist would have been thrilled to take a sail on a real Viking longboat, even a giant-sized one.

Presently, they were in the middle of arctic nowhere, the carved wooden dragon-head on the prow forging on northward, always north. They had left the shores of Jugenheim two hours ago, with Snorri and Kaia heave-ho-rowing through the waves at top speed.

Jake could hardly believe they were going to Valhalla. Breaking in, to be exact.

He was excited for the adventure, which probably meant that he was as much of a loon-bat as Loki. But the flutter of anticipation in his stomach to see the land of myth was mingled with a prudent dose of fear.

Other than that, he was numb. The cold at this latitude was unlike anything Jake had ever experienced—or Archie, for that matter. Each breath stung a bit in their lungs. Ice crystals kept forming on their lashes, and neither cousin could stop shivering, despite the sealskin coats that Kaia had given them. (The smallest size available, for toddler-aged giants.)

She had also provided Red with a thick plaid horse blanket (foal-sized, for giant baby horses) held in place by a strap under his chest. She had cut two slits in the top of it for his wings. She had also offered him a set of horses' leg wrappings to protect his paws from the extreme cold, but the Gryphon wouldn't wear them.

In any case, Red was half eagle, and eagles could thrive in frigid climates. The boys took shelter from the wind under his wings, one on each side of the noble beast; the three of them huddled together for warmth on the deck while the hardy Norse giants rowed, navigating by starlight.

The dragon boat glided past glaciers that sparkled in the night. Gigantic slabs of ice as big as buildings crumbled off the glaciers now and then without warning and crashed into the sea.

Archie whiled away the time with an explanation. "Th-th-the glacier is c-constantly re-m-making itself," Jake's shivering cousin informed him. "The ice f-forms farther north, and when it g-gets to the end, called the t-t-terminus, it c-calves, or b-breaks off, and floats away, f-forming ice-b-bergs."

Jake nodded, stifling a yawn. He had not planned on staying awake all night, but he was too cold to sleep. It would be morning soon. This far north, there were only a few hours of darkness this time of year. He'd be glad when the sun rose and warmed them up a little.

Though the nighttime made their arctic surroundings look even more dramatic and mysterious, it also made the going that much more dangerous. The large oil lamp attached to the front of the ship cast only a small beam of light ahead. The rocks, the passing whales, and most of all, the icebergs Archie had mentioned made their path an obstacle course through the sea. Unfortunately, they did not have the luxury of waiting until it got light out. The clock was ticking on the time limit to answer Loki's riddle.

After a while, Kaia took a break at the oars to rest her arms while Snorri kept rowing. Her blond head was draped in the fur-lined hood of her cloak as she looked up to consult the map of the stars.

All of a sudden, she pointed skyward. "Look!"

Swirling ribbons of color danced across in the sky.

"The Aurora Borealis!" Archie burst out in excitement.

The green, pink, and yellow glow of the Northern Lights bathed their faces, etched with wonder.

"Odin's battle-flag," Kaia said somberly at length. "That means we're almost there." With that, she sat down and took up her oars again with renewed determination.

The mysterious swirling lights in the sky mesmerized Jake. He watched them until they faded half an hour later, vanishing as inexplicably as they had appeared.

But the Northern Lights had no sooner abandoned the sky than the sun peeped over the icy horizon. As it climbed higher, it lit the arctic landscape with incredible colors of a wintry dawn.

Brilliant blues and otherworldly greens shimmered amid a hundred shades of white and silver ice; here and there, the snow looked lavender and pink.

They laughed at the sight of a polar bear standing on an ice floe. It roared at them as the dragon boat glided by. The beast looked ferocious to Jake, but Snorri and Kaia just laughed. The hulking polar bear was only the size of a dog to the giants.

At length, they entered a narrow passage between two towering rock faces. The height of the cliffs blotted out the morning sunlight, casting them in shadow.

The waves crashed between the two sides of the narrow strait they had entered. Jagged rocks were everywhere.

Snorri used all his strength to steer with the oars.

As the boat tossed, Jake and Archie held on in dread, while Red dug his claws into the deck to keep himself anchored.

The longboat angled every which way in the wild currents trapped between the high sea cliffs.

Aside from feeling queasy from the ship's bucking, Jake was terrified at how easily the vessel's hull could be damaged. If they hit any of these rocks and the ship went down, even the giants would be dead in minutes in this icy-water—provided they weren't eaten first by whales or polar bears or something worse.

Sweat stood out on Snorri's brow as he used his massive strength to maneuver the dragon-boat safely through treacherous rocks.

As they approached a sheltered inlet where the foaming waters calmed, a strange clamor filled the air, like a flock of a hundred restless seabirds. The din came from somewhere up ahead, echoing to them down the long narrow corridor between the cliffs.

"What is that?" Jake exclaimed.

"Penguins? Puffins?" Archie guessed.

Kaia and Snorri exchanged a worried glance.

The constant noise of the birds grew louder as the boat drifted deeper into the stone passage.

"I think we're almost there," Kaia murmured. And she was right. The strait ended ahead in a rounded hollow in the rock, a dead end.

The water here was an otherworldly shade of bright aquamarine. The back wall blocked their way in the form of a towering cliff, with twin glaciers reaching down both sides of it like great white arms.

Indeed, the gray cliff ahead was carved with runes taller than two giants. Jake realized he was looking not at a cliff, but at the gate to Valhalla—even as he heard Archie gasp.

"Jake, look!"

He turned as his cousin pointed at the birds, and his eyes shot open wide.

There were creatures clinging to the bare rock face of the cliffs on either side of them, like a huge flock of puffins. Sitting there on the rugged outcrops of stone, some tucked in to little cliffside nests. But they weren't puffins. No, they weren't birds at all.

They were women.

With wings.

"Valkyries," Kaia said reverently. "The Guardians of Valhalla."

Jake was nearly speechless. "What are they? L-like Viking angels?" he stammered with a nervous gulp.

"Of a sort," Kaia told him. "Odin's battle-maidens, hand-picked to go and collect the souls of warriors fallen in battle. They escort them here, to a hero's afterlife. When they're not doing that, they guard the gates to the realm of the gods."

It took a moment for Jake to absorb this. "You mean we need to get past all these hundreds of Valkyries in order to get inside?"

Kaia nodded grimly.

"There's no way," Archie whispered.

"There's got to be," Jake said. "We didn't come this far for nothing."

As Snorri brought the ship to a halt in the calm waters of the inlet, sheltered from the wind, one of the Valkyries pushed away from her perch on the cold rock cliff and flew toward them.

The boys' eyes widened. She *did* look like an angel, except she was armed to the teeth.

Wings pumping, the Valkyrie flew to the front of the ship and hovered there, a ray of morning sun illuminating her exquisite Scandinavian beauty: high cheekbones, brilliant blue eyes, flowing strawberry-blond hair.

Odin had good taste in battle-maids, Jake thought in wide-eyed admiration.

She had sleek, white-feathered wings. Her athletic frame was lightly draped in a short, pale-pink slip of a dress over high, laced boots. But Jake doubted most angels carried a silver sword like the one at her waist, let alone had rune tattoos twining up her arms like this battle-maid of Odin did.

"Noble giants!" she intoned in a forceful voice full of stern dignity. "You must turn back. You are too near the Gates. You have no business in these waters."

Snorri made the boat shake, he was trembling so much in terror of the pretty creature, but Kaia stepped forward and answered in equally formal tones. "Oh, battle-maid of Odin, please grant us passage. I am Princess Kaia of Jugenheim, and I'm here because our land is besieged by the trickery of Lord Loki. We must outwit him in his mischief to prevent a great evil—"

"None shall pass!" the Valkyrie cut her off. "We have our orders!"

"If you please, ma'am," Snorri spoke up, humbly removing his horned helmet, "there's not enough room in these narrows to turn our ship around."

"My sisters and I will assist you. We will steer you back out to the open water, so you may return to your homes or go where you will."

"We can't! We need to solve a riddle!" Archie cried.

The Valkyrie narrowed her eyes at him. "You must go or you will die. None of the living may trespass in Valhalla." She flew back to Kaia to issue her final warning. "I asked you with the respect due your rank, Princess of Jugenheim, to leave. But if you give us no choice, we will turn you away by force."

To emphasize her point, the Valkyrie let out a loud birdlike call, at which, twenty more winged beauties joined her, flying over to surround their boat.

They took hold of the edges of the bulwarks. The leader gave the order and the Valkyries began to fly, driving the dragon-boat backwards.

Snorri tried to work against them with the oars.

Jake turned to Red, "Are you thinking what I'm thinking?"

The Gryphon cocked his head to the side and nodded.

"Good. Let's go, then. C'mon if you're coming, Arch," Jake whispered. "Can't promise we won't get Blood-Eagled for this, but Red can get us past them."

"Of course I'm coming with you!" he whispered back. "These girls are too pretty to Blood-Eagle anybody."

Don't count on it, Jake thought.

Snorri was begging the gorgeous Valkyries to let go of the ship, but Jake exchanged a glance with Princess Kaia, whose hand was inching toward the bow hung across her back.

The princess gave him a subtle nod, understanding his intent. The boys slipped onto Red's back. "Hold on tight," Jake warned his cousin. "He'll have to fly in an unpredictable pattern to get us past this lot."

"Will do."

Red took two running steps across the deck of the ship and leaped into the air, taking flight.

Several of the Valkyries split off from the others, coming after them. "Back to your ship! What do you think you're doing?"

Red kept going, flying swiftly to scale the massive gate ahead. The boys held on tight, but Jake glanced over his shoulder when he heard a piercing, bird-like screech.

The leader of the Valkyries screamed out the summons to her sisters; it was answered by every other winged woman on the cliffs *and* the ones pushing the boat.

As the enraged shriek from all of them echoed through the narrows, the sound was so loud that the vibrations from it cracked a chunk of ice off the end of the glacier.

When the huge slab of ice fell and splashed into the sea, it sent plumes of freezing water arcing high into the air—high enough to spatter Red and the boys.

As a result, ice crystals formed on Red's wings here and there and made it harder for him to fly, especially with passengers.

Behind them, meanwhile, the dragon-boat rocked wildly from the splashing of the ice. Snorri was thrown back from the oars and Kaia went sprawling onto the deck.

Red continued climbing into the sky.

"Good boy, keep going, we're almost there!" Jake urged his Gryphon, riding low over his neck like a jockey on a racehorse.

Meanwhile, Archie glanced behind them. "Uh, Jake?"

"What is it?"

"Remember how the Norns had a bad side?"

"Yes, why?

"Something's happening to the Valkyries!"

"What do you mean?"

"They're—changing!" Archie paused. "Uh-oh. I-I think now they're really mad."

As the Valkyries' terrible screeches reverberated through the chasm, Jake glanced back and saw that Archie was right.

The Valkyries were transforming from beautiful winged women into hideous harpies with great, bony claws. In place of angelic white feathers, they now flapped aloft on leathery, black batwings, their pastel dresses magically changed to wraithlike tatters.

Instead of gorgeous blondes and redheads, they changed into skeletal hags with stringy gray hair. *Now* they looked like creatures fit to haunt a battlefield, Jake thought in shock.

The Valkyries unsheathed their weapons.

"Fly, Red," he whispered to the Gryphon. "Fly as fast as you can. Hold on, Arch."

Sitting behind him, Archie gripped Jake's shoulders and shouted, *"Here they come!"*

CHAPTER THIRTY-NINE
The Land of the Dead

Red flew valiantly with half a dozen harpies on his tail. Holding onto the Gryphon's collar with his left hand, Jake looked over his shoulder, stretching out his right hand.

His jaw clenched, he focused on summoning up his telekinesis to knock their pursuers away, driving a few of the tattered wraiths into the cliffs with bolts of energy that flew from his fingertips.

But for one thing, using this power tended to weaken him, and for another, for every fierce Valkyrie that fell behind or spiraled toward the water, more kept coming.

"How high does this gate go?" Archie cried.

"I don't know. Keep flying, Red. We've got to clear it!"

Clouds cloaked the top of the ominous stone cliff that formed the gate to Valhalla.

The Gryphon kept racing skyward, but the harpies were gaining on them.

Meanwhile in the boat below, Snorri was swinging the oar to knock the Valkyries back, while Princess Kaia continually brought new arrows up to her bow and kept firing away, shooting the screeching harpies out of the sky.

"Keep fighting, Snorri!" Kaia yelled. "We've got to hold them off! I'm not going back to Jugenheim without the answer to that riddle! And if these girls want to stop me, they're going to have to kill me!"

Snorri blanched at her ferocity, but held his ground beside her. "Don't worry, Your Highness, I won't let them get you!"

"How sweet," Kaia muttered as she shot another arrow and hit the screeching, wraithlike harpy in the eye.

"Uh, Princess..." Snorri clubbed another with his oar. "Just one question."

"What?" she panted with exertion.

"Are we goin' to get in trouble with Odin for killing some of his battle-maids?"

"Don't be silly, Snorri! They can't die."

He realized in surprise that she was right as he watched one of the hideous creatures land on an ice floe, an arrow sticking through her.

But in just a minute or two, the Valkyrie roused herself to sit up, pulled the arrow out of her body, shook herself, and then returned to the fight.

"If they can't die, then how are we supposed to hold them off until the dwarves get back? There's so many of them!"

"We're bigger." Kaia drew her sword, back to back with Snorri. "Come on, you little gnats!"

Far above the embattled giants, Red kept on flying as fast as he could, his wings beating hard in the thin, frigid air.

His breath clouded around them.

Archie pulled a hammer out of his tool-bag and whacked the hand of a snarling harpy who was trying to grab the Gryphon's tail.

The Valkyrie howled and fell back a few feet lower just as two more appeared ahead, their swords drawn.

Jake cast them both away with an invisible shock of energy from his fingertips. But still more were closing in, and though the top of the cliff finally came into sight, he was starting to feel fairly sure that the three of them were going to die soon.

He could already feel the Gryphon laboring beneath him. Red swatted away a harpy with his front lion claws, then, suddenly, one of the harpies sliced at the noble beast with her sword. Red roared as the harpy's blade slashed him across his haunches.

The Gryphon whipped aside to kick the harpy in the face with his back paw, claws bared, and indeed, the harpy fell away.

But the awkward motion sent the boys lurching to the right; the sudden shift in the weight he was carrying threw off Red's balance, and the next thing Jake knew, the flying Gryphon went into a horizontal roll—a midair crash!

They went slamming through the flock of harpies, falling. Jake and Archie slipped off Red's back in the chaos and plummeted toward the water, screaming.

Red tumbled end over end in a chaos of wings and tufted tail; Jake looked down at the rocks and icy waves zooming up to meet them and was sure they were all doomed.

But Snorri saw them coming and grabbed one of the boat's nearby fishing nets. While Kaia held off the harpies, he opened the net wide between his massive arms and leaned out over the side of the ship to catch them.

They screamed all the way down, but one by one, they landed safely in the fishing net, even Red—though he was bleeding from the cut on his hip.

The Gryphon didn't seem to care. Snorri set them safely on the deck. While the boys lay in the fishing net for a moment, panting with relief, Red leaped free with a furious roar, pounced across the deck, and immediately started slashing at the harpies like a cat chasing sparrows.

"Red! Come back here! We need to try again!" Archie called as the boys climbed out of the fishy-smelling net on shaky legs.

But despite the boys' attempts to call him back, the Gryphon paid no attention. Red was utterly absorbed in his quest to catch and bite or scratch as many harpies as he could. His fighting instincts had kicked in.

"He's out of control," Jake murmured, watching him.

"Can't you calm him down?" Archie turned to Jake, who continued to stare at his rampaging pet. "I hope that cut's not serious. How's he going to fly us up there now that he's hurt?"

Jake shook his head. "I don't think it's going to work. He's done his best, but he can't get past them. We're too outnumbered. Besides, look at him. I've never seen him so furious."

Even now, Red had a harpy in his beak and was shaking her like a rag-doll.

Jake turned to gaze up again at the looming gates of Valhalla. "We're going to have to find another way up there."

Snorri also looked up at the cliff, shading his eyes. "There's only one way," he announced at length, while Kaia kicked a trio of harpies into the water and Red caught another one by the wing and tossed her.

"How?" Archie asked.

"Remember at the feast?" Snorri prompted.

Jake groaned. "I remember. Very well, if you think it'll work."

Snorri nodded. "It's got to."

"What are you two talking about?" Archie exclaimed.

"Dwarf tossing," Jake said grimly, flipping his forelock out of his eyes with a resolute toss of his head. "I'll go first."

"Now, hold on just a minute!" Archie protested, wide-eyed. "That's just daft! At least with Red, you have some control over your flight path—"

"It's our only choice! You don't have to come if you don't want to," Jake cut him off impatiently, then he turned to Snorri. "Throw me as high as you possibly can."

The giant nodded. "I will."

"But how are you going to get back?" Archie cried.

He shook his head. "I'll cross that bridge when I come to it. Let's just get this over with."

Jake balled himself up like a human cannonball, his arms wrapped tightly around his bent legs. In this form, Snorri picked him up in both hands, taking a firm grip of him.

Then the giant began to swing Jake between his legs, forward and back, gathering momentum. All of a sudden, Snorri released him, hurling him toward the sky.

Jake flew up into the air, whipping past or rather *through* the flock of Valkyries; all the while, he kept his forehead tucked against his knees, his arms tightly clutched around his bent legs.

Jaw clenched, he cleared the flock of Valkyries and promptly disappeared into the clouds.

He opened his eyes to slits against the whipping wind created by his velocity, but all he could see now were white clouds around him. He caught a glimpse of the cliff's edge tapering up into a wall as he flew over it. He was going over the gate!

At about that moment, he reached the top of the arc on which Snorri had hurled him. And then he started falling.

He stretched himself out to his full length, unfolding from his balled-up pose.

His shout streamed out behind him as he plummeted over the mighty gate and toward the ground of Valhalla, plunging through the mists.

Arms and legs flailing, he saw that he was heading for what appeared to be a grassy green meadow far below.

The ground was racing up swiftly toward him, while behind him, he could hear Archie yelling as his cousin followed a moment later.

Then Jake squeezed his eyes shut and prayed he did not splat when he hit the ground. Otherwise, he might have to stay forever.

Here in the land of the dead.

CHAPTER FORTY
Viking Heaven

Whatever pains or broken bones Jake expected when he hit the ground, he was about to learn that the normal rules did not apply in the afterlife.

As he came careening down from the sky at blinding speeds, spread-eagled, he saw the ground racing up toward him and threw his arms up to protect his head.

But when he hit, to his astonishment, instead of hard-packed earth, the grassy meadow gave way, cushioning him with the soft texture of a giant green marshmallow.

He sank down into the softness and was bounced back up again, though not nearly so high.

Archie followed seconds later, and let out a whoop of shock as they both continued bouncing up and down helplessly on the soft spongy turf.

"I don't believe it!" Archie yelled as he soared by. "Woooo hoooo! I'm flying!"

"Quit foolin' around!" Jake scolded, though with each bounce, the boys flew not as high.

"This is wonderful!" Archie turned a somersault in midair before he landed in the green pillowed mattress of the field at last.

"Crikey," Jake panted when they finally came to rest. At last, the boys found themselves sitting in a meadow full of tall grass and wildflowers. They exchanged a glance of amazement.

"I guess we made it," Jake remarked.

Archie grinned.

Looking all around them, the boys climbed to their feet, grateful that the arctic cold had disappeared. Valhalla seemed to exist in its own protected bubble of spring-like warmth, neither too hot nor too cold. Just perfect. As the wildflowers blew on the light breeze, Jake savored the soft, translucent quality of the light. It was gold and white, with a rosy glow.

"I can't believe it. Viking heaven," Archie said with a hush in his voice, looking around.

"I think I want to stay here," Jake replied only half seriously.

His cousin snorted. "You're not a Viking. And you're not dead. As for me, I still have to give my speech tomorrow morning, remember?"

"Is that tomorrow already? Huh." Jake nodded, scanning the pristine landscape of lush meadows and alluring woods. "Come on then, we'd better find this pool. We daren't leave Snorri and Kaia and Red to battle the Valkyries much longer. No telling how long they can hold out."

"Look, over there—a path!" Archie pointed. "That must lead somewhere."

"Let's follow it," Jake agreed. They hurried over to the delightful grassy footpath and started walking.

The path followed alongside a beautiful babbling brook that meandered through the meadow and then passed some orchards. Gorgeous trees along the way offered every kind of fruit. Antlered deer grazed in the fields, while rabbits frolicked in the shade. They heard a whine and Archie looked back, stopping in his tracks.

"Puppies!"

A small troop of adorable, clumsy puppies were trying to catch up with the boys, yipping happily as they tumbled through the grass.

"Where did they come from?" Archie exclaimed.

Jake laughed at the merry sight. "Well, it wouldn't be any sort of heaven if there were no dogs, would it?"

"You sound like Dani O'Dell."

Jake grinned, but they didn't have time to play with the puppies, no matter how adorable.

They hurried on down the grassy path, still feeling a slight marshmallow-like give underfoot. It made each step springy, and the wildflowers they pressed underfoot perfumed their passing.

Before long, the boys spotted two buildings in the distance: one, a smudge of silver to the north; the other, a large wooden lodge to the south—a great hall not unlike King Olaf's back in Jugenheim—but on a human scale, rather than for giants.

The southern building was closer, and the stream was taking them straight towards it. Archie took his spyglass out of his tool-bag and lifted it to his eye. While he studied the nearer building, Jake caught a distant hint of song and chanting.

"Do you hear that?" he asked.

Archie paused. They both listened harder and could just make out deep male voices singing, accompanied by thundering drums. It was a vaguely terrifying sound. The boys held very still, listening. The breeze carried the distant music to them across the meadows— ancient songs that had once struck terror into the hearts of monks and villagers along the British Isles.

Viking songs.

"That must be Odin's mead hall for the warriors!" Archie whispered.

Jake beckoned to him, and the boys ran for cover in the woods.

Concealed by the trees, they continued moving closer to the mead hall, with its huge timber beams and gabled roof. It sounded like quite a party was going on inside. Jake trembled to realize the place was packed with ruthless Viking warriors.

Archie, meanwhile, exchanged his spyglass for his hammer, just in case he needed to defend himself again.

He offered Jake a wrench for the same purpose.

Jake shook his head and frowned. "I don't think that'll do you any good, anyway. The people here are already dead."

Archie shrugged. "Well, it makes me feel better, anyway."

"Come on." Jake nodded. The boys crept stealthily toward the Viking mead hall, scanning the place and wondering how to proceed.

Just then, the door opened. They ducked behind a huge tree as a Viking warrior stepped out. They could hear him singing to himself. The clamor of the music from inside was muffled again when the doors swung shut behind him.

The slight weaving of his steps made the boys exchange a knowing glance. It seemed the mead flowed as freely here in Valhalla as it did in Jugenheim.

Full of drink, the golden-haired Viking went over to the edge of the woods to relieve himself, singing crude lyrics about some ladies all the while.

A moment later, he fastened his leather trousers and turned around, swaggering back toward the party, but one of the war-horses tied up outside the great hall whinnied to him. "And a good day to you, as well, noble steed!" the Viking warlord answered cheerfully. When he stepped over to give the horse a pat, Jake saw his face and gasped.

"It's Ragnor the Punisher!" he said in astonishment.

"Who?" Archie whispered.

"The Viking ghost who was haunting Miss Langesund's ship museum!"

"That man there? What? I'm seeing a ghost?" Archie exclaimed.

"Aye."

"I've never seen a ghost before." He stared, then turned to Jake. "Is that how they always look?"

"Not at all. They're usually sort of bluish-gray and see-through down on earth. Sometimes they look like orbs or just a mist—never mind. Stay here a second. I'm going to go and talk to him. Maybe he can help us."

"Jake!" Archie whispered frantically, but Jake was already in motion, leaving his hiding place behind the tree. "King Ragnor! Sire! Ragnor the Punisher!" he yelled as loudly as he dared. He had to catch the warlord before he went back inside.

Hearing his name called, the Viking chief stopped and scanned the woods. Out of habit, he reached for the hilt of his gigantic sword. "Who's there?"

"Sire!" Jake stepped out from the woods, emerging into the sunlight. "Remember me? Jake—Lord Griffon," he reminded him as he approached the towering warrior. "We met at the museum. I spoke to you there about the people who dug up your ship? Making a monument to your glory?"

"Ah, yes! Clever lad. Excellent advice, to rejoin my shipmates and fellow princes here in Valhalla." Then he frowned. "But what are you doing here? It's a tragedy for a boy to die so young."

"Oh, I'm not dead, sir," Jake hastened to assure him. "Just visiting. In fact, I'm here on a very important mission, my cousin and I." He beckoned to Archie, who stepped nervously into view. "I was wondering if you could give us a little help."

"Mission?" Ragnor echoed. "Why, I haven't been on a mission in nearly a thousand years..." A wistful look came into his fierce eyes. "What sort of mission, may I ask? Have you come a-raiding?"

"No, sir, nothing like that. I'm afraid it's Loki causing trouble again."

"Loki?" Ragnor growled, instantly bristling at the mention of that name. "What's that troublemaker up to now?"

"He's trying to get control of Giant Land."

Ragnor the Punisher looked shocked. "You know you can't let that happen," he said at once.

"I know, believe me. But he's already infiltrated Jugenheim. He tricked King Olaf and his court by posing as a local shaman called the Ice Wizard. In that form, Loki put forth a terrible riddle that we have to solve within a few short hours or he's going to take over Giant Land. But if we do solve it, we can send him packing."

"How can I help?" the Viking warlord asked at once.

As Archie joined them, it was just the answer Jake was hoping to hear. "We found an ancient manuscript that gave us our best clue. Apparently, there's some sort of pool inside Odin's palace that we believe is the key to solving Loki's riddle. But we need to get in there and see it for ourselves, so we can be sure. If we give Loki the wrong answer, then he wins and we're all doomed. If he gets control of the giants, he'll lead them on an invasion of Midgarth and all the other worlds."

"I understand. Hmm." Ragnor stroked his golden beard in thought. "I can get you to the palace and distract Odin's hunting dogs so you boys can sneak in. The All-Father's not at home right now, which should make your task a little easier. But his son's there, so you'll have to watch your step."

"His son?" Jake echoed.

"Thor, of course," Ragnor said grimly. Then he turned away, beckoning them. "Come! To the horses."

Before long, they were mounted up on three of the great war-horses tied up outside the Vikings' mead hall. Jake chose a gray and Archie swung up onto a chestnut. Ragnor's horse was black.

"Follow me!" The Viking squeezed his horse's sides with his knees and the animal leaped into a canter.

Jake hung on for dear life as his horse followed. Being a city kid and until recently a pauper, he was not the most experienced of riders.

He was nervous about whether he could even stay on the war-horse's back. But to his delight, the marshmallow effect made the ride as easy as sitting in a rocking chair.

The horses' galloping strides bounced them lightly over the spongy ground. Still, he held on tightly to the gray's mane, just to be extra safe. It didn't occur to him that riding a gryphon was much harder.

Ragnor glanced over his shoulder to make sure the boys were all right. Archie wore a grin from ear to ear.

Thanks to their fleet-footed mounts, within twenty minutes they were already approaching the castle of Valaskjalf. Odin's palace radiated the soft light of Valhalla with a lustrous gleam.

The walls and battlements were pure silver, but the front steps and four soaring towers were of white marble. The whole castle glittered in the sunlight.

The All-Father must have been a great dog-lover, Jake thought, for not only did Valhalla offer puppies to play with, but two giant statues of wolf-like hunting dogs carved of smooth gray stone framed the castle doorway.

Slowing his horse, Ragnor held up his fist, signaling the boys to halt in the shadows at the edge of the woods.

Jake's heart pounded as he got a better sense of the daunting task he and Archie somehow had to accomplish, sneaking into Odin's fortress.

"Everything looks quiet," Ragnor remarked, nodding in approval. "I'll distract the guard dogs. When the way is clear, you boys sneak in. But you won't have time to dawdle before his hounds return."

"Good luck, Ragnor," Jake answered. "We're grateful for your help. If I don't get the chance to say it later, I thank you."

The Viking nobleman saluted them, then signaled his horse forward. The boys stayed in the shadow of the woods, watching him ride toward the castle.

The spectacle they beheld next gave them some inkling of the nearly-insane bravery that Ragnor the Punisher must have possessed in life. He was using himself as bait for the two giant wolf-dog statues, which came alive as the boys watched.

Ragnor urged his horse up the front steps with a wild whoop.

The dog statues opened their eyes. Their pointed ears pricked up, then they bared their fangs at the intruder.

When Ragnor urged his horse off the stairs with a leap back onto the ground, the guard dogs licked their chops, the stone of their carved bodies turning into muscle and fur. It seemed the dogs could not resist the chase. Barking as loud as cannons, they rose, each as tall as buildings.

The Viking chief rode wildly, zigzagging and leading the giant dogs away from the castle in wild figure-eights.

Watching them, Archie was as white as alabaster, and Jake was almost too terrified to move. But somehow he found the nerve to elbow his cousin and whispered, "Let's go!"

Archie shook off his daze and followed. Then the boys were in motion, sprinting across the field to reach the entrance to the castle before Odin's dogs came back.

The spongy texture of the ground slowed them down a little, but since Ragnor had led the dogs out of earshot, the boys wasted no time.

The last running step off the green grass up onto the white marble staircase was particularly bouncy, and Jake was surprised when he went flying all the way up to the top of the steps in one stride.

He landed on solid marble before the front door. In a heartbeat, his cousin was right beside him.

Immediately, they teamed up to push the palace door open just a crack. Just wide enough for two skinny boys to sneak through.

But for a second, they almost didn't dare go in.

Surely it was madness to trespass into the home of the fierce Norse gods. If this didn't get a person Blood-Eagled, nothing would.

Exchanging a worried but determined glance, the cousins shrugged off their fear and ran inside.

CHAPTER FORTY-ONE
The Silver Palace

The boys sneaked into the castle with no idea of what they might find. The first thing Jake noticed was that the vaulted ceiling above them must have been fifty feet high.

"How big are these gods, anyway?" he whispered. "Human sized or giant-like? Even bigger?

"No idea," Archie breathed as they stole along the corridor. "I think they can change to be as big or as small as they wish. Just depends what they want to accomplish."

"Loki, too?"

"I should think so."

"Great," Jake muttered.

Hurrying to the end of the white entrance corridor, they arrived at the doorway of a vast, rectangular room.

The boys crouched cautiously beside the wall. If anyone came along while they were in that sparse chamber, they'd be seen right away. It offered no place to hide, empty but for a Persian rug in the middle of the room with a round table directly beneath a crystal chandelier. On this table sat a thriving potted plant, lit up by a beam of sunshine slanting in through a high window.

Jake furrowed his brow, studying the scene before him. "Doesn't look very Viking-like to me."

Archie nodded. "Strange."

But Jake shrugged off the modern décor. In dealing with immortals, who could say? Maybe Odin and his royal family liked keeping up with the times.

More important to stick to the business at hand.

"Let's go find this pool from Loki's riddle, then."

"Where do you want to start? We've got three choices." Archie pointed to the three hallways that opened off the vast chamber, each leading, presumably, to a different wing of the palace.

The three elaborate doorways were each as tall as Snorri. Carved symbols above each one gave tantalizing hints of what might lay beyond. The doorway to the left was adorned with graceful, painted flowers, while the one to the right was marked with the symbol of a mighty hammer.

The largest doorway, straight ahead from where the boys crouched, had the ominous symbol of two ravens displayed above the arch.

Glancing around at each of the doorways, Jake knew that the hammer was the symbol of Thor. The flashes of lightning and low rumbles of thunder coming from his wing of the castle confirmed that the god of sea and sky was indeed at home.

But the flowers? Then he recalled Kaia saying something about a goddess queen named Freya, Odin's wife. He could just make out the sound of babies crying, toddlers laughing, and lullabies coming from that direction.

Archie heard it, too, and gave him a wry glance. "I think Freya's the goddess of marriage and motherhood."

"Ah. The one straight ahead must be for Odin, then," Jake whispered. "Why ravens?"

"God of death?" Archie breathed.

"Great. And we're about to go invade his private rooms," Jake muttered. "Let's go."

The boys darted away from the shelter of the wall, racing down the few stone steps into the large sunken chamber to sprint across the room. Passing the table with the plant, Jake caught a glimpse of the brass nameplate on the flowerpot and nearly skidded to a halt for a closer look.

Yggdrasil?!

A baby one! he thought. Immediately, he wondered if there were newborn worlds already budding in the twig's little branches. But there was no time to stop and study it or even to ponder this mystery.

Odin's hunting dogs might return at any moment—or worse, Thor might come out and take a break from doing...whatever it was he did, exactly. Making the weather or ruling the ocean or some such. Passing the table, the boys raced across the other half of the room and managed to dash up the few steps into Odin's personal hallway, still thankfully unseen.

Having made it that far, they paused briefly to catch their breath, exchanging a dire glance.

"Now what?" Archie panted.

Jake's heart pounded as he gazed down the corridor ahead. There were several closed doors along the hallway. The pool they were looking for could be behind any one of them.

"Now we start our search," he whispered.

The boys began checking each of the rooms they came to along the hallway. This was no easy task, since Archie had to stand on Jake's shoulders just so they could reach the various doorknobs.

The rooms themselves offered more, strange types of jeopardy, considering who they were dealing with. The first door they opened revealed a dimly-lit library so huge they could not even see to the ends of it. It must have held millions of books. Of course, Odin was the god of wisdom.

Archie stared greedily at the library's countless shelves, but Jake was more intrigued by another, highly unusual feature. It was said that Odin the Wise had invented the Viking alphabet of runes. Therefore, in his library, each of the runes was proudly displayed.

The mysterious letter-symbols stood several feet tall and glowed with golden light as they revolved slowly, levitating over their pedestals.

"All that knowledge," Archie whispered. "Can't we just go in and take a peek—"

"No!" A flicker of motion near the dark, shadowed corner caught Jake's eye. "Hurry up," he urged his cousin. "There's something moving around in there."

"What? Where?"

"Somethin' big, creeping along the floor. Hurry up! It's coming closer! Archie, quick, get the door!"

"What is it? I don't see any—"

"Ahhhh!"

All of a sudden, a giant snake reared up in front of the boys, its white fangs gleaming.

The boys bit back shrieks as it hissed at them, having slithered out from where it had lain coiled in the corner of the library.

"Get the door!"

Briefly paralyzed with terror, Archie snapped out of his trance and lurched forward to grab the doorknob. He pulled the library door shut with a bang just in time to escape the giant serpent's lightning-fast strike.

The boys ran up the corridor, clearing the area, only to pause at a safe distance, panting and in shock.

"What the deuce was that?" Archie cried.

Jake shook his head in belated dread. "No idea. Come on, we need to keep going."

"Cheese it," Archie muttered, but he followed.

As Jake jogged ahead to check in the next room, he *did* recall Dani reading something to him from her Norway book about an old Viking legend concerning a very nasty giant serpent. Unfortunately, he hadn't been listening very well and couldn't remember the details.

In any case, at the next door, Archie climbed once more onto Jake's shoulders to reach the doorknob, as if they were a pair of circus acrobats. Jake stepped closer to the door so his cousin could get a better grip on the handle.

"That's weird. The doorknob's cold," Archie remarked.

"Hurry up!" Jake whispered in annoyance, supporting his cousin's legs. But when Archie succeeded in pushing the door open, it swung inward upon a black, windy void, and Jake beheld the strangest room he'd ever seen.

If you could call it a room.

It looked to him like the mythical realm of Limbo, the space between life and death.

Beyond the threshold of the doorway, the room had no floor, nor walls nor ceiling, for that matter. The threshold stood as a high ledge looming over dark empty space as black and vast as a moonless night sky; one step forward and you might fall forever.

The boys backed away instinctively—but the room was not entirely empty.

As the rushing winds sighed through the void, everywhere there floated ticking clocks. Ghostly spirits, faceless in their hooded black cloaks, flew among the clocks, haunting the inky room.

"What is this place?" Archie whispered in wonder.

"God of death?" Jake quietly reminded him.

They stared at the clocks and spirits drifting by for a long moment.

"I think those clocks are people's lives," Jake said at length. "How much time we've all got left."

"Well, that's depressing," Archie muttered, hauling the door shut. "No pool in there."

Glad to be gone from the grim place, they kept searching.

Jake's shoulders were starting to hurt from his cousin climbing up and down on them, but he clenched his jaw without complaint, waiting for Archie to get the third door open.

When his cousin succeeded, however, neither of them were prepared for what they saw: a large room full of ominous equipment, gadgets, and machines.

Archie drew in his breath in excitement.

"What is all this stuff?" The boy genius couldn't seem to help himself.

He jumped off Jake's shoulders and took a few paces into the chamber, looking all around him in amazement.

"What are you doing? Get back here!" Jake whispered loudly from the doorway. Had the glock-wit already forgotten the giant serpent guarding the god's library? No telling what nasty booby-traps might await an intruder in here.

His cousin walked farther into the room like a person in a trance, gawking at everything.

Jake wanted to wring his neck. "Do you see a pool?" he whispered impatiently.

"No. This must be Odin's most important room." He turned and stared at Jake, wide-eyed. "God of war."

"It's war stuff in there?"

Archie nodded, marveling over the ancient set of horse armor near him. There were wall arrangements of hatchets and swords, gun cases filled with neat rows of innumerable long guns, from ancient blunderbusses to Brown Bess muskets with bayonets and much stranger, futuristic weapons, silver and black.

High up on another wall, the sharp-tipped prow of a mighty eighteenth century warship protruded, mounted there like a deer's head.

Against his better judgment, Jake followed Archie into the room, passing some huge armored vehicle the likes of which he had never seen.

But most astonishing of all was the back wall of Odin's war room.

It was covered in dozens of flat, rectangular screens with moving pictures on them.

Jake had no idea what sort of magic this might be, but unlike the newly-invented moving pictures he had seen back in the Exhibit Hall, these were not flickering black and white images without sound. On the contrary, the sleek screens before him were as true-to-life as looking out a window, sharp pictures in full color, with all the sounds you'd hear if you were there.

The scenes they showed, however, were terrible, windows onto every war taking place around the world—not just at the present time, but past and future, too...

Roman legions on the march. Knights whacking each other with maces. Tribal warriors in Africa burning each other's villages to the ground. Muddied young Englishmen entangled in barbed wire.

In the upper corner, another screen or window showed some horrific cloud in the shape of a mushroom blooming over a vast modern city before flattening it. The shapes of people bursting into flames...

Beside that, a brightly uniformed cavalry charged across the fields of Waterloo and horses fell, screaming. Below that was a jungle lit up with flashes of gunfire, and to the left of that, a nightmare scene showed a pile of skeletal bodies being dumped into some sort of mass grave.

Sickened, Jake turned to Archie, eager to be gone from this shocking place, but he found his cousin mesmerized by a particular moving picture that showed unimaginable flying machines screaming through the clouds.

Rocketing through the air so fast they left white trails across blue skies, Jake saw they must have had some sort of cannons attached beneath their silver wings.

The boys watched in half-horrified wonder as the pilot, his face hidden by a black, inhuman-looking mask, released his missiles over his target and cheered as something on the ground exploded.

"This can't be right," Archie whispered hoarsely, his gaze still glued to the screen.

"What is it?"

"The future. But they can't...they wouldn't..." He turned to Jake with a stricken look, his eyes wide behind his spectacles. "Mankind finally learns how to fly and this is what they use it for?"

Jake didn't know what to say.

Archie had always seemed to view the human race as basically good, but he knew better. You learned that living on the streets.

Good took effort. Something human beings had to work for. But bad, mean, selfish? Those came naturally.

"C'mon," he murmured, grasping his younger cousin's arm. "We need to keep moving before those dogs come back."

"The dogs of war?" Archie echoed bitterly.

"Probably so," Jake answered in a low tone. He felt sorry for his cousin, who still seemed to be in shock, but they had already wasted enough time.

As he pulled Archie out of there, he couldn't help remembering Isabelle's words back at the Exhibit Hall after seeing Dr. Galton.

One day, she had said, Archie would have to choose what sort of scientist he'd become. No doubt this glimpse into Odin's war room would stay with the boy genius and factor into his decision when the time came to choose his future path.

Jake used his telekinesis to draw the giant door of the war-room shut. Archie was unusually quiet as they turned their attention to the final chamber at the end of the hallway.

The last door was taller than the others, and when they got it open a crack, they soon found out why.

They peered in on a lofty chamber filled with white light. They saw the back of a huge, empty chair ahead, facing away from them, and realized they had discovered the very seat of Odin's power: the throne room.

Not all of the room was visible yet, however. First came a short passageway that served as the entrance—it was only about fifteen feet long. The passage then opened up into the bright, soaring chamber beyond.

"Let's go. This has to be the place!" Archie whispered, leaping down off Jake's shoulders.

"Be careful. Let's keep our eyes open," Jake warned.

As they ventured in, he was more nervous about trespassing into this chamber than any of the others.

They had no choice.

As they went down the passageway and stepped out into the larger throne room beyond—there it was.

"The pool!" Archie whispered.

Before the elevated throne lay a round pool, carved into the pristine white marble of the floor.

As the boys warily stepped closer, Jake reached into his pocket for the scrap of paper with the riddle written on it.

But before he could start checking the throne room to see if all of the clues matched, he glanced down into the crystal-pure pool.

With a sudden gasp, he pointed at the water. "Look!"

This was no ordinary pool. Instead, its placid surface reflected things happening in the world.

The boys stared in wonder at the hazy images that materialized and faded again among the ripples.

The longer they stared, the more specific the visions became.

Perhaps it showed what you wished to see, because the faces of those they loved began appearing. Jake saw Dani O'Dell brushing Teddy while she sat in the dormitory room. Isabelle was nearby, peering out the window through the Lie Detector Goggles.

The empath suddenly paused and glanced around, as though she could sense Archie and Jake's presence somewhere nearby.

Then the picture changed.

"Aunt Ramona!" Jake breathed. They now gazed down upon the patrician, wrinkled face of the dowager baroness back at Bradford Park in England.

Archie chuckled. "Ah, she's playing with her bees."

"Everyone needs a hobby," Jake said with a grin.

The grand old lady also played the harmonium for enjoyment in the evenings, and it always mystified Jake that such beautiful music could come out of nothing but crystal goblets filled with varying amounts of water.

But despite Her Ladyship's being one of the Elders of the Order of the Yew Tree and a personal friend of Queen Victoria, no less, Great-Great Aunt Ramona's pride and joy (aside from Isabelle, her favorite) was without a doubt her beehives. The honey her hives produced was magnificent, but the elder witch insisted that she used no magic on her bees, just a little charm. She had a complicated opinion of magic, didn't altogether trust it.

Oh, she could wield any sort of spell as needed, but she preferred not to whenever it could be avoided.

As they gazed into the reflection, she was talking to her bees—rather more fondly than she usually spoke to the children, for she was strict. They watched her pull down the netting from her beekeeping hat to cover her face, then she opened the door to the hive with a thickly-gloved hand. "And how are all my little friends this morning? Bzzz, bzzz, yes, yes, I know. It was rather cold for you last night, wasn't it?"

The picture dissolved again and showed them a forest scene. Beside a babbling brook, a certain wolf of their acquaintance was gnawing happily on a stick, while a black leopard lazed on a tree branch above him, her tail flicking with contentment.

"The twins! Well, they seem to be all right," Archie murmured.

Then, to Jake's delight, the picture turned again, this time showing them the familiar streets of home—London, just outside Westminster Hall, the famous buildings of Parliament.

"It's Derek!" Jake said in excitement, leaning closer.

On the bustling avenue of Whitehall in the shadow of Big Ben, the rugged, dark-haired warrior was scanning his surroundings with brooding glances in all directions. He was obviously still on bodyguard duty, escorting some little mustachioed foreign dignitary into a waiting carriage.

"Well, he looks annoyed," Archie remarked.

"I'm sure he is," Jake said with a grin.

Then the picture changed again and there was little Gladwin, Queen Victoria's own fairy courier, speeding through the air with a tiny scrolled message strapped across her back, secured between her wings. Her golden fairy trail sparkled behind her as she zipped across the sky.

"Message for somebody, it seems," Archie murmured.

"I wonder who," Jake said, his voice a bit strangled by an unexpected wave of homesickness. What if he ran into trouble in this strange place and never got to see them all again?

When Archie turned away, glancing around the room, Jake froze at a final, fleeting image of a blond man and a dark-haired woman sleeping peacefully side by side under glass lids—or rather, coffins. He stared. *"It can't be."*

"What is it?" Archie turned back to him. "What's wrong with you?"

Jake pointed at the pool, his heart suddenly pounding. "Did you see that?"

"No, what?"

"I...I think it was my...my parents."

"Your parents? What, in their graves?"

"No, they weren't skeletons or anything! They looked just like they do in their portrait above the fireplace back home at Griffon Castle."

"But...how is that possible? Doesn't this pool only show people in the here and now? I mean, everyone else we saw reflected in these waters is alive and well."

"Aye," Jake whispered, swallowing hard at the implications.

"W-what does it mean?" Archie asked.

He shook his head dazedly. "I have no idea."

"Maybe you were mistaken. What were they doing?"

"Sleeping. Just lying there. Under glass."

"Are you sure it was them?"

"I think so," he said uncertainly. Jake had no memory of his parents, of course, considering how he'd been ripped away from them as a baby.

Archie looked at the pool with a frown, but Jake's head was suddenly spinning.

In his recent battle against Fionnula Coralbroom, the sea-witch who had helped Uncle Waldrick betray and murder Jake's parents, she had taunted him with a tantalizing hint that there was more to how the crime had played out than even Waldrick knew. She was a wicked, untrustworthy, old hag who would have said anything to trick him or deceive him if it gave her a chance to escape, and so he had not dared believe her when she had tossed him a crumb of hope that his parents might still be alive, somewhere, magically...

Unfortunately, the Order and the authorities of the Yew Court had locked the sea-witch away in a dungeon cell at the bottom of the ocean before Jake had had a chance to question her and get the truth.

Of all times to receive a clue about his parents' fate! It was maddening. Jake stared at the pool, willing the watery image of them to come back.

Instead, the picture turned dire, showing him Snorri and Kaia and Red still waging a desperate battle against the deathless Valkyries back on the boat. They were obviously tiring. He glanced at his cousin. "How long do you think we've been gone?"

Archie pulled out his fob watch and gave it a shake. He listened for its ticking, but then frowned. "I don't know, it's quit working. Maybe there's no time here. Could be minutes. Maybe as much as an hour?"

Jake nodded and strove to push his countless questions to the back of his mind for now. "Let's hurry and figure out this blasted riddle so we can get back before the Valkyries cut them to ribbons."

"No worries," Archie answered abruptly. "I've already solved it."

CHAPTER FORTY-TWO
Escape From Valhalla

"Have you?" Jake turned to his cousin in shock. It was never a bad thing having a genius around. "When did you do that?" he cried.

"Oh, the moment we walked in."

"Really?! What's the answer, then?"

"Open your eyes, coz. You can count." Tucking his fob watch back into his vest pocket, Archie nodded toward the giant throne.

"Just tell me! We don't have time for games!"

"Very well." Archie vaulted up onto the elevated marble dais on which Odin's magnificent, solid-silver throne looked down on the pool. "Behold! What has four wings but never flies?" He pointed at the twin ravens carved on the back of the throne. "Stands twelve feet above the pool?" He patted the head of one of the twin hunting dog statues on the front of the massive chair. "Twelve *feet*. You see? It's not a distance or a length, it's actual feet! The dogs each have four paws. That's eight feet. And both of the birds have two feet—that's four. Four plus eight equals twelve, simple, count 'em."

Jake stared. "Archie, you're a genius."

"So I'm told." He continued: "The riddle further specified, 'What has four wings but doesn't fly?' Each of these birds has two wings, obviously, and they're statues, so I daresay they're not going to be flying anywhere soon. In short, the answer is: Odin's throne."

"Brilliant. Honestly. Well done."

"Thank you, sir!" Archie took a modest bow, then jumped off the dais.

But Jake was still amazed. He shook his head with a widening smile. "Figures the answer to Loki's riddle is the thing he covets most.

Odin's throne!" But then he had a new thought. "Hold on. If we just say 'Odin's throne,' is that going to be specific enough?"

"What do you mean? It's correct," Archie replied as he walked back over to him.

"Didn't Miss Langesund tell us the Vikings always named their most prized possessions? Or maybe Dani read it to me from her Norway book... I can't recall. But either way, they did, didn't they?"

Archie nodded uncertainly. "Yes. They did like to name their swords and knives and boats and castles..."

"The throne could have a name, see?" Jake said. "And if we don't get it exactly right, Loki may disqualify our answer. He *would,* knowing him. He'll take any excuse to say we lose."

"Hmm." Archie leaned nearer to the throne for a closer look. "There are runes here, all over this front part." He gestured to the carvings. "This might spell out the name, but I can't begin to read it."

"Kaia should be able to. Let's copy it down and show it to her," Jake suggested.

"Excellent thought. I'll make an etching." Archie took out a pencil stub and a little notepad out of his tool-bag. Then he held a sheet of paper over the runes and started coloring over them quickly with his pencil, creating a replica of the mysterious letter shapes beneath.

Jake took a final look around to see if there was anything else he should remember from their trip here, when all of a sudden, the sound of barking filled the air.

The boys gasped and looked at each other.

"The dogs!" Jake tore off running for the doorway.

Archie was only half done with the etching. "Where are you going? Wait for me!"

"Finish the runes. We left the door open!" Jake yelled over his shoulder. He raced toward the door to the throne room as the vicious barking grew louder.

He could hear canine claws clicking on the polished marble floor, coming closer. He'd never make it in time. The god-sized room was too big. Still a ways off, he brought up his hands and used his telekinesis to fling the towering door shut.

The moment it banged closed, a pair of giant black snouts arrived, sniffing wildly under the bottom seam of the door. Odin's hounds scratched at the door, barking up a storm.

Jake backed away, his heart pounding. *We're trapped.* He ran back into the main part of the throne room just as Archie finished with the etching.

"Where are the dogs?"

"Blocking the door."

"Then how are we going to get out of here?" Archie cried.

Jake shook his head. "I-I don't know."

But things could always get worse, and in the next moment, they did. *Boom-boom, boom-boom...*

"What's that?" Archie squeaked.

"Footsteps," Jake breathed.

"Quiet, you dogs!" a deep voice thundered into the hallway. "How am I supposed to concentrate with you two making all that racket? Shut your snouts! Back in your places! I'm trying to run a cyclone in the Pacific, if you don't mind!"

The boys exchanged a look of utter terror.

Archie mouthed the word: *Thor.*

Jake nodded in dread.

Archie clapped his hand over his own mouth to hold back a shriek. Jake grabbed his arm, shushed him, then pointed toward a distant window on the far end of the throne room.

Archie lowered his hand from his mouth and blanched, but nodded. As they ran toward the wall with the window, Odin's hounds continued barking.

"Pain in the rear end dogs! Why doesn't Father take you with him when he goes out wandering?" the weather god grumbled in annoyance. "Sure, leave you here so I get stuck taking care of you..."

Boom-boom, boom-boom. His footsteps were coming closer. Jake broke out in a cold sweat.

"What's wrong with you two? Why are you so fixated on that door?" Thor paused while the boys scrambled to climb up onto the window sill.

Jake zoomed his startled cousin up to the window-ledge using his telekinesis, then Archie tied off a rope from his tool-bag and threw the other end down to him. Jake climbed it faster than he would have thought humanly possible.

"What is it?" Thor asked his father's hounds. "Is someone in there?"

The dogs howled in answer.

"Intruder?" Thor boomed in fury all of a sudden. "Why, I thought I

heard a door slam somewhere down here!"

Jake and Archie combined all their strength to pry the huge window open. They hauled it up just wide enough for them to roll under it; then they stood on the narrow sill just outside the glass.

Jake gulped as he looked down.

Archie glanced at him in fright. "It's too high!"

"Don't worry, we'll bounce. Remember?"

"Oh, right! I forgot." With that, Archie leaped immediately, showing rather more faith in Jake's assurance than Jake had himself.

While Archie plunged toward the spongy green turf of Valhalla, Jake glanced back over his shoulder just as the throne room door burst open and Thor came striding in.

Though Odin's firstborn son had not yet seen them, Jake stopped breathing at the sight of him.

The red-haired god of thunder made Ragnor the Punisher look like a delicate flower, the puniest weakling.

For one thing, he was taller than two giants. Thor gusted into the room, a barrel-chested titan of a man like a force of nature. His *muscles* had muscles, and from beneath his winged helmet, his long red hair flowed down his back.

He had a red beard, a cloak the color of storm clouds, and in his wake, a salt wind followed. Jake gulped as he noted Thor's famous hammer tucked into his thick leather belt.

Meanwhile, Archie had landed safely on the marshmallow ground and stood below, beckoning to him to hurry.

But Jake delayed, wondering just for a heartbeat if Thor might be able to help them with Loki.

The things Miss Langesund had told the children about the Vikings' favorite hero came rushing back into his mind.

Thor was the god of the weather, the skies, and the sea. Like the elements he ruled, he was moody and changeable—sometimes jovial, other times deadly—but always fearless and proud.

At least with Thor, unlike Loki, Miss Langesund had told them, what you see is what you get. The god of thunder was frequently the butt of Loki's jokes. Oftentimes, he took Loki's pranks in good humor. But when Thor got angry, she had told them, he usually made short work of the trickster.

Jake wondered if Thor would make short work of *him* for intruding in Valhalla, or if the thunder god might be willing to listen about their Loki problem.

On second thought, judging by the fierce looks of the Viking god, Jake decided, the likeliest outcome for *him* was being Blood-Eagled. *No, thank you.* Better safe than sorry, he thought, and with that, he jumped off the ledge.

Thor noticed the flicker a motion at the window.

"Who's there? Who dares invade Valhalla?"

The mighty Norse god rushed after him like an ocean gale as Jake plummeted to the ground. All of his experience in darting away from Constable Flanagan back in the rookery paled in comparison to this.

"Run!" Jake yelled at Archie, while the spongy turf of the afterworld received him without injury, bouncing him back up into the air as if he had landed on a trampoline.

Thor leaned out the window and made a grab for him. Jake somersaulted, pushing off the thunder god's metal wristband as the giant hand whooshed under him.

"Agile for a dwarf," Thor muttered, then he yelled for the dogs.

Jake finally landed and used his momentum to kick off immediately for the woods. Archie was already sprinting well ahead of him. The boys raced for the cover of the forest.

Once hidden by the trees, they ran as fast as they possibly could, tearing through the underbrush. There was no sign of Ragnor the Punisher, but they spied their horses from earlier grazing in a field. They ran over to them, climbed aboard, then galloped, full-tilt, back the way they came. In the distance, they passed the huge wooden lodge where the Viking warriors were still celebrating.

They rounded the woods, clattered onto the path beside the stream, passed the puppies, and rode hard for the edge of the cliff-gates over which Snorri had thrown them.

Meanwhile, in the distance, they could hear Odin's war-dogs barking. The sound was coming closer, along with more *boom-boom* footfalls of the angry Thor following his father's hounds.

"Please don't tell me we're going to have to jump off the cliff, too!" Archie yelled as they approached the cloud-swathed edge of Valhalla.

"I think...I may have an idea," Jake answered uncertainly.

Earlier, back on the boat, he recalled the giant white arms of ice that had wrapped around the cliff-like gate of Valhalla, all the way down to the water.

With all the trouble from the Valkyries, he had barely paid attention to the playful penguins frolicking around the glacier.

"Well, what is it? Don't keep me in suspense!" Archie cried as they reached the edge of Valhalla and slowed their blowing horses.

"There!" Jake pointed at the penguins sunning themselves on the top of the glacier.

As Archie glanced over, furrowing his brow, one of the penguins hopped over to a smooth, silvery-blue hole in the upper end of the glacier.

The comical bird flopped onto its belly and slid into the hole with an eager squawk.

Archie turned to him. "The penguins have an ice slide!"

"Exactly," Jake said in relief. He flung himself down off his horse and ran to the hole in the glacier, Archie right behind him.

"Go!" Jake waved his younger cousin into the ice-slide first. There was no time to lose. "Yell loud on the way down so Red and the giants hear you coming. They'll catch you."

"If I don't break my neck," Archie muttered as he climbed feet-first into the penguins' slippery ice tunnel.

"Beats getting eaten by those dogs."

"True." In a seated position, Archie folded his arms across his tool-bag, hugging it protectively against his chest. "All right, I'm ready. Give me a push, coz."

Jake planted his hands on his cousin's shoulders and shoved him hard; Archie let out a yelp as he went slip-sliding down the luge on his back, feet-first.

Archie whooshed out of sight into the ice-tunnel, his hollers, half-excited, half-terrified, streaming out behind him.

Meanwhile, the barking of Odin's hounds and the footsteps of the angry Thor were getting louder. In another moment, they'd be upon him.

Jake waited as long as he dared to give Archie a head start so they didn't crash inside the glacier, but he had to get out of here *now*. The penguins squawked indignantly as he cut in line ahead of them and jumped feet-first into the hole at the top of their ice-slide.

He gave himself a push, shoving off from the top of the round hole with the ice stinging his bare hands. But in the next moment, he was zooming down the slippery aqua-blue tunnel at impossible speeds, arms folded.

Whoosh! Whoom!

He slid up the walls a bit as he went careening toward the sea. His heart pounded. The wind whipped his cheeks and blew his hair as he hurtled down the twisting, turning slide through the middle of the glacier.

Jake could not decide if this was the most terrifying experience of his life or the most fun he'd ever had. He was moving so fast he could hardly see anything. Tears from the wind of his speed stung his eyes. He felt totally out of control.

Then he glimpsed daylight ahead, and in the next second, came shooting out into the empty air.

"Caw!" Red saw him coming and realized he was going to overshoot the boat. The Gryphon flew swiftly to intercept him, grabbing the back of Jake's coat just in time to save him from a tumble into the frigid waves.

Red dropped him in the Viking boat beside the waiting Archie, who was already wrapped in a blanket and beaming now that he'd recovered from the terror. Jake knew exactly how he felt.

Snorri and Kaia were still battling the Valkyries. By now, even the powerful giants looked exhausted. "Go, go, we got the answer! Let's get out of here!" Jake yelled to them.

"Sounds good to me," the princess muttered.

"How long have we been gone?" Jake asked her as she whacked another clawed hag into the waves.

"About an hour and a half. See all the fun you've been missing?"

Jake snorted, but Red took Snorri's place in the battle with a roar so that Snorri, in turn, being the strongest, could take up the oars again.

With all his remaining strength, Snorri began to row, pulling the long-ship away from the flock of vicious harpies.

Thankfully, Odin's angry battle-maidens did not pursue them past the narrow strait between the tall cliffs. As soon as Kaia's royal dragon-boat hit the open seas, the Valkyries let them go, content that the intruders were finally retreating.

And so, they escaped Valhalla with their lives—and with the answer to Loki's riddle.

As the ship barreled through the tossing waves, Jake kept looking over his shoulder, waiting for Thor to appear, but he never did. At least not yet.

Perhaps Thor's chief concern right now was finishing up his typhoon in the Pacific. But as an immortal, Odin's fierce firstborn had all the time in the world to hunt down the intruders, and worse, he had seen Jake's face.

Aye, after their trespass into his father's palace, Jake had a grim feeling that they had not yet seen the last of the thunder god.

CHAPTER FORTY-THREE
To the Victor, the Spoils

"Quarter to nine!" Archie yelled, glancing at his fob-watch. Washed in morning sunshine, the shores of Jugenheim were in sight. The twelve hours given for the final challenge in the contest were almost expired.

"It'll be close," Princess Kaia murmured, hauling on the oars right along with Snorri. She had Archie's paper with the etching of the runes tucked into the neckline of her gown. She had translated the symbols easily, revealing to them in awe the sacred name of Odin's throne.

Snorri could barely pronounce it. Jake hoped their shepherd friend didn't butcher the long Viking word when the moment came for him to give Loki the answer.

"It's so far," Snorri panted. "We're not going to make it." Even for a giant, he had to be exhausted after so many hours of rowing to Valhalla and back again.

"We'll do it," Jake encouraged him. He cast about to find within himself some of the Vikings' type of bragging to bolster up his allies' courage. "We've come this far, haven't we? I can't wait to see the look on Loki's face when he realizes we've solved his unsolvable riddle!"

That cheered them up a bit.

"Aye," Snorri agreed. The clock kept ticking as the giant gave a final heave on the oars and brought Kaia's royal dragon boat up to the wooden dock.

"Just go!" She waved Snorri on. "I'll take care of the boat! My father's great hall is about five miles away. You'll have to run to get there in time. Hurry! We'll be right behind you. Good luck!"

Snorri didn't argue. The whole ship rocked when he jumped out onto the land. Jake and Archie fell and rolled around in the bottom of the boat. Climbing to their feet a moment later, they could still hear his footfalls thundering in the distance as he sprinted off through the forest.

Princess Kaia lowered the sails, then threw down the anchor. "Let's go, boys!"

Jake did not know where she found the strength to run after her battle against the Valkyries and their long, draining journey across the sea.

The cold alone had exhausted him and Archie.

Fortunately, Red still had enough energy to give the boys a ride. When they climbed onto his back, the Gryphon kept pace with the princess, flying beside her.

Her yellow braids whipped behind her, as thick as the ropes on a ship of the Royal Navy. Her bow and quiver of arrows bounced against her back. The ground shook beneath her feet. With the enormous stretches of ground that she covered with every running stride, Red was hard pressed to keep up.

Luckily, they arrived outside her father's great hall just as the sundial in the middle of the village pointed a shadow onto the nine.

"Time's up," Archie murmured, confirming it with a final glance at his fob watch.

Kaia strode through the crowd of people who had come to see the outcome of the contest and to learn whether Gorm or Snorri would be their next king.

The villagers parted to let the princess pass. Meanwhile, Red landed on the giant handrail where Jake had taken his dinner the night before. It gave them a good vantage point of all the proceedings and safeguarded them from the danger of getting stepped on.

Jake gave the Gryphon a grateful pat as the boys slid off his back, then all three of them waited to watch matters unfold.

Princess Kaia joined her father, King Olaf, on the same raised platform where the riddle had been given—and where the Ice Wizard now waited.

Loki. Jake narrowed his eyes, scrutinizing the trickster god in his shaman disguise. *He had better not try any funny business.*

The Master of Ceremonies nodded to one of the king's guards.

The Viking warrior stepped forward and blew into a great horn, calling everyone to attention.

The king and most of the giants looked rather groggy.

When the summoning notes of the horn faded, the Master of Ceremonies lifted his baton. "Ladies and gentlemen, the time for the final challenge has expired!" He gestured grandly toward the crowd. "Let the contestants come forward!"

They did: Snorri the Shepherd, looking nervous and exhausted; and Prince Gorm, wearing a dark scowl that barely covered his panic. He kept glancing around like he wanted to fight anybody who looked at him wrong.

As the two rivals stepped up to the platform, Jake noticed Gorm's band of followers huddled nearby. They were exchanging whispers, sending evil looks toward the Ice Wizard.

Jake instantly suspected they were plotting something.

Maybe the brawny bullies thought they could take on the sorcerer if, or rather when, their leader Gorm lost the contest. Which just went to show that they still had no idea who they were really dealing with.

Standing beside her father, Kaia gave Snorri a private nod, looking scared but hopeful.

"This is nerve-racking," Archie whispered. "What if we got it wrong?"

Jake gave him a dirty look, the only fitting answer for his last-minute doubts. This was no time to say such a thing!

Ignoring his cousin, he folded his arms across his chest and continued watching the proceedings.

"Gentlemen!" the Ice Wizard called with a note of glee in his voice. "Time's up. So I ask you once again: What has four wings but doesn't fly, stands twelve feet above the pool but never swims, and though surrounded by wisdom, is often vacant?"

The words of the riddle now made perfect sense to Jake, but the rest of the crowd mumbled, as baffled as ever.

"Which of you will be the first to give your answer?" Loki asked in anticipation.

"Prince Gorm deserves that honor," Kaia spoke up quickly. "After all, he is a prince. Snorri is but a lowly shepherd."

Gorm obviously did not want to go first, but he could not escape the privilege due to him because of his high rank. Especially after the way he had been rubbing it in Snorri's face since the day the tournament began.

The Master of Ceremonies turned to Gorm. "Very well, Your Highness. What is your answer, Prince Gorm? Speak it loudly, please, so all can hear."

"Yes, do," the Ice Wizard drawled.

Gorm cleared his throat with a wince of excruciating awkwardness. Indeed, the uncomfortable look on his face seemed to suggest that the warrior giant would have rather been in the jaws of Old Smokey at this moment, rather than standing there having to answer a brain-twisting riddle.

"Ahem, can I ask a question?" he said, probably stalling for time.

"If you must," the Ice Wizard replied impatiently.

"What happens if the dummy and I both get it wrong?"

"Hey!" Kaia protested.

"Why, then, I win, of course!" Loki answered. "In that case, you both forfeit, as I said."

"That's not going to happen, though. Is it, Gorm?" King Olaf warned. "You promised me you'd find the answer."

"Yes, er, sire. I believe I have."

"Well?" Loki prompted. "I haven't got all night! Chop-chop! What is your answer?"

"It's, um—" Gorm faltered, but his friends started cheering him on, and he found his courage again. "The answer is... Yggdrasil!"

Jake stifled a snort.

Everyone looked at the Ice Wizard.

Who smiled from ear to ear. "No. I'm afraid that is incorrect."

Gorm let out an angry growl while King Olaf drew in his breath sharply. The giant king wobbled a little, as though he might well faint. "My kingdom!" he croaked.

It all rested on the village idiot now.

Loki-as-Ice Wizard turned to the hapless shepherd with a sly, snaky smile. Clearly, the trickster god was enjoying this.

He'd already tricked Snorri once, after all, down in Midgarth. "And for our second contestant..."

The crowd began to whisper among themselves: "He'll never get it! We're all doomed!"

"Snorri, speak your answer loudly so everyone can hear!" the Master of Ceremonies instructed once again.

Snorri drew himself up with a visible gulp. Jake could see him mentally practicing how to say the complicated name. He took one last, longing glance at Kaia, as if to bolster his resolve.

She nodded at him.

"Tick-tock," Loki said in rude impatience.

"The answer is..." Snorri took a deep breath, then shouted: *"Hlidskjalf!"*

Silence.

"Bless you," someone in the crowd offered.

"It wasn't a sneeze, it was my answer," Snorri said. "Hlidskjalf," he repeated, his voice sounding more confident. "The name of Odin's throne!"

Everyone turned to the Ice Wizard, whose face contorted with shock, which quickly turned to rage. "What? How?! How do you know this? You can't know this!" he hissed at Snorri.

"You mean he's got the right answer?" King Olaf shouted in disbelief.

Loki couldn't even speak. He was too furious.

"It *is* the right answer!" Snorri informed the whole crowd. "And I can tell you why. Odin's silver throne overlooks a crystal pool where he can watch everything going on around the world. It's surrounded by wisdom, because his throne sits in the center of Odin's home, and he is the god of wisdom. The throne has two dogs and two ravens carved on it—that's twelve feet standing above the pool. The two birds have two wings each—four wings—but they'll never fly, because they're statues."

"H-how do you know this? You went to Valhalla?" Loki stammered in outrage.

"None of your business!" Jake yelled, sensing the time was right for one of the winner's coaches to speak up on his behalf. "Snorri gave the right answer! That's all you need to know. He won fair and square despite your trickery, and there's nothing you can do about it now!"

"You!" The Ice Wizard turned and glared at him. *"Cake..."*

"That's right, we've met before," Jake flung out.

"What are *you* doing here? You're not allowed in Jugenheim!"

"Neither are you! Or shall I tell them who you really are?"

Loki narrowed his eyes at him in warning. "How dare you interfere in my plans? You cheated!" he accused him. "You gave this dolt the answer, didn't you?"

"It was a team effort, which is perfectly within the stated rules,"

Jake retorted. "The contestants are allowed to work together with their coaches and advisers."

"You're the one who cheated!" Archie chimed in. "Giving them a riddle that was meant to be unsolvable! Why don't you try playing fair once in a while?"

"What fun would that be?" Loki shot back. "I'll get you for this. You think this is over? You'll be sorry—all of you!"

"You're just mad because you lost. Now, go away!"

"You heard the dwarves!" the king agreed. "I think it's time the Ice Wizard returned to his home glacier."

"Go...home! Go...home!" the giants started chanting, waving their arms in rude goodbyes, and booing the Ice Wizard until he got so angry he disappeared in a sudden *Poof!* of smoke.

"And don't come back!" Snorri hollered.

As soon as he was gone, the giants' boos turned to cheering.

For Snorri.

Jake and Archie beamed as their humble shepherd friend finally got the recognition he deserved.

Snorri smiled bashfully at everyone and scratched his baldish head in self-consciousness at all the attention.

The only one still angry was Prince Gorm, especially when the king turned to Snorri. "Well, my boy, it appears, against all odds, you are the winner. You have won this competition fair and square—"

"Fair and square?" Gorm shouted. "He was disqualified in the first round!"

"Well, Gorm..." The king looked over at him in surprise. "You're the one who insisted he be let back into the contest."

"Just so you could make fun of him!" Jake reminded him. "You treated him like a joke, but now he's beaten you! Too bad!"

"Jake!" Archie muttered, grabbing his arm to rein him in. "Stifle it before you start a fight!"

"The dwarf speaks truly. Come, Snorri." King Olaf beckoned the winner up onto the platform. "Take your rightful place."

"This is ridiculous!" Gorm exclaimed as Snorri mounted the steps to the platform. "Sire, this is no way to run a kingdom!"

"Mind your tone when you're speaking to your king!" Kaia warned him.

Gorm glared at her from the ground before the platform. "This is all your fault, you spoiled princess! If you would've agreed to marry me from the start the way you should have, all this could have been avoided! Now you're stuck marrying a dolt! Well, you got what you deserve!"

"For your information, you braggart, Snorri the Shepherd is far superior to you!" she shot back.

"I am?" Snorri echoed.

"Oh, really?" Gorm barked. "And why is that?"

"Snorri has a giant-sized heart! All you've got is a big mouth."

Gorm glared at her, then huffed away, his weapons clanking at his sides. His followers hurried after him, but he was so angry that he waved them off.

When he had gone, King Olaf turned to the victor. "Now, then. Snorri the Shepherd, the Norns have woven your destiny! You will be my successor and our people's next king. This very night, you shall marry my daughter—"

"Uh, excuse me, Your Majesty!" Snorri interrupted, holding up a finger. "Might I make a few remarks?"

The king smiled broadly. "Of course. Listen up, one and all! Your future king will speak!"

Snorri turned to address the King and the whole crowd, but anyone could see that most of his attention remained, as always, fixed on Princess Kaia-of-the-Yellow-Braids.

"Ahem," he started, only to falter. Then he tried again, more loudly. "Your Majesty, Your Highness, friends. There's only one reason I entered this tournament—because of Her Royal Highness."

Kaia tilted her head with a beaming smile.

"I wouldn't have had the nerve to try if it weren't for my coaches, the noble dwarves. But they gave me the courage to do what I knew was right. I never wanted to see the princess forced to marry a giant she didn't love. Not Gorm, and not me, neither," he said in his usual humble way. "I just want her to be happy. I may not be the smartest giant here, but I do know one thing." He turned to the king, and his voice turned much more forceful. "Princess Kaia has what it takes to rule this kingdom by herself. She doesn't need a husband to do it for her when the time comes. And so, Your Majesty, now that I've won your contest, I choose to forfeit the crown in favor of your daughter."

"*What?* B-but you can't do that!" her father spluttered. "She's a female!"

"If I'm the next king, I can do whatever I want," Snorri replied with a pugnacious thrust of his chin. "I won the right of succession fair and square, and I choose to hand over the crown to the one I know will do the best job for our people—your royal daughter, sire."

The king huffed and puffed and looked nonplussed.

"Oh, come, Your Majesty," Snorri cajoled him. "Kaia's been learning from you how to rule ever since she was a wee small giantess. The people love her. She's as smart and brave as she is beautiful."

"Awww," said the crowd.

"She can do this! And if you don't mind my saying, you shouldn't have put her through all this in the first place."

"Oh, really?" King Olaf exclaimed, turning angrily to his daughter. "Did you put him up to this? Force him into the contest from the start—"

"No!" Kaia explained.

The princess appeared to be in shock at Snorri's public refusal to marry her.

"It's not her fault," Snorri assured King Olaf. "She had no idea that this was my intention all along. Ask the dwarves if you don't believe me." He paused. "I know I don't deserve somebody like her."

Kaia gazed at him with tears of wonder in her eyes. "No one's ever done anything like this for me before."

"I believe in you," Snorri told her.

But the king remained befuddled. "A woman for a leader? Who ever heard of such a thing?"

"There's a first time for everything. Sire, won't you just give her a chance?"

Teary-eyed, the valiant warrior princess could no longer restrain her emotions. "Oh, Snorri, don't you *want* to marry me?" she burst out.

"Of course I do!" he exclaimed, bashfully lowering his head. "Everybody knows how much I love you."

"Awwww," Archie said with a grin, elbowing Jake.

Princess Kaia shook her head. "I wanted you to win the contest, Snorri, but not so you could set me free. I wanted you to win so I could marry you!"

"What?" His eyes flew open wide.

"Oh, maybe you are just a big, dumb oaf if you never realized how much I like you, too!"

Snorri turned bright red.

"Oh, you," she scolded him fondly. Then she threw her arms around him in a giant-sized hug and kissed him on the cheek.

King Olaf was scowling. "Well, if you're going to end up married either way, what do I care which one of you is officially in charge?" he grumbled. "You should manage well enough between the two of you."

Meanwhile, the Master of Ceremonies, after all that he had been through, was eager to bring the nerve-racking matter of the contest to a neat conclusion.

He gestured to the happy couple with a courtly flourish. "Ladies and gentlemen, allow me to present the next King and Queen of Jugenheim!"

He started applauding loudly in the hopes that everyone else would follow suit.

The giants did—uncertainly. Most of them still looked rather confused about what was going on.

Jake and Archie cheered wildly, however.

But when Snorri gave Kaia a big, wet smooch on the lips, the boys looked away, laughing, even as they exchanged a slightly revolted grimace.

"Oh, that's disgusting," Jake mumbled, still clapping.

Archie chuckled while Red cawed in approval. "And they all lived happily ever after."

At least, for a little while.

PART V

CHAPTER FORTY-FOUR
A New Alliance

After the triumphant solving of the riddle and the victorious conclusion of the tournament, the boys and their large friend dragged themselves back to Snorri's cottage to rest and recover from their exhausting voyage to Valhalla.

While Snorri scrubbed himself in the pond (with soap) to clean himself up for his wedding, Jake tended Red's scratches from his battle with the Valkyries, still brooding on his vision of his parents that he had glimpsed in Odin's pool.

What could it mean? What if they were still alive somewhere, somehow? What if, after all this time, he wasn't really an orphan?

He didn't dare let himself hope...

Meanwhile, Archie went out to the shed to continue repairing the Pigeon. The boy genius worked on his contraption for an hour before he finally fell asleep right on the floor of the shed.

That was where Jake found him.

Jake called the eager bridegroom in to pick the little fellow up and carry him back inside. Snorri lifted Archie gingerly in one hand, then tiptoed in and deposited him on the same huge chair where the boys had slept before. Archie never even stirred.

Since his cousin was out cold, Jake took a nap, too, before it was time to go to the feast and stand as witnesses at Snorri's royal wedding.

Unfortunately, not everyone was as happy as they were about the outcome of the competition.

* * *

Hours later, Loki was still fuming. Indeed, he was outraged. How could he, a god, have been outwitted by two meddling boys and a giant with the intelligence of a soup spoon?

It would not stand! No, he vowed to himself, this defeat was only temporary. In a little while, he'd have the giants surrendering to him completely, begging for mercy.

But first he would need a little assistance...some brute muscle.

Still disguised as the Ice Wizard, Loki stepped into the garden behind the great hall and found himself staring at the only other person who was as angry about all of this as he.

Prince Gorm sat alone and sulking. He glanced over, hearing him approach. Oh, the arrogant warrior appeared to be in a terrible mood after losing to the village loser.

"What do you want?" he growled.

"The same thing you do, I wager." Loki leaned on his gnarled wizard-staff. "Wouldn't you like to get back at them, just a little?"

Gorm glared in the direction of the feast. He'd heard Kaia was set to marry that idiot Snorri in the town square this very night. "Of course I would. You don't have to be a sorcerer to figure that out. But what can I do? It's too late now."

"Well, it may cheer you up to hear that I know a way to punish those fools as they deserve. But I'd need your help to carry it out."

That was the secret curse of his devilish existence. He always needed a willing accomplice to get anything really big done.

Gorm turned to him slowly, a gleam in his eyes. "What did you have in mind?"

Loki gave him a crafty smile. "Come with me and you'll find out."

Gorm thought it over for a second. "Why not," he muttered. Then he rose and obeyed, following Loki into the shadows.

CHAPTER FORTY-FIVE
Nightmare From the Volcano

At the wedding feast that night, the giants would bang their cups every now and then to insist that Kaia and Snorri have a kiss, and Jake would nearly lose his appetite.

He and Archie looked away, gagging, every time.

But now it was official: the princess and the winner of the tournament had been married for about an hour.

As the night wore on and the mead flowed and the giants got up to lurch around in their comical dances, the boys and the Gryphon stayed out of harm's way, safely perched up on their handrail to avoid getting stepped on.

Watching all the proceedings, Jake reflected on the first time he had seen Snorri outside that mountain cave on the day that Archie had been kidnapped. It was hard to believe that their silly giant friend would be the next king of Jugenheim, but at least now no one would have to worry about the end of the world.

Or so Jake thought.

But then, as all the giants were enjoying the feast, without warning, a distant rumble of thunder filled the night.

"What was that?" people exclaimed.

Jake instantly jumped to his feet, fearing Thor had finally tracked him down. "Time to go!" he yelped to Archie and Red.

Then a flash lit up the dark sky, but when Jake looked toward the mountainous horizon, he saw it wasn't really lightning.

His eyes widened as the rumbling noise continued on and on.

"Hold on," he murmured to himself, heart pounding. "That's not thunder..."

The giants stopped dancing. Somebody silenced the musicians

and everyone turned to look toward the mountains.

In the distance, a sinister, red-orange glow cast a weird illumination over the landscape.

"What is it?" the giants asked.

Hearing the frightened murmurs go rippling through the square unnerved Jake a little. The boys exchanged an uneasy glance, both wondering what could have the crowd of big, powerful giants so spooked?

But King Olaf quickly took control, stepping up to the platform. "Settle down, everyone! There is no need for alarm. The volcano is far enough away that you won't be in any danger."

"Volcano?" Jake turned to Archie, wide-eyed.

"Brilliant!" Archie whispered, instantly going into scientist mode.

"I assure you," the king continued, "our ancestors were too intelligent to place the village in striking distance of the lava. Don't worry, every fifty years or so, the volcano gets a little indigestion and must let out a belch." He patted his stomach with a grin. "Happens to the best of us!"

The villagers laughed nervously, reassured.

"It must be a sign from the gods that they approve of the match!" someone suggested.

"Indeed!" King Olaf raised his drinking horn in a toast to the happy couple. "Cheers!"

The villagers followed suit, but just as they all started to calm down, another loud boom came from the distance. This time, a plume of bright red-orange lava spurted up into the black sky.

"Ohhh, ahhh!" said the giants.

"What a rare treat!" Archie exclaimed, reaching for his tool-bag. "I hardly expected we'd be so lucky as to witness a volcanic eruption on our trip to Scandinavia!" At once, he lifted his telescope to his eye and settled into position to watch the fiery show. "Incredible..."

Jake looked at his scientific cousin dubiously.

For one thing, he was not sure if Giant Land, balanced on some great branch of Yggdrasil, still counted as Scandinavia.

For another, a mountaintop bursting into flames seemed rather dangerous to be viewed as entertainment.

But after staring through his telescope only a moment longer, Archie lowered it from his eye, turning pale. He pointed at the volcano. "What...is *that?*"

Jake turned to look and all the watching giants gasped in horror as *something climbed out* of the volcano.

Everyone stared in disbelief as a huge, fiery creature like a dog, but flaming red, crawled out of the hole in the mountaintop and shook itself, bracing all four paws atop the volcano.

Then it threw back its head and howled.

The long terrifying notes of its dire baying echoed through the night.

And with that, the fiery beast jumped off the volcano and disappeared among the hills.

Archie turned to Jake. "What was that?" he yelled over the sudden screaming of all the giants.

Pandemonium had broken out in the square.

Jake shook his head dazedly. "I have no idea!"

The feast turned to chaos as panic took hold; the giants overturned the tables and tore down the wedding canopy in their scramble to escape.

Kaia was yelling at them, trying to tell people to exit the square in an orderly fashion, while Snorri stayed near his new wife.

The boys stood frozen with shock on the handrail outside of the great hall.

Archie turned to Jake, his eyes wide behind his spectacles. "Do you think it's Loki?"

"But my dear children, I'm standing right behind you," a nearby voice drawled in amusement.

They whirled around to find the trickster god back in his mad prince form; he was leaning casually against the wall, watching things unfold.

Red growled at him, but Loki's devious smile never wavered.

"What have you done, you loon-bat?" Jake demanded.

"Oh, I just thought I'd bring my little doggy out to play."

"What?" Archie cried.

"His name is Fenrir. Isn't he adorable?" Loki feigned a frown. "Oh, but I'm afraid he's not very friendly—or obedient. In fact, he only listens to me. So you can tell your giant friends that I'll be waiting, whenever they want to surrender."

"Nobody's going to surrender to you," Jake said warily.

He smiled. "They will if they want to survive, Cakey, old boy. When they're prepared to swear allegiance to me, then I will send the

Fire Wolf back into the volcano. If not, he will soon turn all of Jugenheim to cinders. Try not to get eaten, boys." With that, Loki turned himself into a crow again.

Squawking with rude laughter, he flapped off to watch the catastrophe unfold from the safety of the dark night sky.

In the next heartbeat, the Fire Wolf reached the outskirts of the village.

Staring at it, Jake could not believe his eyes. The beast was nearly as tall as the giants—a terrifying monster with blood-red eyes. Its body was made of fiery orange lava, with plates of cooling black rock instead of fur that shifted when it moved.

Its tail was pure flame and had set the forest on fire as it had leaped from hill to hill heading this way.

Then it leaped over the buildings into the square and began tearing the village apart.

Gorm and his warriors came running. Perhaps the prince saw this as his chance to play the hero and show up Snorri for once and for all.

He waved his men into a semi-circle around the beast, but screams ensued as the Fire Wolf ate them one by one.

Gorm was the last survivor, but he only lasted a moment more. He tried to run away, but the Fire Wolf bounded up behind him and gobbled him up in one bite.

That was all Red had to see.

He cawed angrily at the boys, nodding toward his back, ordering them aboard.

"We can't just fly away! A Lightrider doesn't abandon his friends!" Jake protested. But Red leaned near and hissed in his face, showing Jake that it wasn't a request—it was an order.

With a scowl, Jake joined his cousin on the Gryphon's back. Red soared skyward, carrying them, at least, to safety.

As they rose toward the clouds moments later, Archie pointed toward the sea. "Look!"

Jake squinted into the distance. "Is that...?"

It looked like a flock of pale birds racing toward the village.

Archie peered through his telescope and confirmed it. "The Valkyries are coming!"

Jake stared grimly into the distance. *This must mean it's really as bad as it looks.* The celestial guardians of Valhalla would not have abandoned their usual posts if the giants were capable of stopping the Fire Wolf themselves. *Maybe there's no way to kill it,* he thought with a chill down his spine.

Red swept higher, lifting the boys out of the way, just as the flock of winged warrior women raced by beneath them, heading for the fight.

Odin's battle-maidens were in their beautiful forms this time, vengeance stamped on all their delicate faces, swords in their hands.

The boys felt the rushing currents from their beating wings as the flock of Valkyries passed beneath them. Their screeches filled the night as they got into attack formation.

Below, the terrified giants sent up a feeble cheer, welcoming the unexpected help.

A staccato series of piercing birdlike cries rang out as the Valkyries circled above the Fire Wolf in the sky.

Then, at their leader's signal, the winged beauties attacked the beast from all directions.

Red flapped higher so the boys could watch the Valkyries' progress in battling Fenrir from a safer altitude.

That was when Jake noticed the giant-sized wild animals fleeing the forest fires that Fenrir had left in his wake. Huge, Jugenheim-sized reindeer, lynxes, wolverines, and badgers the size of ponies stampeded out of the burning woods, trampling the farmers' crops as they galloped in a panic through the fields.

As for the Valkyries, it did not take long for them to discover that their swords could not even make contact with the Fire Wolf.

Any metal blade that got close enough to pierce him simply melted before it ever touched his hide.

The best the Valkyries could do was to swarm around the savage monster to keep him from eating people, try to keep him contained.

The Fire Wolf fought back, snapping at the beautiful warriors with his jaws, swatting them with his tail, and setting a number of them on fire.

Here and there, the flaming warrior women spiraled to the ground like sparks popping out of a bonfire.

As Jake glanced across the landscape, he suddenly had an inspiration. "Go back down, Red!" he ordered. "I think I may know how the Valkyries can deal with the Fire Wolf. Hurry!"

Red let out an unhappy growl at this command, but he seemed

willing to give Jake the benefit of the doubt. He carried the boys back down to the ground, landing out of the beast's sight behind a corner of the great hall.

"I'll be back before you even miss me," Jake promised in a breezy tone, jumping off the Gryphon's back to slip cautiously around the corner. Then he went running over to where one of the singed Valkyries had landed.

She had obviously gotten too close to the beast. Her sword had melted, her short pastel dress was smoking, and one of her wings was on fire.

Thinking fast, Jake grabbed a leftover pitcher of water from the abandoned feast and splashed it on the gorgeous creature, putting out the flames.

The poor, burnt Valkyrie groaned a little, but a minute later, she was already regenerating, slowly getting up to return to the fight. "Thank you," she panted.

"You're welcome. Wait, don't go!" he shouted as she turned to fly away. "I have an idea that might just help you defeat that thing!"

The Valkyrie paused, cocking her head to the side. "Yes, what is it? Quickly."

"Drive the monster that way!" Jake pointed toward the forest where Snorri had undergone the terrifying test of courage. "A dragon lives in those woods! Old Smokey will be more of a match for Fenrir than any of us will. At least he's fireproof! He's also highly territorial. If you can herd the Fire Wolf toward the dragon's lair, Smokey should come out to fight him!"

"Yes, I see...fight fire with fire. Excellent. Thank you." The Valkyrie nodded. "I'll tell the others." She took a few running steps, leaped into the air, and flew off to rejoin her warrior sisters.

Jake paused, watching the Valkyries, and noticing in the meanwhile the clusters of frightened giants hiding around the village square—some behind overturned tables, others cowering beside broken walls. He gathered they had not been able to escape during the Fire Wolf's attack and now were trapped in their hiding places.

The giant children were among them. Peter, the giant boy who had dwarf-tossed Archie, and his giant little sisters, who had thought Jake was a doll.

Fortunately, Kaia and Snorri were still on hand. They were hiding with some of their people, but Jake had a feeling that Kaia was already making a plan to get everyone out of there.

Stealthily retreating from the edge of the square, he ran back to Red and Archie and told them his suggestion for the Valkyries. Then the three of them remained on the ground, watching and waiting to see if his plan would work.

"Even if Old Smokey can't actually *kill* Fenrir, he should be able to weaken him, or at least it'll buy us some time to get these people out of here," Jake said in a low tone, watching everything.

"But then what?" Archie countered. "What if he comes back?"

Jake considered this and shook his head grimly. "I have no idea."

CHAPTER FORTY-SIX
The Irresistible Call

The boys watched from around the corner of the great hall as the Valkyries began working together to herd the Fire Wolf toward the dragon's cave.

"Tough girls," Archie remarked in admiration.

Zooming around the beast's head like a swarm of insects, they pushed Fenrir back yard by yard to the edge of the woods that marked the dragon's territory.

"C'mon," Jake said to his cousin when the Fire Wolf had cleared the village. "Let's get those giant kids out of the square where they were trapped."

They ran out to join the effort that Princess Kaia already had underway, collecting the giant children into a cart to be driven off to a safer location. She then directed Snorri to start a bucket line of giants to start putting out the fires raging everywhere around the village. Even the top of the great hall was burning.

Jake glanced around in dismay at all the blazes the Fire Wolf had left in his wake. Surely this village would not last long when all the Viking-style buildings were made of wood or thatch.

Looking on in dismay, he wasn't sure where he and Archie could be of use. He felt helplessly small.

Kaia's commands had helped create some order from the chaos, but panic still gripped the people.

With the giants running around nervously in the dark, Jake feared he and Archie were more in danger of getting stepped on than ever. As much as he wanted to help, he realized they had better just stay out of the way this time.

In the distance, a sudden flare of fire with an earthshaking roar told them Old Smokey had come out to fend off the intruder who dared invade his territory.

Jake turned to Red. "Will you take us up again? I want to see what happens! Then I can warn the giants if the Fire Wolf heads back this way."

The Gryphon bobbed his head and soon they were off. As they soared across the face of the moon, nearing the dragon's woods, they saw the Valkyries also hovering in the sky ahead, watching the battle between the two huge monsters below.

The dragon and the Fire Wolf leaped at each other, snarling viciously. The night reverberated with the crash as the beasts hit the ground and rolled.

Huge trees snapped behind them like twigs. The volcanic heat emanating from the Fire Wolf, paired with the dragon's blasts of flame, set more sections of the forest ablaze.

Through the trees and billowing smoke, the boys caught glimpses of the awesome death-match. Leathery wings flapping, Smokey leaped onto the Fire Wolf's back and clawed him with his talons; Fenrir whipped his head around and sank his teeth into the dragon's wing. The dragon gave way with a mighty roar, and they tumbled off in the other direction, slashing at each other with fangs and claws.

A piercing squawk sounded from above them.

Jake looked up to see Loki in crow form swooping out of the sky toward the Fire Wolf, circling him. "Fenrir, stop fooling around!" he scolded his dog. "Get back to your mission, now! I didn't let you out of that volcano so you could wrestle with this brute! Get back to the village! Go! Do what you were born to do! *Destroy!*"

Reluctantly, Fenrir untangled himself from his fight against the dragon.

Old Smokey stood panting, surrounded by burning woods. While the dragon caught his breath, the Fire Wolf backed away. But the great lizard only cared about guarding his territory; satisfied that the intruder was retreating, Old Smokey did not renew his attack. Instead, the golden-eyed dragon merely watched in satisfaction as the lava-dog turned around and trotted out of the clearing.

"Hurry, Red!" Jake cried. "Fenrir's heading back to the village to finish the job! We need to get there first to warn the giants! Fly as fast as you can!"

"Caw!"

314   E.G. FOLEY

"Hold on!" Jake warned his cousin as the Gryphon banked to the left, circling back toward the village.

Red's wings beat the air with powerful strokes.

They only just managed to beat the Fire Wolf to the village because the beast stopped to stomp a few farms along the way.

The Gryphon landed in the square, where the giants had made some progress bringing the fires under control.

Snorri saw them and came running. "Master Jake, Archie! I was so worried about—"

"The creature's right behind us!" Jake shouted. "He's coming back! He'll be here in a moment! Everyone, get ready!"

"How?" Princess Kaia cried in despair. "How do we fight it? Is there any way to defeat that thing?"

"I don't know." Jake hesitated, but when he spotted the king in the square, he realized he owed it to the giants at least to deliver Loki's message. "Sire!" He went running over to King Olaf.

"I have no time right now, Master Dwarf—"

"Sire, I know why this is happening!"

"You do?" This got the king's attention. His brow furrowed, he bent down to Jake with an inquiring look. "What can you tell me, lad?"

"Loki is the one behind this, Your Majesty. He loosed the Fire Wolf to force the giants to surrender to him. He wants control of an army of giants, so he can go to war against Odin. He was here, Sire, disguised as the Ice Wizard. That was Loki."

"*What?*"

"That's why he gave Gorm and Snorri an impossible riddle! He wanted them both to fail. That way, they both would've lost the contest, and Loki would've married your daughter himself. He thought he could get control of your people through Princess Kaia!"

King Olaf's eyes narrowed. "Did he, indeed? Well..." The king of the giants stood up to his full, towering height, glaring into the distance. "My people will never be the slaves of that vile trickster!"

"I was hoping you'd say that," Jake said under his breath. He wasn't sure what he would've done if the king had opted for surrender.

Kaia and Snorri approached.

"Father, what would you have us do?" the princess demanded.

"We are giants!" he replied, drawing his sword. "We fight!"

In the next heartbeat, the Fire Wolf was upon them.

King Olaf made a bold stand. The Fire Wolf slashed at him with its razor-like teeth, but each time it tried to bite him, the king of the giants parried the blow with his blade, and it didn't melt because it was made of dragon scales.

It was a most impressive display of warrior prowess, and it made the Fire Wolf furious.

The beast suddenly lost patience with its stubborn target, opened its jaws wide, and came straight down on the king, swallowing him in one bite.

"Father!" Kaia screamed.

Jake and Archie stared in horror as the beast licked his chops, then eyed up Snorri with a hungry snarl, and started creeping toward him.

"Oh, no, you don't." Furiously, Kaia nocked an arrow in her bow. She brought her weapon up again and again in rage, shooting countless arrows at the beast while Snorri backed away.

Unfortunately, most of her arrows simply caught fire and disintegrated into ash before they even reached the beast's hide.

Still, the flying missiles annoyed the creature. Fenrir whipped around, seeking out the source of the vexing arrows. His glowing red eyes homed in on Kaia.

Too far away to help, Snorri yelled her name as the Fire Wolf bounded straight toward her.

Considering they were standing right beside her, Jake and Archie gasped in terror and leaped out of the way.

Kaia dove aside with them, avoiding the monster's charge, and landing on her stomach nearby. The earth rocked as the giantess crashed to the ground, but to their relief, the Fire Wolf had missed her.

Snorri took matters into his own hands, picking up an enormous boulder from the charred foundations of one of the ruined village buildings.

Lifting it over his head, he hurled it at the Fire Wolf. The boulder lit up like a meteor hurtling earthward, but it was big enough to get through the monster's heat shield.

When it conked the Fire Wolf on the head, the beast apparently saw stars for a minute or two, weaving on its paws.

This gave Kaia a chance to get up, but first she glanced at the boys. "Are you two all right?"

Jake and Archie were both staring at her in shock.

Being a thirty-foot tall giantess, she was rarely on eyelevel with them, and so this was the first they had seen her new necklace.

The special gift from Snorri after he had been so embarrassed about bringing her a book from the dragon's cave.

They had forgotten to ask her about it in all the peril of traveling to the land of death and all.

But now, there it was, hanging right in front of them, dangling from her neck.

Gold and shiny, with the shape of a dog's head on one end.

"Is that—?" Archie blurted out in shock.

Jake nodded dazedly. "I can't believe it."

"Snorri must've found it in the cave back in Midgarth."

She saw them staring and touched it. "What's the matter?"

"Your necklace!" the boys said in unison.

"What about it?" she countered.

But Archie ignored her, elbowing Jake. "Do you think it might actually work?"

He swallowed hard. "Only one way to find out."

"I don't understand! What's the matter?" she asked in alarm.

"Your necklace," Archie said again.

"We need it. Now!" Jake added. "Take it off! Hurry!"

"Why? Whatever for?"

"Please!" Jake cried, frantic all of a sudden at their first glimmer of hope.

"We'll give it back!" Archie promised. "We just need to borrow it for a minute."

Confused, Kaia did as ordered, while a short distance away, the Fire Wolf recuperated from being hit in the head with Snorri's boulder. He shook himself, then continued his rampage in the opposite direction.

"Here." Her brow furrowed, Kaia handed them her necklace. "I still don't understand."

"You will, shortly." Jake took it from her and raised it to his lips.

The infamous Dr. Galton's silent whistle for training animals.

He had thought it was long gone, lost along the way, after he had stolen it from the Exhibit Hall.

Jake turned toward Loki's monstrous dog, took a deep breath, and then blew into the brass whistle.

He didn't hear anything.

But the Fire Wolf paused.

Turned slowly...

And snarling, looked straight at him with his red, glowing eyes.

Jake gulped. "I think it works."

Archie and he started walking backwards slowly and carefully, not taking their eyes off the savage beast. "Er, Jake, he's coming this way... Jake?"

"Red! To me!"

The trusty Gryphon was by his side in a pounce.

"Dwarves? What are you doing?" Kaia exclaimed.

"Sorry, Princess. I need to borrow this for a while. Trust me! I'll explain later!"

"Should I come with you?" Archie asked.

"No, Red can fly faster with just one of us. Stay here and tell the giants to get ready. Once I lead Fenrir back into the volcano, they'll need to seal him in. Have them throw boulders on top of it or something to plug up the opening so he can't get back out."

"I'll take care of it. Jake—you need to be careful up there," he warned, nodding at the sky. "Volcanoes belch out all sorts of poison gases. When you get close, don't inhale them or you'll die. Stay above the smoke clouds. I should also warn you the forest fire will be sucking the oxygen out of the air. That'll make it harder for Red to gain altitude. Without normal oxygen levels, you'll both tire faster."

"Then we'd better do this quick."

As the Fire Wolf stalked closer, growling, Archie sent the beast a frightened glance, then backed away. "Be careful, coz. Don't go dying on us, now that the family has only just found you again."

"Don't worry. You lot won't get rid of me so easily. C'mon, Red, let's put this dog back in his cage!"

"Caw!" the Gryphon answered with a fighting gleam in his golden eyes.

Swinging onto his back, Jake grasped Red's collar; the Gryphon took a few running strides across the cobblestones, then unfurled his wings and launched into the air.

The Fire Wolf leaped after them, chasing instinctively.

Each powerful beat of the Gryphon's scarlet-feathered wings brought them higher over the forest. They set their sights on the fiery mouth of the volcano ahead.

Jake blew into the dog-whistle again and again.

Unable to resist its piping call, the Fire Wolf followed.

CHAPTER FORTY-SEVEN
An Angry God

J ake's hair blew in his eyes as he and Red raced across the sky, the Fire Wolf bounding along the ground below them. Clouds of drifting smoke from the forest fires and heavy ash from the volcano made his eyes water. He coughed, his lungs burning. But as he pulled his scarf across his nose and mouth to help filter the air, his greater concern was keeping an eye out for Loki.

He doubted the trickster god was done playing with them tonight.

In the distance, the volcano, like a great, burning wound in the earth, oozed with blood-red lava flows dripping down its sides. Occasional plumes of fiery molten rock shot up into the dark sky and left huge smoke clouds towering in the distance.

Jake hoped those clouds of poison gases didn't drift in his direction.

While the rumble in the mountain echoed like thunder in the distance, the immediate danger was closer. Through the swirling smoke, Jake could see the Fire Wolf racing through the forest, following them.

The Galton whistle had worked to get Fenrir's attention, luring him to follow. Still, it was terrifying being the focus of the monster's attention.

The Fire Wolf was half as tall as the trees. It kept leaping up as it ran, trying to lunge at Red and him like a cat chasing a butterfly.

"Keep going, boy," Jake urged his feathered friend. "We can't lose altitude or that thing might jump high enough to grab us."

With a cough, Red valiantly flew on, racing toward the volcano as fast as his wings would carry them. The heavy film of the ash and smoke in the air made it hard for both of them to breathe. Jake knew the smoke was bothering Red, for he could feel the Gryphon starting to strain a little under his weight.

Glancing over his shoulder, Jake kept blowing the dog-whistle, luring the Fire Wolf toward the volcano that was apparently its home.

But as he looked forward again, up ahead in the distance, Jake saw a familiar figure standing in the barren wasteland between the lava flows.

Loki was dancing a jig of glee in anticipation of his victory over the giants and all the Nine Worlds soon to follow. No doubt he was delighted at all the chaos he had caused.

But when the Lord of the Shapeshifters looked up and saw Jake and the Gryphon coming, he stopped dancing and stared up at them in disbelief.

They flew over him at top speed.

Jake glanced back to see Loki's reaction when the trickster god realized what was happening. He blew the Galton whistle again, and in the next moment, the Fire Wolf emerged from the forest into the naked lands around the volcano.

Fenrir looked even larger without the trees crowding him in. As the beast leaped closer, Jake uttered a curse under his breath.

Terror made his heart tick like the second hand of a watch, but he could not afford to let fear cloud his mind. He had to focus on getting that monster back into the volcano before Loki interfered.

"Fenrir!" the trickster god bellowed. "What are you doing? You're going the wrong way! Come back here! Bad dog! Fenrir!"

The Fire Wolf ignored him, focused on the piping tones from the Galton whistle that only he could hear.

Loki lost his temper at his dog's disobedience.

Through the drifting smoke, Jake could see him changing into something. "Hurry, Red! I don't trust that glock-wit. I think he's comin' after us."

Red struggled to climb higher on the thin air, heading for the mouth of the volcano. He had to dart and bank this way and that as it spewed lava and hurled liquefied rock thousands of degrees in temperature into the air at them.

Jake quickly concluded that this was by far the most dangerous thing he had ever done or ever cared to do in the future. He tried not to dwell on that fact, though, because panicking wasn't going to help.

But when Loki came winging out of the smoke clouds after them in a terrible new shape, Jake squinted in confusion. *What the—?*

A flying monkey?

Loki cackled as he sped after them disguised as a flying chimpanzee; he wore a little red pillbox hat and a vest, like some sort of demented mechanical toy. "Oh, Cake," he called, "where do you think you're going?"

Apparently, he could still talk in that form.

Jake shook his head, refusing to react to the strangeness of Loki's appearance. The trickster had obviously chosen that bizarre shape to try to shock and confuse him, and thereby gain the upper hand.

It wasn't going to work.

"Hurry, Red, he's gaining on us," Jake warned.

But it was already too late. Zooming up from below them, the flying monkey launched his attack, grabbing for the Galton whistle. "Give me that trinket! You don't get to ruin my fun!"

Loki grasped Jake's arm with his leathery monkey fingers and tried to drag him off the Gryphon's back.

They struggled while Red flew on towards the volcano.

Jake smacked the monkey's little hat down over his eyes. Loki screeched in his face and bared his monkey fangs in answer; then he doubled his attack, buffeting Jake not just with his hands now, but his weird monkey feet, too, his black wings flapping all the while.

"Ha, ha, you're going to die!" the flying monkey chattered gleefully as they neared the volcano, but when he nearly threw Jake off Red's back, Jake punched him across his face.

Loki lost his balance and slipped off Red's back, plummeting toward the ground.

Unable to get any lift in the thin air, the Loki-monkey plunged and tumbled through the sky, disappearing through the drifting clouds of smoke.

Jake peered toward the ground. He had a feeling Loki wouldn't stay down long.

He murmured to the Gryphon to steady him, but as glad as he was to be rid of the unpredictable trickster god, the moment he looked over his shoulder to check on the Fire Wolf, he gasped to find the beast right behind them.

"Higher, Red—fast!" he yelled as the monstrous dog leaped into the air, snapping its jaws right beneath them.

At that moment, the Fire Wolf had reached the edge of the volcano's mouth, where it leaped into the air one last time to try and catch them—and fell straight down into the volcano.

* * *

"Now!" Archie yelled, watching through his telescope. The instant he saw the Fire Wolf plunge back into its fiery home, he gave the signal. "Release!"

Snorri let loose an enormous catapult.

The trebuchet had been King Olaf's pride and joy.

The second he released the tension on the arm, the catapult swung a huge rock forward, aiming straight at the volcano.

* * *

Incoming!

Jake ducked and Red dove out of the way as a hunk of stone the size of a Greek island flew through the night and landed in the center of the volcano, capping it with a huge boom.

"Yes!" Jake punched the air with a jubilant fist.

But the giants didn't stop there. They continued firing great stones from the catapult and working in groups to throw more boulders into the crater of the volcano until they had well and truly stoppered it. The mountain groaned, but it spewed forth no more fire. There was no way the Fire Wolf was getting out of there.

"Look at that, Red! They did it—and so did we!"

"Caw!" the Gryphon answered in triumph, but then the poor creature started coughing in the smoke.

Jake reached down and gave Red a pat. "You can land now, boy. You must be exhausted."

Red did not need to be told twice. He dipped his right wing lower, banking back toward the giants' village.

Unfortunately, they had not yet seen the last of Loki.

When the trickster god had hit the earth, thrown down by a mere mortal boy, a rage filled Loki, the likes of which he had never known.

Snapping his fingers on the way down, he got rid of his amusing flying monkey shape. By the time he hit the ground with a thud, he was back to his usual, preferred form of the mad prince.

Being an immortal, he was, of course, unfazed by the fall, just a little bruised. But as he climbed to his feet, his dark eyes were glazed with fury, for the greatest wound tonight was to his pride.

Loki lowered his head, closed his eyes, and brought up both of his fists at his sides, willing himself to grow.

And grow he did.

Through the drifting clouds of smoke and rivers of lava coursing past him, the forest an inferno around him, he grew and grew, until he stood higher than the trees, taller than three giants.

Taller, indeed, than the volcano.

He was a god, after all.

He was not about to be undone by a mortal brat and his pet lion-eagle-thing.

"Oh, Cake!" he called ever so pleasantly. In his gigantic size, Loki's voice reverberated through the mountains. "Come back here, you brat. I've had enough of your mischief. You've been a Very. Naughty. Boy."

Then Loki stepped over the trees and went after him.

CHAPTER FORTY-EIGHT
Son of Odin

*A*h, *crud.* Jake glanced over his shoulder in terror and saw the gigantic Loki coming. He was kind of hard to miss.

Red flapped his wings frantically to try to stay ahead of their towering pursuer, but it was no use.

With a laugh, Loki caught them between his cupped hands and trapped them like a firefly. "Now I've got you!"

Jake tumbled off the Gryphon's back and struggled to get his bearings, while Red immediately put up a fight.

"Ow!" Loki exclaimed as the Gryphon pecked his palm, hard, with his beak. "Bad birdie! You think you can hurt me? Why, that was nothing but a pinprick." He opened his hands just enough to pluck Jake up by the back of his collar, dangling him between his finger and thumb.

Hanging precariously over the ground so far below, Jake kicked his legs while the trickster god took Red in his other hand in similar fashion. Compared to him, they seemed no larger than toys: miniature soldiers, chess pieces, tiny figurines.

"Dear little Cake. You are quite an interesting fellow," Loki said. "But you've wrecked my plans and now you'll have to pay."

"I'm not afraid o' you!" Dangling from his fingers, Jake tried to take a swing at him, but Loki laughed in amusement.

"Then you're more stupid than the giants."

Jake had to admit it was hardly a fair fight. Indeed, at Loki's current size, dwarfing the giants, the mere breath from his lips when he spoke was enough to blow away the plumes of smoke that curled around him. "Ow! Stop that!" he snapped, turning his attention to Red, who had scratched Loki's huge finger with his hind claws.

"*You* are beginning to annoy me," he informed the Gryphon. He lifted Red higher, inspecting him more closely. "Hmm, when I was a wee boy, do you know what I liked to do? I really enjoyed pulling the wings off dragonflies."

"No!" Jake screamed as Loki started gently pulling on one of Red's wings. "Leave him alone! Take me! It's my fault! Don't hurt him! Please! He was only following my orders!"

Loki paused, glancing over at him. "How very noble of you, dear lad. But don't worry, you're next—"

His words were suddenly drowned out by a BOOM! so loud it seemed to crack the earth.

"LOKI!"

The reverberating bellow seemed to come from everywhere at once.

Jake glanced around in a panic but saw nothing.

Loki's eyes narrowed as the biggest lightning bolt Jake had ever seen came rocketing out of the dark sky. Suddenly, Thor was there, catching his balance after his huge, single leap between worlds. He, too, had made himself gigantic, but unlike Loki, the thunder god was covered in muscles.

"Caw!" Red called to Jake, who nodded eagerly.

"I know!" Thor must have finally tracked them here after he and Archie had broken into Valhalla and then escaped.

He came striding across the mountains toward his nemesis.

"Releasing the Fire Wolf?" he demanded in fury. "Half of Jugenheim is burning! I should've known you were behind this. You have no right to be here, Loki. Leave. Now. Before I *make* you leave."

"You might actually scare me if you had a brain, you muscle-bound numskull." Loki sneered, though he backed away as Thor approached.

"Help! Help!" Jake yelled in the meanwhile. "Help, please! He's goin' to kill us!"

"So! There you are, intruder. I'll deal with you next. Loki, release the human and his creature."

"Who are you to give me orders?" Loki fairly screamed. "I am just as much of a prince as you!"

"Don't make me tell you twice," Thor warned.

Backing away, Loki cast about in frustration for some escape, only to realize he was trapped. "Meathead!"

For some reason, Thor *really* didn't like being called a meathead. Maybe deep down, he knew that Loki was smarter than him. But slyness and brains didn't always trounce brawn, and this was one of those occasions.

A look of wrath came over Thor's broad, ruddy face.

At least it was an honest face.

"Aaaargh!" With a mighty growl, he hurled his hammer at Loki. "Go back down to Neiflheim where you belong, devil!"

Loki shrieked, letting go of Jake and Red to try to dive out of the way.

But Thor's shining hammer followed him, spinning through the air, end over end, passing with a deadly *whoosh*.

Meanwhile, Jake and Red, dropped by Loki, were tumbling through the air. Somehow, before they hit the river of lava beneath them, Red righted himself and caught Jake in his beak at the last minute, swooping him to safety.

Wide-eyed, Jake dangled from the Gryphon's mouth as Red glided down to a small patch of the forest that wasn't burning. The second they landed, Jake turned to see what would happen to Loki.

At just that moment, when Loki turned to see if he might escape, Thor's hammer struck the trickster in the belly. It kept flying, carrying Loki off his feet, until it sent him crashing back onto the huge capstone the giants had tossed up onto the top of the volcano.

The slab of rock cracked under his gigantic weight. Loki fell into the volcano with a shout, butt first. His feet were the last to disappear. Jake could still hear the echo of his yell as he plunged out of sight.

A puff of smoke and tongues of flame shot into the dark sky as the Lord of the Shapeshifters was forcibly returned to his underworld realm.

Meanwhile, Thor's hammer flew back into its owner's hand. Thor grasped the handle, striding over the forest to the volcano.

Taking no chances that Loki or his dog might get out again, Thor smashed the volcano with his hammer, making the whole thing cave in. The mountain turned to rubble—the top of it flattened, Loki buried within.

Watching in the distance, Archie and the giants cheered, but Thor was not yet finished with his cleanup job.

Jake stared in awe as the Viking god of the weather reached up into the skies and pulled down a handful of storm-clouds. He flung them around, then pointed at them, commanding them in the ancient Norse tongue.

With a huge crackle of lightning and a deafening roar of thunder, the storm-clouds released a torrent of rain.

Jake cheered and hugged the Gryphon in excitement as the rain drenched them and all of Jugenheim, putting out the raging fires burning farms and forests.

Clouds of steam rose as cold rain doused red-hot surfaces; the downpour also helped to clear the smoke out of the air.

Thor puffed out his cheeks and blew away the poison gases still lingering over the now-defunct volcano.

Meanwhile, the sheets of rain drummed the charred forests and cooled the lava flows into bizarre, black forms of twisted, misshapen stone.

The rain continued drumming them all as the mighty Thor bent down to have a word with Jake.

Jake cowered from him.

"You! You're the intruder who broke into my father's fortress."

Jake didn't dare attempt to lie to him after Thor's display of awesome power. "I am," he admitted with a gulp.

"How dare you?" he demanded.

"I'm sorry, I had no choice!" he yelped. "I had to go into the palace to find the answer to Loki's riddle, or he'd have taken control of the giants and led an invasion of the earth! Please don't Blood-Eagle me!" he shouted, lowering his head and throwing his arms up to protect himself from the mighty Norse god.

"Now, now," a new voice interrupted from nearby, "nobody's going to Blood-Eagle anyone. The truth is, we don't really go in for that sort of thing much anymore."

Slowly, Jake looked up, lowering his arms, raising his head. He was almost afraid to look. But when he did, he saw a rugged old man with an eye-patch walking toward him from out of the clouds of steam that hung over the half-burnt forest.

He was human-sized, with a shock of white hair and the leathery, tanned complexion of an outdoorsman or an old soldier.

Approaching, he moved with a slight limp. There was something so familiar about him, Jake thought. But for a moment, he couldn't place him.

The old man waved off the sky god. "It's all right, Thor. I'll take it from here. I've been watching this young warrior for quite some time," he said in a deep, gravelly voice.

"Me? A warrior?" Jake echoed. Why, no one had ever called him that before.

He was only twelve, after all.

"Father," Thor said, bending his head in respect to the old man.

"Thank you for your assistance, son."

Jake drew in his breath, realizing that if this was Thor's father, then that meant it could only be Odin.

The king of the gods himself!

And at that very moment, he remembered where he had seen the old man before.

The one-eyed janitor from the University!

"You!" Jake blurted out, wide-eyed. "You were the one who warned me when Archie got abducted!" He stared in shock. "Odin?"

The old man flashed a wolfish grin and Jake suddenly recalled something Miss Langesund had said about Odin roaming the world in disguise, looking for warriors to recruit for Valhalla...

"Why, you've been watching all along, haven't you?" he burst out. "You knew from the start that Snorri broke the seal between the worlds! You must have seen it in that pool! But sir—! Why didn't you say anything?"

"How dare you question the king of the gods?" Thor thundered.

But the old All-Father of the Vikings smiled shrewdly, studying Jake. "Why, indeed?"

Jake stared back at him, amazed and just a wee bit irked at his non-answer.

It figured the god of wisdom would answer a question with a question.

Odin cracked a stony grin and clapped him on the back. "Come along, lad. Let's get you and your genius cousin home."

CHAPTER FORTY-NINE
A Fair Wind

Odin accompanied Jake and Red back to the giants' village, as did Thor, who had also shrunk himself down to human size to avoid any awkwardness.

Archie ran to Jake when he saw them coming. Jake assured him he was all right, then he introduced his cousin to the gods. The giants scrambled to pay their respects to the visiting deities.

While Archie stared in wonder at Odin, and Thor called off the rain, now that the fires were out, Jake congratulated Snorri on his excellent aim with the catapult. Then Jake gave Princess Kaia back her 'golden jewelry,' the Galton whistle.

As she smiled at him in thanks, Jake felt confident that Giant Land would be in good hands henceforward.

At length, Odin gathered everyone around and made a brief speech. "Well done, giants, gryphon, and, ah, dwarves!" He sent the boys a knowing wink, but kept their secret. "You all fought bravely against the Fire Wolf and Loki. It was a splendid victory against a very pesky foe. But you dwarves cannot remain in Jugenheim," he said to Jake and Archie, "unless you wish to stay forever. I must repair the seal, you see. I understand someone broke it." The old man arched a brow at Snorri.

"Accidentally, sir!"

"Hmmm," Odin said. "Once the breach is repaired, no one will be able to get through either way."

"I'm sure we'll be happy to be going home, sir," Jake assured him.

"The sooner the better!" Archie piped up.

"As I expected. But first, I cannot let such brave dwarves leave empty-handed. You may have heard that Odin the Wise is a great giver of gifts!" the king god proclaimed.

Jake recalled Miss Langesund telling them that gift-giving was a point of honor among the Vikings. Any Norse chieftain or king who did not reward his friends or followers with generous presents would have been considered a cheapskate.

Jake was all in favor of rewards.

"Now, then," Odin began.

"Father, wait!" Thor complained. "How can you reward these two when they trespassed in Valhalla? Into your very throne room?"

"Ah, Thor, I am the patron god of wisdom, am I not? I can't help but respect people who would go to such lengths to find answers. Besides, why should I punish them? Because they went a-raiding into dangerous territory, where unknown perils lurked? In that light, I daresay they would have made excellent Vikings."

Jake and Archie grinned at each other.

"They could have turned their backs on Snorri, and on the threat that Loki posed. But instead of walking away and leaving someone else to solve it, they took responsibility.

"They acted as heroes," Odin continued, "and they deserve rewards. In fact, you boys have a standing invitation to join me and my army in Valhalla when you die. Of course," he added, "my Eye, the one I left with the Norns, tells me that won't be for many, *many* years to come yet. Still, the offer stands. I'll send my Valkyries to collect you on that day, if you wish them to escort you to my hall."

"Honored," Archie said at once with a gentlemanly bow.

"Very generous of you, sir." Jake followed suit, though, privately, he already had firm plans to go to Heaven when he died so he could be with his parents.

If they were really there. After what he had seen in Odin's reflecting pool, he was beginning to wonder.

"Very well! Now, then. To your rewards." Odin clapped his hands twice, and a bevy of Valkryies flew down to attend him.

Odin beckoned to the one who was holding a small wooden box. As she stepped forward and opened the lid, Odin turned to Jake. "For the young Earl of Griffon, I present you with a magical dagger." The king-god gestured at the box, and the Valkyrie turned to Jake to let him see his prize. "Its name is Risker. Seems fitting for you."

"Thank you, sir," Jake breathed in awe.

The sleek knife was covered in intricate Viking runes. It had a curved blade and a mysterious gemstone set into the base of the hilt. A leather scabbard came with it, attached to a good, sturdy belt.

"This is a very powerful knife," the chief god informed him. "The handle was carved from the wood of Yggdrasil, and the blade was forged in Asgard by Wayland the Smith himself."

Jake lifted the dagger from its velvet cradle in awe. He curled his fingers around the hilt, testing the weight of it in his grasp. When he carefully touched the edge of the blade to see how sharp it was, he jerked his hand away with a tiny cut on his fingertip. "Ow!"

Everyone chuckled.

Odin arched a brow at him. "Do be careful with it, Lord Griffon. Risker has many amazing properties. Not even I know all of them. I'll leave to you to discover the rest, but what I do know is that it can cut through stone as easily as fabric; it'll never rust; and it will return to your hand the way Thor's hammer does. Learn to use it wisely," Odin advised him. "A day will come when it may save your life."

"Thank you very much, sir. I am more honored than I can say. Truly!" Jake buckled the belt on around his hips and then secured the dagger in its sheath, delighted with his gift.

Odin nodded, pleased by his thanks. "And for you, Master Archie." The king-god turned to the boy genius, who had been snapping a few final photographs. "I understand your flying machine is still in need of repair... Or is it?"

He clapped his hands again, and this time, one of the Valkyries gave a piercing birdcall to her sisters.

A moment later, a group of the winged women came flying through the sky, carrying the Pigeon from the direction of Snorri's farm.

Archie lifted his eyebrows as they set it down before him.

The Pigeon was unscathed. All the damage Snorri had done to it while kidnapping him had been mysteriously fixed.

The broken wing was newly welded; not even a dent nor a scratch marred its polished surface. It had even been washed, waxed, and shined until its brass fixtures gleamed in the silvery dawn twilight.

"I took the liberty of repairing it for you," Odin said to the wonderstruck Archie. "I added a few...how do you say? Bells and whistles. I think they might jar some new ideas for you to explore in your future research."

"I don't like being given the answers," Archie blurted out. "I mean—finding them myself is half the fun."

"I understand that," Odin said with a nod. "Trust me, you'll have to study it well to understand my contributions. But in the meanwhile, I couldn't have you breaking your neck on the way home."

"So it works, then?" Archie asked skeptically, no doubt recalling all those deadly silver flying machines he had seen on the screens in Odin's war-room.

"Does it work?" Odin echoed with a slight huff. "I am the god of wisdom, last I checked. I should think it jolly well works! Well enough to carry you home, cheeky pup. Now then, if you are quite ready to go, the time has come."

"Could we have a moment, please, to say goodbye to the giants?" Jake asked.

Odin nodded. "If you hurry. Your being here upsets the balance of things as much as Snorri's visit to your world did." Then he stepped aside, joining Archie and Thor, who were examining the Pigeon.

Jake turned to Snorri.

The gentle giant shepherd-king bent down and met his gaze sadly. "I can't believe I'll never see you two pips again."

"Maybe someday." Jake faltered. "It's been quite a journey, hasn't it?"

Snorri smiled. "It has."

"You see that? You did win the crown and get the girl without the help of Loki's potion. You *were* smart enough to do it all along."

"Ah, you boys figured out the answer to the riddle, not me."

"Pshaw, but it was you who had the good sense to befriend us," Jake countered. "You got the book from the dragon's cave that gave us our best clue. We couldn't have done it without you. You know, Snorri, it seems to me a leader doesn't have to know how to do everything himself, as long as he knows how to pick his friends and allies. Besides, after all we've come through, I've concluded that you are a good deal cleverer than you think."

"So are you, Master Jake. So are you." Snorri cast a discreet glance at Archie.

Jake gave him a wry smile. It was true, he was no genius, and he still did not have much formal education. But somehow the prospect of returning to the University with all those geniuses seemed a lot less intimidating now, after defeating the Fire Wolf and outwitting the trickster god himself. Of course, he'd never have the world-class brains of an Archie, but at least he didn't feel like a blockhead anymore. His life among the aristocrats was still new to him, but he was beginning to feel more and more like he could hold his own.

"Thanks." Jake stuck out his hand, Snorri offered one finger, and they shook on their friendship.

Archie followed suit. Though he had detested Snorri early on, now the boy genius looked sorry to be leaving their large friends.

With a final goodbye to Kaia, at last, Jake and Archie waved to the other giants. "Good luck to you all!"

"Goodbye, dwarves!" they called, cheering them. "Good work with the Fire Wolf!"

"All set, then?" Odin asked.

"Yes, sir. Thank you. And thank you, Thor," he added, turning to the red-haired Viking hero. "You saved our lives. We could not have beaten Loki without you."

"Humph," Thor grunted, folding his bulging arms across his chest. "You would do well to stay out of places where you don't belong, boy."

Jake gave him a penitent look, but obviously, he had no intention of taking that advice.

With a final wave farewell, the boys and Red left the village. In the company of the father-and-son gods and their entourage of beautiful Valkyries, they walked down to Snorri's sheep meadow, and the original site of where the seal had been broken.

Snorri and Kaia followed to see what would happen.

Thor carried Archie's new-and-improved flying machine on his shoulder, setting it down in the field.

The boulder still sat atop the breach, but the problem wasn't fixed; it was only covered up.

Odin gave his son a nod, then Thor rolled Snorri's boulder away from the hole between worlds.

While Odin inspected the problem, Archie made his final checks on the Pigeon. Then, his tool-bag on his shoulder, he vaulted into the cockpit and started her up.

As the engine purred, the propellers on the stern whirled; the wings began to flap; and the young aviator pulled his goggles down over his eyes. "She sounds good!" he yelled over the noise, adjusting knobs and levers on the dashboard.

Jake climbed onto Red's back.

The two cousins glanced at each other. "You ready?" Jake called over the clamor of the machine.

Archie gave him an eager thumbs up.

Jake grinned, gesturing toward the hole between the worlds. "After you!"

"See you at the bottom, coz!" Archie called. Then Thor gave the Pigeon a push, and Jake watched with his heart in his throat as it plunged off the broken edges of Giant World. The weather god indulged the boy navigator with a puff of wind from his lips.

Archie let out a whoop of excitement as the new-and-improved Pigeon with its slight modifications sped along, swirling through the sky.

Whew. It worked. But of course it worked, he chided himself. Archie's prototype enhanced with Odin's improvements?

He put all worry for his cousin out of his mind. Archie looked to be having so much fun that Jake was eager to join him. "Let's go, boy," he murmured to the Gryphon. Red launched off of the edge and then dove through the hole in the crust of Jugenheim.

Jake glanced back and waved a final farewell to the Norse gods and giants.

Then he held on tightly to Red's collar as the Gryphon descended through the branches of the mighty tree, Yggdrasil.

It was exhilarating to soar like this between the worlds. Behind them, Jake heard noises similar to the rumbling he remembered from the volcano.

Mighty forces were in motion as Odin, arms out, chanted to repair the breach, growing back rock and dirt and stone and turf to cover the hole in the same way that a person's body mended itself after some cut or scrape.

The pieces grew back together again, but within seconds, the bottom surface of Giant Land was hidden once more behind the clouds.

Far below, Jake glimpsed the Norns having their breakfast tea in their meadow, while ahead of him, the Pigeon chugged along steadily through the sky.

Soon they flew away from Yggdrasil, and its massive trunk disappeared into the mists.

As the boys soared earthward, rejoining the world of mortals, a golden sunrise was just breaking over Norway.

A new day waited.

CHAPTER FIFTY
The Travelers' Tale

The boys zoomed and swirled through the gold and pink and baby blue morning sky, enjoying themselves far too much to rush their landing.

Jake supposed this was a longer and more exciting descent than Archie had ever hoped to experience. But the ground was coming up quickly, so he urged Red closer to the Pigeon.

"I can't let Red be seen!" he hollered to his cousin. "Might as well part ways now, if you're going to be all right?"

Archie gave him another thumbs up, his hair flying wildly. "My speech isn't till nine, but no harm in giving the gents a little demonstration, what-hey?"

Jake laughed. He supposed the boy genius deserved to show off a bit for once.

"Could you send the girls on with my notes?" Archie called.

Jake nodded. *They'll love that.* "Are you sure you know how to land that thing?"

"No worries!" he yelled back cheerfully.

"Good luck!"

Archie bade him farewell with a wave. His whoop of joy trailed out behind him as he zoomed down toward the college. "Woooo hoooo!"

Jake stayed up high, obscured behind the puffy pastel clouds so no one on the ground would see the Gryphon. But he watched with a grin from ear to ear as his cousin finally came to a perfect landing on the green in the center of the University buildings.

The boy genius knew how to make an entrance, he thought with a wry laugh as the scientists on the ground came running. Archie hadn't even climbed out of the Pigeon yet as his adult colleagues crowded around his invention, applauding.

Just then, against the white clouds ahead, Jake spotted a trail of golden sparkles heading his way. "Gladwin!" he cried in surprise as his favorite royal messenger fairy came zooming out of the clouds. He immediately wondered if the message she had been en route to deliver when he had seen her in Odin's reflecting pool might have been for him.

"Oh, thank goodness you're alive!" she cried in her tiny, tinkling voice as she reached him. "I was that worried!"

"No need. Archie and I are both safe."

"Good!" She landed on Jake's shoulder as lightly as a dragonfly and crouched down against his neck, shielding herself from the wind by tucking back behind his coat collar.

He furrowed his brow as she held on tightly to his earlobe to keep from being blown away. "Derek Stone sent me. He got one of his warning feelings about you. That you were in danger. The Guardian instinct, you know. But he couldn't come himself on account of his bodyguard assignment, so he sent me to check on you."

"Did he happen to send a message with you?"

She nodded. "I have it back at the room."

"As soon as I'm on the ground, I'll send a telegram to let him know I'm all right. Are Dani and Isabelle safe?"

"Oh, yes. They're in the dormitory, still waiting for Henry and Helena."

"No sign of them yet?" he asked with a frown.

Gladwin shook her head sadly. "No."

Jake pondered this news in concern.

He still had only a small amount of experience in magical dealings, but he would've thought that when Thor had defeated Loki, the spell the Lord of the Shapeshifters had cast over the twins would've been broken. That was how it usually seemed to work.

"Would you mind looking after Red for me while I go and see the girls?" Jake asked the fairy as they coasted down into the clearing in the woods above the fjord, where Archie had first tested the Pigeon on the day they had arrived. "He's been through an awful lot over the past few hours. We could've died."

"I knew you weren't safe!" Gladwin scolded, pinching his ear.

"Ow!"

"Humph, that's what you get for fibbing to me. No worries, my foot!"

"All right, so maybe I deserved that. But don't take it out on Red. It wasn't his fault; he was only doing what I asked. He needs some food and water, and some sleep. He inhaled a lot of dangerous gases over the volcano."

"Volcano?" Gladwin cried.

"I think a few of his feathers might've got singed."

"I want to hear *all* about this later."

"I'll tell everyone the whole tale on the boat ride back to England," Jake promised as he slid off the Gryphon's back. "You'll stay with us till then, won't you, Gladwin?"

"Of course."

"Thanks. It's been a little unnerving without Henry and Helena."

"I know, lad. You go on now." The fairy fluttered down onto Red's head. He looked up at her with a curious roll of his golden eyes. "I'll see to him," she promised with a nod.

Jake thanked her again, then gave his trusty Gryphon a pat on the neck. "See you again soon, Red."

With what was left of his strength, he jogged back down the same mountain trail where he had originally heard the *BOOM* that he had thought was an earthquake.

Well, now he certainly knew the truth! Giants were real. And as he loped wearily down the path, it occurred to him that he never did get to ask the Norse about the trolls that they claimed lived in these woods, too.

After everything that had happened, he had no desire to meet one at the moment. He just wanted rather desperately to get back to normal life.

Fortunately, he made it back to the dormitory without encountering any more magical creatures.

Dani and Isabelle jumped up from where they were sitting in their room and ran to him the moment he arrived, both hugging him at the same time.

"Jake!"

"You're alive!"

"Blech, you smell like sulfur and smoke!" Dani said, stepping back from him with a grimace.

"Ha, wait till I tell you why," he answered with a grin.

"Where's Archie?" Isabelle asked, clutching his arm in worry.

"He's fine. I think he might end up giving his speech early today. Also, he needs his notes. He wondered if one of you could bring them to him."

Dani snorted. "Figures!"

Isabelle shook her head. "Thanks for bringing my brother back in one piece."

"Any news of Henry and Helena?" he asked in concern.

The girls exchanged a guarded glance.

"What is it?" Jake prompted, worried anew when he saw their pained looks. "What's happened? Are they still in animal form?"

"Oh, yes," Isabelle said with caution.

"What, then? Has something happened?" he cried. "Did a hunter shoot them?"

"No, no, nothing like that," Isabelle assured him. "It's just...well, they are enjoying their freedom in the forest so much as wild animals that they...well, Jake...I'm afraid they don't want to come back."

"What?" Jake stared at her in shock. "Don't *want* to come back? What do you mean?"

"The last we saw them, they had started reverting to the wild. They were afraid if they came around us again, they'd attack us, like real wild animals. They didn't want to hurt us. Please, it's not their fault..." Isabelle kept trying to explain, but Jake was hardly listening, outraged to think the twins would abandon them.

Angrily, he strode over to the window and scanned the edge of the woods beyond the pleasant campus grounds. "This can't be right," he murmured to himself. "When Thor hit Loki with his hammer, I'd have thought..." His words trailed off as he continued studying the landscape.

"Thought what?" Dani prompted, stepping closer in concern.

"Ha!" Jake suddenly shouted. "I knew it! There! Look!" He pointed toward the trees, then ran off without explanation.

"What the—? Jake?"

"Where are you going?" the girls exclaimed, hurrying after him.

He went into Henry's room. "They've changed back—whether they like it or not. They're outside! I knew it," he said as he grabbed an armful of clothes for their tutor and dodged back out of Henry's room.

"They are? Wait! Jake!"

"Where did you see them? Where are you going?"

The girls followed again as he ran back to the window in the girls' room and beckoned them over impatiently. "There! Look." He pointed at their tutor in his human form, concealing himself as best he could behind a leafy mountain laurel bush.

"On second thought, maybe you shouldn't look," Jake added with a roguish glance.

The girls shrieked and averted their eyes, not that you could see anything, really.

Poor Henry! With a mortified expression, their bookish tutor was staring toward the dormitory, waving discreetly, and obviously hoping in desperation that one of them would see him and bring him some clothes.

"I'm sure Miss Helena won't be far away," Jake added.

Isabelle gasped. "I see her! Over there!" She pointed to another section of the woods, more to the east, where their governess, like Eve in the garden, was trying to shield herself from view with her long black hair and several leafy branches.

"Blimey, she's starkers," Dani uttered.

"Derek will be so upset he missed this," Jake drawled.

Dani smacked him on the arm. "Be good for once."

Jake laughed, but Isabelle had turned red on behalf of their governess.

"We've got to bring her a dress or something! Hurry!"

With that, the three of them scrambled to help, running off to their separate tasks. Jake raced out to bring Henry his clothes; Isabelle ran to the rescue of the mortified Miss Helena; and Dani dashed off at top speed to bring Archie his notes for his big speech.

Jake couldn't help laughing to himself as he ran. The magical life might have its perils, to be sure.

But it was never dull.

EPILOGUE
Return to Albion

Several days later, the Invention Convention ended for another year, and the geniuses of the world headed home to their far-flung points of origin from all around the globe.

Which was why Jake was sitting, presently, in the dark, noisy cargo hold of the steamship next to a large wooden crate marked: 'DANGER! LIVE ANIMAL! KEEP HANDS AND FEET AWAY.'

From inside the crate came the unpleasant and peculiar sounds of a Gryphon feeling seasick: occasional feline groans, pitiful tweets. Yacking coughs now and then, like a cat thinking about coughing up a hairball sometime soon.

"Becaw."

"Oh, stop being a baby. You'll be fine," Jake assured his feathered pet. He reached through the open end of the crate to drape a handkerchief wetted with vinegar over Red's large, leathery beak.

Miss Helena swore this was the best traditional remedy for the queasy mal-de-mers.

"How's he doing?" Gladwin came buzzing through the darkness, her fairy trail sprinkling the surrounding piles of luggage as she approached.

"This is definitely not Red's favorite mode of travel," Jake replied.

Since the Gryphon was half lion, he couldn't swim, and sensibly, he did not dare fly for long distances over the ocean. He had no choice but to go by boat, but this steamship really did not appear to agree with him.

Jake was a bit puzzled because Red had had no such trouble on the Viking longboat when they had traveled to Valhalla. But maybe it was because there had been ice floes all around them, like little bits of land where he knew he could stand on solid ground (or rather ice) any time he chose.

Or maybe it was being confined in the crate to avoid being seen that made him queasy. Whatever the cause, the noble Gryphon was a pitiful sight at the moment.

"Poor boy." Gladwin landed atop Red's crate. "I'll stay with him. Go on, you're wanted topside."

"What for?"

"The others want to see you."

"All right. Thanks. I'll be back soon, Red. Hang in there, boy."

"Becaw," Red said miserably.

Jake paused, frowning to leave his loyal pet in this condition. "Gladwin, do you suppose gryphons like ginger tea? I could bring some back for him from the ship's galley if it would help to settle his stomach. It always helps me when I get one of my horrid telekinesis headaches."

"Couldn't hurt to try it," she said with a shrug. "Mind you, I'll stay and watch him, but just to be clear, I *don't* clean up gryphon puke."

"*Royal* garden fairy. I should think not. But all right, duly noted," Jake said with a smile. Then he strode through the cargo hold, passing Archie's flying machine, safely stowed nearby.

The Pigeon had caused a sensation when the boy genius had presented it at last to his scientific colleagues.

For his part, Jake would never forget how happy Archie had been flying down from Jugenheim. If Archie hadn't decided to come along on the adventure, he would've missed out on the flight of a lifetime.

Quickly climbing the ladder up from the cargo hold, Jake stepped out into a plain, gray, metal corridor in the lower deck. This level housed much of the steamship's machinery as well as its sprawling galleys, or kitchens.

From there, he hurried up through various levels of mid-decks, where the army of uniformed crew and staff bustled about their work; up past the red-carpeted hallways lined with elegant passenger staterooms, through the public areas—the dining hall and the ballroom, with its chandeliers and grand piano; until, at last, he arrived outside on the main deck, where he found his party standing at the windy rails.

They were watching the craggy shores and green hills of Norway receding into the hazy blue distance.

The twins gazed wistfully at the forest, chastened by their return to civilization. Jake gave them a sympathetic smile as he approached.

Henry and Helena smiled back.

Nearly losing the twins had made the kids appreciate their dear shapeshifters even more.

Perhaps before, they had taken Henry and Helena for granted, but now they understood how lucky they were to have a skilled governess and tutor who cared for them so much.

After all, Henry and Helena could have run off if they wished and done whatever they pleased, making use of their abilities as shapeshifters like Loki to enjoy a life of ease and pleasure without responsibility.

But instead, their two dedicated teachers had chosen to come back and remain with the kids and look after them. They had given up their freedom for the four of them, and the children loved and respected them all the more now that they understood their dedication and unselfishness.

Jake left the pair to their thoughts, however, turning to Archie.

The boy genius wore a dreamy smile, still privately savoring his scientific triumph. Mr. Edison and Alexander Graham Bell had personally come up to shake his hand after his speech.

Beside him, Isabelle was holding Teddy in her arms, the ribbons on her hat blowing in the breeze. She kept trying to ignore a boy about her own age who kept smiling at her from the far end of the deck. She really was quite shy.

Dani, on the other hand, dashed over to Jake when she saw him. "There you are! I've got something for you." She reached into the pocket of her pinafore and handed him a little slip of paper. "Derek sent you back a telegram just as we were leaving! I kept it for you, since you were already down in the cargo hold with Red."

Jake furrowed his brow. "What's he say?"

The message Derek had sent earlier with Gladwin had been a simple inquiry asking if Jake and the others were all right. Jake had already telegraphed him to say they were.

Dani handed him the warrior's reply. "He's done with his bodyguard assignment. But look, here's the exciting part! He wants to know if he should start making the arrangements for our next trip!"

"Where?" Jake asked eagerly.

"To Wales! So we can tour your goldmine!"

"Brilliant," he murmured, glancing over the telegram, his eyes aglow at the thought of seeing all that gold.

His gold!

It was enough to warm the heart of any ex-thief.

"That sounds grand," Jake murmured. "Though...to be honest, I wouldn't mind staying at home for a while, after all this." He looked at her again. "You'll be coming, too, right? All of you must come with me."

"Ye better believe it!" she said with a grin. "I might've missed out on the giants, but I can't wait to meet the dwarves!"

"You already know one," he countered with a grin.

"Actually, she knows two," Archie chimed in, throwing his arm around her shoulders in chummy fashion as he joined them.

Dani looked skeptically from one boy to the other. "What are you two talking about?"

"Didn't we tell you? That's what the giants thought we were..."

While Archie started telling Dani some of the funnier details about their trip to Jugenheim, Jake tucked the telegram from Derek into his vest pocket, intrigued by the prospect.

He had never been to Wales.

But as he glanced around at the others in affection—still recalling those terrifying moments when he feared he might never see them again, might not make it back from Giant Land alive—his glance caught on Henry.

He was a little concerned about their tutor. Henry was staring down at the waves, looking lonely and forlorn. Jake frowned, though he wasn't sure what to say.

After seeing Snorri marry Princess Kaia, he had no doubt there was somebody out there for everyone. Miss Helena and Derek Stone seemed to like each other. But poor Henry could not be with Miss Langesund, whom he obviously fancied, because of his being a shapeshifter. That was some secret for a chap to have to keep.

But how could a lady scientist ever accept something she couldn't even comprehend?

And yet, before they had left the University, Jake had had a private meeting of his own with Astrid Langesund. And perhaps what he had told her had helped to expand her awareness of matters that lay beyond the realm of what could be scientifically proved.

He owed a debt of honor, after all, to a certain Viking warlord.

Jake had given Ragnor the Punisher his word that he would tell the "grave-robbers" about the real historical owner of the Viking ship the Langesunds had found.

Considering how the wild blond warrior had helped the boys survive their visit to Valhalla, Jake didn't care if Miss Langesund thought he was a loon—it was a promise he meant to keep.

It was scary, though, admitting to an outsider that he could see ghosts. Aside from Dani, he had never willingly told any non-magical person about his abilities. He had not dared to tempt fate by proving it to the lady-archeologist with a demonstration of his telekinesis, either. It was up to her, whether she would take him at his word or not.

"I know you probably won't believe me, and I can understand that," he had said when he had gone to see her in the little ship museum after all the excitement. "I only ask that you at least hear me out..."

She had looked at him in astonishment when he had told her he could see ghosts, that he had been born that way.

"And when you brought us in here that day, I saw the spirit of the king who owned this ship. He was furious that you and your father had dug up his grave. That's why everything kept falling down around you. It wasn't clumsiness. He was haunting you, throwing things around..."

Miss Langesund had sat down slowly, her pretty blue eyes wide behind her ugly black-rimmed spectacles.

Jake had shared more details. "His name was King Ragnor the Punisher. He never told me exactly where in Norway his lands were, or in what century he lived, but he gave me great boasts to describe himself. He said he made the Gauls tremble, and he tattooed the face of Loki to help identify him when the trickster god changed shapes."

"Oh, Jake, but Loki's just a legend," she had protested with a confused and disbelieving smile.

"Right." He had ignored the remark. "Ragnor also said he slew the terrible ice grendels. You don't happen to know what those are, do you?"

"Ice grendels?" she had echoed. "No, I've never heard of them. Grendel was a monster in the story of Beowulf...but that was just a story, too."

"Right," Jake said again, more quietly, smiling in spite of himself at her unbelief. He had considered showing her Risker, his magical dagger from Odin. But he was afraid she would deem it an important historical artifact and refuse to let him take it out of Norway. But it was a personal gift. So he had left it safely in its sheath back in his room.

He had practiced with it a little, and like the king god said, it would return to him when he threw it, only he was too scared to grab it out of the air yet for fear of accidentally slicing off his own hand.

At length, having shared his information, he had stood up to leave the lady-archeologist to her studies. "Well, that's all I wanted to tell you, Miss Langesund. Do with the information as you see fit. But trust me, Ragnor will be back if there's no honor given to his memory here. The only reason he and his men agreed to stop haunting the museum was for the glory of being remembered for their great deeds."

She had thought it over, still smiling uncertainly like she thought this might just be a boyish prank. "Well, it couldn't hurt to put up a plaque about him here, I suppose, if we say it's just a legend. It might even help sell tickets to the museum. We can always use the funding."

"Oh, he'll like being described a legend, I'm sure. That should suit his ego very well."

Even now, Jake still did not know what ice grendels were, but after all the mysterious things he had seen, it seemed all right to leave some mysteries unsolved.

At least for now.

It was only the one about his parents that still really haunted him. Perhaps someday he'd know the truth.

For the time being, not wanting Miss Langesund to think him either a prankster or a loon—especially since he'd have to see her again at Archie's next Invention Convention—Jake *did* give the lady-archeologist a small but interesting piece of proof.

He presented her with one of the grainy, black-and-white photographs that Archie had developed after their return from Jugenheim.

A picture of Princess Kaia's royal Viking boat.

He had left the lady-archeologist marveling over it in confusion.

The other pictures, the kids kept for themselves. Dani had already started making a scrapbook, but Jake had no plans of parting with the photograph of himself standing on a table beside a smiling Snorri.

He'd never forget his gentle giant friend.

But as he turned to gaze across the sea, leaning against the ship's rails with the others, his hair blew back from his face in the sea wind, and Jake could already feel a bold new wave of excitement rising in him.

More adventures waited for him and his friends and of course, his Gryphon.

Many more.

A daring smile curved his lips.

Wales, eh? he mused. He could hardly wait to hear the dwarves sing.

The End

Want More Gryphon Chronicles?

Come along with Jake and his friends on their next adventure—to Wales—to tour Jake's (or is it Red's?) goldmine and meet the dwarves who work there! The kids receive a grand welcome from the little folk. But when the local miners accidentally dig too deep, an ancient evil long trapped underground breaks free...and Jake will have to face his most terrifying enemy yet.

The Gryphon Chronicles: Book Three
THE DARK PORTAL

The Pickpocket Who Inherited a Goldmine

After his harsh beginnings as a rough-and-tumble orphan on the streets of London, Jake Everton takes his rightful place as the long-lost heir of an aristocratic family with magical powers–his personal quest, to follow in his slain parents' footsteps as a Lightrider in the age-old battle of good versus evil. In the fantastical nooks and crannies of the Victorian Age, Jake and his friends (including his pet Gryphon!) find no shortage of adventure–righting magic-related wrongs, solving supernatural mysteries, and exploring wondrous new worlds.

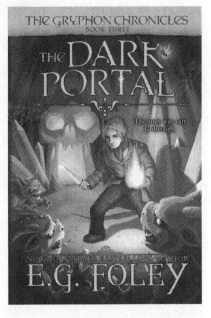

A Dark Presence

Something stalks a quaint town in the misty mountains of Wales, attacking humans and magic folk alike. Jake and his friends must get to the bottom of it–and in the land of deep, dwarven mines, the bottom can be very dark, indeed.

Turn the page for a Sneak Peek...

PROLOGUE
The Sorcerer's Tomb

A hundred and fifty feet underground in perfect darkness, a labyrinth of black, twisty tunnels snaked beneath the mountains of Wales. And in one such little-explored passage of the Harris Mine, a simple man called Barney had just discovered a curious phenomenon.

He angled his handheld wedge against a big, tough knuckle of coal and gave it a whack with his hammer to show his fellow miners. "See what I mean? Got a funny sound just there, ain't it?" He tapped again, harder. "Sounds...I dunno, hollow."

"Yer head's hollow," grumbled crew chief Martin. Nevertheless, to Mr. Martin's experienced eye, the problem was plain: They'd hit a stubborn section of the coal seam. He gave his men a nod. "Let's blast it."

Crawling about awkwardly in the narrow, claustrophobic space barely four feet tall, the men fetched the heavy hand-cranked drill and started churning it.

The tip of the drill slowly pierced a thin hole into the rock face, where they would soon pour in the blasting powder. Cranking the drill was backbreaking labor, just like every other job in the coalmine and its sister company, the Harris Ironworks. But coal made the steam that forged the iron that ran the British Empire, which, in turn, ruled the world. And so these rough, rugged miners saw themselves as unsung heroes of a sort. To be sure, not a one of them was ever afraid of the dark.

Even when they should be.

At length, the skinny hole into the bedrock was drilled, the blasting powder carefully poured in.

Daredevil Collins volunteered to light it—always a dangerous job. Cocky as ever, he held the squib carelessly between his teeth and lit it as if it were a cigar instead of a type of firecracker. Swiping it quickly out of his mouth, Collins shoved it into the hole the men had drilled.

As it burned its way toward the little pile of blasting powder, he scrambled after his crew, who had already scuttled out of range to wait for the explosion.

All four men held their ears and opened their mouths slightly, waiting for the shift in air pressure.

BOOM!

"Ha, ha!" The miners cheered out of habit at the blast. "That'll teach her!" said Martin.

With pickaxes and hammers at the ready, the men crawled back to harvest the chunks of coal that had been knocked loose from the mountain's grip by the explosion.

As they approached, the air was so thick with dust and smoke that it blackened their faces until all they could see of their mates was the whites of each other's eyes. As the men pressed on, the tiny oil lanterns on their hats glowed like four lonely lighthouses in that thickest type of fog, known as a London Peculiar.

Martin whistled for Jones to bring the coal cart so they could load up their fresh haul and carry it topside.

The more coal they brought up to the surface each day, the more money they made for their families. Of course, their pay went right back to the Company through the rent on their houses, owned by the Harris Mine, or through the goods they bought at the Harris Company Store.

The Company, in short, was more powerful around here than Queen Victoria.

"Look!" Barney suddenly burst out with a gasp. "I don't believe it! I-I was right! It *was* hollow!" He pointed as the smoke cleared to a *hole* they had blasted in the underground wall.

It should not have been there.

Indeed, it was impossible. There shouldn't be a hollow space left after their controlled blast, just an indentation exposing deeper layers of the earth's solid bedrock holding up the mountain.

"Well, beggar me," he murmured, marveling at it.

Bending forward to shine his headlamp in, Barney peered through the hole that opened into a darkness ten times blacker than even the rest of the mine. Then he waved his crewmates over. "Fellas, come and see!"

"What is it now?" Martin grumbled, coming up behind him.

"You got to see for yourself. There's some kind of room in there!" Barney said in wonder, pointing.

"Don't be daft. A room? Underground cavern, maybe..."

But as the others crowded round, even stern Mr. Martin had to admit that it was, indeed, an ancient-looking room with smooth, chiseled walls.

Smith squinted into the midnight darkness beyond the hole. "What's a room doing all the way down here?"

"How should I know," Martin said. An uneasy chill ran down his spine, for Wales was not just the land of coal and mist and unexpected spellings. It was also a place of legend. The sacred homeland of countless bards and sorcerers of old; the birthplace of Merlin himself, according to some; a land of ancient magic, mighty castles, and time-forgotten kings.

Collins had that daredevil gleam in his eyes once again as he glanced around at the others. "Fancy a look, boys? C'mon, let's go in!"

"I'm not so sure that's such a good idea," Barney warned him, but coalminers as a rule were not afraid of much.

Even when they *really* should be.

"C'mon, leave it. We've got to cut our support timbers to prop up that hole," Martin said. "It ain't stable."

"Ah, just for a moment." With a laugh, Collins vaulted through the hole, and so was the first to see the ancient, heavy table in the center of the mysterious chamber and the chair...

With a skeleton sitting in it.

A skeleton decked in strange jewelry and wearing the floppy hat and moldy velvet robes of a Renaissance-era scholar.

Collins stopped in his tracks when he saw it and pointed, aghast. "Bones!"

Barney, who was following right behind him, ran into Collins's back on account of not watching where he was going. He was too busy staring all around at the strange subterranean chamber, his eyes wide.

The rest followed, and when they all saw the skeleton, they let out exclamations of wonder and shock; the four big, fearless coalminers unconsciously started huddling together with a creeping, superstitious sense of doom.

For they now realized that they had just disturbed the dead.

"This is no ordinary chamber, my lads," Martin said in a hushed voice, taking control of the situation, as their leader. He looked around at all the odd things inside the chamber, and the bones. "It's a tomb."

"But whose?" Smith murmured, while Barney just gulped.

"His," Collins whispered, staring at the skeleton. "Whoever he is."

The skull's empty eyes stared right back at them from the darkness, giving them no answers.

Sitting upright, as if he had died right where he sat, whatever soul had once owned those bones had left this life surrounded by his books and papers.

This seemed odd to Barney. "But surely not a tomb, Mr. Martin. I mean, folk ain't usually buried at their desks, is they?"

"Well, you do have a point there," the crew chief admitted, growing ever more aware of some unseen evil lurking in this place.

"Maybe he died alone down 'ere and nobody ever noticed," Collins opined.

"Likely so," Martin quickly agreed, but Smith shook his head and whispered, "Maybe he couldn't get out."

Somebody gulped in the inky darkness.

"Maybe we'd better leave," Barney squeaked, but unfortunately, Collins had now recovered his nerve.

"Wonder who he was, poor bleeder." As he ventured closer, his hat-lamp shone on the long-dead occupant of the crypt.

Strange jewelry hung around the scholar-skeleton's neck, an intricate metalwork necklace with all sorts of arcane insignia. They had no idea what all the strange little symbols meant.

A chunky ring hung loosely off the skeleton's bony finger. The thick band was probably made from locally mined gold, but none of the men recognized the unusual black rock in the center, though they unearthed gems and semi-precious stones in the Harris Mine nearly every day.

None of them could explain it, either, when the black stone took on a cloudy green glow...

The Complete Gryphon Chronicles Series:

Book 1 – THE LOST HEIR
Book 2 – JAKE & THE GIANT
Book 3 – THE DARK PORTAL
Book 4 – RISE OF ALLIES
Book 5 – SECRETS OF THE DEEP
Book 6 – THE BLACK FORTRESS

And don't miss out on the holiday fun...

It's Jake's first Christmas with a family, but nothing's ever quite what you'd expect. Celebrate a Victorian Christmas with a Gryphon Chronicles holiday novella.

JAKE &
THE GINGERBREAD WARS

Peace on Earth, Goodwill to Men...And Gingerbread Men?!

ABOUT THE AUTHORS

 E.G. FOLEY is the pen name for a husband-and-wife writing team who live in Pennsylvania. They've been finishing each other's sentences since they were teens, so it was only a matter of time till they were writing together, too.

Like his kid readers, "E" (Eric) can't sit still for too long! A bit of a renaissance man, he's picked up hobbies from kenpo to carpentry to classical guitar over the years, and holds multiple degrees in math, science, and education. He treated patients as a chiropractor for nearly a decade, then switched careers to venture into the wild-and-woolly world of teaching middle school, where he was often voted favorite teacher. His students helped inspire him to start dreaming up great stories for kids, until he recently switched gears again and left teaching to become a full-time writer and author entrepreneur.

By contrast, "G" (Gael, aka Gaelen Foley) has had *one* dream all her life and has pursued it with maniacal intensity since the age of seventeen: writing fiction! After earning her Lit degree at SUNY Fredonia, she waited tables at night for nearly six years as a "starving artist" to keep her days free for honing her craft, until she finally got The Call in 1997. Today, with millions of her twenty-plus romances from Ballantine and HarperCollins sold in many languages worldwide, she's been hitting bestseller lists regularly since 2001. Although she loves all her readers, young and old, she admits there's just something magical about writing for children.

You can find the Foleys on Facebook/EGFoleyAuthor or visit their website at www.EGFoley.com. They are hard at work on their next book.

Thanks for Reading!